IN THE
Cold, Cold
Ground

AN ANTHOLOGY OF NEW ENGLAND
HORROR NOVELLAS

Trade Paperback Edition
ISBN: 978-1-58767-940-7

Cemetery Dance Publications
132B Industry Lane, Unit #7
Forest Hill, MD 21050

www.cemeterydance.com

CEMETERY
DANCE
PUBLICATIONS

In the Cold, Cold Ground

AN ANTHOLOGY OF NEW ENGLAND HORROR NOVELLAS

EDITED BY

ED KURTZ

CONTENTS

ALL THE STRANGERS CAME TODAY

BY ED KURTZ

CHAPTER ONE

The apartment was unusual, to say the least. Yawning out over the entire second floor, the space appeared to have been converted for office use at some point in recent history, complete with fissured ceiling tiles, fluorescent ballast lighting, and a sparse breakroom. There were two doors that led to nowhere at all and another door that had been sealed up; beyond it stretched a second staircase to the first floor that was no longer in use, closed like a tomb.

Upon being reconverted into a living space, what was once a laundry room now hosted an oven and sink, separate from the rest of the breakroom/kitchen, in a cramped space abutting the bathroom. One had only barely room enough to turn around in the peculiar little space, which would make cooking and washing dishes an odd and delicate procedure.

The rest of the house was divided into two other apartments; one on the first floor and another in the cellar. There was a decrepit old shed out back and a narrow path through a dense network of crawling English ivy in the backyard that pushed all the way to the Quinnipiac River beyond the property's terminus. According to the broker who found the place for Eun and Jim, the house was first built in the 1880s, though clearly renovated so many times since that little if anything of the original house remained. The original owners, Eun thought grimly, would likely spin in their graves to behold the Frankenstein oddity their home had been turned into. There were probably thousands of old houses in Connecticut that had been transformed into multi-family dwellings, but she had never seen one so herky-jerky, so jarringly patchwork as this one.

Still, the apartment was nearly twice the size of the one they were being forced to leave due to the criminal rent increase they were facing, and for nearly three hundred bucks less than they would otherwise be forced to pay. Weird, yes, but neither of them could turn up their noses at the rent. It was a steal, at least when compared to literally every other option they had.

"It'll take some getting used to," Eun conceded. "But then again, so did you."

She smirked and Jim played the role of the offended party, pouting and swiping at her with his hand. "We'll make it work," he said.

They signed the lease the following morning.

THEIR FIRST ORDER OF BUSINESS, EVEN BEFORE MOVING THEIR belongings into the new place, was to do something about the ragged Barcalounger and hideous coffee table the previous tenants had left in the middle of the living room. Eun had explicitly requested these be taken out before moving in, but no promises were made and the day they received the keys, they inherited the damn chair and table, too.

"We'll just haul them up to the attic, then," Jim said.

Eun made a face. She hadn't really gotten a look up there when they toured the place. It was Jim who ascended the narrow steps to take a glance, and all he'd said upon coming back down was, "It's damn hot up there."

"Is there room for this crap?" she asked.

"We'll make room."

She could feel the heat through the closed door in the room they designated for their office. Jim propped it open and the heavy, humid air seemed to unfurl at Eun like grabbing tentacles. Even the window unit, not four feet from the attic door, seemed incapable of making a dent in that unpleasant aura emanating from the mysterious space above.

Eun said, "Maybe we could just use them."

Jim wrinkled his nose and shook his head. "Forget it. Come on, it won't take us long."

The steps were so dusty their shoes slipped here and there, increasing Eun's anxiety about ascending into the strange, unpleasant attic. Even as his own feet skidded and the unwieldy armchair slammed against either side of the close, cobwebby walls framing the staircase, Jim kept up his mantra: "Careful, careful, careful."

At the top of the stairs, a rectangular hatch on rusty hinges wobbled, threatening to slam shut on top of them. Opposite that stood a railing, but the moment Jim's hip brushed against it, the entire structure collapsed in a cloud of dust. Eun could have sworn she caught sight of something skittering away from the scene in her peripheral vision, but she dared not dwell on it. Instead, she shifted her grip just enough so that she could push the Barcalounger up the last few steps where it finally came to rest on the bare, dirty floorboards right next to a small pile of animal shit.

"Oh, gross," she said.

"Christ," Jim groused. He wiped the sweat from his forehead and scanned the dim, crowded area. When his eyes landed on the window at the far end facing the street, he said, "Look. It's been left open."

"Raccoons?" Eun tilted her head at the feces left on the floor.

"Probably. I'll close it later."

11

They went back down for the coffee table, and Eun quietly hoped this would be the last time she ever climbed up those stairs.

FOR THE FIRST SEVERAL NIGHTS, EUN PARK LAID AWAKE FOR HOURS ON end, staring at the fissured ceiling tiles in the low light from the streetlamps outside. It was by no means unusual for her to get the new place jitters; she couldn't think of a time when, after moving into a new place, she didn't have trouble sleeping until she gradually grew accustomed to the new surroundings. Yet there was something different this time around; something else, apart from the novelty of a new home. She couldn't stop imagining what lay beyond the tiles, on the other side of the ceiling, stalking the attic floor. Jim never did get around to closing that window, and Eun had resolved to quit asking him altogether since his replies grew terser and more irritable each time she did so. Instead, she was going to have to do it herself, no matter her unease with the notion of running afoul of an unfriendly and potentially rabid animal—or worse.

On the one-week anniversary of properly living in the apartment, surrounded by boxes and tote bags yet to be unpacked, Eun walked past Jim on the living room floor, trying to make sense of the sundry cables needed to connect half a dozen devices to the television, and went directly into the office to the eerily warm attic door. She was armed with a broom and dustpan, along with a small white garbage bag, for any unpleasant surprises the raccoons undoubtedly left along the path from the steps to the window. The broom, she figured, might also double as a defensive weapon in case of a raccoon-related emergency.

The trapdoor wobbled precariously when she stepped on the first stair inside the balmy doorway. Eun held the broom above her head like a torch as she went up. The steps creaked beneath her feet, annoying her that she couldn't better listen for unwelcome sounds in the attic above.

All she wanted to do was shut a window and she was acting as though she was preparing for war. Eun let escape a small chuckle.

The worst thing up there, she reminded herself, was the crap on the floor. Just watch where you step and you'll be—

Something slammed, a near-deafening crack that echoed in Eun's head as her entire body tensed and she lost balance just long enough to fall back against the stairway wall. The wall quaked and the trapdoor swung down, crashing into the rectangular frame and only barely missing the crown of her skull by a matter of centimeters. She was instantly plunged into darkness and gave a long, shrill cry as her knees buckled and she crumpled to the stairs like a marionette with her strings cut. The broom and dustpan went clattering down to the bottom of the steps and the attic door swung gently back and forth on its own hinges below, permitting brief pulses of dusty light into the otherwise dark, hot, musty space.

"*Fuck!*" she screamed.

"What is it?" She could only faintly hear Jim's voice, muffled and distorted from the swinging door and her own blood pounding in her ears. Moments later, he gently pulled the attic door all the way open and beheld her in the shadows, cowered on the steps, as though he couldn't quite understand who or what she was. "You all right?"

"No, I'm not fucking all right."

Jim leaned back, affronted. "Okay, Jesus. Whatever it was, *I* didn't do it to you."

With that, Jim stalked off, letting the door swing back into the frame, where this time it stayed, leaving Eun in the dark. She fumed for a full five minutes in there before she felt at all ready to come back out again.

At least, she thought, the anger staved off the fear.

CHAPTER TWO

The truth of the matter was that Jim had always been a relatively patient guy, quiet and easy-going for the most part. He was a guy who rarely lost his cool and never lost his temper. But just as things were changing for Eun in their new domicile, they were changing for Jim, too. Or rather, *he* was changing.

When they met online, he was living in Council Bluffs, Iowa, though within the year he arrived in Connecticut with all of his worldly belongings stuffed into his Toyota from floor to roof. Most who knew them feared they were both making a terrible mistake, but five years in, Eun and Jim had certainly proved such fears groundless. Things weren't always perfect — they never were — but both of them had learned from a lifetime of mistakes and they agreed that meeting as they settled into middle age was actually the best thing all around. Neither of them wanted children, they had the same basic goals and needs out of life, and they genuinely enjoyed one another's company. Eun never believed in any new agey bullshit about soulmates and the like, but she rested well knowing she made out all right with Jim.

And then they moved, and everything seemed to be changing now. In the span of a few short weeks, they were somehow becoming strangers, more roommates than anything else, and Eun fought against her own plain and simple awareness of why that was happening to them.

It was this place. It wasn't *right. They* weren't right.

Nothing was.

And Eun had no clue what she could do about it.

AFTER RECEIVING HER FIRST WEEKLY TEXT REMINDING HER THAT THE trash would get picked up in the morning, Eun traipsed down to drag the cans to the curb. She had never owned a home, so the routine was anomalous to her; in the past there had always been a property dumpster for her to use. To further aggravate her, there were only two sets of garbage cans for the three apartments in the house, and whoever it was that did *not* pay a quarterly fee for the service was using *her* cans. She scanned the vehicles in their assigned slots as she rolled first the trash and then the recycling away from the house to the curb, right next to the trio of mailboxes facing the street. It was tempting to blame the owner of the creepy white van emblazoned with right-wing stickers on the rear bumper—people tended to assume Connecticut was all rich liberals, and boy, were they ever mistaken—but she had to admit to herself that she simply didn't know. A word would have to be had with the property manager about it. Eun did not like to be taken advantage of, even for something as seemingly small as a foreign bag of trash in her garbage can.

When she finished with that task, she pivoted to return to the house, where she froze.

From her vantage point in the front yard-turned-parking lot, Eun could clearly see that the attic window was now closed. As she had surmised the previous afternoon, that must have been what slammed and caused the trapdoor to fall on top of her, nearly frightening her to death. It was an old house, she reminded herself. A *very* old house. There was every possibility that all it took was a light breeze to tip the scales and send that thing crashing down. As things stood, she figured she ought to be glad the glass didn't shatter.

The problem was solved, however it happened. Eun felt she ought to be happy.

She wasn't happy. Nothing about the new apartment, nor the house it was in, made her feel anything remotely near to happy. And just because that damned window was closed didn't mean that the attic no longer existed for her.

The attic existed. And Eun's problems with it were far from over.

EUN RETURNED HOME FROM WORK A GREAT DEAL LATER THAN WAS typical for her; everything seemed to be piling up on her ahead of the audit for the end of the fiscal year, and then 91 was utterly gridlocked due to an overturned semi. She texted Jim from where she sat parked on the highway and zoned out with the radio warbling the same hundred or so songs they always circulated. Thoughts of all the things she needed to get done filled her head and battled for primacy, from the TVs she and Jim wanted to get mounted on the living room and bedroom walls to the portable kitchen cart they needed to acquire to help link the stove room with the rest of the kitchen. There were pictures to be hung, curtains to buy, and about a million books that needed to be put away. She didn't think about the attic at all—at least not until she finally returned home at a quarter to six.

That was when she happened to glance up from that same vantage point in the parking lot to discover that the attic window was wide open again.

Eun stopped dead, her purse and laptop swinging from her shoulders, and stared open-mouthed at the gaping space, yawning into the darkness. Just below it, Jim stood at one of the kitchen windows, grinning and waving down to her. Eun didn't register his presence there at all. His smile melted and he went away, leaving the oblivious Eun to remain where she stood, wondering with something akin to mounting outrage who had dared to go up there and open that goddamned window.

There weren't many suspects.

"God, that traffic must've—" Jim began when she came through the door.

Eun cut him off. "Why did you open that window?"

"Sorry?"

"The attic window," she said. "It's wide open again."

Jim's face pinched. "It can't be."

"It is."

"Nobody can get up there but us."

"That's why I'm asking you."

"But it wasn't me. I haven't even been up there."

Eun dropped her bags and stormed off to the office, leaving Jim to close the door before following her in there. "Maybe you were wrong," he offered weakly when he caught up to her.

"About what?" She pulled the attic door open and squinted into the oppressive heat. The weather was slightly better outside, but somehow the attic felt even hotter than before.

"I don't know," said Jim. "Maybe it wasn't closed. Maybe you were looking at the wrong window and just thought it was."

"It wasn't the wrong window."

She began to climb the steps, craning her neck to look where she needed to push the trapdoor back up. Jim said something else, but she couldn't quite hear it and wasn't sufficiently interested to ask him to repeat it. Instead, she threw the trapdoor open and emerged, already beginning to sweat, into the dusty, smelly attic with an impossibly open window.

The Barcalounger and coffee table were both positioned exactly as they'd left them, as was the animal shit on the middle of the floor and the collapsed railing. She stepped over the scat and advanced a few feet further than she had to date, stopping in the center of the floor, halfway between the stairs and the open window. Jim was still calling up to her in a raised voice, but it was impossible to make out. Eun's ears felt like they were stuffed with damp cotton and her skin was beginning to itch terribly all over.

Maybe, she told herself, that same damn raccoon got trapped in here when the window slammed shut. Could a raccoon open a window like that?

She sincerely hoped so, but doubted it.

A large, bulbous black spider clung to a half-destroyed web that stretched from the disused red-brick chimney in the middle of the space to the arched ceiling. Eun shuddered, stepped away from it, and in the process tripped over her own feet and pivoted on her way down to try to break the fall with her hands. Instead, she crashed shoulder first into a cracked plastic tub full of moldering newspapers, which she sent sprawling across the floor as she landed. She cried out in pain and rolled over, off of the now shattered tub, her shoulder throbbing hotly and her clothes caked with dust and cobwebs and worse.

"This goddamn attic," she moaned.

Eun sat up. Her hairline leaked sweat from her scalp in rivulets that ran down the length of her face. Above her, the spider was now gone. And beside her, she brushed the fingers of her left hand against something soft and hairy that made her instantly recoil. She scooted away and got to her knees, her wide eyes falling upon the still form of a medium-sized raccoon.

Leaping to her feet, Eun kept her eyes locked on the animal— quite dead, by the look of it—and tried in vain to make sense of what she was seeing. When she felt the texture, she expected a wig or maybe a fur coat, but what she got instead was something that made her stomach lurch. With one foot pointed toward the stairs in the event that she needed to run, she nudged the animal with the tip of her other shoe. When it didn't move or make a noise, she nudged it harder, with the same result. The thing was dead, all right. And when she cautiously drew close again to get a better look, she could plainly see how that came to be.

The raccoon's head was twisted all the way around so that its snout was aligned almost perfectly with its spine.

It fell, Eun told herself. *It fell and broke its neck.*

Of course, she knew perfectly well that would not have turned the poor creature's head 180 degrees, but the only other possibility was that someone, or some *thing*…

"No," she said aloud. "No."

She knelt down and pulled away the entire front and back page from a musty old newspaper. With this, she picked the carcass up from the floor by its broken neck and started back for the stairs, but then paused to look back at the open window she'd forgotten all about.

The raccoon, she thought. *Opened the window and…died.*

Whether or not it was capable of opening a window, she gravely doubted there was any way it could possibly have ended up as it was without the violent participation of something else. Something else in the attic.

The thought did nothing to raise her spirits.

She brought the raccoon downstairs with her, holding it out at arm's length the entire way, and leaving the window as it was for the time being. In the moment, it just didn't seem particularly important to her anymore.

"I ADMIT," JIM SAID, HIS EYEBROWS TIGHTLY SQUASHED TOGETHER, "IT'S odd. And pretty gross."

The dead raccoon lay on top of the newspaper, which was now at the bottom of a reusable shopping bag nobody would ever use again. Jim and Eun stood together looking down at it as if neither of them could quite determine what it was.

"It looks," Eun began, trying to tease out the words from her befuddled mind, "well, like a fresh kill."

"It's not a *kill*," Jim protested. "It's a dead animal you found in the attic. It's not very pleasant, but it happens all the time."

"How would you know it happens all the time? When did you ever have an attic before?"

"The house I grew up in had an attic. Two of them, as a matter of fact."

"And you found dead animals with their heads turned all the way 'round up there all the time?"

"That's—look, that's not the point."

"Look at it, Jim. Something purposefully killed this poor thing."

"Something?"

"Someone."

"Who, Eun?"

"I don't know, Jim! But accidents don't do this. It's too—*violent.*"

"Come on," he said, his voice approaching the quality of a whine. "What are you, a forensic animal death scientist now? You're watching too much TV."

"It's common sense."

"Eun…"

"Look at it, goddamnit!"

Her voice had grown so loud so suddenly that it startled them both into momentary silence. Eun was rarely one to raise her voice, and for a few seconds neither of them quite knew how to react to it.

"Just throw it out, okay?" Jim said after collecting himself. "Double bag it and throw it in the trash outside. And please—stay out of the attic. I'll shut the window. I'll nail it shut is what I'll do. And then nobody ever has to go back up there again, all right?"

"Jim—"

"Just throw it out." He said this as a kind of final punctuation to the discussion as he turned to walk away, leaving her standing over the carcass in the shopping bag.

"Something did this," Eun said again, softly.

She left it where it was, almost a form of protest, and watched as Jim vanished into the office with intent stamped onto his face. She heard him swing open the attic door and begin to stomp up the stairs until she couldn't hear him any longer. She then set up the coffee maker, and while it began slowly dripping into the pot, she slipped into the bathroom for a quick shower to scrub away the itching dust and spiderwebs that she'd accumulated in the fall.

And, after she dressed and returned to the kitchen for a cup of coffee, Eun froze midway with her widening eyes locked on the animal in the bag.

In the short time it had taken her to shower and throw on a t-shirt and shorts, the carcass had gone from freshly dead to putrefied beyond recognition. Most of the gray, black, and white fur was gone, laying bare blackened and moldering flesh crawling with writhing white maggots. The animal's face was reduced to gaping cavities where the eyes were only moments before, its terrible fangs exposed in a rictus grin that rested upon the highest vertebrae of a partially visible spine. The pungent, vinegary bouquet of rot displaced the erstwhile pleasant smell of the coffee in her nostrils, whereupon she fell staggering toward the sink to vomit.

Thereafter, the rotting carcass went into first one garbage bag, then another, and ultimately downstairs in the outside bin on the curb. She did not tell Jim about it when at last he returned from nailing the attic window shut.

CHAPTER
THREE

The following Sunday, Eun drove up to the Naugatuck Valley to visit her parents while Jim stayed home, determined to finish a work project before the start of the new week. Her mom and dad, both immigrants, were getting along in years and finding it harder all the time to navigate their small world without Eun's assistance, either physical, lingual, or most commonly both. The time was fast approaching when she would have to make a decision regarding their immediate future, being the last stage of their lives, and as much as she knew they simply couldn't go on living in a three-story rowhouse when neither of them could manage the stairs to either the basement or second floor, the sheer finality of moving them into an assisted living facility made Eun feel as though she was pushing her parents right into their graves. It wasn't only the best thing for them, it was the quite simply only choice to make, and she knew it. Still, she dragged her feet as though she could somehow stave off the inevitable.

After she paid their bills and made certain they had food enough for at least a week, Eun headed back to Yalesville before nightfall, as usual, due to her worsening night-blindness. Her mood was low and morose, and she'd been driving nearly twenty minutes before it occurred to her she had been cruising along in total silence, drowning in her own heavy thoughts and anxieties. The moment she realized this, she switched on the radio and let her speakers blare Van Halen throughout the SUV despite her lifelong aversion to that particular band. Anything to silence her own mind.

Fortunately, it was not long before Eun was turning onto Main Street at the intersection with Route 68, by which time she could see Jim's car in the parking lot just half a block up the road. And as she pulled into the slot directly next to it, she realized she could see Jim himself, standing in the window with the light at his back.

Except he wasn't standing at the kitchen window as he sometimes did when he saw that Eun had come home. Jim was standing at the attic window.

She backed into the space and let the engine idle for a minute or two, her eyes locked on Jim's silhouetted figure in the window. The attic light—little more than a bare bulb suspended on a wire from the beams above—was too bright behind him for her to see whether he was looking at her or even noticed that she'd come back. She wondered what on earth he was doing up there in the first place, and she concluded that something must have gone wrong for Jim to have bothered climbing back up after the apparent finality of nailing that damned window shut earlier in the week.

Another dead raccoon, she figured. *Or worse. Rats.*

He'd heard something moving around, Eun wagered as she switched off her headlights and then the motor. Now he was up there trying to figure out what he was going to do about it, so lost in his thoughts that he hadn't even realized…

She came to a dead stop halfway between her SUV and the front door, dropping her keys to the asphalt with a noisy jangle. She didn't even hear or notice it. Every sensory resource at her disposal was focused solely on the only thing in the world she knew or understood in that moment, which was the fact that her boyfriend had just appeared in the kitchen window, smiling and waving down at her.

At the exact same time, the dark figure in the attic window directly above him swept back as though suddenly pulled away and the light went out.

Whoever it was Eun saw in the attic, it wasn't Jim.

"Oh God," she said, her voice barely a whisper.

She was at the glass front door to the house before she could take another breath and halfway up the carpeted stairs leading to the apartment's front door before it occurred to her that she did not have her keys. Eun froze, temporarily unable to choose between running back for them or hoping Jim would open the door if she just banged on it—assuming he *could.*

Her hand curled tightly around the doorknob before she knew she'd made a choice. The door was locked because she had locked it when she left, so Eun slammed the heel of her palm against the peeling paint and shouted Jim's name. Each second that passed without a response of any kind felt like a dagger digging another inch into her chest.

"Jim, *please,*" she bellowed. "Open the *door!*"

It must only have been thirty seconds at most, but by the time she finally heard the deadbolt unlock, she would have sworn it had been thirty minutes. The door swung open and Eun all but collapsed right into Jim's arms.

"The attic," she wheezed. "There's somebody in the attic."

Jim had to plant his left foot firmly behind him to keep from being bowled over, and he grasped her by the shoulders to keep her upright, as well.

"Eun!" he said, his voice a bit louder than he intended it to be. "What's going on? What are you talking about?"

"I saw," she said. "In the window. Somebody is *up there,* Jim."

"Nobody's up there."

"I saw."

"Eun…"

"*I saw, goddamnit!*"

She wrested free of his grip and hunched slightly, her eyes wide and wild. Jim thought she looked almost feral, but he dared not say as much. Instead, he held up his hands, palms out, and said, "There's only the one way up there, and I've been four feet from the door ever since you left."

"It's been hours," Eun protested. "You must have gotten up to pee."

"Nobody snuck into our attic when I was peeing. For Christ's sake, what's gotten into you? What is it about that damned attic that's got you acting so—"

"What," she said, "crazy?"

"I didn't say that."

"You were about to."

"No," Jim said. "Odd, maybe. You've been acting odd, you've got to admit."

Eun straightened up. She drew in a deep breath, slowly, and then released it even slower still. She gently shut the front door and twisted the knob to lock the deadbolt. She then said, "I saw someone in the attic window. I thought it was you. Then I saw you in the kitchen window, and that was when whoever was in the attic window went away. If there is really only one way up there..."

"Then they're still there."

"Yes."

Now it was Jim's turn for the deep breath. "Okay," he said. "All right. Fine." He made a thin, straight line of his mouth and went silently into the kitchen, where he pulled open the utility drawer beside the refrigerator. After sorting through the sundry items therein for a moment or two, Jim found what he was looking for and returned to Eun with a mini flashlight in hand. "Let's go see."

A LOT OF YEARS HAD COME AND GONE SINCE THE LAST TIME ANYBODY called Eun Park crazy. The last time was so long ago that she was still telling people her name was *Janet* and had never heard of Jim and had never so much as held a mobile phone in her hand. She was barely 22 years old, still living at home in the Naugatuck Valley, and she lost what was left of her mind over the course of one terrible summer.

"You're crazy," was what her mother told her in the awful quiet minutes after Eun had finally stopped screaming at the dinner table. In the morning, her parents drove her and her suitcase to the Yale New Haven Psychiatric Hospital, where nobody called her crazy but most everyone treated her like she was. For the following five weeks, she spent her days in grippy socks, wandering from solo therapy sessions to group ones, sleeping ten to twelve hours a day and being experimented on with a battery of tests and drug cocktails. Ultimately, it was determined that Eun "Janet" Park wasn't suffering from major depressive disorder, bipolar disorder, or borderline personality disorder, as had all been suggested at one point or another. It was just good old fashioned schizoaffective disorder that was disrupting her fragile mind, conjuring the odd hallucination here and there, and all but annihilating any chances of getting a decent night's sleep.

What Eun saw at the dinner table that night was, as she eventually felt comfortable enough to discuss in private therapy, a root-like network of grabbing hands free-floating throughout the entire first floor of her parents' rowhome. The hands were all interconnected, twisting and wriggling as though in a vain attempt to free themselves from the impossible knot of fingers and thumbs and wrinkled palms, jutting here and there as one or more of the hands won control of the knot and then lost it again to another. And though this was hardly the first time either of her folks dealt with their only child's skittish anxiety over something neither of them could see or hear, it was the first time she kicked away from the table and began screaming as she flailed her fists at the monstrous abomination tumbling through the air directly at her.

It was by far the worst hallucination she had ever experienced up to that point, and the stress of it was so severe that she fainted dead away on the linoleum floor only minutes after she launched herself away from the table. Her mother later told her with tears streaming down her weary face that she had been all but certain in that moment that Eun had died.

Added to her already steady diet of antidepressants and benzodiazepines was risperidone for the hallucinations, and even after she was released back into the care of her parents, Eun stayed on the same cocktail well into her thirties when at last she was determined to have managed a balance that meant the disorder was controlled if not conquered, and she no longer required the antipsychotic. She never saw another horrible Gordian knot of reaching fingers, nor any of the other terrible strangers that preceded it.

She was seven months free of them on the day she met Jim.

And nobody ever called Eun crazy again. At least not for a while.

IT WAS TWILIGHT WHEN EUN SAW THE FIGURE, BUT BY THE TIME SHE AND Jim went through the door to march single file up the dusty steps, night had descended and the attic was almost completely dark. As she had noted only a quarter of an hour earlier, there was an attic light, but it was in the middle of the space with only a pull-chain to switch it on, so the flashlight was necessary to make their way that far. Yet being little more than a keychain light for the direst of emergencies, the flashlight provided only the meagerest light by which to see. Eun doubted it could be much darker if Jim switched it off and they depended on the weak light from the moon and streetlamp outside, but she was hardly willing to see if she was right.

Jim took two long strides as soon as he was on the attic floor, but Eun seized a handful of the back of his shirt, restraining him and all but forcing him to fall backward.

"What are you doing?"

"You're going too fast," she said in a low whisper.

Jim chuckled derisively. "You're frightened of nothing."

"I sure fucking hope so," she said.

The floorboards creaked beneath their feet as Jim, still tethered to Eun's tightly gripped fist, made his way toward the hanging light. He reached out clumsily, knocking the bulb into a pendulous swing when he meant to grab the chain. The weak beam from the miniature flashlight shot herky-jerky around the space, illumining dust motes in a way that reminded Eun of bioluminescent fish and clouds of tiny plankton. Beyond that, she caught glimpses of supporting beams dripping with cobwebs like pearls, cardboard boxes sinking in on themselves like rotting November pumpkins, cracked trunks with rusty latches, stacks of magazines and newspapers…

And a tall, narrow figure standing at an odd, canted angle between an upended headboard and a broken easel.

Eun screamed.

"There! He's *there!*"

Jim said, "What?" But before he could gather his wits, Eun snagged the flashlight from his hand, thrusting its light in the direction of the man she saw in the dark. Jim let out a gruff noise of offense, but she paid him no mind; she was focused solely on proving him wrong, showing him that she was absolutely not crazy. That she saw what she saw.

A stranger.

She found the easel, so Eun prepared herself before sweeping the area with the light to reveal the stranger in the attic.

The figure hadn't moved, still standing still at that same eerie angle. And when Jim saw it, he erupted into a fit of high-pitched giggles. Upon first hearing it, Eun momentarily considered the possibility that her partner had lost his mind at the worst possible moment, but that didn't last long. He had barely started laughing before she realized they were both looking at a dressing mannequin with a frayed scarf festooned over its shoulders and a checked hat resting on its faceless head.

Immediately, her entire body felt overheated as the embarrassment rushed through her body like a quick-acting virus, upsetting her stomach and forcing tears into her eyes. The best thing she could think about the situation was that she had not hallucinated anything, but merely mistook an innocuous object for a human-like shadow. At the very least, the damned thing was *real.*

Still chuckling, Jim found the chain at last and yanked it, flooding the attic with the unpleasant yellow light of the bare bulb. In the fuller light, the mannequin looked sillier still, a mere thing, hardy noticeable given its environment. Nonetheless, it remained somehow disquieting to Eun, who found herself unable to look upon it for longer than a few seconds at a time before she had to look away again.

"See?" Jim said, triumphant. "Nothing. Okay? Nothing."

"No," she countered. "It was something. Just not what I thought it was."

"Eun..."

"I didn't—it was there. It *is* there. It's *something*, Jim."

"Right," Jim said with a bit of a sigh. "I know. You're right." He pursed his lips in a way that might have been intended as a smile, but he only looked annoyed. With that, he pulled the chain again, plunging the attic once more into near-total darkness. A small gasp escaped Eun's mouth. Jim aimed the flashlight at the stairs and said, "After you."

It was the smallest victory she could have achieved in the moment, but still a victory. She wasn't imagining anything, and she hadn't hallucinated. It was only a mistake. An honest—sane—mistake.

He followed behind her, keeping the light ahead of them, and continued to chortle to himself every step of the way, enjoying his own, much broader victory. *Was this how it was supposed to be?* Eun half-wondered, despite knowing perfectly well that it wasn't.

Just as she knew so perfectly well that the figure she saw in the window wore no hat.

CHAPTER

FOUR

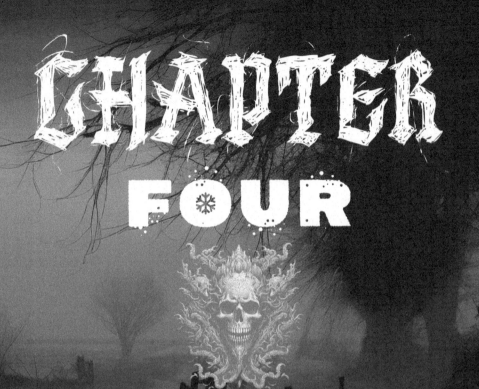

Despite the crushing late summer heat, life inside of Eun and Jim's apartment had grown decidedly chilly. She spent her days at work, he spent his at the home office, and the texts were few and far between, perfunctory. In the evenings, suppers consisted of scavenging the pantry and fridge, everyone for him or herself, after which Jim typically hid himself away in the same office where he spent his days, scrolling social media or playing military murder games on the spare television he never managed to get on the wall. Eun kept a series of nineties favorites spinning on the turntable in the living room, which she listened to through headphones that reduced the incessant machinegun fire from the office to a minimum. Her grunge classics had done a lot of the heavy lifting for her in the long days following her stay in the psych ward, and she hoped the warm familiarity of the music would help her now.

The stark truth, however, was that little could assuage the dull ache in her chest that had persisted since the night she saw the shadow in the attic window. She recognized it for what it was—anxiety—and feared it was only a matter of time before it worsened into something resembling full-on panic. And how long after that before panic transformed into madness?

"I'm *not* crazy," she said aloud, though she couldn't hear her own words over the comforting scream of Chris Cornell in her ears.

From the office, on the other hand, she *could* hear Jim bark a laugh. At the game? At *her*?

Eun's face reddened with the hot blood of embarrassed anger and before she could give it a second thought, she yanked the headphones off of her head and let them drop to the floor as she rushed from the living room to the office to ask that smug son of a bitch what exactly was so fucking funny. There was a time, some years now gone, when he'd told her it didn't matter in the least to him that she'd struggled with her mental health, that she'd spent a little time in a nuthouse. *Everybody fights their own mind now and then,* Jim had said. He was so empathetic then—but now it was all some big joke? Eun the loon, jumping at shadows again?

"God *damn* it, Jim," she began, storming into the home office, "I am not going to be laughed at in my own—"

The word *home* got caught in her throat at the sight of him, splayed back in his ergonomic office chair, arms dangling limply on either side of him and his head back at a severe angle. His mouth hung open and his glossy, gray-green eyes glared unseeing at the ceiling above him. It was almost as though he was attempting to look *through* the ceiling, past the barrier between himself and the attic above.

To Eun, her partner looked frozen solid in a state of absolute terror.

"Jim?" she said. "*Jim!*"

In lieu of reply, a hollow clicking emanated from his throat, like a baseball card taped to a child's bicycle spokes spinning inside of a deep well. The sound was so thoroughly inhuman that Eun found herself scanning the room for some other possible source of the grating, unnatural noise, a desperate attempt to convince herself that it wasn't Jim doing that, that it *couldn't* be him. Yet the clicking continued, and there was no mistaking its point of origin. She could even see his Adam's apple bob in time with the clicking, as though something was pushing it up and down inside of him.

Eun physically shook herself free from the grasp of her fear-induced paralysis and surged forward, nearly tripping over a box of books she'd been meaning to donate to the library but never seemed to get around to it. Instead of tripping, she half-hopped the rest of the way across the room to Jim, who she seized by the shoulders just as something moved in the murky periphery of her vision to the right.

The attic door, slowly shutting. No, that wasn't completely right. The door was *pulled* shut, by a thin, dark hand curled like autumn vines around the knob, until the latch caught with a click not unlike the one rhythmically cranking out of Jim's mouth. Only Jim had gone silent, and all Eun could hear now was the soft, almost imperceptible creak of the steps beyond the door, on the other side of the wall, leading up into the attic.

And then there was silence.

"Eun?"

Jim's voice snapped her attention away from the door and for a blissful instant, she forgot all about it. "Jim! Are you okay?"

"Me? Are *you* okay?"

He appeared genuinely puzzled, perhaps even a bit annoyed. His brows were tightly knitted, the game controller grasped with both hands as though he'd been holding it the entire time. But Eun knew he had not been. She never saw the controller until that very moment.

"He was here," she squeaked.

"What? Who?"

"The man in the attic, Jim. The *stranger.* He was just *here.* And you…"

She whipped her head to look at the attic door, which remained closed.

Jim said, "Oh, for God's…"

But she *shushed* him harshly, cutting him off, and listened carefully with wide, watery eyes searching the paneled ceiling as though it might somehow give away the attic's secrets to her.

"No one was here. I've been sitting here the entire time, playing…"

"You were—I don't know! Unconscious? In a trance or something? You weren't *here*, Jim. You didn't *see*."

"Jesus *Christ*, Eun!" Jim roared, and he hurled the game controller at the floor, causing the back panel to snap off and the batteries to jettison in two separate directions. Immediately, the screen froze and a message appeared, instructing the player to check the controller's power, but Jim ignored it. He leapt to his feet and glared down at her, their faces no more than a few inches apart. "That's enough, do you understand me? That is *enough*."

By now, she could hear her own elevated heartbeat slamming in her ears. Her knees were threatening to buckle and it took the lion's share of her focus and strength to keep from crying. But Jim had never raised his voice to her, not like this, and the hurt it caused was almost enough to overpower the fear she was feeling about whatever it was that was happening in that house.

Almost, but not quite.

"I'm not crazy," she said low.

Jim exhaled a sharp laugh. He said, "You sure about that?"

Eun closed her eyes. She drew a long, slow breath in through her nostrils and exhaled just as slowly through her barely parted lips. Experience had taught her that shit stuck better than sugar, so as a rule of thumb she typically did her level best to prevent saying anything to anybody she cared about that could not be unsaid. Compliments were often forgotten, but harsh words lasted a lifetime, like scars.

"Get fucked, Jim," she said anyway, and with that, she went briskly out of the room. Shortly thereafter, the office door slammed behind her.

At last, she let the tears flow. She cried so hard she could hardly find her way back to the living room couch. And once she did, and she sank deeply into the cushions with her face buried in her hands,

Eun heard the door squeal back open again. Quickly, she wiped at her swollen eyes with her shirtsleeves until she could see clearly enough to look through the short hallway to the office, but the office door remained shut.

It was the attic door she heard, inside the office, opening up.

Eun remained perfectly still, her hands on her knees, mouth agape and eyes streaming, for what felt like hours while she listened and stared until, at some point, she simply passed out from exhaustion. She never heard a thing after that door opened. She didn't hear Jim, his game, or anyone else make a single sound. She never heard the door close again, either.

Upon waking around six in the morning, still sitting up, Eun discovered that Jim was gone.

HE WASN'T IN THE OFFICE, AND THE ATTIC DOOR WAS CLOSED. EVERY other room in the apartment was similarly quiet and unoccupied. And when Eun peeked out one of the kitchen windows to the parking lot below, she could see that his car was gone, too. For a full minute she stared at the dark stain on the asphalt where his Toyota had dripped rainwater or oil or some combination thereof, and she struggled to recall whether Jim had said anything about going anywhere that day. She was sure he hadn't. He left because he was angry with her, and he was angry with her because he believed she was losing her mind again.

Eun was not inclined to agree with that assessment. She knew how it felt, what it was like. She'd been down that awful, terrifying road before and she knew this was an entirely new and different awful, terrifying road for her. This wasn't her brain falling apart on her all over again. But thinking about something one of her shrinks told her in the psych ward, she feared it just might be something far worse.

Just remember, he'd said, *that so long as they're just hallucinations, they can't really hurt you.*

Which meant this—whatever *this* was—could.

Her eyes shot away from the window, sweeping the kitchen until landing on the door to the office that she'd left slightly cracked after checking for Jim. All she could hear was the fairly distant sound of cars rushing past on 68, which sounded so hollow and removed that Eun felt like it occupied a different plane of reality than the apartment. The house.

Above her, something creaked in a way that gave a long, low groan, like old wood straining to bear weight. Eun closed her eyes, drew in a slow breath, and reminded herself that old houses settled and creaked just as a matter of course. She then stepped into her flats, grabbed her purse and keys, and got the hell out of there.

CHAPTER
FIVE

hough not expecting her, Eun's parents were delighted to see her when she arrived later that morning unannounced. It wasn't something she often did, and she didn't have the heart to tell them she hadn't come because she missed them, but rather because she was afraid. Worse still, when her father asked how the new apartment was coming along, Eun lied and said it was all perfectly fine. She loathed the guilt that crept over her like a deep chill for lying to her folks, but it was so much easier sometimes than navigating the tricky language barrier that existed solely as a result of their stubborn insistence that in America, one needed only to know English. She knew less Korean than a first-year language student at mid-term, and though her father's command of English was competent, her mother had always relied on them rather than improve her less-than-perfect language skills. Accordingly, Eun opted for the path of least resistance more often than not. In cases like that morning, that path led directly to mistruth. Whether or not it was detected this time around she couldn't say, but neither her mother nor father let on if so.

She helped them pay their bills and balance their checkbook, hauled their air conditioners out of the windows and stowed them in the basement, and double-checked that they had sufficient supplies to last at least a week before the buzzing anxiety building just beneath her skin began to grow unbearable.

Still no word from Jim. Not so much as a text or even a social media post that might let her know that he was at least all right.

And she was beginning to face the fact that running to her parents for a few hours was not going to solve anything between them—nor between her and whatever it was occupying the attic above their apartment. Whether she liked it or not, she still had to go home eventually.

Home. The word seemed suddenly foreign to her, indecipherable. Her parents' townhome was no longer home to her, yet she recoiled from the thought of calling the second-floor apartment she shared with Jim home, either.

The buzzing beneath her skin intensified. It was not helped much by the unexpected vibration of the phone in her jeans pocket, which caused her to yelp and shoot up straight like she'd received an electric shock.

Thank Christ, she thought, fumbling to get the phone out of her pocket and into her hand. The tone that accompanied the vibration was from her text messages, which she rarely ever used. For most people, she preferred the messaging options through social media, but Jim eschewed those services and could only be reached by text. In all likelihood he had come to his senses about his tantrum and was texting to see where she was. Maybe he was still mad, but in the moment that only faintly seemed to matter; Eun just wanted to know that he was okay.

She tapped in the four-digit code to unlock her phone and hurriedly swiped open the texting app, but only to find a new text from their trash service reminding her to put their cans out for the morning. There still was no word from Jim.

Eun opened up her chat with him, and she typed, *You home yet? I'm at my folks'.*

She then pocketed the phone, said her goodbyes to her mother and father, and made the long drive back to the apartment on Main Street.

Even from where she sat at the stoplight at the intersection some forty minutes later, she could clearly see that Jim's Toyota was still missing from his parking slot. She pulled in next to the empty space a couple of minutes later, and then she climbed out of her SUV. She then headed for the front door but stopped cold halfway to look at the mess on both the asphalt and rhododendron beneath the first-floor apartment windows. At first, she thought it was ice, but she was quick to realize ice would have melted in the late summer heat, so it couldn't have been that.

It was glass. Small, glittering slivers and chunks of broken glass. She hardly needed to look to confirm, but she did so anyway. Craning her neck back, she narrowed her eyes in the bright afternoon sun at the attic window, which had been smashed to pieces, frame and all.

From the inside.

When she was small, it was the man beneath her bed. That terror seemed to last forever, though in fact it was only five or six months before her phantom graduated to the closet. This was in some ways more frightening to Eun, but from another perspective she felt some small modicum of relief; at the very least the closet could be obstructed by her desk chair. In time, she worried about something lurking on the slight ledge outside her bedroom window, and for the preponderance of her childhood, Eun learned to withstand the most intense discomfort from having to pee badly rather than risk the dark hallway beyond the bedroom door. Darkness, to her mind, hosted untold horrors without exception, and she would go to nearly any lengths to avoid it.

But no one could stay away from the darkness all the time. Nightlights and flashlights could only do so much, which was practically nothing at all, and for all the blessed relief she experienced at dawn's first light, it always came with the horrid knowledge that the light could never last. Night always came back.

And when the night came back, so did the strangers.

It was a catch-all term for her, something that seemed to capture the general form and intent of that which frightened her most, the unknown and, perhaps, unknowable. At school, she had been warned about strangers, and to hammer the point home they paired the alarming word with a rhyming descriptor to both ensure she remember it and ratchet up the terror it invoked: danger. Strangers, those she did not know or understand, represented danger, a real, salient threat to her well-being and continued existence. Something out there was trying to hurt her.

Or something in *here*.

At the time, she was merely a sensitive child. Her parents banned scary movies and fretted that Halloween would be too much for her. Adolescence only made the strangers double down in their attacks, however, which inspired Eun to devise places to hide from them. She hid in the pantry and she hid behind the water heater in the basement. At school, she missed classes because she was hiding in the bathrooms or the janitor's closet. A guidance counselor levied an accusation about drugs, which was taken seriously enough to warrant testing that revealed nothing of the sort. Her grades fell and her friends melted away from her. And she learned the best way to hide was to hide it all from anyone and everyone. To hide herself, even *from* herself.

Which worked, at least until the strangers began manifesting in broad daylight whether others were present or not: at the supper table and in the middle of Spanish 201. That was when Eun couldn't hide any longer. And that was when she found herself medicated and under constant supervision until she finally learned how to hide herself from the strangers by being too doped up to perceive them. She did that until the strangers finally went away.

But the strangers were back. They had found her again, and they had learned some new tricks since last they came. And if there was one thing Eun Park knew perfectly damn well about hallucinations, it was that they couldn't smash windows.

This, to her, signaled one of two things; either that this was emphatically different from every visitation she suffered before, or that it was *not* different, and that there never had been any hallucinations in the first place.

The strangers, Eun worried now, were *always* real.

WHAT LITTLE GLASS FELL INWARD CRUNCHED BENEATH THE SOLES OF Eun's shoes when she reached the window. The sash and rail looked as though somebody had taken a baseball bat and a great deal of rage to it. The only obvious and reasonable suspect was Jim, but that would have meant that he'd come back home while she was out, climbed up into the attic, obliterated the window for some reason, and then left again. It wasn't completely outside of the realm of possibility, but it failed to make much sense. Sure, he'd been upset about what she'd seen in that window, but she found it hard to believe he would take his frustration out that way. That just wasn't Jim.

Then again, she considered as she kicked at the glass and fragments of splintered wood at her feet that the horrible trance he'd fallen into the night before wasn't exactly Jim, either. She was kicking herself now for not insisting they go straight to the emergency room right then and there, but his attitude toward her precluded that. For all Eun knew, Jim could have gone to the hospital himself, but why wouldn't he have told her as much? The longer he was out of contact with her, the more she worried something terrible had befallen him, and yet she couldn't help but feel that his being away from the house was the safest thing for him. Still, she was beginning to wonder if she shouldn't call around to the area hospitals just in case, while continuing to try to get a hold of him directly.

She pivoted to return to the staircase, having left her phone downstairs on the kitchen table, but fell still as soon as she was facing away from the ruined window. The light was on, its bulb swinging slightly on its chain as though just pulled on. Beyond the opposite window facing the back of the property, all she could see was stark blackness. Outside of the sickly yellow light of the bulb, the periphery and corners of the attic were similarly dark, and she felt a cool breeze tickle the back of her neck and arms from the gaping hole behind her. Eun turned to look back through the broken window and emitted a papery gasp.

It was pitch black outside. In the time it took her to turn around, it had gone from late afternoon to what looked like the middle of the night. Even the streetlight was out, as were the lights on all the houses across the street. There wasn't a star in the cloudless sky. Just darkness, everywhere she looked, apart from the weak sphere of light emanating from the hanging bulb in the middle of the attic.

She'd lost hours, somehow, and she'd done so standing in one place. Peering into the endless pitch outside, she couldn't really make out the outlines of things, and there was no traffic to be seen or heard. Behind her, something made a rusty-sounding creak. Eun spun back around to find the bulb had begun to swing from side to side, gradually swinging in a wider arc with each pass. The wider the arc, the closer the bulb got to the brick chimney that rose up from the bowels of the old house to the roof above. It wouldn't be long before the light smashed against the brick and plunged the attic— and seemingly, the world—into total darkness.

Eun lunged for the bulb. She planned on grabbing it with her bare hand, no matter how hot it might be. In that moment, she prioritized the light over the fear of being burned. Burns healed. She did not know if she would ever overcome whatever it was that awaited her in the dark.

The pads of her index and middle fingers brushed the grimy surface of the bulb when she swung her hand out, and indeed the heat was intense enough to sting her skin, but she wasn't close enough and the light swung away from her hand. She said, "*No,*" and watched helplessly as the bulb careened toward the brick surface of the chimney, against which it lightly clinked before the momentum was interrupted and the entire apparatus spun off toward the staircase. A urine-colored halo of light moved over the steps like a scudding storm cloud.

A small sigh of relief escaped Eun's lips, but it turned quickly into a gasp when she realized there was movement at the bottom of the stairs. The bulb was already swinging back toward her, its trajectory altered by its brush with the chimney, but she was certain there was something—or someone—down there by the door leading into the office.

"Jim?"

He came home, saw my car, went looking for me, she thought rapidly.

The momentum was slowing now, the reach of the bulb's arc shortening, but on the next pass it still managed to toss a brief blanket of light over the sunken steps, where for half a second she saw the shadow ascending. And it was quite definitely not Jim.

The shadow belonged to an androgynous figure, vaguely human or at least human-shaped, with long, gangly legs that stepped high as it climbed the steps. It spread its arms out to feel along the walls with long, soot-black fingers while keeping its wide eyes trained, unblinking, on Eun. The white eyes were the only part of the figure that wasn't inky black, like bright twin moons appearing from behind a contrail of oily smoke. That was what it looked like—smoke—crawling over the figure to keep it hidden even as it moved up into the attic, step by step, staring directly at her until the light returned to the opposite direction, plunging the steps into darkness again.

Without thinking about it, Eun shot out her right hand to bat the light back toward the stranger on the steps, but she hit it much too hard and shattered the bulb with the heel of her hand, extinguishing the light after a single bright flash.

From the top of the staircase, in the absolute darkness, she could hear the stranger croak, "*Hello…*"

"Go away," Eun said, stumbling backward. "Go *away.*"

Her hand throbbed from what she thought were probably shards of glass embedded in her skin, and she could feel a warm trickle of blood sliding down. Between the pain and the terror, her stomach lurched as she continued to take backward steps.

"*Helloooo…*"

Her heel struck the wall beneath the broken window, startling her into momentarily losing her balance. To keep from falling through the window, Eun leaned forward, overcorrected, and collapsed onto the floor atop the broken glass and splinters and dust and animal shit. Immediately, she planted her palms on the floor, driving the jagged shards from the bulb and, she suspected, a few from the window deeper still into her palm. Ignoring the hot pain as best she could, she pushed herself up until her left shoulder hit something that curled around it.

A cold hand. Ice cold.

"*Hello, Jaaaaaaanet,*" said the stranger right into her ear. Its voice was high and crackled like static. The hand tightened its grasp on her shoulder, sent icy shocks of pain shooting into her neck and back, and Eun screamed.

She tried to shrug free of the grip, but the hand held fast, its bony fingertips sinking into her skin. When that didn't work, Eun reared back, pushing into the hand rather than pulling away, and brought up her right hand from the floor. She then shoved the bleeding heel of her hand hard into the stranger's face, which felt like hard-packed snow when it gave beneath the force of her strike. The hand relented at last and she wasted no time scrambling away from the stranger on her hands and knees.

"*Stay,*" it moaned behind her. "*Staaaaaay Janeeeeet.*"

Eun said, "Fuck *you,*" and launched herself up to her feet in time to hit the first step down, but she missed the second completely and toppled forward, barking her right knee on the edge of a stair before reflexively pulling herself into a ball for the rest of the fall down to the bottom.

When she slammed against the wall with her hip and shoulder, the impact sent the door flying open so hard the doorknob punched a hole into the wall behind it, lodging it there. Eun groaned, leaning against the wall and trying to focus on one pulsing pain at a time, but there were so many all screaming at her at once. She was afraid to move—afraid she wouldn't be *able* to move if she tried—but realized if she didn't at least try, the stranger would be upon her in seconds.

"No," she grunted, and she used the wall to brace her as she rose, shakily, to her feet and opened her eyes.

And not only did she find nothing on the steps above her, but the office in front of her was bright with the late afternoon light streaming in through the leaves of the trees to the side and back of the house. The attic too was perfectly visible in the sunlight, and there was no sign of the stranger or anything else lurking up there.

Her knee throbbed, her hand and wrist sticky with drying blood, and as much as she didn't want to think about it, her shoulder still ached from the stranger's cold grasp. She held her hand up to the light and saw bits of glass sparkle in the light when she turned it. A couple of them were easy enough to extract, but the rest would require the precision of tweezers. But this part she almost didn't mind; it was proof that it happened. She didn't know if it was the next day or the same one it had been when the world suddenly turned dark, but the glass embedded in the flesh of her hand was *real*.

She wagered the bulb was still broken up there, along with the window. And when she gathered sufficient courage to yank up her shirt sleeve to expose her left shoulder, she was far from surprised to find a reddish-pink welt rising there, the same size and shape as that thing's wretched black hand.

It happened. The stranger was real.

I'm not crazy. I'm not.

"I'm not," she said aloud.

"You're not what, hon?"

Eun jumped and yelped. Standing in the office doorway, Jim raised his eyebrows at her.

"Jim," she said. "Jesus Christ."

"Nice to see you, too."

"Where the hell have you been?"

"I had a doctor's appointment. I told you."

"You told me?"

"It's on the calendar."

"Jesus Christ." Her heart was thudding against her ribs. "Jesus Christ, Jim."

He walked to the middle of the room and looked her up and down. She was sweaty and covered in dirt and grime. Her jeans were torn at the right knee and he could see blood crusted on her palm.

"Eun, what the hell?" he said. "What in the world happened to you?"

CHAPTER
SIX

He agreed that the window was an alarming mystery, but of course Jim refused to entertain any notions about anyone or anything living in the attic or invading their apartment. (He said *home* rather than *apartment*, but Eun let it go.)

"There's a perfectly logical explanation for everything," he said, his tone more patronizing than usual. "Even if we don't know what it is."

"I know what it is," she said.

"I'll call the guy—what's his name? Brian? Ryan? The property manager we're supposed to call. I'll leave him a voicemail. Probably a branch hit it or something."

"What branch, Jim? There's no branch anywhere."

"Fine, then a bird."

"A bird did that?"

"A fucking big bird, all right? It slammed into the window, smashed it out. Happens all the damn time, Eun!"

"From the *inside*?"

"Christ!" he shouted, throwing up his arms. Eun flinched and stepped back. "What do you want me to say? That I believe you that there's—what? A lunatic hiding in the attic? Or is it a ghost? We've been through all of this already, and you know—goddamnit, you *know* that isn't true, Eun. It's not true because it's not fucking possible. Why can't you see that?"

"It called me Janet," she said, wrapping her arms around herself.

"What?"

"I said it called me Janet."

"It—someone *spoke* to you? You're hearing things too?"

"I heard it because it spoke to me. Right in my ear." She pointed aggressively to her left ear, where the stranger had been poised when it said her old nickname, the American-sounding name she chose for herself in the fourth grade to feel less like an outsider. "And there's no way it could have known that. Even if it eavesdrops on us, we never talk about that. There's no reason to. It *couldn't* have known, Jim."

Jim shut his eyes and sighed deeply, his mouth downturned so dramatically it almost looked to Eun like he was trying to be funny. But there was nothing funny about any of this and nobody was laughing. Eun was traumatized, and Jim simply seemed disappointed, which in turn saddened Eun. Even if he did believe that she was backsliding into delusions and hallucinations, his reaction should have been one of concern, not disappointment as though she'd done something *to* him. She hadn't done anything to anyone, save the stranger in the attic whose face she pushed in when she escaped its awful hold on her.

She perked up a little upon recalling that. The welt—she hadn't shown Jim the welt.

Rather than pull up her sleeve this time, Eun pulled the top off altogether so that she was standing in the kitchen in just her bra. She jutted the shoulder at him and said, "Look at that. *Look* at that, Jim."

"Shit," he said, narrowing his eyes and getting closer to examine it. "That looks pretty bad, baby. Is it a rash or something?"

"It's fucking frostbite is what it is," she barked back. "It put its hand on me and clamped down. Felt like it was solid ice all the way through. Look, Jim. Look—it's the shape of its goddamn hand."

At this, he pulled a face, the concern melting away from it. Eun knitted her brow and looked from Jim to her own shoulder. The welt was still very much there, but it no longer looked like much of anything apart from an amorphous splotch. It had swollen in the time since the stranger grabbed her, and the shape of the hand was now lost.

Jim said, "A hand."

"I should've taken a damn picture. Shit!"

Tears welled up in her big brown eyes, at the sight of which Jim finally began to soften. He nodded, touched her gently at the elbow, and kissed her on the forehead before helping her slip back into her top. "We can get through this," he said quietly. "We are *going* to get through this."

"How," Eun wondered aloud, "when you don't even believe me?"

DESPITE HIS PROTESTS, EUN REFUSED TO SEE A DOCTOR FOR HER injuries, convinced that it would just look like Jim had been knocking her around. Instead, she treated herself as best she could, applying antiseptic cream to her cuts and scrapes and keeping a warm washcloth on her shoulder until the swelling went down. Even then, it still didn't resemble a handprint like it did at first.

Strangely enough, it was Jim rather than Eun who acted like a nervous wreck all evening. He paced from room to room, starting tasks he would then abandon in favor of something else, while constantly checking in with her. She'd told him she didn't really want to talk any more about it until she had time to give it all some more thought, but what she really meant was that she needed to come up with a plan that in all likelihood would not involve him. She scrolled through social media on her phone without paying any attention to it, all the while pivoting in her mind between running away and facing this son of a bitch down.

But how could she face something down when she didn't even know what it was or what it wanted?

Me, she told herself. *It wants me.*

It told me to stay.

"Stay," she whispered. "Janet, stay."

"What was that?" Jim called out from the bedroom.

"Nothing," she said. But she hoped it just might be everything.

THE URGE TO RETURN TO HER PARENTS WAS STRONG THROUGHOUT THE rest of the day, but Eun resisted. She had already run away once, and of course that hadn't changed a thing. It wouldn't change anything now. There were only two options available to her: leave permanently and never come back, or do something about the stranger terrorizing her.

Jim went out like a light almost as soon as they went to bed. It was uncommon for him, but Eun figured his day-long anxiety must have worn him down. She almost felt guilty, but she kept reminding herself that it wasn't her fault he refused to have faith in her. Perhaps, she allowed, it was a big ask, believing a fantastical claim from a woman with a history of severe mental illness with no evidence apart from her word, but sometimes love made huge requests. Love, to Eun's way of thinking, had to mean making sacrifices or it wasn't worth anything at all. And was it really such a terrible sacrifice to just listen? To believe?

Maybe it was. She really didn't know. Apart from some baseline depression and generalized anxiety issues—and the odd panic attack once or twice a year—their five-year relationship had been entirely free of her more extreme issues from the past. He only knew about them because she told him, so as far as Jim should be concerned, they were ancient history. Yet here it was, a relic of the distant past rearing its ugly-ass head once again and metamorphosing into a wedge between them. It was far from fair, and the inequity of it all made her want to scream where she lay beside him.

Jim began to snore, so Eun rolled onto her side and gently rubbed the small of his back with her uninjured hand which, as it usually did, soothed him into softer breathing. He brought his knees up to his round beer belly and sighed contently, still fast asleep. Eun wished she was, too. She hadn't particularly expected to sleep well that night, as she hadn't any night since they moved into that godforsaken apartment in that godforsaken house, but she still had the smallest glimmer of hope. Now that she was beginning to put the pieces together in the chaos of her mind, she felt like one good night's sleep would be just the thing to keep her together to the end. She had even considered taking one of Jim's over-the-counter sleeping pills, yet she was too afraid that she wouldn't be able to wake up again if she really needed to. Jim could sleep through the apocalypse most nights when he took those damned things, and that wasn't at all what Eun wanted or needed.

She needed rest, of course. But she also needed to be ready.

And as if to prove the point, when Eun rolled back onto her back, she was met with a familiar pair of sightless white eyes peering down at her from the ceiling. The stranger had somehow slid into the space between the attic floor and the paneled ceiling and pulled one of the panels away just enough to poke its night-black head through. Its eyes appeared bigger, rounder than they had before, and though they had no pupils she could tell it *saw* her. It was all but looking straight through her, to the heart of her.

The stranger's head tilted to one side, as though trying to get a better vantage point, whereupon it started to scratch at the underside of another panel with its jagged fingers, an arrhythmic scraping noise that caused the ceiling apparatus to tremble above her.

Eun said, "No—I'm not ready. Go *away*."

To this, she could have sworn she heard the thing quietly chuckle before withdrawing back into the ceiling, away from the half-open panel. For an astonished second, she almost thought the admonition actually worked this time, but that was until she heard the sound of another ceiling panel being shaken out of its frame.

The panel was directly above Jim.

This time, the stranger pulled the panel completely out, leaving a hole large enough for it to spill its entire torso through. Dangling so, the creature canted its head to gaze at Eun as its spindly right arm extended like a spider's leg toward Jim's head.

"No," Eun said, determined to fight if she had to, but when she tried to sit up, she found herself frozen where she lay, utterly paralyzed. Her eyes traced the stranger from the right hand reached toward Jim up to its staring face, then down its left arm to the single, pencil-thin forefinger touching her own hand. The cold emanating from the touch worked its way from her hand to her arm, across her chest and stomach, down her spine, and throughout her muscles and nerves.

It locked her in place, helpless to watch while the stranger turned to face Jim, when the bottom half of the stranger's face split open into a broad, toothy smile. To Eun, it looked like rotted fenceposts appearing from behind fire-blackened shrubs. She tried to shout at the damned thing, but her voice was as inoperable as the rest of her. Only her eyes seemed free to roam, but they stayed focused on the terrorizing scene playing out beside her.

The stranger's fingertips settled, one by one, around the periphery of Jim's face, and when the last one touched him, his legs shot out and his entire body went rigid. From the creature's gaping grin a long, solidly black tongue appeared, writhing like an eel, lapping at Jim's neck and shoulders until Jim began to moan—softly at first, but it quickly morphed into that same terrible clicking he had done the night before in the office.

The cold reached Eun's bones and, achingly, she longed to shiver, but even this was denied her in her paralysis. She wondered if Jim felt the dreadful cold too, or if he felt anything at all. There was no way for her to tell if the clicking was Jim's response to what was being done to him, or if it was the stranger somehow communicating through him. All she knew was her fear; fear for Jim and fear that her developing comprehension of these horrors would count for nothing.

I know you, she thought. *I have always known you.*

And that, it seemed, was enough.

The stranger quickly withdrew its hand from Jim's face as a child might whip a hand away from a hot surface, and it wound its disgusting black tongue back into the crevice of its mouth. Jim fell limp and immediately resumed snoring.

"*Yes*," the stranger said, turning back to her.

You were under my bed and in my closet.

"*I wassss.*"

You were in every shadow. You found me where I hid.

"*Alwayssss*," it said. "*Always find Jaaaaanet.*"

You found me again, from wherever you went. Wherever you come from.

"*Stay Jaaaanet. Staaaaaay.*"

You don't want me to stay, she thought. *You want me to go. You want me to go with you.*

To where it came from. The place where night had no stars, no moon, no clouds. No sky at all. A place of absolute darkness and the coldest cold she could imagine. A place of death, yet beyond death.

Darker, deeper, and colder than a grave.

"*Jaaaaanet.*"

I'm not Janet anymore.

"*Euuuuun*," it said, mockingly. "*Eun the looooon.*"

Fuck you.

"*Staaaay.*"

"I can't," she said, startled to hear her own voice. "I *won't*."

The stranger's eyes seemed to widen at this, as though it was surprised, but they then clouded over with what certainly looked to Eun like rage when it bellowed, "*YOU—WILL—STAAAAY!*"

It removed its hand from hers, but rather than withdraw again, the stranger lurched at her, its yellowing eyes bulging and smoky black flesh swarming over its form as it sailed first at and then *into* her. Headfirst, the stranger sank into Eun's mouth, wide open for a scream that would never come, filling her throat like thick, brackish graywater. She threw both hands to her neck, clawing at her throat now that she could move again, but there was no stopping it.

In a matter of seconds, the stranger had disappeared into her mouth and spread throughout her veins and organs, so cold that it burned like fire. It seeped into her leaden muscles and invaded her flesh. Her ears and nostrils filled with it, and soon thereafter so did her lungs. At first, she struggled to breathe, believing herself to be suffocating, or more likely drowning, but she wasn't. This was only a new way of breathing, colder and slower, thick and heavy. And by the time she realized she wasn't drowning, the stranger permeating her body filled her eyes, coating them with a frozen darkness that wiped out the room's weak light like it was blowing out the world's only candle.

In time—hours, perhaps, or only minutes—the painful sting of the cold gradually subsided, and for a blissful instant, Eun hoped this meant the stranger was releasing her. But the darkness remained, stark and absolute, and she began to realize she hadn't grown warmer. Rather, she felt nothing at all.

She couldn't tell if she was still in bed or standing up. She tried to swing her arms, turn her head, but whether or not she succeeded was a complete mystery with no sight, no hearing, no feeling. It was how she imagined a sensory deprivation tank might feel, only worse, with her airways and lungs and mouth and stomach all plugged up with the shapeless entity that possessed her. She wasn't even sure if her eyes were open or not, but she decided it didn't much matter either way. There was nothing to look at. There was only *it*.

The stranger, which had found her at long last.

It can't end this way, she thought. *It isn't fair.*

It isn't fucking fair.

Eun, rasped the stranger.

Eun the looooon, came the voice again. Or was it another voice, adding to the first? *Loony Euuuun.*

They had chanted that at her in school, when she came back after her time "away," as her father insisted on calling it. They sniggered and shied away, almost as though afraid of catching what she had. They whispered in huddles and defaced her locker, and the only time she ever fought back she was suspended for a week and her history teacher demanded she be moved to private study for the safety of all involved. They thought she was dangerous. They thought she was poisoned. They all thought she was out of her fucking mind.

She had gone from "the Korean girl" to "the crazy girl who sees things that aren't there."

Do you see? she wanted to scream at them now. *I was right all along. They* were *there.*

They're here.

Don't you see?

CHAPTER
SEVEN

She crouched inside the pantry, knees to her chin and her fingers interlaced over her shins. In order to fit, she had to remove the pots from within as well as the little shelf, most of which she piled up on the counter beside the toaster. Would a stranger notice the clutter and understand something was amiss? Janet sincerely hoped not.

And yet, given how nightmarishly awful her week had been so far, there was at least a miniscule part of her that wondered if letting the strangers take her could be much worse. The week prior she had gotten so spooked by something crawling in the shadows of the locker room showers after gym, something she could have sworn grinned at her, that she ran back out into the gymnasium in just her underwear and bra. First thing Monday morning, her locker was festooned with panties and bras like bunting for a parade. She stopped dead in the middle of the hallway when she saw the cruel prank, and if there was a single soul within earshot who didn't laugh, she didn't know about it.

By Tuesday, the narrative had evolved to describe Janet as a sex maniac, deliberately flashing everyone from students to faculty, and on Wednesday afternoon she heard the first rumblings about affairs with teachers and secret abortions. Some were saying she had to be on drugs, but nobody could really agree upon which drugs she favored. The one thing everyone appeared to agree on was that Janet Park was a psycho, best avoided, fun to mock.

Janet from another planet.

Eun the loon.

The bitch was just crazy, that was all.

And for all her efforts to hide it from them, from everyone, it never took long for one of her strangers to throw her for a loop, to show up when her defenses were down and frighten her so badly the façade went to pieces. It seemed like any time the abuse started to dwindle, any time the bullying and crass accusations began to wane, the strangers took notice and decided to ratchet things back up again. It was bad enough when it was the strangers at home and the bullies at school, but by now she had no bigger or worse bullies than the strangers themselves. They only ever let up on her when they were planning something. Of that much, she was certain.

Just as she was certain that their endgame, their ultimate goal, wasn't to kill her, but to ruin her. To make her *really* crazy. And maybe, she worried frequently, something worse still that she hadn't quite figured out yet.

So, she hid. Anywhere she could find and fit into, any time she so much as sensed their presence, Janet hid. Yet even as she pressed her spine against the inside corner of the cabinet in which she crouched, she knew it was only ever a temporary solution. The strangers always found her.

What meager light leaked into the cabinet from the kitchen through the narrow cracks around the doors abruptly dimmed, signaling the sudden appearance of something just outside. Janet's eyes popped wide and she held her breath, hating herself for trembling lest she made a noise and be discovered.

"*Dodaeche?*" Janet's mom, undoubtedly wondering why all the pots were stacked up on the counter. "*Eun?*"

Janet's eyes shut gently and her lungs emptied with a sigh of relief.

"*Umma,*" she said. It was one of the few words from her parents' homeland they ever bothered to teach her.

"*Umma* is here," her mother said. "No worry, Janet. *Umma* is here."

Janet's shoulders relaxed and she released her white-knuckled grasp on her shins as she leaned forward to push open the cabinet door. It was only as she was already doing so that it occurred to her that her mother just called her Janet. Which her mother would never, ever do.

"Oh, God," Janet said as the billowing plumes of black consumed the light of the kitchen.

"*Umma is heeeeeeeere, Jaaaaaanet,*" mocked the stranger. It threw open both cabinet doors and rushed inside, all huge milky eyes and smiling black teeth, like a jar of ink spilled into a pond. "*Always heeeere. Alwaaaayssss heeeere.*"

She opened her mouth wide to scream but the stranger was quicker; it shoved two long, knuckled fingers into her mouth that bent down into the opening of her throat, silencing the scream that was building there. The fingers twitched, scratching at her larynx and gagging her so badly her eyes spilled tears. The scream that died in her throat was reborn in her mind, shatteringly loud inside her head as she vainly fought to free herself from the shadow stranger's invasive attack.

Even as her throat started to go numb from the stinging cold of the clawing fingers in her throat, she felt the almost fluid cold seep into, and then behind, her eyes. Her skull became a receptacle for its darkness, its empty chill that overtook her mind, her body, her spirit if ever she had one. It was as though it wasn't merely taking her over, but *replacing* her, from the inside out.

Piece by piece.

Until there was nothing left of her.

"Eun?" her mother said, her voice a faint echo from far away. "Eun, honey? Where you go?"

I'm here, Umma. I'm right here.

"Eun?"

Help me, Mom. Please. Help me.

"*Michin yeoja.*"

I'm not a crazy girl, Umma. *It's real. It was always real. Please, Mom. Please.*

Umma?

Mom?

"Eun?" Jim said.

Jim?

"Eun, where are you?"

She didn't know. Not exactly. She *had* been in the cabinet, in the kitchen, in the rowhouse she'd grown up in. But where had the stranger taken her? She tried and failed to comprehend if this was a memory or a dream, if she was Janet or Eun. Both or neither.

She couldn't even be sure if she was alive anymore. Everything was so dark. So cold. And she couldn't feel herself anymore. That tight little ball of incessant anxiety that resided in her chest seemed to be gone. Before, she would have celebrated its disappearance, but she couldn't remember not feeling it there, compressing and expanding, buzzing against her ribs, and she was terrified to think of what its absence might mean.

"Eun? Are you here?"

I don't know, Jim. I'm nowhere.

And nowhere was so terribly empty, so hollow and lonesome. She sensed space open around her, wide open, and she stood up, no longer in the cabinet if ever she was, impossibly minute in the gargantuan breadth of so much nothing.

Nothing around her, above her. Nothing beneath her feet. She stretched out like a starfish, Michelangelo's Adam-cum-Eve, and had to wonder whether or not she was crying because there was no way to be sure.

I'm nowhere, Jim.

I'm sorry.

"THERE YOU ARE," JIM SAID WITH AN ANXIOUS CHUCKLE. "JESUS, I thought you'd up and left there for a second."

"I couldn't sleep," she said. She sat up on the couch and stretched her back, cat-like. "You wouldn't believe the nightmares."

He scrunched up his face the way he tended to when he was concerned, and he walked over to sit down beside her. "Things have been a mess since we got here, haven't they?"

With a sardonic half-grin, she nodded. "You can say that again."

Jim wrapped an arm around her and pulled her toward him. She sighed, half-contentedly and half-frustratedly. He rubbed the small of her back and, after a moment, said, "We could leave, you know."

She blinked several times and leaned away so that she could look at him. "Wait," she said, "what?"

He squinted, gathering his thoughts, at the living room window and the bright, late summer morning beyond the glass. "Things were fine. I mean, *everything* was fine. For five years. And then we came here. I don't know what it is, and to be honest with you? I don't even fucking care. I just know we'd be better off someplace else. Jesus, *anyplace* else. So—I think we should leave."

"You're—you're serious?"

"Dead serious," Jim insisted. "It's not worth it, is it? So we'll eat the fee for breaking the lease. Big deal. We'll still have *us*, and what's more important?"

"Us," she agreed. "Always us."

"You're goddamn right," he said with a smile, and he leaned in for a kiss.

When the kiss was done, she whispered into his left ear, "Thank you, love. Thank you."

That morning, they made love for the first time since moving into the old apartment house on 68, after which they lay side by side on top of the comforter and idly discussed where they might go looking for a better place to live, and how silly they had been for ever agreeing to the current apartment in the first place. She admitted at last it had been only stress that had conjured visitors from the attic and the shadows, and he assured her it was all over now and no score was being kept. It was as good as forgotten, or at least as soon as they rid themselves of the worst mistake they had ever made as a couple. Jim apologized for the lousy attitude he'd had of late, but she wouldn't hear it. It was all in the past. Only their future remained. Only their future was real.

The light melted the shadows away, and the nightmares receded into the foggy banks of distant memory. Everything was going to be all right.

JIM SMILED WANLY AFTER HE FINISHED SHOVING THE VERY LAST DUFFLE he could possibly fit into the back of his Toyota. It was only his first carload, but with the destination being only twenty minutes across town, he was feeling pretty good about getting everything done before the end of the month. He felt slightly less assured that the mere act of moving house would be sufficient for restoring his partner's delicate mental health, but he was hopeful and, better still, open to some ups and downs on the road back to where they were.

He closed up the back of the SUV, locked it with his remote, and headed back upstairs for a bottle of water and a breather before taking his first haul to their new home.

Home. Again. At last.

Same town. Same them.

But no more shadows.

No more strangers.

The bathroom door that never quite closed all the way squealed open, and she walked past the absurd stove room, into the kitchen where Jim stood by the refrigerator gulping down cold water. She approached from behind and wrapped her arms around his midsection. At the beginning of their relationship, she could do so easily, but with every passing year it grew a little more challenging to touch her fingertips around his belly.

"Are you ready to go?" she asked him.

"Let's make it happen, cap'n," he said playfully.

Jim pivoted, still within the circle of her arms, and kissed her forehead before they went hand-in-hand for the door and to begin the next chapter. A better chapter.

Together.

THE PROPERTY MANAGER HAD BEEN A FRIENDLY AND EASY GOING SORT when first Jim and Eun moved into the helter skelter apartment on 68, but upon learning that they meant to break their lease—and worse still, the news about the attic window—his attitude quickly became chilly. He sent a couple of guys to assess the damage to the window, after which they covered it with a sheet of transparent plastic that they securely taped around the edges.

It was through this plastic that, as the soon-to-be-former occupants of the second floor apartment pulled out of the parking lot one by one in their respective cars, Eun Park watched them go. She grasped what was left of the window's inner casing with branch-like ink-black fingers that scratched at the paint while she glared through wide, milky eyes at the life she used to have, slowly driving away from her.

All around her, at the periphery of her senses, the darkness hovered and swirled and crept like cigarette smoke, curling around her and seeping inside so that it could pulse within the cold of her. She had not yet mastered the art of detaching from the pitch, from the shadows and all the others in that place where light and warmth never penetrated, so Eun knew it was only a matter of seconds before she would be reclaimed from the window, from the attic and the house and the world of love and hope and second chances. Back to the infinite black, where all strangers gathered and waited and conspired to find the ones who could *see*, the ones like Eun.

Or Janet.

Or whomever, whatever she was now.

"*Jiiiiim,*" she croaked. It hurt to speak, her throat still clogged with the frigid viscosity of the endless night. *It's not me, Jim. That thing is not me.*

But Eun knew that wasn't strictly true. She understood how it worked. That thing *was* her—now. And as for her, she was something else. Something unknowable even to herself.

She was a stranger. At long last, she was one of her own terrifying strangers.

If she could have, she would have cried. Instead, she barked a sharp, raspy laugh.

They were long gone now, out of view. And in the ensuing moments that followed their departure, the world around the old, odd house commenced disappearing, as well. Day turned to night, the clouds melted away, all the lights blinked out as the other world washed over all of it, a tsunami of total darkness that swallowed it all up in one massive, greedy gulp. Thereafter, there was no window, no attic, no house on 68. No Yalesville, no Connecticut, no difficult parents or angry neighbors. Nothing at all.

Nothing but the cold she could sense but not feel, the heavy dark, and all of the other strangers moving aimlessly, hopelessly through the stark emptiness of what she could only think of as hell itself. They all came when she did, apart from her but the same as her, a vast network of lost souls clambering for the light, the warmth of another's life. Empty and afraid, hungry and alone. Always so terribly alone.

Someday, she would try again. She had escaped once; she could do it again. And again after that, if necessary. She didn't have to be Eun or Janet, or even Jim. After all, a starving dog would eat most anything.

She wouldn't be a stranger forever. But until she could find another opening, another one who could see and hear her, there would be nothing. Hollow, silent, empty nothing. And in an obscene way, she almost welcomed the respite.

She almost felt at peace.

Almost.

THE ART OF DEVASTATION

BY MORGAN SYLVIA

The storm isn't supposed to pick up until later, but by the time I reach the restaurant, the wind is already gusting hard, ripping orange and crimson leaves from swaying trees, sending bits of litter across the parking lot. It lashes my hair with icy fingers as I get out of my beat-up Subaru, then slams the car door open into the side of the expensive SUV I've parked beside, leaving a minuscule scratch. Hoping no one notices, I hoist the old leather satchel over my shoulder, then pause for a moment, taking in the scene before me.

The restaurant perches on a rocky point overlooking the harbor, offering picture-perfect Maine seafood and, on nice days, picture-perfect Maine views. This is not a nice day. Grey clouds hang thick above the rugged, rocky cliffs that hug the harbor. Here and there, ancient, weather-beaten houses peek out from the green-black woodline topping the craggy bluffs. I find myself frozen in place, disoriented, off-kilter. I haven't been downeast in so long that it seems new to me. The bite of the salt wind, the eternal crash of waves against rock, the screech of seagulls: these things are familiar and alien at once.

Beyond the mouth of the harbor, open ocean waits, deep and dark and full of ghosts. The waters are black and choppy, and the endless line of froth-capped waves rolling in are already dangerously high. Simply looking out at the churning Atlantic triggers the old fears. My heart pounds with anxiety, and my breaths come quick and shallow. Cold black fear churns in my gut.

I force it down. I can't let nerves rule me today.

The next gust of wind carries both the icy promise of winter's cold and droplets of salt spray that sting my face. I pull my old army jacket in close and scurry inside, passing thick double doors that sport lobster buoys for handles. Inside, I stamp off the stormdrops and look around. Soft yellow lights glow against wooden walls hung with fishnets, lobster traps, and taxidermized sea creatures: requisite décor for these forgotten places that dot Maine's rocky coast. A bearded, flannel-clad millennial stands behind the bar, polishing glasses and watching the weather channel on a flatscreen TV. Onscreen, a vividly colored radar image shows the approaching storm: an ominous blob that will soon cover all of New England.

Aside from the bartender, the place is nearly empty, though whether this is due to the storm, the hour, or the economy is anyone's guess. Behind the empty hostess' station, someone has scrawled the week's specials in rainbow chalk on a blackboard. *Hurricane Betsy Specials! Blueberry Scones, Lobster Bisque, Steak Bomb Poutine, Steamahs. Best Chowdah On The Point!*

It doesn't matter that there's no one to greet me.

Elle Sanders sits perfectly straight in a cracked leather booth tucked into the restaurant's northwest corner, silhouetted against a huge, rain-splattered window. Steam rises in tendrils from the generic white mug before her. She hasn't seen me yet. I cross the room, passing empty, scarred tables, floor-to-ceiling windows, and a lobster tank where unfortunate but delicious crustaceans await their fate. Nerves churn in my stomach. I spent the whole drive up trying to convince myself that my final grade—and therefore, my future— do not actually depend on this interview, which I'm still surprised she agreed to. I glance out at the storm-tossed sea as I am pulled into the aging ballerina's orbit. The sight of the breakers crashing into the granite bluffs terrifies me. I fight back another wave of anxiety.

Elle glances up as I approach. The face I've seen in so many magazines and television screens is suddenly real, framed by gleaming pine walls and taxidermized lobsters. She's aged since her last movie. Though she still sports her trademark crimson nails and lipstick, her ash blonde hair is steel grey now, and fine wrinkles pull at her eyes and lips.

Surprisingly, it's the rescue photo she reminds me of, the one they took when they pulled her off the island. In that picture, her mouth is stained with corpseblood, and her neck is draped not in diamonds, but in seaweed and intestines.

"You're late," she says coolly as I reach the booth.

I'm immediately annoyed. Even before the storm turned this way, I wasn't thrilled that she insisted on meeting here. The cost of the gas and room I rented absolutely drained me. I'll be eating cheese sandwiches and ramen noodles for weeks.

A retort rises to my lips, but I catch myself in time, bite the words off at the root. "There was a tree down on Route 1," I tell her, swinging the satchel into the chair. "Weather's coming in faster than they said. It's a Cat 3 now."

"I heard they're calling for 40-foot seas," Elle sounds almost nonchalant, as though this wasn't a record-breaking anomaly. "I imagine the roads were rough. That last stretch is a bitch in winter."

The storm isn't the only thing looming over the state. I counted five empty businesses in this tiny fishing town alone. With the economy soured, fisheries limited and/or dying, and tourism slowed to a trickle, Maine is struggling. Beloved mom-and-pop places are closing their doors, and the touristy spots are either raising or slashing their prices, rolling the dice either way. Even the bars are failing.

Outside, the wind rises to a scream.

Elle looks me up and down, her perfectly made-up eyes raking me over as I put my purse down atop the satchel and take my rain-soaked jacket off. I'm immediately self-conscious, painfully aware that I am everything she's not: casual, poor, slouchy. Her leather

Gucci purse probably cost more than I make in a month. She's sporting designer clothes: I'm wearing black combat boots, woolen tights, a dark floral ditzy skirt, and a cable-knit fisherman's sweater that is only new to me: I picked it up at a thrift store last fall.

"You look tired," Elle says politely, as I slide into the booth.

I don't need reminding that there are dark circles under my eyes, that my skin is pale and grey. I haven't had a decent meal or a full night's sleep in weeks. I'm not about to tell her why.

The night terrors have returned. The green-eyed, scaled specter that has haunted me since childhood reappeared out of the blue last month. With every nightmare, the wraith gets closer, clearer, more menacing. Every night in my dreams, I sink again through cold green waters, only to find her waiting for me, screeching pelagic curses in a language I do not know but somehow still understand.

But it is daytime now, and the aquatic monsters are sleeping.

I take a deep breath of fried-seafood air, then sit back and settle in, getting a better look at the photos on the varnished wooden walls. Pictures and paintings of lobster boats and seals sunning themselves on the rocks are interspersed with a series of sailors' knots in fancy frames. Their names are etched into small metal plaques: *Clove Hitch, Bowline Knot, Becket Bend.* The configurations remind me of the sea lore book my mother read to me as a child. *Three knots a tempest brings.*

Someone in the kitchen snaps on a marine radio. The voices are broken by static, further distorted by the sound of frying food and an old Elton John song on the radio. I wonder if the restaurant staff has friends or family caught out in the storm.

Elle watches me calmly, waiting. There's something familiar in her gaze. I've seen enough of her movies and interviews to warrant that, but it still unsettles me.

I tuck a stray lock of hair behind my ears. "Thank you for meeting me, Mrs. Sanders."

"Ms." She corrects me calmly. "I'm divorced. Thrice, now. Of course, I've lost far more important things than the *R* along the way." Her eyes meet mine. "But you would know that, wouldn't you? You've done your research."

"I have. Not that there's much to find on Giselle Sanderson."
I fold my jacket, place it atop the satchel. "There's plenty on Elle
Sanders, of course: Interviews, reviews, and more 90s gossip column
fluff pieces than I can count. But as far as Giselle Sanderson…there's
very little after the rescue. You've done well at scrubbing your early
life from the internet."

Elle smiles. "My publicist is a bear. Though it helps that certain
things happened before the internet made keeping things private
difficult, if not impossible. We didn't have smartphones or social
media back then."

I tilt my head, immediately curious. "Do you ever think about
that? If you'd had cell phones…the others may still be alive today."

"No." Elle shakes her head. "*Possibilities* aren't real. What
happened, happened."

Fair enough. I fish into the leather satchel, pull out the magazines
and stuffed manilla folders, and set them on the table. Everything in
the pile is familiar: the magazines, clippings, even the articles printed
from websites. *Elle Sanders' Shocking Mental Break. Elle Sanders and Matt
Dobbs Split Confirmed. Elle Sanders "A Terror On Set." Ballerina Breaks
Down On Biopic Set. Ballet Coven: Fact Or Fiction? Behind The Scenes Of
The Tragic Heather Winters Photo Shoot. Elle Sanders Breaks Silence About
Witchcraft Rumors. Did Elle Sanders Kill Heather Winters?*

Most of the articles are useless to me. I no longer care about her
frenemy/rival/costar's tragic death. (Or murder, if the speculations
were true.) I'm not interested in the charity scandal, the feud with
the Miss It starlet, or her affairs with rockers and actors and foreign
kings.

I just want to know what happened on that island.

Elle reaches out with a crimson nail to adjust the magazine on
top, turning it to face her. Her younger self stares out from the cover.
This must be around the time she danced *Dracula*. The chunky blonde
streak and thin eyebrows she favored in the 90's are clearly visible. "I
haven't seen this one," she murmurs. She turns to the feature article,
which I've bookmarked with a Hannaford grocery receipt.

In my earliest memories, I am stumbling around my bedroom in
my pink tutu, pretending to be her.

"My mother used to take me down to Boston to see you dance," I say quietly. "I've seen you in so many ballets. *Dracula, Sleeping Beauty, The Rite of Spring, Undine,* and *Giselle.*"

Elle looks startled and suddenly uneasy, as though I've breached her privacy.

A short, tanned waitress with bleached blonde hair approaches. (A true Mainer: she's still wearing shorts.) As she puts menus on the table, I notice she sports a nautical compass tattoo on one toned forearm, a tentacled sea monster on the other.

"Good morning, ladies! Looks like we're in for a true nor'easter." She tops off Elle's coffee, and rattles off the specials I saw listed on the board. "We're on a limited menu today, but if there's something specific you want, just ask."

Elle orders wheat toast with avocado. I opt for coffee and a blueberry scone. Another gust of wind lashes the windows as the waitress speed-walks away. I glance at the docks again, noticing for the first time the flowers and lanterns set around the granite monument at the edge of the dock.

Elle follows my gaze. "Those that go down to the sea in ships," she says quietly. "Lobster boat sank last week. Three lives lost. No idea what happened. The EPIRB went off, but the Coast Guard found nothing but flotsam." She sips her coffee. "The ocean will always take its claim."

The memory strikes immediately. I am a child, leaning over the rail of the boat taking us to a clambake on Cabbage Island. One moment, I'm staring down into dark green waters, looking for mermaids, happy and innocent. In the next, I'm falling into the ocean, which is black and bottomless and filled with monsters. Icy waters close in over my head, and I am pulled down into cold liquid darkness. My nose and throat fill with salty brine as I sink from the light.

I force my anxiety down and busy myself by setting up the phones and making sure the apps are recording properly. When I'm set, I find Elle calmly waiting.

It's time to begin.

I take a deep breath. "Can you introduce yourself?"

Elle looks into the phone, speaks without missing a beat. "I'm Elle Sanders. I'm 48 years old, and I am an award-winning dancer, actress, singer, and choreographer, founder of the Sun Road Dance Academy, patron of the arts."

She left out a few things: 90s It girl for a hot minute, tabloid fodder for years, a blazing star who fell as fast and as far as she rose. Former girlfriend of controversial singer said to have sold his soul to the devil. A renowned dancer, she was the star of her generation until an accident ended her dance career. She moved from stage to screen, starring in a few blockbusters and a string of flops before returning to dance, this time as a choreographer. She now owned a ridiculously overpriced makeup line, co-hosted a very scripted 'reality' dance show, and ran a prestigious ballet camp.

But I can fill these details in later. *Keep it moving,* Tommy told me. *Like a live podcast. No dead air.*

I clear my throat. "I was surprised that you agreed to the interview. You've turned down so many that I only reached out as a formality. Why are you breaking your silence now, all these years later?"

She turns the question back on me. "Why do you think?"

I pause, considering. "Well, the obvious answer is that the statute of limitations ran out. Though I suppose the rules are probably different for crimes that happened offshore."

Elle raises a perfectly-shaped eyebrow. "The rules for *everything* are different offshore. And your research should have shown that I was never charged with any crime. Any applicable statute of limitations would have run out decades ago."

"True. But there are recent developments." I flip through the files, pull out the snippet, and push it towards her. "What are your thoughts on this?"

The story was a blip buried in the weird news segment, sandwiched between the giant albino moose, the blue lobster, and a UFO sighting over Vassalboro. I can pretty much quote the piece word for word. *A team of researchers digging for artifacts found more than they bargained for when they stumbled across a forgotten cemetery on an uncharted island off the coast of Maine. The site had been desecrated, the bones of the dead strewn about and covered in toothmarks. And in one open grave, a 200-year-old body tied in knotted ropes was sporting the class ring of Chris Matthews, who was lost at sea in 1993.*

Elle's face pales as she reads. I see the tiniest tremor in the hand holding the page. "No one...no one contacted me."

I watch her, puzzled. "You didn't know about this?"

"No. I had no idea they found it." Elle breathes as though she is exhaling her strength. Even her voice sounds weaker.

"They returned it to his brother," I offer gently.

Her eyes lock onto mine. "I didn't mean the ring," she snaps. "I meant the island."

I frown. "I don't understand."

"No," Elle says. "I suppose you wouldn't."

She carefully pushes the paper back to me, using only her nail, as though she doesn't want to be contaminated by it. She looks angry, and I can't puzzle out why. Maybe she misses the attention? But that doesn't set right. No blip in *News of the Unexplained* would ever return her to her former golden girl paparazzi-fodder status. The world has moved on. Even the gossip columns have forgotten her.

The sea hasn't, I think.

Then I wonder where the thought even came from.

"If you didn't even know about this," I ask, "Why *did* you agree to talk to me?"

She looks me straight in the eye. "Because the tarot cards told me to."

She is mad after all, I realize. Seeing the dark gleam of her eye, I am reminded of her grainy black-and-white biopic, *The Art of Devastation*. The film was a box office flop, panned by critics and audiences alike, but my mother and I loved it. We watched it over and over again when I was a teen.

In my favorite scene, Elle dances on top of a cliff, her bloody feet staining sharp shells and rocks crimson-black.

The waitress returns with our order. Elle looks at her toast as though it were moving. "This is burnt. And I'd like some garlic butter."

I glance at the toast before the waitress apologizes and whisks it away. There's one tiny speck of blackness. *Drama queen*, I think. I break a piece off the scone, pop it into my mouth. The blueberries are tart and sweet, bursting with flavor, reminding me of the blueberry barrens I passed coming up. The fields stretched red and lifeless against the grey skies, boulders jutting into churning clouds.

I wonder if they will survive the storm.

Elle refuses to look at my plate. She notices me noticing, and gives a tiny half-smile. "I've been retired for years. But I still see food as numbers; calories, carbs, fat."

This surprises me. "Even after what happened?"

Her eyes flash. "*Especially* after what happened."

The wind raises to a scream.

"Let's start at the beginning," I tell her. "You were born in Manhattan to a very wealthy family. Your father was a hotshot agent, your mother an heiress and model."

"That isn't relevant." Elle points outside the window. "The story you want me to tell starts right *there* on that dock. What happened before doesn't matter."

"But it does," I have to coax her a bit. "There is a saying that the end is always the beginning. The beginning of your life here was the end of your privileged life in Manhattan, after your father fell from grace."

Elle gives a bitter laugh. "It was more of a swan dive than a fall."

She's not wrong. I have those articles too.

I sip my coffee. It is dark and bitter. "What do you remember about your early life?"

Elle glances at the snippets, then refuses to look again. "Not much. It's a blur now. Trips to Bloomingdales, the Russian Tea House, and the Met. Art galleries and dance school and fancy galas. Summers in the Hamptons, winters in Milan. I didn't realize how lucky I was until it fell apart. One day, I was on top of the world. And then suddenly there were cameras and news crews everywhere: outside our building, at the museum, at my father's office. Our phone rang so much my mother unplugged it." She puts her spoon down. "Things got really ugly after the newspaper ran the photo of my father with the strippers. I remember a lot of screaming, shouting, camera flashes everywhere. And then I was brought here, to my mother's family home. That was all she had left. Everything else was either seized or sold off in the divorce."

The sun briefly peeks out from behind the clouds. The diamond on her finger catches the light.

Poor little cannibal.

Keep it moving.

"You were sixteen when you moved here, and already turning heads as a dancer. I suppose going from Manhattan to downeast Maine would have been a bit of culture shock."

"Very much." Elle speaks with a raw honesty that surprises me. "I was in dance school, I had the cute boyfriend, the high-end clothes, the good life. And then it all got ripped away from me. We lost it all. Even my sweet sixteen gala was cancelled. After the scandal broke, we lived in darkness. Kept our shades drawn, so the paparazzi couldn't see in. I completely shut down. That's why I kept returning to the role of *Sleeping Beauty*. I was sleeping, when I got here. I was sleeping for a long time after the rescue."

I can't help but feel for her. "You said in your autobiography that you hated Maine at first."

"That's one word for it. I used more colorful terms at the time." Her voice seems to rise and fall with the wave pounding the rocks below. "I hated the accents, the wilderness, the long, cold winter nights. The huge dark stretches of unbroken forest unsettled me. Still do. I was used to skyscrapers. This cold remote coastal forest felt like another planet. I hated the ice in January, the mud in March, the mosquitoes in July. I missed my friends. I missed malls and ballet school and late-night subway rides to nightclubs we weren't supposed to go to. And I stuck out like a sore thumb at first." Elle's voice is bitter. I hear the resentful teen she once was. "That's the thing about small towns, you know. When a new piece of the puzzle drops in, well, you may as well move in under a microscope. I went full rebel. Dyed my hair black, started wearing leather and ripped jeans, all of that. And then I met Jason."

I pull out the *Morning Sentinel's* cover story. *Witchcraft and Cannibalism on Remote Island.* The sidebar features Jason's senior photo. It was taken at Thunder Hole in Acadia, on a rocky crag overlooking the same seas now churning and crashing against the docks below us. I study his face. Dark hair falls into scowling eyes, leather jacket. "Jason Kerriault. Northport's bad boy heartthrob."

The tiniest shade of a smile lifts her blood-red lips. "Mother *hated* him. He had long hair and wore leather and listened to heavy metal and smoked cigarettes *and* pot. She thought he was Satan personified."

I flip to the obituary. *Jason loved hunting, fishing, and exploring trails on his ATV. He also enjoyed music and was a talented artist.*

Elle gazes out at the sea.

I open her autobiography. "There's a passage here that struck me as rather insightful. '*It's strange, now, looking back on that time. The last traces of the old world were giving way to the new. Change hung so heavy in the air you could taste it. We saw the cracks appearing in society, the wars and social issues and pollution and drugs, but we were foolish enough to hope we could fix things.*'" I put the book down. "Is that still how you see that era?"

Elle pauses, considering. "I suppose so, yes. It was a different time. Clinton was president. Waco, Texas was all over the news, and the Seattle grunge scene was exploding. We had just graduated. Well, most of us. Sara had one more year. Kevin and Jason were going for their GEDs. They were already making money on the lobster boats. We pretended we'd be friends forever, but we were all going in different directions. We could feel things pulling us apart." She pauses, her voice almost wistful. "We were young, dumb fools, taken by a dream. But the dream had other ideas."

I pull out the rescue articles. The bloody, mad-eyed girl in the grainy newspaper photo bears little resemblance to the poised, coiffed dancer sitting across the table from me. Elle's eyes are sunken and wild and mad in that picture, her neck and face stained with gore. The leg sticking out beneath the Coast Guard blanket is skeletal.

The article's main photo shows the six of them on the dock outside this very restaurant, tanned and windblown, laughing. Beyond them, lobster boats float atop much smaller waves than those crashing below. Elle's face is turned towards the sun: she is in that bloom of youth, strikingly beautiful. She hasn't changed much physically, but the laughter has gone from her eyes.

I clear my throat. "Tell me about the others."

Elle looks at the photo, points faces out with a crimson fingernail. "Kevin Drake, Jason's best buddy. He had a good heart—or, I thought he did—but he was always in trouble. Probably would have ended up in jail. Chris, well, he just wanted to get out of here. He'd already enlisted in the Marines. Sara, Kevin's girlfriend, was a wild child, always down for a party. I think she would have stayed, settled down, had kids, eventually become a soccer mom with some wild stories and a wine habit. Zeke…he was very quiet and sweet. A gentle soul. He wanted to become a marine veterinarian and rehab seals. Anna was this bubbly, goofy girl. A Mainer girl-next-door type. She was going to be a nurse." Elle hesitates. "I envied them, you know. The honesty of their lives. In Manhattan, it seemed like everyone was wearing masks. They were allowed to be themselves. I had no concept of what life was like. They taught me…reality, really. Before I met them, I thought the worst thing about poverty was not having brand-name clothes or new cars. I didn't understand what it meant to struggle until my first husband left me penniless. I had to dance for a living." She carefully stirs sugar substitute into her coffee. "Of course, that was easy compared to what I went through on the island."

A dark head pops out of the water, then submerges again.

"I can imagine." I take a sip of coffee. "Let's move on. You set out on August 25th, 1993."

"Yes." Elle gives a faint smile. "I suppose I can put an exact date to the last day of my youth."

They'd found her three months later, covered in blood, with Chris's rotted right calf in her stomach.

"Did any of you think of the danger? Six teenagers out at sea, unsupervised?"

She laughs. "Our entire *generation* was unsupervised. And the guys had all been on lobster boats since they could walk." She pauses, thinking. "It was Jason's idea. His parents were assholes. You know, he told me that when his mom asked when he'd be back, he said October. She never even batted an eye."

"That's sad."

Elle laughs. "Mine didn't even notice I was gone. But you have to understand...island hopping was normal for us. We practically *lived* on boats. Anna and I waitressed on a whale watch tour, and Kevin, Jason, and Chris all worked on lobster boats. Any time we could get any of our parents' boats, we took off. If we had to stay on the mainland, we camped or went to my place or Chris' family's cabin at Moosehead." She looks out over the bay, pointing at a rocky outcrop that juts out from the harbor's curving sides. "You see that point? That was where we hung out when it was warm. High school kids still hang out there now. We would smoke a joint, and then want cookies, so we'd bring our milk cartons from school. I remember the picture on mine that day. Timmy O'Donnell, a smiling, freckled boy with chubby cheeks." She hesitates. "They never found him."

I raise an eyebrow. "You have a good memory."

She's quick to agree. "It's why I learn choreography so quickly."

My phone buzzes with weather alerts. Rain splatters the window beside me. "What did you do on those trips?"

"Whatever we wanted. That was the whole point. We were young and wild. The longer we were out on the water, the more we wanted to stay there. We were free there. Not tied to anything. The *freedom of the seas* isn't just a metaphor. Land began to feel like a cage. So, that summer, we decided to have one last trip. A banger, I think they call it these days. Summer was winding down, and the future was bearing down fast. We knew we'd be sucked up into the real world soon. The guys were usually on the lobster boats all summer, but they had a week off. We just went for it."

"But you didn't take a lobster boat. You stole your mother's yacht. A Catamaran Cruiser named *The Sapphire Dream*."

Elle raises a perfectly-shaped eyebrow. "You also have a good memory. That can be a blessing or a curse."

I ignore this. "You spent several days island hopping and camping. The *Bangor Daily News* article mentioned that you deliberately sought out haunted islands."

She laughs. "There are over 4000 islands off the coast of Maine. Most, if not all, of them have ghost stories attached to them. But to answer your question, yes, we did. Sara was interested in witchcraft. Ouija boards, seances, all that. She was goth before goth had a name. Jason, too."

"You also dabbled in witchcraft."

Elle's smile is bloodless, vampiric. "Strong women are always called witches, no matter what century we live in."

The waitress comes back with the replaced toast, tops off our coffee. "Bring us a pot," Elle tells her. "We're going to be here a while."

The waitress smiles and retreats. I wait until she's gone. "In your book, you mentioned that even approaching the island, things seemed off."

"Oh yes." Elle bobs her head. "I still remember the way the ocean was swirling and churning in eddies below us, the sound of the engine straining. Kevin had a hard time getting the boat into the cove. But he wasn't one to back down. He loved the rush of danger. I really realized that earlier that week, when we had a run in with the Old Sow."

I try not to sound as confused as I am. "What's Old Sow?"

"The biggest whirlpool on the eastern seaboard. Been swallowing ships and souls for, well, probably as long as ships have sailed these waters. We were sailing along, and suddenly these walls of water rose on both sides of us. We were all terrified, but Kevin was whooping and laughing. He got a rush out of it. I think he did it on purpose." Elle fixes me with a cold stare. "Can you swim?"

The query catches me off guard. Memory strikes hard and fast. *I am five, waking from another nightmare of salty black-green depths, the scaled, gilled being with the cold, gleaming eyes. I sob into my mother's chest, choking on words I don't understand, rambling about the locks and the wards.*

Elle is watching me, her gaze sharp and cold.

My throat tightens involuntarily. "No."

"You should learn," Elle says, casual again. "It's a basic life skill everyone should have. I was a good swimmer. But as soon as I looked down into those waters, I knew I was dead if we went down there. Even right offshore."

I put the cup down, hide the tremor in my hand. "Tell me about the first night on the island."

Elle sits back, her voice haunting, musical. "I remember feeling unwelcome. The woods were very, very quiet. Too quiet. No birds, no crabs, no bugs. We were used to islands. Usually, we'd see seals sunning themselves on the rocks, osprey and eagle nests in the pines, puffins and gulls on the shore. But there was nothing there, nothing alive in that place except for us. We never even used our bug spray, the whole time we were there. We never had to."

I tilt my head. "Did anything unusual happen that night?"

"No." She shakes her head. "We didn't even explore that much. There was an old lighthouse, and a small, ruined cabin beside it. That was as far as we got that day. The stonework was very different than what we usually see around here. There was this really thick, ancient door, and it was locked. I looked through this cracked, grimy window, and saw this old table and chairs, all neatly laid out. It felt off. I was immediately uneasy. I think we all were. We didn't stay long. We went back down to the beach and set up camp early, and then Sara, Anna, and I laid out the rest of the day. That night we had a campfire and cooked almost all of our food. We were *trying* to use the supplies up, so we didn't have to bring them home. Can you believe that?"

I murmur in sympathy. "Hindsight is 20/20."

"Definitely," Elle agrees. "We decided to play this drinking game we used to do at parties. We wrote confessions on scraps of paper and dropped them into a bucket. Then we'd read them out loud and try to guess who wrote it. If you guessed right, the person who wrote it had to drink. If you were wrong, *you* drank. Typical Blackport high school stuff, like going to the quarry in summer or snowmobiling in winter. It was usually pretty silly. I think so-and-so is cute. I once made out with this person. That kind of thing. But this place...just brought out the darkness in us."

"What did you confess to?"

"Wanting to disappear." Elle is surprisingly candid. "I wanted to fade away into nothing. They knew it was me right away."

"Because of the eating disorder."

She sips her coffee. "You won't have trouble finding material on that. I've been open about it in several interviews. There are also essays and resources in my cookbook, and on my dance academy website. And I support several health programs." She pauses. "Of course, those will be buried in the back pages. Charity work isn't very headline worthy."

"What did the others write?"

"Sara broke some heirloom and let her kid sister take the blame. Chris almost drowned his baby cousin. And Zeke." A half smile turns up her lips. "That was one of the sweet moments. Chris pulled a card that read 'I want to suck your dick.' And he looked at Zeke and said: 'Come on, Zeke, we already know you're gay.' We all held our breath for a second, but then Zeke just took this long drink and we all cracked up." Her voice becomes wistful. "I think that was the last time we really laughed."

A *thunk* startles me. The wind has pushed a garbage can against the side of the building. The bartender goes out to retrieve it. The gusts shove him sideways.

Elle speaks quietly. "I still remember sitting before the fire that night, wrapped in a plaid blanket, watching the flames flickering on their faces. Anna had the giggles and she just laughed at everything. Several boats went by. Chris had one of those huge old boom box radios, but we were too far offshore to get WTOS or WBLM, so we played cassettes until the batteries died. I can't even tell you how much we regretted that later. The last human voice aside from ours that I heard for months was Danzig." She stirs her coffee. "You know, the sight of sitting across a fire from someone is probably the oldest collective memory known to man. It immediately puts us into a primal state. So does staring out at the sea."

I glance out the window. At the docks, a woman kneels before the memorial. The wind takes the flowers and casts them into the froth.

Elle continues in a quiet voice. "I didn't sleep much that night. I had terrible nightmares. I was very relieved when the sun came up. I already wanted to get off the island. Kevin and Jason set some lobster traps that morning. I don't know if it's still the same, but back then anyone with a boating license could set five traps. We'd picked up clams before setting out, so we were going to have a clambake that night. Our last hurrah. It was Labor Day weekend, and we had to get on with our lives." She hesitates, recalling something. "That was the morning they saw the other boat."

I sit up straighter. There's no mention of this in the files. "Another boat? Did they get its name?"

She shakes her head. "No. I remember Jason saying that they didn't seem very friendly. Didn't wave or anything, just sat there and stared at the guys. It really rubbed Kevin the wrong way. He thought they were poachers."

"Lobster poachers?" I raise my brows. "That's a thing?"

"Oh yes." Elle sounds almost benevolent. "They pull other people's traps and take the lobsters. If they're *really* being jerks, they'll cut the lines. Some of them sell the stolen lobsters, then come back here and drink with the guys they stole from. Some of them vanish, and it's probably safe to say they're out there under those waves somewhere. But anyway, Kevin got really drunk that night, and started acting up. It killed the mood. Jason and I went down the beach, but that wasn't much better. We'd been together almost three years, but we were at a crossroads. I didn't want to stay in Maine, and he didn't want to leave. I'd already been accepted to ballet school. We hadn't really faced it until then, but we knew we had to break up, even though we didn't want to. It was a very sad and sweet night."

I recall her dancing *Romeo and Juliet*, the passion in every line of her body. The performance was captivating, won her instant recognition. I wonder what Jason would have thought, if he'd lived long enough to see it.

Elle speaks calmly. "The next day Anna and I went out on the boat with Jason, Kevin, and Zeke to go get the traps. It was a gorgeous day. Mid 90s, I think. The water was flat calm, and this vibrant blue. The day started out great. We lay out on the boat while the guys fished off the side. But once we got to the spots, they found that only one of our buoys was still attached to a trap. The others had been cut. Kevin was pissed. Livid. He completely flew into a rage. I remember Jason trying to snap him out of it by joking around. He was doing this whole schtick in his Mainer accent. 'Hey Poseidon! Can we have a few lobstahs? Give y'ah bee-yahs.' Then he turned around and I saw his face go white. I turned to see what he was looking at, and that was when I realized. Zeke wasn't there. He'd gone overboard."

I think again of the cold, green-black waters closing over my head, the clawed hand pulling me down, the silver eyes glaring at me from the gloom. *A dream,* Mother always said, ignoring the scars on my foot.

I try to keep my voice from shaking. "You didn't see what happened?"

"No." Elle shakes her head. "None of us did. He never made a sound. We all started looking over the sides of the boat, calling for him. We thought maybe he was swimming, pulling a prank, but he didn't come up. I happened to look up and I saw, in the distance, a hand and arm going under. I don't know how he got so far away so fast. Kevin drove the boat closer and cut the engine, in case he got caught, and we all looked over the sides. I'll never forget staring down into that green-black water. And then Jason yelled and dove in. It seemed an eternity that he was under. I was so scared that they were both gone. That water...even in August, it's freezing cold. You've only got minutes before hypothermia hits."

I fight the nerves back. The cup shakes in my hand. Coffee sloshes over the side, splattering onto Elle's *Vogue* cover.

"Jason almost drowned, saving Zeke," Elle continues. "He didn't have the strength to climb back into the boat. Zeke was unconscious. We had to haul them both over. Anna started CPR right away. Time froze. I swear it was an eternity before Zeke coughed and sputtered and puked out this black water. It was absolute chaos after that. Everyone was upset and shouting about what to do next. Anna and I wanted to go to the mainland and get them to a hospital, but Kevin didn't want to leave Sara and Chris on the island. I think he knew

THE ART OF DEVASTATION

there was something off with the maps, but he didn't want to tell us. We tried the Coast Guard, but there was no signal. The radio just stopped working. That's when the storm hit."

This isn't in her memoir, either. "A storm?"

She motions outside. "Not like this one. It was a very strange storm. We were all half arguing, half discussing what to do. And then Kevin looked past me and pointed, and said we had to get back onto the island. I think the term he used was 'right fucking now.' He was right. The weather looked really weird. The clouds were this sick yellowish green, and the light was...off. It was kind of blurry, like smoke. Every hair on my body stood on end. It just felt unnatural. And it was moving fast, like a tornado or something. Kevin gunned it towards the island. The water got really choppy, even though it had been calm before. I came up off the seat a few times. Every time I looked back, that strange miasma was closer. All the instruments on the boat went crazy."

The sea has its own magic, its own secrets, she said in her biopic.

"Kevin didn't have trouble getting into the cove that time. He just pulled right up. And Sara and Chris came running down to us. They were furious. Livid. They both insisted that we'd been gone overnight. I know it was only a few hours. But we didn't have time to argue. The storm was coming in fast, and our tents weren't made for that kind of weather. The best thing—the only thing—to do was to carry Zeke up to the old lighthouse quarters. The guys figured they'd have to break the door down, but it swung right open. The place was eerie. There were dishes in the cupboard, but no mice, no spiders, no flies. Nothing. Chris and Kevin cleared the chimney as best as they could and got a fire going. Luckily, the well pump worked. And then we cuddle piled."

You did more than cuddle, I think, *if the scene in that cable movie is true.*

Elle's gaze latches onto mine. "The storm broke over us. It made *this*"—she motions outside, at the rising tempest—"seem like a summer rain. We couldn't see anything past the sheets of water. We heard the sounds that night for the first time."

"What sounds?"

"Music. It sounded like singing, but it was very discordant. Atonal. And then there was a sort of howling going on behind it. The guys insisted that it was the wind and the water, but I could tell that they were unsettled too. I was terrified. I really, really, really wanted to go home. All I could think of was my room and my comfy bed. But there was no leaving in that tempest. The storm seemed to last forever. We slept and woke twice." She draws a breath. "That's when we noticed that Zeke wasn't right."

I look down at the obituary, at the dark-eyed boy who never got to experience manhood. "What was Zeke like?"

She drums her fingers over the table. Her nails make a tapping sound, like rain. "Very quiet. Intelligent. Soft spoken. I thought he came from abuse, perhaps, but his parents seemed very meek when I met them. He was always off in his own world. But whatever happened to him under those waters changed him."

"What do you mean?"

"He kept saying he was fine, but his skin was ice cold whenever we touched him. He wasn't shivering. I mean, his breathing, everything, looked okay, but he seemed off. Anna was basically hysterical, screaming that we needed a doctor, that he could still get sick and die. And then he spoke in this kind of monotone and said he *had* died. We assumed he was joking, but his eyes were...empty. He barely said another word all night. Just stared out the window, muttering about locks and wards."

I freeze in place, the blood draining from my face.

If Elle notices my unease, she doesn't mention it. "When we woke the next day, I couldn't wait to get the hell out of there and go back to the city. We were all ready to face the world again. We grabbed our gear, opened the cabin door, and walked into the most stunning sunrise I've ever seen. It was absolutely beautiful. The last days of summer always are, you know. We were in pretty good spirits. Zeke was quiet but he seemed okay, and Kevin seemed more like himself. I remember going over choreography in my mind as we went down the trail to the cove. That was the longest break I had taken from dance since getting mono in junior high. I really wanted to get back to the studio. We were talking about what we were going to do when we got back: hot showers, pizza, that kind of thing. Anna and Sara wanted to go see *Jurassic Park*. I had a hair appointment." She looks out the window, thinking. "You know, small everyday luxuries become huge when they're stripped away from you. Food and warmth are most important, of course, but after that, it's the little things you miss. Hot showers. Clean clothes. Chocolate. Coffee." She smiles. "Anyway, we were going single file. I was behind Jason, and he suddenly stopped short, so fast I almost walked into him. He was just standing there, staring out at the water. It took me a minute to figure out why." She looks at me, her eyes piercing. "The boat was gone."

"That must have been terrifying," I murmur.

"*Terrifying* doesn't begin to describe it. One minute you're standing in the sun on this perfect summer day, healthy and happy, and then a second later you're in a life-or-death situation. You feel death breathing down your back. The weight of mortality is an anchor. I felt that terror sink down through my gut."

"You said in early interviews that you thought you'd be found quickly. Did you believe that? Or was that...something you told yourselves?"

"Oh, we believed it. Once we calmed down, we took a breath and kind of thought, 'Well, this will be a funny story.' There's a lot of traffic on the Atlantic in summer. We'd heard and seen plenty of boats. And we were just a few miles offshore."

I blink. "No, you weren't. You were halfway to Nova Scotia."

She tilts her head. "Then explain to me how we left at nine in the morning, and were camped and unloaded by noon?"

I look down at my files, push the *Portland Press Herald* article towards her. "This says you were rescued off Cutter Island. But the ring was found on Banister."

There's something chilling in her smile. "Exactly."

"*You're crazy*," I want to tell her, but the words are pointless. Anyone who has seen her dance knows she is beyond mad. "What do you mean?" I ask instead.

She makes her point by pointing. "We got clams from Joe's lobster pound, right *there*, right across the harbor. Then we left from *this* dock, right outside. We sailed northeast. The mainland was on our left. And even I can roughly tell direction by the sun. Cutter Island is south of here. We were only out of sight of land for long enough to listen to *The Wall* and *Master of Puppets*. A few hours, at most. Banister Island is in sight of the mainland. And neither of those islands has a ruined lighthouse."

I tap the article. "It says here that the Coast Guard logged a distress call from a male who identified himself as Jason Kerriault. He said you were all on Banister Island. A team went out and searched the island, but found nothing."

"Yes. And you can ask Jack about it, the harbormaster. He was on that crew." She points at a building alongside the docks. "His office is right down there, though I expect he's a bit busy today."

I frown. "Then where *were* you?"

"That's the question, isn't it?" Her gaze is hard. "Where were we. A place with a forgotten name. A place that remains hidden, save for those it lures in."

Ballerina drama. I want to roll my eyes. But something in her voice chills me.

Elle leans forward. "Cutter Island has been here all along. Maine's islands were very important during the war. But the island I was on isn't on any list of them. It isn't on any map, either. Not new ones, anyway. It appears on maps as The Isle De La Mole or The Isle De La Morte from the 1500's until 1945. Then it vanished. It was taken off maps, until it reappeared on Google maps last summer."

"You're...saying it disappeared. And reappeared."

"Yes." She tops off her coffee. The knot diamond flashes in the light. "Have you ever heard of Hy-Brasil?"

I shake my head.

"Hy-Brasil was reported in sightings as far back as 1325. It appeared on maps until the 1860's. In 1674, Captain John Nisbet and his crew got stranded there. They thought it uninhabited, but woke to find themselves met by a very old lord and ten naked men, who imprisoned them for the 'art of devastation.'"

I stare at her. "*That's* where you got the title for your biopic?"

She smiles sardonically. "My agent wanted to call it *Dance of Death*."

"You must admit this is…" I struggle for the word.

"I believe *paradox* is the term you're looking for. And there are plenty of them in these parts. But there were no old lords or naked men on this island." Her voice drops. "What dwells there is…unholy."

I look at the map, at the area I've circled in red. *Not possible*, I think, and privately decide it must have been a fata morgana: a mirage caused by layers of different air temperatures. But I need to let her talk. *Keep it moving.* "What happened after that?"

"We hauled everything up to the lighthouse. There was no point staying in tents on the beach. No one said a word that whole time. Things were very tense. We were living under a cloud of anger and misery. Kevin and Jason got into a terrible fight. It took all of us to pull them apart. They blamed each other for not securing the boat properly, even though they'd both checked it. They'd been best friends since kindergarten. But they were really trying to hurt each other. There was this rage in Kevin's eyes. He wasn't there.

"The next day we decided to check out the light room. The stairs were rotted out, and part of the roof had caved in. I was elected to go up: I was the lightest, and had the best balance. I scaled the edge of the steps, holding the rail. When I got to the top, I could see for miles. There was no sign of land. No ships. No planes. Nothing but ocean, as far as I could see, in every direction. I stayed there for hours. Didn't see a single boat or plane. But then I looked down and noticed this pale shape in the water below. At first, I thought it was a whale or a shark. Then I realized what it was. Our boat. It wasn't gone after all. It was underwater…on the opposite side of the island from where we had landed, perched on the edge of an underwater cliff. There was a drop-off just beyond it…a line of sheer blackness. It made no sense for the boat to be where it was. I decided 'Oh, the storm must have pushed it there' but I knew that didn't make sense. I kinda pushed the thought down and went to tell the others. We all went to check it out. It was very slippery and difficult to get to it. It was about, maybe ten or twelve feet down. But when we got close enough to really see it, we realized that it wasn't our boat, but a different one. It was rusted out and covered in slime and barnacles. It must have been there for years."

"Did you see a name on the boat?"

"No. But the police figured it probably belonged to Bob and Terry Taylor, a couple who was lost at sea back in the 70's. They were some sort of new age gurus. Zeke somehow knew their names. He wrote them in his notebook. Drew their faces." She pauses, pondering. "I suppose that book is still sitting there."

"What happened after that?"

"We started looking into the water from various spots. And we did find our boat. Sunken, like the other one. On the edge of the abyss, like the other one. We knew we had to salvage what we could. Chris and I were the strongest swimmers, so we dove down to it. That dive was *terrifying*. The water was ice cold, and the boat was just deep enough to where we could only barely get in before running out of air. I could feel the currents pushing and pulling me. We knew there were scuba suits and tanks in the deck box. We got those out first, then put the scuba gear on and went down for the rest. Chris wanted the radio. He thought maybe he could fix it, once it dried out. I felt watched, the whole time I was down there. Sometimes I thought I saw a face staring at me from the black depths. And I kept hearing this strange sound, like music. Oh, and then I saw the steps."

"Steps?"

"Carved into the ocean floor. They were clearly ancient, as they were very worn, but you could tell they had been very elaborate. There was a sort of ethereal, almost rib-like shape to these arches further down. They went down, over the drop-off, into this watery black abyss."

I can taste the salty brine again. My heart pounds in my chest.

Elle's brow creases the tiniest bit. "Do you remember the day you drowned?"

My voice hardens. "How did you know about that?"

"Medical records."

"Those are confidential."

Elle's lips turn up, and I understand the meaning of the phrase *crocodile smile*. "Nothing is confidential if you have the right...means." She pauses, thinking. "They say it's peaceful."

The pale face again leers through my thoughts. My foot bounces on the floor. "It's not."

"I'm inclined to agree. Nothing about those waters seemed peaceful." She takes a deep breath. "The next thing I remember is everyone sitting around the fire, outside the lighthouse, because it was still nice enough. And then, just beyond the light, I saw this pale face staring at me. I was so startled that I fell off the log I was sitting on, kicking up a little cloud of sand. When that curtain fell, she was gone. I tried to tell the others, but only Zeke believed me."

Two men come into the restaurant, shaking off the rain, and sit at the bar, speaking in somber tones. The sound of human voices is oddly soothing.

"You said something was off about Zeke."

Elle glances out the window, as though looking towards the island. "He was never the same, after he went over. He always had this blank look on his face. He saw things we didn't. Heard things we didn't. We were all doing the best we could. Every day, the guys took the dinghy out to set our one remaining trap to try and catch what lobster they could. They kept the signal fire going, tried to fix the roof. Us girls handled the cooking and cleaning, gathered wood and seaweed. But Zeke...Zeke had checked out. He found a spot on the cliff overlooking that drop-off, and he would sit there on the rocks all day, drawing and looking at the sea. I remember I asked him once why he wasn't helping, and he asked me why I wanted to leave. I knew something was really off the moment he said that, but I didn't admit it to myself until later." Her voice drops. "It wasn't Zeke, came back with us that day. I don't know if Zeke opened the watery gate of death and something swam through, or if he drowned and the sea gave us something in his stead. But that something still walks those shores."

Her words raise the hairs on my neck.

"It was getting cold at night by then. It's never *not* cold, on those islands. Even in August, the wind smells of ice. No one said it aloud, but we were all thinking the same thing: that we wouldn't survive a winter there. We were scared, and hungry, and cold, and angry. And that was when we really started hearing things. Thuds. Distant wails. Your mind plays tricks on you. Was that a branch? Was it the wind? It was unnerving. And we still hadn't seen even so much as a fly there. We took to playing silly games every night, to lighten the mood. One night, Chris was imitating a seal. He was really funny when he wanted to be. We were all crying with laughter. And then right after, we heard something laughing *outside*. This was not, 'Oh did you hear something?' We *all* heard it. Very loud, and very clear. My spine turned to ice. It immediately killed the mood. We were all quiet after that." She pours black liquid into her cup. "That was when it really began to sink in."

The waitress comes by to check on us. "Getting wicked windy out there! Do you ladies want anything else? We got a fresh batch of whoopie pies."

I try to imagine her home: old wood-paneled walls. Thick flannels hanging from the doors, winter boots beside them. In the kitchen, old dishes and white winter light against windows filled with plants that, like me, cannot help but reach for the sun, though they only absorb its light but never its warmth.

I scan the menu, check my account balance on my phone, and order a cup of chowder.

Elle goes for the lobster bisque. "Please send Danny and Todd a drink on me," she says. "My condolences."

The waitress shakes her head sadly. "It's so heartbreaking. I saw Carter's little girl at the memorial this morning. She thinks her daddy is at sea, and the candles will help him find his way home."

Elle clucks in sympathy. I realize they're talking about the lobstermen at the bar.

As the waitress moves off, we are silent a moment. "That's Anna's nephew, you know." Elle says. "One of the men, went down. They never met."

I'm not sure what to say. "That's so sad."

We are silent a moment. Below, the waves crash into the rocks.

I open Elle's book. "You described a memory very vividly in Chapter 3. *'We were runaways, once, and then castaways, and then we went mad. But we were happy savages. We danced in the surf and in the showers of campfire sparks. We fucked in tidal mud, lived by the rise and fall of the sea and the sound of the waves.'*" I put the book down. "That sounds quite…"

"Hedonistic?" Elle gives a half smile. "My editor wanted a very primal take on that part. We absolutely *were* hedonistic. But we were also pragmatic. We did everything we could think of. We lit signal fires, wrote 'SOS' on the beach in rocks and seaweed, used our mirrors to signal planes. Chris even used the last of the oxygen in the scuba tank to get the bathroom mirror out of the yacht. He almost died doing that, you know. When he was coming up, the boat moved off the cliff and tumbled into the blackness below. It almost pulled him down with it. But it was for nothing. No one saw us. No one came. Days went by. And then weeks. We rationed the supplies, but it wasn't enough." She stares out at the water again, as though entranced. "I used to walk down the beach in the morning and stretch. No matter how cold it got, the sunrise was always so beautiful. In those moments, I felt almost at peace. But then I would look out at the sea and realize there was nothing out there but water that was miles deep and ice cold, and the terror crept into my bones. I'd grown up in Manhattan, surrounded by millions of strangers. The isolation was terrifying to me."

"You told the police that several ships passed by."

Elle frowns. "How did you know about that?"

I'm puzzled now. "It was in the files that you sent."

"I never sent you any files."

I open my mouth to question this, but she continues before I can speak. "We did see ships. Planes, too. At first, every night, at least one passed by. Though we always had the fire ready, they never noticed. Sometimes we heard engines, even though we couldn't see anything. One ship came so close I could see people dancing on the deck, and hear strains of jazz trailing over the water. The sea was very calm that night. I still remember how beautiful the lights looked, reflecting on the water."

"Did anyone else see it?"

"Sara. We both screamed and yelled for the guys to build up the fire, and she ran up the beach to get them. But it was too late. That sort of thing happened a few times. One day, Anna and I were on the beach, and Kevin came racing down to us, completely out of breath. When he could talk, he asked why we'd signaled him. We hadn't. We were looking for crabs. But he insisted we'd been waving to him. And as we were arguing, we heard the distant thrum of an engine. We all turned just in time to see a boat passing by. If he'd stayed where he was, he might have gotten the fire lit in time. You could cut the tension with a knife after that one. We were all so angry. Kevin started punching walls. Anna just withdrew, became very quiet. She didn't laugh or joke anymore. She barely spoke.

"One day, I decided to go for a walk, and I went into the woods. I found an old trail and followed it, and when I came around this bend, there was this lean-to. A sort of primitive cabin or survival shelter. There was a fire lit inside, and a pot bubbling with soup, and a bowl. I remember the bowl: it was a gray clay bowl with this intricate orange knot pattern around it. I stared at it and...I kinda went into a daze. I...I don't remember moving forward. But suddenly I was sitting at this makeshift log table, shoveling soup into my mouth. I can still taste it. Leeks and lentils and potatoes and onions. Suddenly I had this sense of something watching me. And then I felt an ice cold finger on the back of my neck, and I looked down and saw a scaly finger on my shoulder, with webbing between the fingers and long black claws."

I recall again the hand grasping my leg, pulling me down into the depths. My blood runs cold.

Elle's voice rises along with the waves. "I have never run so fast in my life. I was absolutely hysterical when I got to the cabin. Of course, the others didn't believe me. I led them to the same spot, but it all looked different. There was nothing there but a foundation and the log. When we got back to the cabin, Zeke was sitting at the table, eating sand from the exact same bowl. He looked up at us and said: 'She wants me back.' As soon as those words left his mouth, the air filled with this terrible keening wail, as though some gate had just burst open. I took that bowl and threw it across the room. It made a dent in the plaster, but it didn't break."

The power flickers out. The wind is picking up fast. Elle is unphased.

"We'd all seen things, by then. Heard things. But we never all saw or heard the same thing. Sara would hear a twig break behind her. Jason would think he saw something in the water. I would feel fingers in my hair, or breath on my neck. But we'd been able to convince ourselves that the laughter and the music was the wind. This was...there was no explanation."

Elle's voice is quiet. "At this point, things become...disjointed. I can no longer track who did or said what, or in what order things occurred. I only know that we became increasingly desperate. Things went from bad to worse...fast. Someone or something cut the lobster trap line. The only axe we had went missing. The dinghy sprung a leak. And we were running out of food. The guys tried making lobster traps, but none of them held together without nails or glue." Her voice drops. "We saw fewer and fewer ships, as time went on. At one point, I hadn't heard an engine or seen a plane in days. And then one day I look up and there was one right offshore"—she points out the window—"As close as that buoy. A windjammer. I thought at first it was one of the replicas, headed for Deer Isle or Bar Harbor. But something about the way it moved was off. It didn't rise and fall with the wind or the waves. It just cut a straight line. And seeing that, my blood ran cold."

Outside, the winds rise, battering the windows. Rainbeads splash, making diamonds against the glass.

Elle is silent a moment. "The records show that we were only on the island for a little over two months. But it was much longer than that. We...stepped outside time. I noticed that the ships we did see seemed to be getting older and older. I saw warships, heading out from Bath. Whaling vessels. Pilgrims, setting out for a new world. Pirates. Merchant ships. Trading vessels. Every night, they went further back."

I glance down again at the rescue photo. Her eyes stare through the camera, wild and mad, her pale face framed by pixelated waves.

"Time can do strange things in those situations." I offer. "You may have hallucinated."

She shakes her head. "This was no illusion. We were there for three new moons. I saw the same ship, passing on the full moon, three times. That's at least two months. My dreams reached further and further back each night. I saw navy men, merchants, pirates, and sailors and fishermen, and then Puritans and settlers. I started seeing shapes, hearing voices. Each night the island whispered these rotting aquatic enchantments into my soul."

I glance out. I can barely see the mouth of the harbor through the rain. "What did you do?"

"Chris spent days trying to dry the radio out and rig it up to one of the lantern batteries. The wires were all corroded. But he did manage to get static one day, and sat there all afternoon, sending distress calls. The next day we woke up to a white, bright, sun, and a frigid room. That was the first frost. We boiled pine needles for tea. I remember it was dead silent. And then suddenly the radio crackled to life, and we all heard this very flat, baritone voice say. 'They are coming for you.' That was all it said. 'They are coming for you.' We thought we were being rescued. We rushed around, packing, leaving our marks on the failing walls, and hauled everything down to the shore. And we waited. And waited. And waited. We were so excited. I did a grand jeté: a jumping split." She dangles her spoon over the coffee cup, stirring absently. "No one came. By nightfall, we were utterly dejected. None of us spoke. We stared at the fire and knew ourselves to be utterly alone. It was devastating."

I look out at the waves and realize that they are full of ghosts.

"We tried to keep our spirits up." Elle takes a tiny sip of coffee. "We made cards and dice, things like that. Then we tried the confession game again. *That* was a mistake."

"How so?"

"The last secret we pulled said '*I didn't mean to kill him.*' It...didn't go over well."

I ponder this. "Was that a reference to Mr. Lee?"

Elle shrugs. "Maybe. I didn't find out about him until later. I don't think the others knew, either. Kevin was very tense, but we were all at our wits' end."

I have those clippings as well. "The camera footage shows Kevin breaking into Mr. Lee's store and stealing food, beer, and coffee brandy. Mr. Lee caught and confronted him...and had a heart attack on the spot. Kevin called 911, then ran off and left him." I hesitate. "Aside from that being a horrible thing to do...why steal food in the first place? You were using your money for all of that."

Elle shrugs. "He felt like he needed to contribute. He had to be the man. That was Kevin. He'd give you the shirt off his back, but never let you forget it. His dad was the same way. Honestly, his parents were jerks. His dad had him out on that boat at 5 AM seven months out of the year, and never gave him a cent until the other captains started scouting him. Looking back, I think he was torn up over what he did, but couldn't change it." She toys with her spoon. "I guess we'll never know."

The waitress comes over and puts a bowl of chowder down in front of me. Her eyeliner is smudged, now, her perky smile dulled. I see the worry on her face, and wonder if she knows someone caught out in the gale.

Elle glances out at the churning sea. "I mentioned earlier that Jason and I were growing apart. Not long after the radio incident, I came around the cabin corner and found him and Sara talking. I was too far away to hear them, but their body language told me everything. They were just looking into each other's eyes with this earnest, honest love. They denied it at first. Told me I was seeing things. But Jason finally admitted it. He begged me not to tell Kevin, at least until we got off the island. And I agreed. Kevin had always had a temper, but he was getting really explosive and volatile. Chris and Anna were fighting a lot as well. We were all on edge. Things kept going wrong. The radio went missing. We lost the can opener. And then Chris fell through the stairs." She draws a shaky breath. "He was trying to reinforce the old lighthouse steps, thinking if we could keep a fire burning up there, maybe it would attract attention. He fell through a rotted step and broke his leg. It was...bad. Really

IN THE COLD, COLD GROUND

bad. The bone was sticking out. Anna and Jason tried to set it, but we knew he needed help."

Her voice is quiet when she speaks, her eyes as cold and dark as the crashing sea beyond, and as full of secrets. For the first time, I see a crack in the façade. "I'm not proud of what I did next," she says.

"Go on."

"I had an eating disorder. As a dancer, I was always under pressure to stay thin, and I was very aware of what I put into my body. I've since learned healthier habits, and I know now how dangerous that was, but back then...back *then* I wasn't healthy. On the island, I always ate the smallest portions. At first that was alright. For a time, the hunger was probably easier than it was for the others. But I also grew weak faster than they did. By then, we were always, always hungry. We were almost out of food, and there was no more lobster. We ate seaweed and the occasional clam or fish. Everything took ten times as much effort. Every step we took was this Herculean effort. The smallest stick of wood seemed super heavy, like this massive weight. And then...I remember the moon was full, and I saw the ship again, the same ship, the same music, and I knew for certain that they were dead and I just snapped." She meets my eyes, her voice calm and even. "I ate everything. Every last crumb of food. I had no control over myself. I was just watching myself gorge. The biggest—and last—binge of my life. And then I went to the furthest point on the island and threw it all up."

I stare at her, unable to comprehend what she's telling me. "You're telling me that you...wasted what little food you had?"

"Every crumb."

I'm speechless, which doesn't happen often.

"When Kevin found out what I had done, he completely lost it. The others were pissed, believe me. But Kevin wanted to kill me. Literally. He came at me with this cold black rage in his eyes, and said that since our supplies were in me that *I* would be the supplies. I froze in fear. Jason stepped in front of me, and everyone was yelling and the rage just spread to Chris and Anna and Sara. I saw them step forward, and I just had this gut-deep instinct that they were going to kill me. I felt it. I could see it in their eyes. Their faces were red with fury. It was this howling intense moment of chaos. And I just ran. I ran for my life. It was getting dark. I remember looking back and seeing Kevin's flashlight beam bouncing as he ran after me. That's when I found the cave."

"Cave?" This isn't in the book, either.

Elle nods. "It was tucked in behind this little outcrop. I went in to hide, but when I got inside, I found a door. It was made out of some strange metal, and covered with runes. Kevin and Jason came in after me, and as soon as they saw that door, they forgot all about the supplies. We figured it must be an old naval base or a pirate's hideout or something. It wasn't even locked. It swung wide open. There was nothing beyond it but a curving rock stairwell spiraling down into blackness."

"That...makes no sense."

"No," she says. "It doesn't, does it? A stairwell, in the middle of an uninhabited island, going down into the sea. Down *below* the sea."

The power flickers again with the next gust of wind.

"When we saw the stairs, we thought it could be something from World War II, possibly going down to a submarine dock. Maybe there was something at the bottom...supplies, blankets, anything. So we went down, and down, and down into that blackness. Every cell of my being wanted to turn and go the other way, but I was afraid to leave Jason's side, so I forced myself to go on. It seemed forever before we reached a landing, with these tunnels branching off into the rock. We must have been under the ocean. The ceiling was wet, and we could hear water dripping above us. And then we found the missing radio, just sitting in the middle of this hall. It crackled into static, and then we heard these garbled voices...every hair on my body stood on end. Kevin smashed it, and then this terrible, bone-chilling howl echoed from the blackness beyond. We ran. I remember we had to grab Jason. He was standing there as though he were frozen, staring in that direction. Climbing up was grueling. I didn't think we were going to make it."

Elle taps her spoon on the saucer, then folds her hands quietly. She can sit immobile, it seems, for hours. I can barely go a minute without fidgeting.

It's a long time before she speaks.

"This next bit," she says finally, "is still hard to accept."

Her voice is calm and soothing, her words anything but.

"I woke up one morning, and everything was very still and frigid. I sat up and saw Zeke opening the door. He was naked, but even in the cold I could see the sheen of sweat on his skin. I sat up and called him, and he paused, but it took him a long time to turn and look at me. I still remember his voice wafting back through this cold white sunlight. 'She's calling me,' he said. 'I have to go now.' Then he stepped out the door. I got up and went after him, and he was standing at the edge of the woods, right at the shadow line, looking at me. He pointed to the cliff on the other end of the island, and I saw a man standing there, silhouetted against the sunrise, with his head tilted back to the sun and his arms raised to the sky. Then he tipped and fell over, in the same position, like a statue someone knocked off a shelf. When I looked back at the woods, there was nothing there. And I realized that it was Zeke on the cliff, and the thing I'd seen in the woods was something wearing his face. My screams woke the others."

Elle taps her spoon onto her saucer. "We spent that whole day looking, but we never found a trace of him. Eventually we had to give up. None of us spoke that night. We just sat there in this awful, weighted silence. I walked down to the beach myself, and I saw one last boat pass. This one was a primitive vessel, a sea kayak, and the men in it wore skins and carried clubs. I knew, looking at them, that none of them had drawn a breath in not hundreds, but thousands of years. I realized only later that they must have been the Red Paint people, one of Maine's earliest civilizations."

The lights flicker again.

"That was when things started to get really bad. Anna stopped talking to everyone, and Kevin and Jason got into some really bad fights. And then I found Sara dry heaving in the woods one morning. She didn't even have to tell me. I looked at her face and knew why immediately. She was pregnant."

"How did you cope?"

"I did what I always do when I'm troubled. I danced. Only there, I danced barefoot on the rocks. That's why my feet were so bloody in the rescue photo." She tilts her head. "I also made knots."

Looking at her in that moment, I see the combination of madness and strength that led her to nearly dance herself to death filming *The Red Shoes* remake.

"You choreographed a piece while you were there." I flip through the book. "*Coilwork*. And you wrote a poetry book about knots and tides later."

She rolls her eyes. "The *New York Times* called it pretentious. *Dancer's Monthly* tried to choreograph it."

"Right." I've forgotten about that. "Didn't the theater they were using burn?"

"Faulty wiring. Rats, probably." Elle refills her coffee again. "Knot magic is one of the oldest spells known to man. It appears in ancient Greece and Egypt, and even in old Norse legends of Odin. Of course, knots were also often used in weather spells. Witches would harness the wind, and sell the threads to superstitious sailors."

I refill my own cup. "My mother was interested in sea lore. I remember a little saying she used to tell me. Releasing one knot brought a mild wind, two a good gust. Three knots a tempest brings."

A dark fire flickers in her eyes. "I danced a knot that night, on the cliff."

My thoughts are suddenly tumbling, rushing with currents and tides and dreams of scaled silver fish spinning in unison through unhallowed tides. I see again the face beneath the waves. Hear her voice, carried on cold churning currents, murmuring about locks and wards.

Elle sounds like she's underwater. "Are you alright?"

I snap out of my daze. "What? Yes." I glance around, and am startled to realize it's gotten dark out.

"You seem pale."

I look down at the table, find it covered with the remains of a feast I don't recall ordering, much less eating. Two lobsters, a pile of clamshells, nearly-empty bowls of chowder, and the remnants of a jumbo shrimp cocktail ring sit before us. Two baskets of rolls flank a heaping plate of fried clams and oysters, all cold with congealed grease.

I am disoriented, confused. "What time is it?"

Elle checks her Rolex. "Almost six." She casually cracks a lobster leg, fishes the meat out with expert dexterity. "You're not driving back to Portland tonight, are you?"

I check my phone and do a double take. We've been recording for five hours, somehow. "I...I rented a room above the bar down the road. Grinsy's?"

She doesn't bother to hide her disdain. "They...rent rooms?"

The world spins. My words are thick and slurred. "The room isn't terrible. It's small, but clean."

"No judgement here," she says. "Some of the accommodations on the *Firebird* tour would make Grinsy's look like the Four Seasons."

I glance out at the sea, which is now cloaked in darkness. She is there, the being, the wraith, on the dock, beyond Elle, beyond the stuffed lobster. I shut my eyes. Tell myself it's an illusion.

She's still there when I open them.

"You look like you've seen a ghost," Elle says calmly, and I stare at her but see the sea witch instead, the unhallowed thing beneath the waves, grabbing my ankle and pulling me down as my last breaths rise to the surface in silver bubbles.

I excuse myself and flee.

In the bathroom, I splash cold water in my face. The wraith is there, behind me in the mirror. I spin three times, counterclockwise, as my mother taught me. She is gone when I open my eyes, but the world is tilting and my eyes are stinging and my face burns with fever.

I stumble back to the table as the waitress finishes clearing the plates. I feel a stab of guilt, realizing that the poor cook probably had to reopen the kitchen just for us.

Elle stands as I approach, guides me into the chair. "You don't look well." I feel her cool hands on my forehead. "You're burning up. Why don't you stay with me tonight? That dive is no place for a young girl."

My head throbs. Words emerge leaden and heavy. "No. No I couldn't. That's too much of an imposition."

The power goes out. Only the candles and lanterns keep the darkness at bay. I look out the window and see that the entire town is cloaked in blackness, save the occasional solar light.

The storm screams in the background.

"Well." Elle gathers her coat. "That's a wrap on this session. You really *must* come with me. My house runs mostly on solar, so the power loss won't matter much. We'll finish the interview there. And I can show you the artifacts."

I try to stand. The room spins around me. I plunk back down onto the seat. "Artifacts?"

"I brought a few things back from the island."

I take a deep breath. The wave of sickness fades. I notice the glass of ice water before me and gulp it down, though I hate cold water.

A blinding light bobs over to us: the waitress is using her phone as a flashlight. "Looks like we're closing earlier than expected, Ms. Sanders."

Elle clicks on her own phone's flashlight, fishes through her wallet, and hands over two hundred-dollar bills. "Keep the change," she says, then jerks her head towards me. "She'll be leaving her car here overnight."

"Thank you, Ms. Sanders." The waitress tucks the bills away. "Can you get home alright?"

"Of course," Elle says curtly. "I'm only right around the bend. And tell Jim he only needs to run the generator for the freezer."

It's only then that I realize she owns the place.

She turns to me. "Come, dear."

I try to protest, but the room tilts and my stomach lurches. Elle holds my elbow and guides me across the room. The lobster tanks are now two residents down. Outside, in the raging night, silvery sheets of rain pour from the sky and the wind shoves at my back. I look towards the ocean, and see only blackness. The pounding of the surf fills my ears, my mind, my thoughts. I'm soaking wet by the time we reach the SUV I dinged earlier. Of course it's hers.

The SUV is like a spaceship inside: the luxury soundproofing immediately dulls the storm sounds. Elle navigates expertly through the maelstrom, following a narrow winding road that hugs the raging shore. A few feet to my right, craggy banks fall away towards the sea, which is silverchurn and blackdeep and snapping at the rocks. Most of the houses are dark, their fences and decks decorated with buoys and lobster traps. Here and there, lights pop on as generators fire up. The lighthouse beam barely cuts the pounding rain.

Elle turns into a drive lined with ancient pines. Two stone pillars sit at the entrance, flanking a wrought iron gate that slides open before us. The three-story brick house beyond sits solid against the storm, its thick walls unyielding, unbothered by the gale.

I follow her up wide marble steps. Above, the widow's walk pierces the turbulent sky.

Elle punches a security code into a keypad and pushes the shining door open. Inside, her place is actually quite cozy, the white walls softened by bright Persian rugs, thick wooden beams, and caramel-colored leather sofas. Three massive fish tanks bubble away, their denizens untroubled by the storm. Knot motifs are everywhere: on throw pillows, wall art, rugs, even the blankets folded over the back of the couch.

Elle takes her leather boots off at the door and hangs her dripping coat and umbrella on a tree, then steps aside and motions me to follow suit.

I glance out the window. The wraith stands in the drive. She opens her mouth, and suddenly everything sounds as though I am underwater.

When I look again, she is gone.

The room spins.

"This way, dear." Elle shows me to the guest room, which is really more of a suite. In the center, a huge mahogany bed is piled with comforters and pillows. "I keep spare clothes in the dressers. I'm sure you'll find something that fits. Why don't you take a nap?"

I manage a nod. She opens her mouth as though to speak, but then changes her mind and leaves, closing the door behind her.

Outside, the wind rises to a howl.

My eyes and thoughts grow heavy, and I am suddenly drained, exhausted. The call of soft, dry clothes becomes too hard to resist. I don brand new leggings, a Bar Harbor sweatshirt, thick socks, and soft slippers, then sink onto the bed. I only mean to rest a moment, but as soon as I lay down, I'm out.

In my dreams, the thing beneath the salty green waves opens her mouth, and earsplitting, unholy screams rise to the moon on silver bubbles.

A HUGE CRASH AWAKENS ME A FEW HOURS LATER. A PINE HAS SNAPPED somewhere. I wake disoriented but clearheaded in what is by far the most comfortable bed I've ever slept in. The ship's wheel clock on the wall reads 9:30 PM. Outside the window, the rain is falling sideways through the gale. There is only blackness beyond.

I pad down to the living room. Elle's muffled voice echoes from another room: I realize she's on the phone. The bubbling fish tanks mask the howl of the storm. I look at the art and photos on the walls. There are photos of her with all the ballet greats—Balanchine, Baryshnikov, Nureyev, Fonteyn—as well as with dozens of actors and rock stars. The glass bookcases are filled with tomes on occult topics, dance, witchcraft, and sea myths.

I pick up a jade figurine. The wraith stares at me from green stone. It is ice cold in my hand.

Elle's voice jumps me. I haven't heard her approach. "That piece was from Beijing," she says. "Would you like some tea?"

I put the figurine down. "That sounds amazing."

I follow her into the kitchen, where stainless steel appliances and mahogany furniture create a magazine-ready atmosphere against sage green walls. She makes tea while I get my phones set up again.

I happen to look over in time to see her opening a pill bottle. She catches my gaze, and looks down, shaking a white dot out of the bottle. "You asked why I'm talking to you. Why I'm being so open." Elle opens the fridge, takes out a bottle of water. "The doctors tell me I have six months."

I don't know what to say. "I'm sorry," I tell her.

"Don't be," she says, downing the pill and swallowing. "I've lived more than most do. I've done all I wanted. Not really interested in getting old and frail anyway."

I look around, and realize she has no one. I feel bad for her, suddenly.

She seems unfazed. "Let's continue the interview."

We sit in the breakfast nook, a bowl of fruit between us.

"We stopped," I say, prompting her, "with you learning about Sara's pregnancy. What happened after that?"

She doesn't miss a beat. "Jason went missing. At first we thought he was getting wood or something, but when he didn't turn up, we knew something was wrong. We combed the island, calling, shouting. We looked everywhere. And finally there was only one place left to check."

It isn't hard to guess. "The cave."

She glances down at her hands. "I took a torch with me that time. There was something different. The energy felt more tangible. I could feel the darkness pressing in. More malevolent. My body... did not want to go in there. I couldn't get my legs to move. Every cell of my being tried to stop me. But as scared as I was, I was more terrified of being stuck there without Jason. We went further into the tunnels than we had before, and down another level. The walls were carved with these intricate patterns. They were hypnotizing to look at. I had to focus on the ground. Eventually we found this strange chapel. There was an ossuary that incorporated the bones of some massive beast. I suppose it must have been a prehistoric whale or dinosaur. We found Jason sitting in the darkness, whispering to this... thing. We had to drag him out. And he came up rambling about this ancient city under the sea. Some sort of drowned prehistoric civilization." She pauses. "There was no howling that night. No screaming. As if the things were...waiting."

The tea is rich and earthy. It tastes like dirt.

"By late October, we were desperate. When we heard the whales pass by, we knew winter was coming, and we had to get off the island before the snow hit. We tended Chris as much as we could with the first-aid kit, but the wound was infected. I can still smell the reek of it, even now." Elle squeezes a slice of lemon into her tea. "Have you ever smelled gangrene?"

I shake my head.

"The stench is a survival mechanism, meant to warn us from eating dead flesh. But when you're starving, it still smells like food. When I ate his leg, it had a sweet taste."

My stomach twists.

"We really started to panic then. We were so cold, and so hungry. Something changes you, in those situations. You become something else. Anna and I talked about death. That was all she talked about, by then, really. We wondered if we would wake up somewhere else, with the others. Kevin wanted to take the dinghy. He insisted we couldn't be too far offshore, as we'd still had almost a full tank of gas when we reached the island. But the dinghy wasn't very sturdy. If it sank with all of us on it, we were done. In the end, we decided that he and I, being the best swimmers left, would put scuba suits on, in case we fell in, and row out. So, we set out, paddling furiously. We made good progress until we reached this...barrier. It was like a wall pushing us back. I remember him prodding me on, promising he'd buy me a salad if we made it. He said that to infuriate me, to pump me up. It worked. I went for it. We both were. We paddled and paddled and paddled and got nowhere. It was as though some unseen force was holding us back. We thought maybe we were in a riptide. We tried all different directions. No use. The only way we could move was back." She puts the cup down. "The island wasn't going to let us go. We didn't even have to row back. Current pulled us right in.

"Kevin didn't speak a single word that night. He just sat there, staring into the flames. In the morning, he was gone. So was the diver suit and dinghy. Sara was crushed. They'd obviously been having issues, and she was planning to break up with him, but she refused to believe he'd left her. I suppose he's beneath the waves somewhere." She trails off, staring out the window. "That night, I saw the first of them. A shadow figure, with glowing silver eyes, coming out of the water, framed against the moonlight. At first, I thought it was a rescue diver, but as it got closer, I realized it wasn't human. Then I saw more of them, those beings, coming out of the water, walking towards me. I could see scales shining in the moonlight on their necks and chests. I ran back to the cabin. The others didn't believe me, but we found the tracks and the bones and the blood in the morning."

Her voice grows small and thin.

"The sea was dark and empty after that. There were no more boats. No more lights. No more planes. No more dreams. And then things started washing up onshore. We started finding body parts. Heads and hands and feet. A severed penis, one time." Her voice trembles slightly, and I see the fear in her eyes. She can't quite keep her hand from shaking. "Then the ocean threw her demons at us. Monstrosities began to wash up. Things that didn't seem...right. Some had two heads, others had fins on their hands. We started seeing lights again. Ships, flying overhead. Boats, moving past very, very quickly. We told ourselves that we were hallucinating. But we somehow always hallucinated the same things." Her whisper holds back the storm. "And then they brought Zeke back to us."

I freeze. "What?"

She nods. "One morning, out of the blue, I came across Zeke, standing on the beach. He was facing the other way as I approached. I remember I stopped, and I said his name, and he turned to face me and I saw that he had no eyes. And there were cuts in his ribcage. Like...gills. Anna saw him and ran up to him. She started asking if he was alright, and he only stood there, quiet. Wouldn't say a word. And then he snapped and lunged at her, and grabbed her by the neck. I somehow pulled him away, and he dove into the sea. When we got back to the cabin, Chris was dead. Not freshly dead. He was bloated and rotting, as though he had been dead for days, though he'd been breathing when we'd left him that morning. We buried him the next day. Anna wanted to put him in the cemetery. So we dragged him up the hill and dug his grave with our bare hands. Anna put his class ring on his finger. She usually wore it as a necklace. A thick fog was rolling in as we finished. I looked back once as I started walking away. Sara was just sitting there, staring over the water as the mist closed in." Her voice drops. "That was the last time I saw her alive."

For a moment, she looks upset, and then she collects herself and looks at me and the witch blood is still there, still true. I see in her the roles she has danced: Giselle, bargaining with the dead; the Black Swan, giving into her dark side. And I realize that she has come to encompass these beings.

"We found her on the beach the next morning, naked, surrounded by a perfect circle of fish. Her mouth was stuffed with seaweed. Her eyes were in the palms of her hands. She was above the tide line, surrounded by tracks that only went in and out of the water. We built a cairn for her, but the next day it was smashed and empty. Something came out of the water, dug her up, and dragged her under the waves. The blood and tracks in the sand left no question. That night, I saw more figures emerging from the sea. They were slouched over the sand, fins scraping, abominations standing against the bright moon, which shone yellow over the waves. They walked over the sharp shells and rocks, and I saw them raise their arms, and I heard this terrible music."

Her words send a chill down my spine. I hear again the traces of music from my dream. Elle's eyes look blank, mad, cold. Delusion, I wonder? Hallucination? But I remember the still from her biopic, the drowned man walking back into the sea. I search her face, her body posture, for signs of lying. There are none.

"Anna and I tried to get through to Jason. He ignored us. He wasn't *him*. He didn't speak, didn't react to us, didn't laugh. He was usually very thoughtful. His eyes were always...full. Full of thought, emotion, mischief. His stare could just trap me. I'd get lost in it. But this was just a blank look. The next day he was gone again. Anna wouldn't go back into the cave with me, so I had to go alone. I don't remember much of it: I was so scared my brain I think blocked it out. I remember finally finding him, sitting there in the dark. Only, he wasn't Jason anymore. His skin was a sickly grey-green, his lips were blue, and his hair was white. I thought he was dead, but when my flashlight beam hit him, he turned his head to me. And his eyes were...bloody. I remember seeing the rip in his AC/DC concert shirt, and thinking he'd be upset about that. And then he...attacked me. I screamed and ran, but I didn't have the energy to go very fast.

He ran after me and tackled me. I remember hitting the ground hard, so hard, but somehow I got free. I felt his fingers on my leg as I scrambled away. They were ice cold. Far colder than any human being's should be." Elle turns sideways and takes her foot out of her slipper. Four scars cross her calf. "They always wanted me to cover these. I did for a while, and then, during the promo shots for *Ondine,* I decided I wasn't going to hide them anymore. You can still see the scars in some of those pictures."

Her words twist my stomach into knots.

Elle looks into her tea. "I've come to think of those last days as the rage hours. The rage days. I don't know what I hallucinated and what is real. I only remember that the howls and the creatures got closer every night, and they seemed to know that Anna and I were unprotected. One of the last things I recall was a storm. We hid in a closet as the wind and the waves lashed everything. We heard the chants that night, the unholy groaning and moaning, and the woods filled with howls and the laughter of ghostly children." She hesitates. "We were very hungry by then. We were both thinking the same thing, but we didn't say it. And then one day I found Anna in the cemetery. She looked up at me, her lips stained red. And then I saw what she was eating."

Nausea churns in my stomach. "Chris."

Elle is silent.

I recall the line from her solo album, an industrial-goth flop which was unremarkable at best. *I turned my face to the sun, holy and tainted. I ate his eyes and become all-seeing.*

"I don't remember waking in the night," Elle continues softly. "Or going to the cemetery. I came to as the sun rose, bloody, surrounded by remains. Body parts were strewn everywhere. Our faces, hands, and arms were stained with blood. And then Anna was gone, and I was alone. The last of it was darkness. I couldn't cut any wood, and there was no more food. Every day I looked for Anna, but I never found her again. I suppose she jumped into the sea."

I blink, stunned.

She doesn't know.

"Actually," I say, "she was rescued by a fishing vessel off the coast of Iceland. They thought she was from Scandinavia, so they never thought to check records here. A nurse made the connection back in 2006."

"*Iceland?*" Elle stares at me. "That's impossible."

"It's true." I lean back. "I thought you knew. Anna Kelly is still alive. She's in a retirement home in Nova Scotia, near where her mother lives now. She's physically healthy, but she only speaks gibberish."

She is quiet as this sinks in. "It's backwards," she says finally. "She's speaking backwards."

I raise an eyebrow. "How would you know that?"

Elle sounds almost casual. "She started doing that in the end."

Thick silence follows.

I pull the newspaper article out. "You were rescued on November 9th, by a lobsterman named Carl Veilleux. He didn't usually go that way, but he'd had a hunch about it. He saw the signal."

"It was my compact," Elle says. "Can you believe that? All the signal fires we lit, and a tiny damn mirror reflecting the sun is what saved us. I was trying to start another fire."

She's lying. I spot the twitch.

Then I remember: she cooked Chris.

"When I heard the boat, it took me a minute to realize I was hearing an engine. And I raced down the beach, screaming and waving. I shredded my feet, but I didn't care. He'd barely pulled in before I jumped into the boat and I just begged him to go, get me off that place. I looked back as we pulled out, and saw Jason standing there. I hadn't seen him in weeks. I could have told the fisherman to go back. But I knew that what I was looking at was no human being. So I turned away. That's one of the things that haunts me now." She takes a deep breath. "Anyway, the fisherman gunned the engine, and we took off. Whatever was holding us back before wasn't there anymore. It let us go. And I once again returned to the land of the living."

For a moment, only the storm breaks the silence.

"The rest is a blur," Elle says quietly. "Flashing blue and red lights, a plaid woolen blanket someone draped around my shoulders. I didn't even realize that I was holding my backpack until the medic pulled it out of my hand. I looked up and saw Jason for a moment, standing with the gathering crowd, and then my mother was there, swooping me away. There was silence and peace in the hospital, for a time. Padded rooms and sterile halls and nurses handing out pills in Dixie cups. A year later, I returned to ballet school." Her eyes meet mine.

"Do you know what *The Rite of Spring* is about?"

I am taken off guard. "The ballet? A virgin sacrifice, isn't it?"

Elle doesn't answer: instead, she gets up and leaves the room. She returns with something in a leather tube, which she pushes over to me. "I did have charcoal. And we found some old paper in the lighthouse."

I unfurl it. It's a gravestone rubbing.

"Her name was Marie de Laurence," Elle says. "She was your great-great-grandmother's great-great-grandmother, several times removed."

I freeze, stunned, then the bloodboil starts. I look up at her, hearing the grit in my voice. "Is this a joke?"

"Oh no." Elle shakes her head. "She was banished from Kennebunkport for witchcraft in 1674. She came north, and apparently chose the island voluntarily. There was no trace of her for the next sixty years, until a small lobster boat pulled ashore for repairs. She killed three of them, though the official records say they were lost at sea. Fourteen more souls died on that island between then and now, including my friends."

I stare at her, feel the temper boiling through my blood. "I drove all the way up here from Boston. You refused to meet in Kittery or Portland or even Brunswick, where I could have taken a bus or a train or a rideshare. I drove here, even though the gas alone cost me two days' wages and I had to take a payday loan to rent the room. Please don't toy with me."

"I'm not toying with you," Elle says. "I needed you to know the truth about who you are and where you come from." She leans towards me, whispering, her eyes glittering and wild. "You saw her that day, didn't you? When you fell off the boat. She told me everything. Sometimes when I was onstage, I would hear her whisper, words wrapped in ice water and bubbles. And I recall once more the price I paid for my escape."

I'm spinning again. "She?"

"The wraith you dream of." Her eyes snap onto mine. Her gaze is cold and dark and full of death. "You were only a child when you first met her. Your father said it was seaweed, caught you, but you know better. Whenever you looked into tidal pools or mirrors or the glass of the windows, she was always there, getting closer, getting stronger."

The blood freezes in my veins. "How...how would you know that?"

Elle looks around the room, almost casual. "The thing you met under the waves? I've danced her for years. Drawn her. Sang her. Played her. The night Zeke died was the first night she spoke to me."

"The woman," I say, my voice shaking. "The sea witch. The one *you* bargained with. What did she look like?"

She doesn't bat an eye. "Black hair, scaly skin, her glowing eyes. You can see her if you turn around. She's on the deck right now."

I think she is joking, but her eyes are serious, weighted with dark truth. I turn and see, through the lashing rain, the being that tried to haul me down into the depths. Terror clutches my throat, chokes my breath.

It is in that moment that I finally understand.

Mother, pointing ever so discreetly, "See her? The Black Swan? That's Elle!"

I look down at the bowl of fruit on the table. The bowl is grey, handmade, with orange knots. The patterns make me dizzy. I force myself to look away.

I swallow. "It wasn't Sara, that was pregnant, was it?"

She is silent a moment. When she finally speaks, her words are as sharp and icy as the waves beyond her. "I was in the asylum for eight months before being transferred. I had to give birth in that place. They took the babe away from me before I ever held her, but they let me pick the parents. I chose a dentist and a schoolteacher, a former dancer herself, in Saco. It wasn't until much later that I had my lawyers track her down."

I fumble, stand up. "We're done here."

But when I move forward, the room spins and my stomach heaves, and I taste something sickly sweet and bile is rising fast so fast and I am running for the sink before the foulness erupts.

Misery slows time. The wind screams, eternal.

I hear Elle's steps moving toward me. "Long before the first human baby raised its fist to the air and cried, the ghosts of another civilization haunted these waters. They were lost to a great upheaval, one that turned the world upside down and buried their cities. In the turmoil, their god slid beneath these waves. He slumbers now, but there are things that serve him still. She isn't the only one. The god of the deep has never seen our world, child, save through their dreams."

When the nausea has passed and my stomach is empty, I splash water on my face, rinse my mouth, and turn around.

The kitchen is empty.

I can see only black night beyond the French doors that lead outside, hidden behind sheets of thrashing rain. A pale figure stands there in the darkness, facing the sea.

I step out onto the veranda. "Elle?"

She does not see me. Does not hear me. Does not turn. Her voice is chattering in a strange, dissonant rhythm. I can only make out some of the words. *Rictus hell night things walking on the beach things walking from the sea the fog closed in so thick and didn't clear Chris' corpse was hovering in midair, grinning at me dance it was always there in the dance they never saw it*

The hairs on the back of my neck rise. "Elle?"

She turns and faces me, madness gleaming in her eyes, the sigil carved into her forehead, blood running down her mouth and then she opens her hands and there are eyes covered in seaweed and I feel the presence in the night beyond.

I turn and race through the house, grabbing my phone off the table as I pass. My shoes are upstairs and all I have are Elle's guest slippers but I don't care I can't stay I am running into the storm, I have to put distance between us, it's late and dark and dangerous but I need to get the hell away from her but even as I tear off into the charnel, hideous night, I know it's too late.

A hideous screech splits the air behind me. I glance back and see them on the rocky shore, scales glistening in the storm. Things are stomping crashing through the woods behind me, and when I look up I see a shape moving through the trees and the boreal forest is lashing and angry and silver and I understand that on such nights things move between worlds.

By the time I reach Grinsy's bar, I too, have become a primitive thing, hunted and hounded. I curl up sobbing in the bed, my feet bloodied and dirty and throbbing, like hers were, visions rolling through my thoughts like waves. Below me, sailors gather by candlelight, singing sea shanties, waiting for word of those caught out in the storm. I'm almost asleep when the bar below erupts in a sudden roar of collective grief and sobbing. I hear the clink of chipped glasses raised in toasts to those that had gone down beneath the waves, and I know the sea has claimed another.

I WAKE TO BRIGHT, STREAMING SUNLIGHT AND A THICK, HEAVY SILENCE. The storm has passed, I think, until I check my phone and realize this is only the eye. The previous day's events seem surreal in the light of day. My memories are blurred, coming in waves. I get dressed, and open the door to go in search of coffee.

My satchel is outside my door. When I open it, I find an external hard drive within.

THE FIRST FILE IS A CLIP OF ELLE DANCING *DRACULA* IN BLACK AND WHITE. She goes through the routine perfectly, nailing the most complicated leaps and spins. She is airborne, weightless, soulless and free. Her eyes flash open, vampire fangs and blood-black eyes. A net is cast over her, and she falls to the ground, immobile, entranced by silver knots.

SHE STANDS ON THE STEPS OF A MANSION, SURROUNDED BY ROLLING green gardens, dressed in some haute couture gown, drinking champagne from a crystal goblet. As she talks to the camera, I realize this is an outtake from the biopic. "Reality is what you feel, is it not? These solid objects. The earth beneath us. The air in our lungs. The water in that fountain. But they are moving too, their atoms spinning through time just as ours do. They only move slower. It's all a dance. Every atom, every planet, every galaxy. Every soul. Dancing."

ELLE SITS BEFORE A LIGHTED MIRROR IN HER DRESSING ROOM, surrounded by blood red roses, applying crimson lipstick. A turquoise betta fish twists in a wine glass before her. "Are you going to ask me deep, philosophical questions? Why am I dancing *Dracula*? Why do I always keep betta fish in my dressing room?" She picks up a second lipstick tube and holds it up. "Why am I using this lipstick tonight, instead of that one? Does this one have blood in it, like they say?" She dabs perfume on her wrists. "I like *Dracula*. I like the idea of immortality. I'm dancing *The Red Shoes* next, you know. And then *The Masque of the Red Death*. After that, *The Cask of Amontillado*. Interesting how Poe is so relevant today, you know. But then, he wrote about death, mostly, and that never gets old."

"Death is quite a heavy topic for such delicate dances," the reporter says.

"Is it?" Elle tilts her head. "Do you know what these ballets are about? They're hardly the stuff of fairy tales. Human sacrifice, witchcraft, trapped spirits. *Swan Lake* is about bondage, and the darkness within. *The Red Shoes* is about madness and/or demonic possession."

The reporter clears his throat. "There are rumors that you and Heather have been at odds. Are the stories about the coven true?"

"Rumors! There are also rumors that I drink blood and dance naked under the full moon." She moves to the camera, perfect teeth flashing. "I have to stretch now. And you must leave."

The video bounces and jerks as she shoos the reporter away. I almost don't catch it. I pause the clip. Rewind it. It takes me a moment to get the shot angled in and freeze it, but there it is. The wraith stares at me from the reflection of Elle's mirror.

I spin clockwise, like the storm.

IN THE FINAL CLIP, ANNA KELLY SITS IN A WHEELCHAIR. SHE IS WEARING pajamas, though it is midday. Her eyes are clear blue, and empty. She stares out a window bathed in cold sunlight, muttering something about locks and wards.

I zoom in on her hand. She is winding knots into a thread.

Elle's face stares out of the magazine on the table beside her.

I CALL MY PARENTS.

My mother tearily confesses everything. They would have told me, she says, but the contract bound them to silence. It all makes sense now: the books, the ballet classes, the trips to Boston. "I felt you should know her," she tells me, sniffling. "It was easier that way, if you thought I was just another fan."

I reassure her, tell her I'll be over for dinner next week, then pull my hair back into a sloppy bun, don jeans and Bean boots, like a true Mainer.

A huge pine has snapped over the restaurant, in the spot where we sat yesterday. The dock is in pieces. By some stroke of luck, my car is unscathed. Before heading out, I walk down to the memorial and look at the framed picture of Carter Kelly. But I don't wait long. I take the turns too fast. My eyes are glued to the road, but my thoughts spin into chaos. Elle's gate is open. I peel into the winding drive, gun it past the pines—two of which have toppled over—then screech to a stop and cut the engine.

Silence closes in thick around me. I slowly step out and approach the massive porch, my boots crunching in the drive. Below, the sea crashes against the rocks, angry.

The manicured gardens are overgrown with weeds. The windows are dark and dusty. I rub grime off the one beside the door and peer in. The furniture is covered with sheets. The fish tanks are foul and fetid, their waters opaque with filth. I smell the faint stench of decay.

A massive cobweb hangs over the door, filled with dead flies.

A siren and the squeal of tires breaks the silence. A police car pulls up, flashing red and blue lights a colorful contrast against the day's drabness.

"Stay where you are," the cop barks. "What are you doing here?"

I freeze, stammering. "I...I'm not breaking in. I'm looking for Elle Sanders."

The cop approaches. "There's no one home here, miss. Get to shelter. The storm isn't over."

My head is spinning. "But I was here this morning. She must have just left."

He remains unimpressed. "Be on your way or you'll be on your way to jail."

I don't need to be told twice. I'm halfway to Route 1 when I get a text from Elle. *Meet me at the dock.*

I lay on the gas. But it's pointless. Not a mile down the road, a huge tree blocks the way. I sit there, staring at it, until the winds pick up again. Only then do I succumb and turn around.

The wraith waits in my rear-view mirror when I look back.

ELLE IS WAITING ON THE DOCKS. BEYOND HER, STEEL-GREY WAVES shatter the sunlight, reflecting it back to the atmosphere. The vista would be idyllic, except that the harbor is a wreck: boats are mashed together, crushed up against the rocks. I see volunteers moving among the rocks, looking for orphaned baby seals.

There is a hole in the sky.

Elle holds a piece of rope in her hands. Knowledge churns in my gut. I look up, meet her soulless eyes.

Three knots a tempest brings.

"Yes dear," Elle says sweetly. "I summoned the storm."

I shake my head. "That's impossible."

"Nothing is impossible. The world works on witchcraft, because witchcraft is nothing more than focused energy. Think about it. Hurricanes often start with the tiniest breeze in Africa. One cannot create a hurricane through witchcraft. But one can move a seed. A pod. And that seed, dear, *is* the storm." Her eyes glitter, like the sea. "It's time for you to come home."

A steady line of residents moves down to the docks, tossing trinkets into the sea. Knots and shells and coins. *They know,* I realize. In the distance, another dark line looms over the sea: the back half of the gale.

I swallow. "I guess I know why you always danced stories about curses and deals."

She smiles. "Bargains made between the devil and the deep blue sea."

My throat is tight. "You promised her my life, in return for yours."

"I wanted more than *life*. I wanted success. That cost double. I don't know what drove me to her. What made me tread that path, with the sharp sea grass, beneath the quarter moon. But this is not a curse, child. It is a gift." She steps forward, traces my cheek almost lovingly. I flinch, but cannot back away from her touch. "There are many worlds out there. And the veil that separates them is both as vast as space and as thin and fragile as a cobweb. In most places, the barrier stands. But there are holes in the fabric. I stumbled through one, once." Elle tilts her head towards the vessel. "Come. We should be out of the harbor before the eye passes."

Despite the rising terror in my gut, I cannot keep my feet from clambering down the dock and climbing into the boat. Someone sees us and shouts. Elle ignores them, turns the boat into the black line over the sea. An old, mustached man run-waddles down the dock, waving his arms. I wonder if this is Jack, the harbor master.

Elle ignores him, gunning the motor. A moment later, the radio crackles to life as the Coast Guard tries to reach us. She tells them we do not need rescue, then snaps it off.

I stand at the bow of the boat as it slices the waves. The shore is soon obscured by the rising waves. In time, I sense the barrier she spoke of give way before us. As we approach the island, deep pulses of red light flicker in the depths below us. Something inside me changes, like a gear shifting. I look down into the waters and see the beautiful monstrosity twisting beneath us in cold green depths. My lips mouth its name.

Then the skies tear open, and the sea churns to rage. All manner of monsters pour through the gap. The worst of them goes by the name of Elle Sanders.

A wall of water approaches. I jump to meet the wave and then sink into salty depths, where my brethren are waiting to welcome me home. I have become as she is, soulless and free.

In the world we've left behind, the storm descends on the town.

AFTER EVERYTHING

BY ERRICK NUNNALLY

PART

I

DEPUTIES & CRICKETS

FROM EDDIE'S NOTEBOOK:

When it comes to creeps, there is one thing you can count on. Every time. When all is said and done, they do not behave like humans. Whatever they do to find and kill living people is merely a function of their built-in drive for murder. They aren't hungry in the normal sense. Their stomachs don't work. Whatever it manages to choke down, a creep will eat to bulging and just kind of shit it out and move on. Gross from the waist down and the waist up.

The shambler came to the playground at the same time every day. During sunset, as the sky turned brilliant blues and purples that bled to red, the dead thing waited at the bottom of a slide, confused. At other times it bumped swings with an awkward, stiff push. When the sun sunk beneath the horizon and twilight ruled the sky, it would leave.

For Jeff, it was the moaning that got to him, not the decrepit rotting humanity. The moaning the dead did, these things that didn't need to breathe, that had no clear need to vocalize. The sound was an awful reminder of their origins. They'd suck air into lungs unused for who knows how long then—depending on how freshly dead—issue a raspy, wet gurgle or a dry hiss. Sometimes they'd follow up with a combination of hissing exhalations and long, even groans. The sounds made every nerve tingle on Jeff's head and coated him in a light sheen of manic energy.

Eddie's composure was a different story.

The end-of-the-day ritual at the playground had become their regular thing about four months ago when Eddie had noticed this particular shambler while on a solo run. On your own, you never rushed into a creep kill until you'd taken a good hard look at the scene. Eddie had time to observe the thing's odd behavior and it was the absolute definition of *odd*.

Eddie's shambler turned dumbly in a circle and moaned its last before shuffling back the way it had come, disappearing into the brush. The young man scratched a few thoughts into his notebook.

Jeff swore openly, frustrated at his inability to kick the panic he felt when hearing the moaning. The terrified clenching in his chest and gut embarrassed him. It was something they'd only spoken about once. It was no secret where the trauma had come from. The feeling wouldn't go away. It was a reminder of their hard shift from past to present.

Eddie didn't bother trying to shush Jeff. They were far enough away that the shambler couldn't hear them. He'd told Jeff on more than one occasion that courage wasn't a lack of fear. He was here for his friend and partner. They were a team. So Eddie decided to worry about other matters.

Jeff cursed again and gathered his pack before scooping the last of the weed back into a plastic baggie for another day. They tried to share a joint at the end of the day and the playground was a perfect spot. Good thing the creeps didn't have much of a sense of smell; those membranes were among the first to dry up.

Eddie watched Jeff for a moment before pushing himself up off the cool soil and brushing pine needles down his front. He'd been getting restless with his hometown—the weird creep notwithstanding—and had been considering making some kind of change. Tucking his notebook away, he turned to his friend.

"Hey, Jeff, you want to pack it up in a few days and try our luck down in Furnham for a couple of weeks? It'll be like a vacation, I hear they still got cows down there." Eddie grinned the way he always did, with about half the effort and a wry pinch in one eye.

Furnham was a town about twenty-five miles south of their hometown. It often seemed like Massachusetts had an unlimited supply of small towns, the next as uninteresting as any other. A detail here and there is what made the difference. In this instance: the rumor of fresh beef. It wasn't a sure thing—creeps tended to take down any living creature that couldn't muster the intelligence to get out of their way—but the possibility was attractive.

Jeff spaced for a moment and Eddie hoped that he was seriously considering the suggestion. His partner pissed all over the idea, instead.

"Naw, man, I've been listening to the reports after the broadcast, and the fuckin' bugs have set up a hive between here and there. They're close. This one popped up and they never even saw it being built, never saw 'em land or nothin'."

"Chrissakes, seriously? Is that what I'm missing at the end?"

"Dude, you pass out right after the recorded message. It's like your lullaby."

Eddie snorted because it was true. He usually fell asleep towards the end of the broadcast, one of the most repetitive and boring things to have ever been sent across the airwaves. Still, it was to promote analysis of an honest-to-god alien language. Repetition had taken the edge off of his curiosity, however.

"I'm starting to think you don't love me," Eddie said.

"What?"

Eddie screwed his face up and chuckled. "Et tu, Jeff?"

"What? No!" Jeff sucked his teeth and said, "I don't—I mean—"

"Fuck's sake, man…"

"No, I—"

"You don't actually think romantic love is the only love. Do you?" Eddie projected as much incredulousness as he could. Jeff wasn't a dullard, but there were holes here and there. They'd been friends a long time and it remained surprising.

Jeff took a breath to say something but instead waved his hands and shook his head.

"Look, Jeff, you're my best friend. And I love you. See? It's not hard. I love beef jerky too. See the difference?"

Jeff tsked and huffed. "Yeah, I get it." He said it like he didn't get it or probably that he'd never thought about it.

Eddie shook his head and smiled, slapping Jeff's shoulder.

Jeff chuckled and sighed. "And I'm sorry. I didn't mean to imply…"

"I know," Eddie said, squeezing Jeff's shoulder.

The two walked in silence until Jeff spoke up, "You think we'll ever see one of the bugs up close?" He stared across the cracked and overgrown parking lot attached to the playground.

Eddie rubbed the stubble on his chin and thought about it. In the midst of the chaos during the early days, some thought the aliens had something to do with the virus, but the visitors seemed to be just as surprised as humanity. "Probably not. Well, maybe. I mean, if the hives keep popping up, the feds won't be able to keep up with the creeps *and* cordon off the bugs. I don't think they're part of the problem, though."

Jeff made a disgusted noise. "Part of the *immediate* problem, you mean. What do you think they've been doing?"

"I dunno. They landed in Canada first, right?"

"Yeah, that we know of."

"Maybe they seek maple syrup."

"Ha-ha. I'm serious."

"Me too, I love maple syrup. But I have not a single clue on the bugs. I am sure that first contact with the goddamned creeps probably ruined whatever plans they had." Eddie hoped the aliens didn't honestly think the walking dead were the best humanity had to offer. The bugs had maintained radio silence ever since first contact with the creeps. That one recorded message went out and nothing much had changed since.

Jeff said, "Yeah, I guess. As long as they're not trying to eat us, they can wait in line."

Frustrated, Eddie shoved his custom-designed, creep cancellation tool—the 'creepwhacker'—through the steel loop on his belt. He'd been thinking more often about a change of scenery and who better to do it with than his best friend? They would both benefit, Eddie was sure of it. But just like that, the plan was ruined, much like everything else since the creeps showed up.

Eddie wondered if maybe the bugs could have helped with the creeps. Their first contact with the walking dead couldn't possibly have endeared humanity to the visitors. If there *was* a hive south of their town, it was the eighth known location, and the fifth inside the United States, hundreds of miles south of the others.

Jeff drew his leatherneck closed and Eddie reflexively checked his. It was Jeff who had copped the idea from a history class. When you're canceling a creep's ticket, you don't want another one to jump on you and sink teeth into the back of your neck. The thick leather could buy precious seconds to recover. What little they'd been taught at the hastily organized deputizing seminars culminated in "avoid unplanned contact with the contaminated." It was the same practical advice they gave about having sex. If you want to avoid unplanned pregnancy or diseases, don't have sex. Then again, with so many parents gone, they had to give some kind of direction to restless teens.

Whatever virus the creeps carried was a pathogen that didn't last long outside of their bodies. Their slowly rotting forms didn't seem to carry any additional diseases, but anything was possible. The sheer, unexplained amount of the restless dead reinforced all possibilities. More so since visitors from outer space touched down in North America.

Both of the boys kept every inch of their bodies covered, right down to a pair of matching leather helmets and clear goggles liberated from the military surplus store on the edge of town. A deep scratch from a deadhead might mean a slow death. A kind of death, anyway. They'd each agreed to cancel the other's ticket and collect the credits if one of them got infected.

Both Jeff and Eddie had contributed here and there to the methods used to cancel creeps in the area, but they'd learned the bulk of their craft from a man whose name they never truly knew. Everyone called him Sensei—even his grizzled girlfriend, Lana.

FROM EDDIE'S NOTEBOOK:

Hickory dickory dock
A creep bumped into a clock
The clock chimed loud
The creep spun round
And Eddie canceled its ticket

We bagged ten creeps today. That's twenty eyeballs, enough credits to eat and resupply with.

Jesus H. Christ, I'm bored.

PART

II

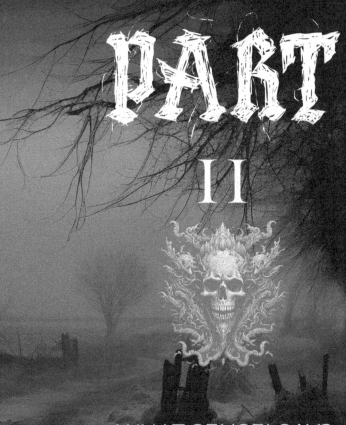

WHAT SENSEI SAY?

It wasn't hard to guess that Sensei had been a martial arts enthusiast in a previous life. No mean feat of deduction there, the man carried two or three unusual weapons for canceling creeps and he used them with flair. The most difficult weapon he employed was a type of flail: ten feet of steel links with a six-inch pipe linked to one end and a four-foot handle at the other. The pipe, filled with concrete, had screws driven entirely through it to produce a series of short, but deadly, barbs around the outside.

He could spin the flail in a blurry arc and bury the end in a creep's head, whip it back and cancel another in the same motion. The loose chain in between served as tangle and control when needed. Four or five lopes meant nothing to him.

Sensei behaved as if his entire life had been spent preparing for this very moment in history. On some occasions, he dropped hints that he'd worked with the government or had a family consumed by the monsters, but he wandered indiscriminately in the hot zones. It didn't seem possible for such a man to lose his own children to the hordes.

It was impossible to verify anything he said. It didn't matter, his actions spoke clearly enough.

Sensei projected a deadly serious menace the way Lana projected cool. He was over six feet of salty baldness and tattoos on a muscled frame built for murder. He referred to the creeps as 'Charlie.' For him, a laugh was a way to control, a comment on misfortune or mistakes. It could serve as a signal for both his students and to telegraph his anger. That laughter held all the sorrow and disappointment he carried. It was a shield and it didn't take long for his students to learn what it meant. He never wrote anything down, never consulted a manual. The man had everything he needed in his brain and chewed out knowledge between ruined teeth. Lana preferred long weapons like pikes and weighted staffs. The sort of things Jeff worked with. She kept her dark braids plaited back from her face and entwined with colorful yarn. Like Sensei, Lana had lean muscle running the length of her tall body. She rarely smiled at anyone but her partner. Most of the time, her eyes were unreadable, like glass. She was the one who suggested that Eddie keep a journal, and she said it without a hint of warmth, just a statement of fact. Whenever she shared, it was the cold steel of experience.

Eddie never got the hang of exotic weapons like the flail, but he enjoyed working with knives and the modified entrenching tool he now carried as a weapon.

Sensei and Lana exited the kids' lives as abruptly as they'd entered it. One terrifying morning they were there. Consoling, directing, instilling discipline and order. *Teaching*. Several months later—yet another terrifying morning—and they were gone, never to be seen again. His last piece of advice echoed in their ears:

The dead deserve nothing outside their graves.

The wandering couple were the primary reason Jeff and Eddie remained alive today. They liked to believe that Sensei and Lana had moved on to another forgotten and abandoned town, between the cities, to take other boys and girls under their leathery wings for just long enough to teach them how to stay alive.

Then to direct them to the Federal Deputies Program for Young Adults.

PART

III

THERE'S NO PLACE LIKE HOME

Jeff and Eddie lived on the top floor of a two-family house. There were so many abandoned homes in the area that they could have lived in any McMansion. A smaller home meant a creep had a narrower route to find its way to wherever you were sleeping. Easier to defend too, if you know what you're doing. The damn things don't sleep, of course, and the worst of them can turn a doorknob or walk through a patio window to get inside.

The boys always chose a place on a corner with a fenced-in backyard. If there were glass patio doors, they had to be able to be barricaded or the house was left empty. A secure fence all the way around the house was a bonus. An escape plan, always necessary.

Creeps weren't the only problem. The distinct lack of law enforcement in the area meant what could only be politely described as vigorous competition between other deputies. Neither of the boys had killed a normal human being—although the concept of a "normal" human being was being redefined more quickly than anyone could keep up with.

When they got to their latest base, there was a lone figure stalking around the house, covered head-to-toe as they were, trying to peer through the windows. It was full dark and the tall figure didn't move like a creep.

Owen.

Owen wanted people to call him 'The Big O' and he frequently referred to himself in the third-person using the ridiculous sobriquet. It didn't help that the boys knew he'd copped the nickname from a Japanese cartoon.

They'd first met during eighth grade—what would come to be their last year of school. The large boy had transferred in, made no friends—but plenty of acquaintances—and created a legend of sorts. Rumors surrounded him: dead animals, vandalism, robberies, arsons, assaults. No one had seen or could prove anything, but that was all there was to know about Owen. His own personal narrative was unreliable. No one still around had ever met his parents either.

Jeff called out first. He hadn't always been the more aggressive of the two, but lately he'd become more assertive.

"Hey, Owen, fuck off. This is our place; you see the flag."

"The Big O sees your numbers, bros."

After a two-week seminar, deputies' numbers were issued along with the eye scoop for Credit Verification Collection, and off they went. When a deputy claimed an abandoned property for the night—or whatever—he marked it with something bearing their license number.

The potential for abuse was horrific, of course.

Canceling creeps was admittedly cathartic, but Owen took a sadistic pleasure in the task. He also enjoyed finding new ways to otherwise abuse the afflicted before shutting them down. Like the boys, Owen wore hodgepodge armor to protect his skin and knew his way around smithing tools. All the successful deputies knew how to use the shop at the high school. It served as neutral territory.

"The Big O reads, boys. I was here lookin' for y'all. Got a business proposition for ya." Owen favored a pitted goalie's mask for face protection. The mask featured two, dirty red stripes on each cheek. Eddie wondered, as always, if Owen had been stupid enough to have smeared infected blood on his gear or if the rival boy had used paint. If the rogue deputy could manage it, he wouldn't take the mask off. It was his wall, the deception he needed to present himself in the manner he wished. It was "The Owen Way," as the disturbing deputy liked to mention.

If he was grinning, Eddie couldn't tell by his eyes. They were in a perpetual dead state as if the top half of his face had seen a recent treatment of Botox.

Creeps didn't blink much, but even they had more expressive eyes, their bodies constantly losing moisture, eyesight failing. They were most dangerous in a dark room or at night.

Owen preferred to consider Eddie as the leader of the two-man crew. Eddie was the only one of them that could bear to deal with Owen with any regularity and for any length of time.

Eddie slung his helmet and pushed his goggles up. "Lose the mask, Owen; if you want to talk, do it like a normal human being."

"Inside, boys, inside."

"Fuck you, Owen, we're not interested." Jeff started for the front steps.

"Didn't hear nothin' from Eddie."

"The mask, Owen."

"Fine!" He snatched the filth-smeared, white plastic from his face, pulling it over his long, dirty-blond hair. "Okay?"

Owen tended to have two emotions: utter calm and utter fury. At this moment, volcanic frustration creased the lines of his face. Just as quickly, the emotion drained away, leaving the large boy's normally dead eyes floating in the middle of that conflicted mess.

"All right," Eddie grinned and clapped Owen on his shoulder pad. He pointed at the taller boy and said, "You got five minutes."

Owen smiled, only the lower half of his face mimicked the emotion. Jeff was perpetually annoyed with the rival deputy, but Eddie instinctively knew there were no good results in getting on Owen's bad side. So he forced cordiality and did what he could to keep "The Big O" at a distance.

Jeff rolled his eyes and let Eddie handle Owen.

The boys tromped up the porch stairs. Eddie took one last look down both streets and followed them inside. From behind, he got a good look at the long, zippered bag that was strapped to Owen's back. It was olive green and had the sheen of a military tarp with official-looking numbers stenciled on the side: *FA-MAS-X NATO*. Eddie locked the door from the inside, and the three quickly canvassed the house for creeps by dint of habit.

They settled in the kitchen, Jeff pulled out a package of beef jerky, placed a strip between his lips, and tossed Eddie the bag. Eddie didn't offer Owen any. Judging by the boy's size, he was eating just fine.

Jeff flicked the power switch on the small portable radio they kept with them. The recording of the daily broadcast from Earth's otherworldly visitors floated in the air. With limited resources, the government—all governments—rebroadcast the message followed by a statement of any decoding progress that had been accomplished. So far, a series of numbers and basic mathematical equations were identified. What may have been the key to the aliens' language was proving difficult to match up with what had to be a recorded message in their native language.

Owen didn't appear to mind the radio chatter. He pulled the olive green bag over his head and plunked it on the kitchen's granite counter with a distinct, metallic *thunk*.

"Check this shit out." The sound of the thick zipper cut eerily loud against the home's placid backdrop and the low volume of the radio. The only power in the area came from individual generators nowadays and most homes were quiet. At least the water still worked.

Jeff hustled upstairs for a lamp, he didn't want to miss this. Owen paused, waiting for proper light. When Jeff returned, another item liberated from the surplus store downtown provided a warm halo of light for the boys.

Owen drew some kind of rifle from the bag, a weapon neither of the other two boys had ever seen. It looked new, oiled, and deadly. Compact, easy to shoulder. The trigger was too far forward of the stock, giving the weapon an awkward appearance. Owen produced two curved magazines from the bag. They were taped together, one upside down to the other. He held the weapon in one hand and the loaded magazines poised in the other with an amused glitter in his eyes. Jeff tensed, glancing at Eddie who managed to get closer to Owen without the blond boy taking defensive notice or, if he did notice, he didn't care. Jeff had seen the rush of what could only be described as light coming into Owen's dead eyes when he'd produced the dyslexic rifle.

Eddie reached out and gently stopped him from loading the weapon. "Okay, that's hot shit, we see. Where the hell did you get it?"

There weren't many true man-killing weapons in the area. Law enforcement and the National Guard mostly carried them. It was Massachusetts so, sure, plenty of folks had access to hunting rifles or an exotic handgun or two, but nothing quite like this. Besides, popping off rounds at creeps only brought more of them out. You'd damn well better be prepared. Even if you had a machine gun, it was a burden to get ammunition for it. Owen had the air of a man who seemed to have plenty.

"National Guard unit got pinched by a horde at a narrow pass on 210. You know, right where the highway collapses to one lane? They got stupid and tried to shoot their way out instead of steppin' on the gas."

"That *was* stupid." Jeff snorted under his breath.

It was true. There was nothing in it for law enforcement or the military to spontaneously engage a horde of creeps. No bounties for them, just duty. Everyone around here knew to never stop on the highways with creeps coming out of the brush. The noise of a Guard unit would have brought plenty of lopes out, for sure, and eventually shamblers.

"You bet it was, Jeff, my man. I heard opportunity knockin' and I got a plan to cancel enough tickets to move to one of the islands where the real action is with real people."

Islands out of sight of the mainland, especially the small ones, were the safest places to be nowadays. Clean an island off and keep it clean, a simple plan. One driven by billionaires, simpatico millionaires, and their sycophantic apologists. Tough to join, the price was high. Although, Eddie wondered, why Owen would want to be around such people when he liked to cancel creeps so much.

"How much of this shit did you grab?"

"There was enough to make my plan a reality, Eddie, but I need a couple of guys to help me pull it off."

Jeff leaned on the counter, eyes on the FA-MAS-X. "You can't just wander around blasting creeps, you'd never get enough of 'em."

"Exactly, that's why we're gonna call 'em to us."

"That's insane," Jeff said. "The creeps would come from every direction, you'd be surrounded. There's no way to control that."

"This," Owen indicated the weapon in his hands, "is only a part of the solution, there's more where this came from, I just need a team to make it work. We could earn enough canceled tickets to buy our way *out*. Check this."

Owen put the weapon down, turned a magazine in his hands and pushed two bullets into his palm. He jiggled them together briefly before tossing one to each of the boys.

"Look closely at the tip."

Eddie peered at his bullet. The casing didn't appear to be anything different, but the bullet itself was something new. The tip looked like a series of stacked bands around a bundle of needles.

"When fired from shoulder height," Owen put the weapon to his shoulder to demonstrate, "these rounds spit those needles out in a wide pattern, penetrating *many* creep brains at once. Way more potent and accurate than a scatter gun. The pattern stays flat. Fuckin' *science*, man." Owen slowly pushed his hand out from the barrel, keeping his palm to the floor and splaying his fingers.

The economy had gone to hell in the last couple of years, stuttering over new ideas, but it was still an economy for those who played. Capitalism wouldn't die. The kind of fantasy that Owen seemed to be dreaming of was certainly possible. Money was money and it still made the world go 'round. Even if the creeps were slowing the rotation. The boys exchanged another glance, and Jeff pulled away from the group to root around for more food to eat. Eddie considered Owen with level eyes and crossed arms.

"You may have something there, Owen, but we're not interested in this plan."

"You've got to be kidding me."

Jeff remained silent, one hand pushing a palmful of popcorn into his mouth and the other on the pike he used against creeps.

"Owen, it's no big deal; we're just not lookin' for the big score right now."

"Then what the fuck are you two doing? This is the fucking way, man!"

Eddie shifted his weight—a casual move—and rested his left palm on the Bowie knife he kept strapped to his hip. Mentally, he went over the move Sensei had drilled into his head: a quick draw slashing across the throat or face and then returning the point of the knife to the heart or head. He never thought he'd have to pull it off, but there was a first time for everything. It was a technique that could potentially drop anyone. Before committing to such matters, however, he casually addressed Owen.

"Hey, Owen, be cool, man. How about we think about it? That's a big move and we like to be careful. Maybe we can come up with something to make it more comfortable for us? It'd still be your idea, so we can say right away it'd be a 60/20/20 split."

Owen seemed to physically chew the idea over, his jaw working, scanning the two other boys and the room.

"Yeah, that's cool." Owen pointed at the boys in turn as he said, "Eddie, my man. Jeff. I'll see y'all later." With a dead-face smile, Owen collected his gear and left the house. The boys watched him jog down the street and didn't say a word until the back of his unprotected blond head disappeared in the shadows. No one knew where Owen holed up. Ever.

Jeff sighed and said, "Let's move tonight. Right now."

A dangerous proposition, but Eddie sighed in return and answered, "Yeah."

They set about the task.

PART

IV

THE GIRL AT THE EDGE OF TOWN

"We need to go see Karen."

Jeff was rooting about in a waterproof, oversized messenger bag. Their supply sack. The container sagged with its mouth gaping hungrily open.

"That's going to bring us up short on credits this month. We'll need to cancel as many tickets as we can in the next couple of weeks to make it up."

"Yeah." Jeff, chewing his lip, looked at Eddie.

"Uh-uh, we're not doing that."

"I know we're not."

"*Fuck no*, we're not."

"Damn straight, but maybe we can find that horde Owen talked about, pick at the fringes?"

"Maybe." Eddie tapped his fingers in turn, wondering if they could be that foolish. If being that foolish was worth it.

The boys headed to Karen's shop without a word passing between them. In the distance, they could hear the rumble of engines. The Guard passed through on occasion, as evidenced by Owen's "good" fortune. This early in the morning, it had to be a convoy, but the sound came from the opposite side of town, well away from Owen's "discovery."

KAREN RAN THE LOCAL, FED-SUPPORTED GENERAL STORE. BEFORE HER old man died, the Feds arranged to set up the shop in an old industrial office area. Wide open, flat parking lot, solid chain-link fencing all around, and encircled by bales of concertina wire.

Karen , barely a couple of years older than the boys, had no taste for combing the area and canceling creep tickets.

A few of the walking dead were tangled up in the barbed wire with arrows poking out of their heads. It demonstrated that she had some talent for cancellation, if not the zeal to patrol the area looking for trouble. It was a solid gig.

Jeff and Eddie paused to scoop one eye out of each creep and collect the arrows. Karen would get the credits for these. Frosting on top of her regular cake. It was an understanding between her and the local deputies: she took care of everything that wandered into her perimeter and they cleaned up outside. If it had an arrow sticking out of it, scoop an eye, pull any bodies out of the wire, and wait to be let in. Eddie gave a little wave to the pole-mounted camera and Karen buzzed them through the outer gate.

The front door had a tiny bell that tinkled when the boys entered. Uncomplicated, the shop featured rows of basic and emergency supplies like first aid kits, various lengths and strengths of cords and chains, dried foods, canned goods, bottles of water, blankets, et cetera.

Karen sat by the door, behind an unassuming desk. Both Jeff and Eddie knew that she kept an arsenal at hand. A woman living on the borders of an unregulated area might occasionally need to create her own law.

Several years ago, she would've been considered a plain girl: light brown hair, puckish nose, round shoulders, and wider-than-a-model hips. *Average*, as the ignorant parlance went. Now, she was "blessed" with a beauty enhanced by dire circumstances. It was doubtful there was a male alive within fifty miles that wouldn't find Karen attractive. And none of that mattered to her. Despite her current circumstance, she was one of the sharpest people either boy had ever met. Like most of them in the area, she grew up in town; they'd all attended the same schools. Karen always excelled; learning came as easily to her as independence. From her perspective, life's pickings had always been slim.

Eddie gave Karen a broad smile, "Hiya, Karen, had a few creeps come up last night?"

"Hey, Eddie. Yup. Hi, Jeff, how's it going?" Karen smiled at Eddie, but her demeanor shifted when she spoke to Jeff. Her eyes crinkled, she touched her hair, and a shade of blush showed along her jawline.

Jeff smiled, mumbled hello, and wandered on into the building. Eddie wondered how his best friend could be so dense.

"Nice shooting. I still can't believe you can hit 'em like that from here."

Karen's skill with a compound bow was legendary in the area. Her father had been an accomplished bowhunter and taken his daughter with him as often as he could. At any distance within range, Karen could be devastating. Jeff and Eddie had seen her take down several creeps in a row, calmly notching, drawing, and releasing arrow after arrow. Eddie placed her three retrieved bolts on the desk.

Karen smiled and snapped on a pair of disposable gloves, scooped up the bolts, and examined them.

"Still good, still good—ugh—bent tip, cracked shaft."

She tossed the busted arrow and set to cleaning the serviceable ones. "You still watching that creep that comes to the playground?"

"Yeah, same pattern every day."

"God, that's so bizarre. Seen many more in the area?"

"Maybe. Last night, Owen told us about a horde up near 210. We're thinkin' about seeing if we can pick up some easy credits off it."

Making an awful face, Karen said, "Owen," and sighed. "That's really dense forest over there, if there's a horde, it's best to be avoided. What does Jeff think?"

"He suggested it."

A look of concern briefly crossed her face. "Well, supplies are a bit low, delivery's late, and, no, I don't know why."

"Could be anything. The country isn't exactly stable."

Karen nodded. Then she rolled her eyes as a dull thud sounded from the back, followed by the tinkle of items rolling across the floor.

Eddie smiled at his feet when he heard Jeff's voice call out: "Sorry."

They both headed for the back, all the while Eddie outlining what they were looking for and Karen trying to play it cool around Jeff while he awkwardly went about the business of cleaning up the mess he'd made.

Eddie looked around and, after surveying the scene for several moments, decided that, yes, the shelves were unusually bare today.

PART

V

PRINCE ALBERT WAS IN A CAN

The boys cruised down the center of Route 12 on the fixies they'd borrowed from Karen, looking to hit 210 close to town and ride northwest up the highway. The knobby rubber tires rolling against the road made a steady hissing noise while Eddie pressed Jeff about Karen.

"Seriously, man, how can you not? You don't think she's cool?"

"Yeah, I think she's cool, you know, but…"

"But what? Just ask her out or, uh, something."

Jeff abruptly stopped his bike. Eddie circled around and pulled up next to him. Jeff looked off into the trees for several moments before speaking.

"I mean…what the fuck would we do? You 'n' me spend all of our time cutting down creeps or smokin' weed and Karen don't do either. There's nothing else to do around here but survive. What's the point?"

Eddie thought about it for a moment, trying to respect Jeff's opinion.

"Then make a point, Jeff. Meaning is what we make it nowadays. Karen's the prettiest girl around—hell, the only girl 'cause I'm not gonna count Marie the Butcher and her Deathbos."

Jeff sighed. "And she's older than me."

"Jeff…"

"Okay! Okay, fine. I'll, uh, talk to her. I guess?"

"It'll be fine, man, you do that. I gotta live vicariously through you, my options are less than zero. Plenty of dudes, most of 'em scummy, none of 'em on my freq."

They rode in silence for the next few miles until their destination came into view.

What was left of the convoy lay plain about a quarter-mile ahead. There'd been no word of the convoy in town and it was clear that they'd been blowing past town on the highway heading east.

The boys stashed their bikes on the overgrown median and continued on foot, melting into the old growth on the eastbound side. They moved slowly, no rush. Both had their weapons at the ready. It was slow going through the brush. No need to stumble into anything, no need to stir up a wasp's nest until it was time to destroy it.

They came to a clearing parallel to where the convoy lay. The grass was trampled and plenty of broken branches led deeper into the forest. They eyed each other and crept up to the grassy bluff overlooking the highway. Eddie slid his pocket scope out and peered at the scene.

There were dead lopes everywhere on this side of the convoy. Soldiers who'd been torn to pieces lay scattered about them, and spent shell casings glinted in the sun. Gear from the humvees lay scattered in chaotic clusters on the roadway—phantom reminders of the living who needed *stuff*. It looked like they'd encountered a horde crossing the highway.

The mess was no doubt partially Owen's handiwork, he'd tossed the convoy. No weapons in sight, also no doubt Owen's handiwork. For several minutes, they lay, and watched, and listened.

Finally, Jeff rolled over and held his fist out to Eddie. His partner matched the gesture, they bounced their fists three times and stopped. Jeff with "rock" and Eddie with "scissors." The loser took point.

Eddie crept over the edge and looked around. Then he stood up and started walking towards the carnage. If creeps were around at this point, there'd be no hiding. After he'd gotten about twenty yards, Jeff rose up and followed, turning in slow circles. Eddie focused on the vehicles in front of him, Jeff focused on everything else. Stillness. The absence of anything living. A light breeze ruffled the trees around them, nature whispered.

Moving in a wide circle around the two vehicles, Eddie came back to the point where he'd begun circling and moved in, stepping gingerly over the gore-strewn corpses. They were going to be up to their asses in cleaning bleach this evening for sure.

The rear vehicle's doors were hanging open, but the first vehicle was buttoned up tight. Eddie peeked into the open humvee and looked around. There was a first aid kit strapped to the dash. He gently loosed it and stood up. Catching Jeff's eye, he held the first aid kit up. If they couldn't sell it, the materials would come in handy at some point. The fact that the kit was still there spoke volumes to Owen's frame of mind. He tossed the strap across his body and headed over to Jeff and spoke quietly.

"What a mess."

"You're right about that. What about the other vehicle?"

"I dunno, it's closed up all the way around. Judging by the mess out here, I don't think Owen would've taken the time to close it up. Besides, there's bloody handprints all over the side of the damn thing."

"Whaddya wanna do?"

"I wanna open it up, check it out, and screw the fuck out of here, but I'm gonna need your help."

Jeff nodded and the two headed back to the closed humvee.

Jeff said, "I can't tell in this fuckin' mess which way the horde may have——" They both froze when they heard the soft thump and stirring sounds from the closed humvee.

"How the hell did a creep get stuck in there?"

Jeff said, "Might be a soldier. Waiting for help."

"Yeah, right. Might've *been* a soldier. That's a creep and we're gonna cancel that ticket."

Jeff nodded. "Okay. Let's hope it's a shambler and not a goddamn lope. Real quiet, you get the door."

Jeff nodded and they moved smoothly, like the team they were. Eddie positioned himself about where they thought the shuffling sounds were coming from. Jeff put his hand on the door handle and rattled it. The violent thump and moans that followed confirmed a stuck creep.

Jeff counted to three and yanked the door open. The lope—no doubt now—sprang out and Eddie swung in a blurry downward arc to cleave the creep's head. It would have been a clean cancellation had Eddie's CCT not rebounded smartly off the helmet strapped securely under the damn thing's chin.

FROM EDDIE'S NOTEBOOK:

Up close, a creep's need to put your lights out is so desperate, you can practically taste it. They hiss if they're older and drier or they gurgle and groan when they're fresher. Incidental noises. It all comes from their disgustingly contorted faces and decaying lungs. The fresher they are, the more they stink in accompaniment to their relative fleshiness. Lopes are way more aggressive, you can just tell how badly they want you dead once they spot you. The virus tended to affect some more than others. Sometimes you got fast-moving lopes and sometimes you got slow-moving shamblers. The shamblers might miss you passing by or take a more "thoughtful" approach to deciding whether to murder you or not. The differences take some getting used to.

We've seen both types up close plenty of times and learned what little science there was on them in the deputy's seminar (what little the gov't has shared with us). Who knows where the science is today? We've tried philosophy to figure out what makes a person become a shambler or a lope. Great love versus great hate? Serious attachments to the world around you? In the end, only one thing makes sense: canceling tickets, collecting credits, surviving, trying not to be too bored with the repetition. Contributing a little to maybe balance the world back out. There isn't much room for doubt.

Especially if a berserk lope gets the jump on you.

THE LOPE DIDN'T EVEN TRY TO BREAK ITS FALL ON TOP OF EDDIE, IT JUST plunged its face at his head and neck. Instinctively, Eddie drove an elbow into the lope's throat as they toppled backwards. There was a dull thunk that echoed through his head and light blossomed between his eyes when the back of his skull met the pavement. The leather helmet took the brunt, but it stung nonetheless.

The lope scrabbled to shift its weight, relieving some of the pressure from Eddie, but still gnawing at the plastic forearm armor of Eddie's gauntlet. Jeff couldn't safely split its skull while the thing was on top of Eddie and, besides, it was wearing a helmet. A fresh creep would leak too many fluids onto his friend. Instead, he drove his pike, at an angle, into its back, planning to manipulate it off of Eddie. At least, that's what he would have done if the damned thing didn't have a flak jacket strapped securely to its torso. The pike bit through the outer fabric, but found no purchase in the underlying Kevlar. It slid off, leaving a tear.

Jeff swore, dropped the pike, crouched, and dove across the dead soldier's back, cupping one gloved hand underneath its chin and the other on the back of its head. As he rolled, the creep rolled with him, its neck cracked with the move. The pair rolled off of Eddie with Jeff on top and the creep face down. Jeff held its face securely against the asphalt, but the creature struggled violently, a broken neck notwithstanding.

"Eddie! C'mon!"

Eddie rolled to one side and forced himself up; the world swam and he could feel the steady spread of an impact headache crackling across his scalp.

"Fucking creep," he muttered, pulling his knife and placing the point just behind its ear, under the helmet. One shove and it was dead-dead.

"Shit. Thanks, man." Eddie wiped the knife on the creep's cammo, sheathed it, and took one knee while he hung his head.

"I can't believe how fucked up this little trip just got. You gonna be okay?"

"Yeah, just whacked my head. Still dizzy."

"Sucks. I know when—oh, shit."

Eddie looked at Jeff, then followed the line of his eyes. A horde of lopes was melting from the tree line, swarming in their direction. Probably migrated from further inland, wandering in a vast circle as they moved across the country.

Not that it mattered where they came from or why.

PART

VI

THE CREEP MARATHON

FROM EDDIE'S NOTEBOOK:

Too often, urban creeps cluster and form a horde. They migrate, moving from more populous areas into the countryside, cutting down every living thing in their path. Hordes are almost exclusively lopes. So they can move fast and generally create chaos wherever they go. The key to dealing with a horde—should you be so blessed to meet one—is to not get surrounded. They move in a big circle according to reports, but that's not so apparent when they're coming at you on the ground.

Run.

Jeff scrabbled for his pike and Eddie scooped up his CCT. They didn't have a plan and didn't need one. It was time to run. They headed straight down the highway, back the direction they'd come from.

Lopes were quick, but all things were equal in the flat. The more they migrated, the more they degraded their already decomposing bodies. Their single-mindedness didn't allow them to focus on more than killing. All the boys had to do was make it to their bikes at a good pace and they could put a decent distance between themselves and the horde.

Eddie's head throbbed so bad he could feel it in his shoulders. He tucked his weapon into the crook of his arm and fell into a rhythm with Jeff beside him. Completely covered in gear, they ran flat out.

In the sun.

At noon.

Eddie focused on the steady slap of his own footsteps and not the discordant thunder of dead feet behind him or the lightning strikes zipping across the back of his traumatized head.

The first pop they heard, neither of them paid attention to. The second and third, however, made them look over their shoulders. The lopes were stumbling over the first rows that had been cut down. Then another row went down, and another. Jeff and Eddie stopped.

The horde turned, attracted to the sound of the weapon, having lost interest or sight of the boys. They milled for a moment, bumbling awkwardly when another pop sounded and four or five more creeps crumpled to the asphalt.

They turned like a flock, stumbling in the rough grass on the side of the road. One more pop and the horde was down by at least an eighth. Owen's fancy new weapon was incredibly effective, canceling creeps as promised. Each blast came spiced with maniacal laughter.

Until the gun jammed.

They could hear Owen swearing sharply inside the tree line. He was slamming the weapon against a tree trunk on top of the berm, struggling to clear it.

Jeff pushed his goggles up and pulled his mask down, relishing the relief of cool air. Around deep breaths he wondered aloud, "What the fuck's he doing? He needs to keep quiet and run."

Eddie, hands on his knees and sweat stinging his eyes, shook his head. "He's a psycho, you know that. God, look at him."

Owen continued to struggle with the weapon as the lopes erratically navigated the berm leading up to his position. By their rough estimate, Owen had already racked up hundreds of thousands of credits.

The air was sharply punctuated by a crisp *boom*, followed by another. The big blond now had two long-barreled revolvers in his hands, targeting the nearest creeps.

Eddie stared incredulously, his goggles and mask off his face. "He's...he's not running, that crazy fucker."

"We gotta go."

"They're gonna get him."

"We gotta go!"

Eddie looked directly into Jeff's face, the only exposed part of his body, and said, "We have to *try*."

"No, we *don't*."

"*I* have to." With that, Eddie pulled his goggles down, the mask up, and headed for the flank of the now much smaller horde, aggravated by the pain radiating from the back of his skull.

"Goddammit, Eddie, I said I'd ask Karen out! I can't do that if I'm dead! *Fuck*." He followed his friend.

EDDIE'S NOTEBOOK:

Note: The back of a creep's head presents a clear and irresistible target. When distracted, several creeps can be canceled from behind with little skill. Luck has nothing to do with it.

BOTH JEFF AND EDDIE WERE SKILLED DEPUTIES. THOUGH IT APPEARED that they headed for the flank of the horde, the movement of the rabid creeps put the boys directly behind the single-minded killers.

Eddie's modified entrenching tool featured no barbed edges. Which meant that it didn't get stuck when burying the business end in a creep's head. The tool came out clean, allowing him to bury it into another with little pause between. Jeff's pike had similar characteristics: the sharp tip and tapered edges thrust cleanly through a skull and withdrew with relative ease. On occasion, Jeff could spear two at once. As long as the creeps remained focused on Owen and his steady firing, they could work from behind, cutting the monsters down as they stumbled into the ditch and up the side of the berm.

They were nearly through several ranks of lopes when Jeff spotted Owen leveling a new firearm at the lopes in front of Eddie. The ploy had been working because Owen had been making so much noise, but if Jeff started shouting now, their advantage would disappear and they'd be overwhelmed.

Jeff bit his tongue as Eddie cut down a lope in front of him; they couldn't risk detection this close to the remaining dead. Eddie drew up short, seeing Owen with a shotgun to his shoulder, and dove to the side as the barrel sounded loud over the moans of the dead.

Eddie ground his teeth together when he got hit with buckshot, but a sharp gasp passed his lips as he tumbled into the grass. The lope nearest him stumbled to a halt and spun its head around, trying to locate the new and closer sound. For a hazy second, it looked directly over its shoulder before looking down. Eddie struggled to his feet, holding his side, as the corpse lunged at him ravenously.

Jeff's attention fell entirely on Eddie. He heard the ominous rack of the shotgun and the subsequent blast. He felt the spread of the shot around him as the lopes directly to his front took the brunt of the ammunition. Another *click-clack* and a spray of shot passed mere inches in front of his head as he closed on Eddie and the lope.

Jeff's pike pierced the creep's skull just as it fell on Eddie. Another lope turned and fell on Jeff's back as a fourth blast from the shotgun sounded. Jeff instinctively planted a foot and turned, twisting his hips and toppling the lope. He caught a glimpse of Owen struggling to bring his shotgun to bear on the creeps in close quarters with him. He was screaming incoherently as several more pushed against the ones who'd reached him first.

Eddie thrust with the sharp end of his CCT and canceled the creep Jeff had knocked down while Jeff swept his pike in a wide arc, crushing the skull of the next nearest monster. The rest continued to descend on Owen, his screams of rage spiraling into a syrupy squeal punctuated by enraged invective. If cursing stopped the dead, Owen would've cleaned up the eastern seaboard. Jeff grabbed Eddie's arm and hauled him smartly towards the asphalt and away from the carnage.

Across the highway, another horde melted from the forest. They'd almost pulled off the largest cancellation in local history, but success likely wouldn't have looked much different than this mess. There were just too many creeps.

PART

VII

THE GHOST OF THE BIG O

Since the rise of the creeps, hospitals have become few and far between outside of the most well-protected urban areas. Inside big buildings, the dead can wreak significant havoc. Nowadays, hospitals are heavily guarded and equipped to go mobile. The chronically ill are shipped to remote, walled locations—fortified former Army bases and the like, as far north as possible, where *it's consistently colder and the creeps are much slower.*

We live in one of the low-priority zones, we have nothing to rely on but each other and the nearest general store. Karen has the most extensive collection of first aid materials and training. If either one of us gets hurt, that's where we're going to go.

I can't imagine an injury that Karen can't help with.

Blood dripped down Eddie's leg and left spatters on the pavement. They'd stopped once, after putting a few miles between themselves and what was left of the horde, to bandage Eddie's side, but it was a field dressing wrapped around an awkward location. Between the buckshot wound and the concussion, Jeff's friend looked pasty and huffed deeply to maintain speed. He knew as well as Jeff did that their only hope was to get to Karen's.

Monthly deliveries supplied fuel for general stores in the network. Each of them had a government-supplied generator if power failed—the Feds' idea of support, a political bone tossed to low-priority zones.

The general store was always a logical point of return. Since it was located in a wide open, industrial parking lot with a few low-lying buildings around it, they'd be able to see whatever was coming. And they could stash their gear for the day since they had no idea where they were going to live next.

Several-hundred feet from the gate, they saw the ragged gang: a mix of lopes and shamblers tangled up in the barbed wire with Karen undercover on the other side, calmly re-notching and firing arrows. Individual creeps kept trickling in from the far tree line.

Jeff snarled, "What the fuck is going on today?"

"I'm really tired, man, really tired, I've gotta stop." Eddie gasped and slumped over his handlebars, but remained on his feet.

"Oh, shit. Okay. Here's the plan: you sneak up, as close as you can without being spotted, when you're in position, I'll ride up and draw the lopes away. Karen will open the gate for you, and I'll circle around and zip in next. Okay? Eddie, okay?" While Jeff spoke, he rummaged in the first aid pack Eddie had pulled from the humvee.

"M'kay, le's do it," Eddie mumbled.

"Uh, one more thing." Jeff jabbed an injector into Eddie's thigh.

"Ow! What the...?" A wash of adrenaline made Eddie's ears ring and the edges of his eyes tingle. "Okay, sure, okay, yeah, let's do this."

"Uh-huh, that's what I thought. Go."

Eddie, with renewed vigor, took off, skirting the outlying buildings and staying out of sight. From his vantage point, Jeff could see where Eddie decided to hunker down with his bike and wait, hopping from one foot to the other. With a deep breath, Jeff stood up on his pedals and started out slowly to pick his angle. So far, so good. He increased his speed and came at the lopes from behind. Yet another creep in the tree line spotted him and broke into a stumbling run as he closed on the pack.

Jeff began to whoop and holler as he passed the group in front of Karen's gate. They turned in unison as he skirted past. Then the creeps not tangled in wire lurched after him in earnest. He caught a glimpse of Karen's confused face as he turned in a wide circle, herding the dead. She'd understand when she spotted Eddie.

Eddie watched Jeff's circuit. When his partner broke pattern and began to ride the creeps away, he left cover and headed straight at the gate. Karen spotted him coming, cross-slung her bow, and rushed to manually unlock the mechanism. The gate swung open and Eddie glided in with a grin. Karen had no eyes for him, however, she looked past his shoulder at Jeff as he rounded the corner of a far building with lopes in hot pursuit.

"He's coming back, Karen, he'll be here in no—"

They heard the sound at the same moment: the small engine of a dirt bike burping along in a high pitch. Rider and vehicle popped into view, careening from the trails in the surrounding forest.

It was Owen. He was not quite dead yet.

FROM EDDIE'S NOTEBOOK:

There are rumors that the creeps can somehow call each other. That their moaning draws others. It's a theory that tends to hold up. Hordes formed, they roamed in wide, circular patterns and slowly migrated. Occasionally, you might bump into a few and several others will come as fast as their dead legs and dizzy patterns will carry them. Other times, loners will stumble around unaware of each other or sporadically attacking whatever moved.

The scientists always say they need more time to study this stuff, but the people wanted no part. We don't want theoretical attempts at cures, we want the creeps gone.

We, the people—the living people of Earth—wish for the dead to die and stay dead. Right now.

OWEN'S BIKE MADE AN AWFUL RACKET. TO HUMAN EARS, THE MESSY engine delivered an ear-splitting annoyance. To creep ears, it was a dinner bell. The majority of the creeps stumbling after Jeff bumbled to a halt, turned, and started moving towards the cacophony Owen was making as he zigzagged across the broken asphalt. The tall deputy barely controlled the bike. At speed, it wanted to stay up on its own. As he slowed, it wobbled, halfway to the gate, and pitched over to leave its rider in a heap. Owen didn't stay down long, dragging himself to his feet immediately after hitting the pavement.

He looked like raw steak in human clothes. Blood stained his chest and legs. The bottom half of his face was unrecognizable, and one eye was either missing or so lost in a mass of torn flesh as to be unidentifiable. The long blond hair Owen normally sported was matted with blood where it could be seen or missing entirely from his head where it had been pulled away in bloody chunks. Of course, the lopes had torn apart the only exposed flesh they could find. The hockey mask he normally wore was nowhere to be found.

As he hauled himself to his feet, he roared incoherently, using his shotgun to stand. As he hobbled towards the fence, they began to make out what he was saying.

"Shoulda fuckin'w orked! Knew they'd come, knew it! Fuckin' fucks, fuckin' dead fucks, fuck all o' you, you're *all* dead!"

Karen stared at Owen as he headed for the gate. Owen's eyes focused intently on his destination. The lopes closed less than half the distance to his stumbling form. Behind him, a horde stumbled from the treeline.

"Kar'n! He'p me, godammi' he'p me, I'm hurt! Kar'n you gotta he'p me!"

Eddie swallowed hard and touched Karen's elbow. "Close the gate, Karen."

"But..."

"Karen, he's infected, he's going to die. Close the gate."

Karen sobbed a deep breath and started to push the gate shut, avoiding Owen's eyes. She heard the action of the shotgun as Owen rammed a round home. When she picked her head up, he fired from his hip.

"Karen!" Eddie dove at her and they both tumbled to the ground. Bits of birdshot pinged off the gate.

Owen chambered a second shell and fired again. Shot ricocheted off the pavement around them. Karen had specks of fresh blood on her hand and face, nicks where the first volley had raked her skin. Owen fired once more as the pair crawled for cover. Their only saving grace was Owen's hampered gait when he wasn't using the shotgun as a crutch.

Eddie spared a glance and noted that the lopes had closed half the distance again. Owen hobbled, stiff-legged, maniacal, determined. He tried not to think about what would happen if they didn't get the gate closed.

BEHIND LOW COVER AND IN RELATIVE SAFETY, KAREN BLINKED RAPIDLY and looked at the blood on her hands. "He—he shot me. That idiot shot me. On purpose."

"Karen, we've gotta close the gate…" Eddie's voice slurred and the world slowed down. His head swam and he lost equilibrium, unable to stay up on his elbows, barely able to hold his head off the ground. He could just see Karen through a hazy purple halo at the edges of his vision.

Karen looked into Eddie's eyes. "Why would he shoot me? I've always been…kind to Owen." She stared right through Eddie then, saw some point miles beyond his face and didn't like what she saw.

"Karen," he managed to grunt.

She pushed away from Eddie, rolling onto her back and palming her bow. Pulling a bolt from the quiver on her hip, she nocked it and took a deep breath.

Eddie's voice slurred. "I don' thin a'ssa good idea, Karrn."

"Shut up, Eddie."

He shut.

She rolled onto her knees, remaining doubled over and close to the ground. When Karen reared up, the scene in front of her froze in her mind, she saw everything at once, a flash of imagery like a photo. The lopes were gaining on Owen. He was half turned, dividing his attention between the creeps and the gate. She tunnel-focused her attention on her target and, with a hissing breath, let fly.

The arrow thunked into Owen's chest, penetrating his body armor. He drew up short, his one good eye aghast at the bolt protruding from his chest, and stumbled to a halt. The old, familiar rage crossed what was left of his features and he raised the shotgun, aiming directly for Karen.

Owen pulled the trigger at the same moment that Jeff slammed into the barrel. The weapon and Jeff clattered to the ground, the bike spilling from under him. Owen poured more contempt into his already rage-contorted features, resembling evermore the creeps he'd hunted so passionately.

A dagger slipped into the Big O's hand, he took one step towards Jeff, and was met with a pike in the soft spot above his body armor and just below his neck. Jeff thrust hard, pushing Owen into the gaggle of creeps approaching from behind. They desperately grasped at Owen as their victim slashed and struggled. The dead, in return, made a puddle of what had only been a fraction of a human being to begin with.

Jeff dashed through the gate and helped Karen slam the mechanism shut. What creeps reached the fence, Karen and Jeff canceled in one fluid shot or thrust after another.

Eddie, unconscious on the ground, missed it all.

PART

VIII

TRAVELING CIRCUS

FROM EDDIE'S NOTEBOOK:

*It's getting harder and harder to understand
what the government is doing. They communicate
less and less with us every month. The credits
keep flowing, we keep canceling creep tickets.
We can only guess what the so-called organized
resistance is up to. The Free Media reports
aren't as accurate as we believed, and they
were frequently being jammed by the federal*

broadcasts. What are the Feds doing about the hordes and their migrations? How are they dealing with the bugs? Our only regular contact is through their radio broadcasts and whatever information trickles to the general store. If we want any kind of information about the outside world nowadays, we have to ask Karen.

Maybe we should move, but where would we go? Far enough south would be a more comfortable climate, but even more of the dead could be active there. Will we ever have the money to get to an island? Are the harbors even operating anymore? (I'll have to remember to ask Karen the next time we see her.)

Jeff said, "We have to leave."

Karen shrugged. "I know how you guys roll."

"No, you don't understand, something's wrong; I think we *all* have to leave."

"I'm not leaving my store, Jeff. Where the hell would we go, anyway?"

Eddie awoke on a cot tucked behind a low partition parallel to the front desk. He felt crusty and weak, his side hurt, and he still had the dull pangs of pain radiating from the back of his head. He pulled himself up to see Jeff and Karen.

His friend was now silent as both he and Karen were staring out the window at something.

"..." Eddie tried to talk, but his throat was raw. There was a bottle of water on the floor, so he took a long drink and spoke up: "Hey, what's going on?"

They both turned at once. Karen smiled, but Jeff was all business. "Eddie, how you feelin'?"

"Raw, lots of aches. Like crap." Jeff glided over and held a hand out. Eddie sat further up with assistance. "What're y'all staring at?"

The two exchanged a look before Karen answered, "The creeps keep showing up. More and more of them. It's weird. Well, weirder than what usually passes for weird around here." She moved to touch her face and hesitated on some of the bandages taped to her neck and cheek. Her hand was swathed in bandages too.

Jeff shrugged. "Ever since Owen went full-on nuts, they've just kept showing up. Sooner or later, that many of 'em will push the barbed wire into the fence and then..."

They all knew the possibilities. That many dead bodies brought a significant amount of weight to bear. Eddie sniffed, rubbing his head and drinking more water.

"Right. Okay. So, how do we—wait. Are they all coming from one direction?"

Jeff peeked out the window. "Yeah, I guess, there's creeps all around, but most are out front here."

"Anything on the broadcasts?"

Both Jeff and Karen made an exasperated sound and turned on the radio perched on the counter. It was all of five minutes before the Free Media reported a massive horde moving southwest, lured from the city by officials using fireworks.

"Shit." Jeff balled his hands into ineffective fists, then picked up his pike. "It's going to be a second fucking apocalypse out here— what are they thinking?"

Karen laid her head down on the counter and Eddie's mind raced. He leveraged himself off the cot and peeked out the window. Then he hobbled to the back and did the same. The dead were thicker out front than back.

"We have no choice, we need to leave. It's only going to get worse. This is far too many for the locals to handle. Anybody know where MacReady and his crew are?"

Karen swung behind the counter and dug out her SAT phone. She punched a few numbers and waited. Inside the shop was silent, the boys could hear the electronic tingle of the phone's ring.

With a taught expression, Karen said, "He's not answering." She ended the call, thoughtful, with her thumb hovering over the buttons.

"Try his mobile."

"Oh, yes, Jeff, thank you, I *am* female."

Jeff blushed, but Karen smiled at his embarrassment. Eddie's brow creased at the normalcy of it all, at what kind of society they'd become. An army of dead outside the fence was only slightly weirder than *what usually passes for weird*.

"Hello, Officer MacReady? Hi, it's Karen. What? Yes, I'm at the store. Why?" Karen's jaw muscles worked as she listened. Color rose in her face and her jaw clenched, the muscles bulging and twitching. She was grinding her teeth hard.

"Yeah, right." She signed off without saying goodbye. Karen was the most cordial person the boys knew, something was definitely wrong.

"What is it?" Jeff asked.

Karen held her hand up and hung her head. Her entire body shook for a moment before she started pawing at things behind the counter, speaking as she moved.

"They're gone, everyone's gone." Her voice, raw and thick, caught in her throat.

"What?"

"They got the order to evacuate early this morning. *They were warned that this horde was coming this way*." Karen paused to let that sink in and resumed stuffing items into her woolly-pete bag. "Fuck." She choked back tears, "Fuck me, fuck us—*fuck*!" She scooped up her archery gear.

Eddie knew, he got it when she said it and moved to start collecting his gear. Jeff, however, was having difficulty processing what had happened.

"But, why didn't they call you? They should have called *you*."

Eddie shook his head, but Jeff didn't notice. Karen paused, rammed the heel of her palm across her eyes, and leveled her gaze at Jeff.

"They abandoned me, Jeff; they abandoned *us*. You, me, the other deputies—big government *fail*."

Jeff just shook his head, mouth hanging slightly open, blinking stupidly. When he looked out of the windows, he could see the creeps piling into the fence, dragging barbed wire with them, each one's behavior encouraging the next behind them. From inside the building, he couldn't hear the chain link hit the asphalt, but it was a motivating sight.

"Shit!"

Jeff summed it up in one word.

EVERY STEP EDDIE TOOK ONLY ACCENTUATED THE THROBBING ACHE deep inside his head and ribs. He felt weak and slow, moving through knee-deep syrup. Jeff got a hand on his back and ducked under his arm to help him along.

"You all right?"

"Hell, no. I ain't going to be able to run far."

"We're not running!" Karen called, ducking through the small door in the back. The boys had never been this far into the building. It was a locked supply closet, but there was a door in the back. Karen burst through it and slapped the lights on before clapping her palms on the giant heap of canvas in the center of the room. Jeff left Eddie leaning against the wall and helped her pull the tarp off a big, shiny, heavy-duty pickup truck.

"Oh, hell yeah," Eddie mumbled, stumbling over and opening the door to tumble into the back seat. Jeff tossed his pack in after his partner.

Jeff grinned at Karen and she grinned right back, winking and snatching the keys from the wall and starting the vehicle. The sound of glass shattering in front accompanied the violent rattling of the corrugated door.

"Is the door automatic?"

"Damn it! No. We have to pull the chain. There!"

For a panicked moment, all three exchanged glances. Eddie had no ideas, but Jeff didn't hesitate.

"Pull up as close as you can to the door. I'll hop in the back and work the chain. When the door's up, gun it."

"Jeff, they'll be all over us before you can crank the door all the way up."

The corrugated wall started to shake from the creep onslaught on the other side.

"So keep the cab's windows rolled up—let's go!"

Karen heaved a breath that came out as a cross between a sigh and sob. She pulled the truck up to the door, they felt and heard the thump as Jeff hopped into the back. Then the rattle of the chain. They both turned at the tapping on the back window.

"Open this one up so I can squeeze in when I need to."

Eddie slammed the sliding window as far open as he could and Jeff began cranking the chain through its pulleys. They could see the feet of the dead meandering back and forth. Creeps didn't tend to realize they could crawl until you knocked them down or they rotted to the earth.

Jeff cranked furiously. The mechanism that allowed one person to move the weight of a large steel door moved slowly by necessity. He cussed under his breath and tried to speed up the rhythm of his hands pulling the chain.

With the door at about waist height, the creeps started to duck in, drawn by the racket coming from the door at the rear of the garage. The wooden door splintered and slammed open. Creeps struggled to come through the small passageway all at once, tripping over cleaning supplies, tangling each other up. The dead outside the building were momentarily distracted by the noise and for a precious few seconds, they missed the exposed Jeff furiously spinning the chain.

Then the lopes rushed the vehicle, slamming against the sides and reaching into the bed of the truck. The door was just about level with the vehicle's roof when Karen panicked. Her foot spasmed and tapped the gas. The truck lurched forward.

Jeff tumbled into the bed of the vehicle, stunned by the sudden motion. Dead hands scrabbled at his body and pawed at his head. He swatted them away, thankful that, unlike Owen, he had short hair tucked beneath a tight helmet.

"Ohmygod, Jeff?" Karen turned in the driver's seat.

Jeff poked his head up and met her eyes. "I'm fine! Go, go, go!"

She slammed her foot down on the accelerator and the truck lurched forward. The right-side mirror tore off on the edge of the garage. The left-side mirror smacked the heads of the creeps pressed together on Karen's side. Her face, drained of all blood, was a ground-teeth rictus of stress. Karen did not normally spend time this close to the creeps. None of them had seen this many since the early retirement of their childhood.

There was a sickening *screech* as the roof connected with the lip of the corrugated door and a wild crack shot down the center of the windshield. Eddie grit his teeth, clawing the seat in front of him, and wished he'd put his seatbelt on.

Jeff curled into his arms for cover as debris from the roof's running lights spattered around him and the truck bounced over the lip of the garage. Lopes fell underneath the big truck's powerful wheels. A sudden turn threw Jeff into the sidewall of the bed, forcing the wind out of him. When the vehicle leveled out in the flat of the parking lot, he scrambled to get inside the cab.

Eddie grabbed his collar and dragged him in, never taking his eyes off the road and maintaining a steady stream of calm and encouraging words with Karen.

"Easy Karen, pick your spots, hit 'em where the crowd's weak, you're doing great…"

Jeff hauled himself into the front seat and clicked his belt on. "Which direction are we going?"

Karen glanced up at the digital compass. "Northwest—shit!" A decidedly large creep went under the fender and the truck bucked.

"Why are they still so thick? Goddammit!"

Eddie chimed in: "They surrounded us! Creeps came in from the east and bled around us to the north."

From Karen: "South, then?"

Both Eddie and Jeff shouted at the same time: "South!"

The sickening thump of bodies against the truck didn't ease as Karen made the wide turn. Losing momentum now might mean the end of it. The seconds dragged as the sound of creeps rebounding off the body panels continued. The ride roughened as members of the horde were crushed beneath the truck's wheels. All this gore would make it all but impossible to exit the vehicle uncontaminated. Jeff spared a glance at his friend. Eddie's eyes were rimmed with red and he was as drawn and pale as his brown skin would allow.

After several sickening minutes, they hit the open road. A few lopes stumbled after them. Karen slammed on the brakes.

"What the hell are you doing?" Jeff asked, his voice shaking.

Karen's only answer was a sharp, "Fuck this." She slammed the truck into reverse, twisted her body to look backwards and hit the gas. A few wet thumps later, they had no pursuers. She laid into the accelerator, putting serious distance between them and the dead.

"Oh, God," Karen said, "where are we going? This thing doesn't have the greatest mileage."

"It does a great job getting through a horde! We were damn lucky you had this truck."

Karen smiled at that and spared Jeff a glance. He had a real smile on his face instead of a polite one.

"Amen to that."

After several moments of silence, Eddie said, "Furnham. Head for the coast. Jesus, I'm hungry." Eddie spent several moments chewing on beef jerky before he passed out again, half the uneaten meat in his hand, dreaming of a past that was gone forever. Again, their world was turned upside down and shaken like a snow globe. The boys and Karen would be in limbo until the debris settled.

PART

IX

ED WOOD TURNS IN HIS GRAVE

A light thumping at his foot brought Eddie around. He heard what sounded like a rush of static and opened his eyes. His water bottle rolled back and forth on the floor, tapping his foot. Outside, a torrential rain fell.

Jeff peeked over the seat. "Dude, check it: carwash."

Eddie grinned and downed the rest of his water. "How long?"

"We're almost there."

Eddie looked out the window and scanned the landscape. Wind whipped the treetops and water cascaded in sheets around them. Storms had gotten worse in the years following the coming of the dead. The atmosphere churned, clouds came in fast, dumped their payload, and left just as quickly. It would be clear soon enough.

He spared a glance at the fuel gauge. Less than three quarters of a tank, two five-gallon cans strapped down in the back. The surviving towns were the only place to get gasoline nowadays. He assumed that their hometown had been completely overrun.

Jeff began thumbing through the radio stations. Precious few remained on the air and most of them simply carried what the Feds were broadcasting. Stations that ran a steady stream of invective, dogma, propaganda, or misinformation found their licenses pulled and their signal eliminated. Only Free Media remained and they walked a delicate line, slipping into open frequencies sporadically. So far, they only reported what was happening without adding opinion, but it was all unverifiable.

Now the trio found themselves caught up in the brutal efficiency that the federal government had brought to bear during the worst disaster in American history. Likely the worst disaster in the world. Apparently, deputies and their support system were highly expendable. Jeff paused on what sounded like the official broadcast.

The eerie guttural sounds of the alien language brought them all to jaw-clenched silence. The language sounded like a cross between gargling with syrup punctuated by sharp clicks and pops. They'd never listened like this: ensconced in a vehicle surrounded by speakers. The language carried a hypnotic, indiscernible quality in its deficit of pauses, merely rumbling on, one sound hardly any different from the others to human ears.

A few more moments of stunned silence and Jeff reached out to change the channel. Nothing changed. He skipped forward again, but still no change.

"What the hell? It's on all the stations." He ran up and down the dial.

That's when Karen saw it first.

THE RAIN TAPERED OFF TO THE OCCASIONAL PATTER AND A THICK MIST enveloped the landscape, obscuring everything. Karen slowed the vehicle down and turned on all its lights. It didn't help much, she still white-knuckled the steering wheel. The truck lurched, an indication of cracks in the road big enough to grab the wheels. More potholes soon appeared, enough that Karen swerved to avoid some of them. In the distance, they could see an ominous domed shape. Bled of any color, a deep shade of grey rose up from the median, cutting across the road.

"What is *that?*"

A rhetorical question, an enduring human habit. Neither of the boys were prone to babbling, so they kept silent. Neither of them were willing to entertain what it was anyway.

Karen slowed down to a crawl and they crept along towards it. The mound had risen up from the median, forcing dirt and grass aside, splitting the asphalt and creating a bizarrely sloped road pitching into the ditch on either side.

"Shit. I don't think we can get around that." She slowed the truck to a stop.

The highway's railing ran several feet up the side of the mound on both sides. They sat and stared at the absurd obstacle for several minutes. Long enough to notice figures standing around the mound. A crowd of creeps had gathered. None of them moved, but for a slight sway. None of them reacted to the truck's engine or lights.

Eddie felt uncomfortable in the silence. He could feel the prickle of something, but couldn't put his finger on it. He sat back in the seat and placed both palms flat to the leather on either side of his hips and closed his eyes. It didn't take long.

"Hey, y'all feel that?"

Karen tipped the mirror to see his face in the backseat and Jeff turned with a quizzical look.

"A vibration or hum or something. You can just…feel it."

Jeff spared a glance at Karen and then placed his hand on the passenger side window. After a moment, he looked at them both. "Yeah. Okay, so, *what* is that?"

Karen let go of the mirror and rubbed her fingers together. "It's the bugs, gotta be. I heard they were down here. You two knew that, right?"

"Sure, we heard it too, but we didn't think they'd be right on the edge of town like *this*."

Karen sighed. "Okay, what now?" Her voice sounded tight, it matched her face. Jeff put a hand on her shoulder.

"Let's just give it a minute. We'll—"

"What?"

Jeff pointed to his left and a little rear of the truck. Some of the mist had cleared and a creep could be seen plainly, standing just outside of the tree line. It swayed gently, as if underwater, chin pointing at the mound.

"Oh, goddammit." Eddie swiveled in his seat. He looked more closely at the surrounding landscape and started to pick out creeps here and there. Standing as the first one did, swaying gently, unsure. No way at this point to tell whether they were lopes or shamblers. Near as he could tell, they stood equidistant from the mound, scores of them faded away into the distance, surrounding the mound thickly on the sides of the road.

Karen rammed her hands into her hair and said through clenched teeth, "This is ridiculous!"

Jeff, with the oblivious cunning of a young, human male asked, "What do you mean?"

Eddie dropped his head into his hands as Karen slowly turned to face him, her eyes wide. "Jeff. Seriously. The dead walk and aliens have landed."

Eddie snorted.

"Uh, right, yeah. Sorry." Jeff grimaced and resumed scanning the landscape. Mist and clouds continued to dissipate as their surroundings became increasingly clear.

They surveyed the scene for several more uncomfortable minutes in complete silence before Eddie announced: "I'm going to go take a look."

"I don't think that's a good idea, Eddie."

"I've gotta move. I feel better. I want to know." He pulled his goggles on, helmet, and clipped his mask on. With that, he popped the lock on the door and spilled out.

"Jeff, you have to stop him!"

"No, I have to back him up." He slid into the back seat and pulled on the gear he'd taken off for the ride. Then he kept his eyes on Eddie.

Karen sighed. "Hand me my bow."

Jeff slid the bow to her and they both watched Eddie's back and the surrounding horde.

FROM EDDIE'S NOTEBOOK:

Creeps are simplistic most of the time. The more decrepit they are, the less likely their eyesight is worth a damn. We've been able to sneak around creeps quietly or remain still while they passed. They constantly move, however, so if you're going to try holding still, it better not be in their path. That's got to be how hordes form and break: they just keep moving until they fall apart. The virus drives them to death and compels them to take as many others with them as possible.

Not that it matters. Not anymore.

EDDIE CLOSED THE DOOR OF THE TRUCK WITH A GENTLE PUSH AND stood silent. He watched the creeps around them. None moved except for the slight sway. Taking a deep breath, he tested his side. It still hurt, of course. Then he rolled his head around his shoulders, loosening the tension. It hurt too. He almost smiled at how pointless it all was.

The mound in the short distance and the swaying creeps painted a sight more bizarre than everything they'd seen before. Eddie looked back at the cab and nodded at Karen and Jeff. Only Jeff nodded back. Eddie drew his creepwhacker and took a few tentative steps. Nothing. He crossed half the distance to the mound and stood inhaling the thick, humid atmosphere.

There was a heady, vegetal smell in the air that he couldn't place. It overrode the musty current of stink that bled off the creeps. The scent was something new to his nose, and it triggered no memories. A cross between pine and rotting grass came to mind. He looked at the surrounding creeps. They stood facing the mound. He could feel the hum in the road and on his skin now. He looked back at the cab again and waved, pointed two fingers at his eyes and then vaguely at the creeps. He brought the tip of his tool smartly down on the guardrail making a loud ping.

No response from the creeps, but Karen appeared to turn a few shades whiter.

Eddie continued his walk up to the mound. The surrounding horde were in various stages of decay, shriveled faces peered dumbly through black rivulets of old blood. He'd never seen behavior like this. The closer he got to the mound, the more it appeared to have risen straight up from the Earth. Details indiscernible from the truck came into focus. The top looked flat and the sides were devoid of any weeds or other random debris, pushed up from beneath the asphalt. At the apex of the bulge, there appeared an atmospheric disturbance, the remaining mist swirled oddly there, a haze of heat-mirage billowed out. Even where the green of the median should have bisected it, there was nothing but clean soil. The guard rail hung in the air near it, peeled backwards in a nautilus' curl. He sheathed his weapon and put both hands on the metal. Giving it a push, he confirmed its sturdiness. Shaking his head, he turned to look back at the truck ensconced in the mists. From this distance, he couldn't see either of his friends inside the cab, just the rows of lights.

Eddie put one foot on the mound and tested the soil. It wasn't soft at all, the dirt had the consistency of sandy concrete. The sides sloped up at what he guessed was less than forty-five degrees. He looked back at the truck again, and decided to head back. He arrived at a trot and opened the door to lean in.

"The mound's solid. I want to go up and see what's on top or on the other side."

Jeff took a deep breath and exhaled loudly. "I dunno, Eddie. What's the point?"

They both looked at Karen.

"Hey, I just want to get out of here."

"Look, we can't exactly head back, we may as well check this out and see what our options are. According to the map, the nearest exit is a thirty-mile drive north of here. Maybe we can figure a way around from the top."

Jeff said, "Fine. I'm coming with," and gathered his gear.

"*What?*" Karen looked at them both with intense skepticism.

Jeff shrugged, hopped out, and hauled his pike out of the truck bed.

Karen stared at the two. It felt safe in the truck, she'd mowed her way through one horde with it, why not another? Then she sighed and put both of her hands on the wheel. "All right, I'm coming too, but I'm pulling the truck closer, in case we have to run."

The sound of the truck slowly moving across the shattered roadway was eerily loud. For this many creeps around, Eddie realized, no moaning could be heard. The dead stood silent, gently swaying to a rhythm they couldn't hear.

Karen shut the truck off, but left the doors unlocked. Pocketing the keys in her vest, she set about strapping her meager gear on. The boys watched her. She was woefully unprotected for any close work.

"Jeff?" Eddie left the rest of the question unsaid, his eyes cut from his partner to Karen.

Jeff stepped close to Karen and told her, "You stay behind me, okay? If anything happens, you get back to the truck or find high ground and get to work. You're not wearing as much protection as we are; don't worry about me or Eddie."

"That's it?"

"Yeah, why?"

"You're not going to tell me I should stay in the truck?"

"No." His eyebrows creased when he said it and his eyes scanned Karen's face.

She suppressed a grin and touched Jeff's shoulder. "All right, then, let's go."

They set about heading up the side of the mound. The surface had enough traction, but without careful steps, one slip and a rough slide awaited. Several feet up, Karen noted that the vibration could be felt in the air this close to the mound. Jeff agreed.

When the hum stopped, they froze.

Eddie whispered, "Don't do anything." He let his knees relax on the sandy surface and brought himself slowly to the side of the mound. Glancing around, he could see a few creeps starting to move. They heard a plaintive moan in the distance and part of the horde swayed in that direction.

Karen did the same, but Jeff had stopped in an awkward position. He began to lower himself when his foot shot out from under him, issuing a loud scrape.

The creeps nearest them started to move in their direction and moan. More of the horde changed its bearing and began a thick landslide in their direction. Several of them were already at the truck.

"Oh, shit," Karen swore, "what do we do? They're coming fast!"

"Up!" Eddie started to climb again.

A few of the fresher ones managed to start climbing the mound's slope. Karen rolled onto her posterior, nocking arrows and letting them fly. Each one bringing a creep down.

"C'mon, Karen, forget that!" Jeff reached back and grabbed Karen's arm.

The three of them were about halfway up the mound when they heard the sharp staccato crack of gunfire in the distance. They paused to look at each other.

Eddie shrugged and said, "That can't be the creeps shooting, keep moving."

As they got closer to the top, it became clear that the shooting was coming from the other side of the mound. Eddie's hand reached the top of the mound and found a flat lip about a foot thick. The hardened dirt pile was hollowed out. The center dropped straight down about fifteen feet to a packed dirt floor. Heat boiled out of the opening.

Eddie tipped his head in for a look. "I can see some light. It looks like there's a tunnel off of this opening."

The mound itself was surrounded by creeps. In the distance, they could see, in the massive swirling tide, a breakpoint where the horde turned in the opposite direction. Bright lights and flashes of activity came from there. A helicopter hovered over the melee in the distance, its spotlight sweeping back and forth. A bomb exploded in the horde that was quickly followed by another and another in a straight line bisecting the highway.

The trio stared, slack-jawed, aware of only the vast depth of shit they were in as moist heat rolled over them from underground. More creeps managed to begin the crawl up the side of the mound. The sound of a car alarm rung brightly in the misty gloom. Lights flashing, alarm whooping on and off, the truck began to draw the attention of the surrounding creeps. Slowly, the moaning horde turned towards the new sounds and lights.

Karen held her keys and pushed the button again, sounding the alarm. "This isn't going to work forever, guys." She spoke through clenched teeth, a tremor of panic barely held in check.

Eddie made the decision first. He took one last look into the mound and made the leap.

"Eddie!" Jeff called.

He toppled when he hit the dirt, falling onto his side in the gloom. Eddie shouted up through pain-clenched teeth: "We can't stay up there, we need to be out of sight! C'mon!"

"Karen, go!"

She peeked over her shoulder, set the alarm off one more time, and rolled over the lip to land nimbly on her feet. Jeff followed, stumbling upon landing as Eddie had, dropping his pike in the dirt with a dull clang. He scrambled to scoop it up as two lights came on.

Eddie held a flashlight and his side where he'd been scattershot. He grimaced. Karen also held a light. Sweating in the gloom, he pulled his mask off and pushed his goggles up. Jeff did the same. Weak light appeared from far down the tunnel.

They swept the space with their lights in opposite directions. The tunnel led off in one direction and nothing but dirt walls surrounded them. A fine grain of what appeared to be sand covered the ground. Only one choice remained and Eddie took the first slow, sweaty steps into the tunnel.

"Karen, point your light backwards and stay between us. Jeff can keep an eye on our rear."

They moved quietly through the tunnel at an angle that Eddie determined cut diagonally across the highway above. They remained silent, the only sounds were their footsteps and breathing. A racket of bombs and guns faded aboveground. The hot air was difficult to breath, but manageable. A steady flow of the muggy atmosphere coursed over them. Between the trio, they didn't have much water, most of their supplies were in the truck. They couldn't continue without their gear for very long.

Soon, Eddie could make out more light in the distance and they stopped to confer.

"I guess no one has any idea what that might be?"

Jeff snorted quietly and Karen shook her head.

"Machinery of some sort, something's got to be making this hot air."

No sooner than he said it, the air's sluggish passage slowed.

Karen spread her fingers and palms against the rough wall. "You feel that? The hum is back."

Gradually, a light breeze of cool air began to seep into the tunnel.

"Yeah," Jeff stood up straight, "I can feel it right through my boots. It's strong in here."

"Ah, *shit.*"

"What?" Karen and Jeff asked simultaneously.

"The hum. It's what captivated the creeps so much."

"Yeah, so?"

"So, it's on again. Meaning we could probably get back to the truck."

"But we can't get out of this hole." Karen rolled her eyes.

"Right. I'm sorry, guys, maybe we should have stayed outside."

Jeff looked down the tunnel. "No, it doesn't matter. We keep moving. There has to be an exit."

They nodded and resumed their journey, flashlights tucked away. The light at the end of the tunnel blossomed and they could hear the erratic sounds of mechanical tinkering. In the low light, an oddly humped figure hunched over a piece of machinery that seemed to grow out of the walls.

The trio stopped and huddled as close to the wall as possible, staying in shadow. They watched tensely as the first alien they'd ever seen went about some sort of repair. Hoses and cords ran from the walls to a device on a cart. A haphazard array of lines, some pumping fluid, others inert, all snaked into the earth around them.

Until this moment, they'd only seen blurry photographs. The bugs stayed inside after their first meeting with the creeps. They might think the whole of humanity was a mindless mass of murderers. Plenty had speculated so, but a more reasonable group speculated that a race which could traverse the galaxy just might be able to suss out the differences between creeps and normal human beings.

The alien stood up straight, extending its limbs in opposite directions, and let out a rattling hiss. They could just make out plates on its carapace that made the noise. People referred to them as bugs because that's what they looked like: tall grasshoppers. Or crickets. Or cockroaches. Or something—it was hard to tell, the few that had been caught on camera were hard to make out. This one, they could see, had no antennae—dispelling that particular report as myth—a greenish cast along its dark blue chitin, and large, seemingly binocular eyes. Only four arms—dispelling another myth—and no tail or wings (myths three and four, gone as well).

The creature piled tools into the three-wheeled cart and sat down on the edge of the machine it had been tinkering with. Using its upper arms, it slid a pouch that was slung across its back around to its front and began rummaging in it. They could see a wrap of some sort crisscrossing its torso, over its shoulders, and down both legs. Various pockets and loops dotted the material here and there. From the pack it produced a metallic pouch and a small tool. It squeezed the pouch and a soft pop could be heard. After a few moments, it ripped the pouch open and started to eat using the utensil.

After a few bites, it issued the soft hissing sound again, rattling its carapace, and crumpled the top of the package down, placing it back in the pouch. It stood up and, with its back to the trio, arranged some things in the cart before disconnecting the various wires and hoses.

Eddie looked at Jeff and Karen. They both shrugged in return. He chewed his lip for a moment and indicated that they stayed where they were.

What? Jeff mouthed silently.

Eddie stood up.

No, Jeff indicated by shaking his head.

Eddie reiterated that they stay put. He stood up, removed his head gear and creepwhacker, then gave both to Karen. Jeff made a sour face, but stayed put.

Eddie started down the tunnel, towards the alien.

FROM EDDIE'S NOTEBOOK:

We don't know why the aliens came here. WHAT. DO. THEY. WANT? All we've got is an undead infestation and a long history of discord.

PART

X

WHAT GOES DOWN MUST COME UP

The aliens had not-so-fortuitously arrived during the peak of an unprecedented outbreak on planet Earth. All attempts at containing the virus failed, nothing could stop its global march.

Private islands were annexed. As capitols moved to islands and strict containment measures were put in place, overpopulation became a thing of the past. It was a sure bet that some governments operated more liberally and less like dictatorial regimes. The majority of any space surrounded by water were filled to capacity with the privileged and their families. Strict measures ensured they weren't overrun in waste disposal alone.

The creeps had been witnessed walking into oceans or lakes, chasing boats or humans smart enough to dive in and swim, but they never got far. Eventually they wandered out or found themselves stuck in the mud and silt, caught in currents, never quite buoyant enough to float. Creeps were easily canceled in the water. Islands became the safest enclaves, but also the hardest to supply. A busy harbor drew hordes, so islands that could handle aircraft were the most popular. The Army Corps of Engineers experimented with moats and other water hazards as protection, but it was hard enough to dig holes without hordes of creeps showing up.

When the first aliens landed, global communications were focused on heading off the march of creeps around the world. Any transmissions from the arriving spacecraft were lost in the mash of panicked calls or emergency broadcasts. There weren't very many people looking out into space for visitors which, considering the circumstances at the time, made sense. If NASA had seen them coming or heard from them, it didn't matter.

The first landing was public. Too public. Hordes of creeps converged on the location as the craft headed for the ground. Of all the living humanity all over the planet, it was the creeps who made first contact. From then on, the aliens' landings were a mystery. These days, the world had lost track of the aliens. The only way to know where they were was when a mound popped up.

HALFWAY TO THE END OF THE TUNNEL, EDDIE STOPPED TRYING TO BE quiet. He scuffed his feet and held his hands out and open, his face plain to see and expressionless.

The alien stopped puttering, stood up stiffly, and spun around to stare at Eddie. For his part, Eddie turned slowly, keeping his hands in view, allowing the alien to see all of him. When he'd completed turning, he saw that the creature held one hand to a small device near what would have been the collar bone on a human being. It was speaking quietly into it. Guttural and fluid, punctuated by pops and clicks, Eddie listened for a moment and then spoke up.

"Uh, hello?"

The alien stopped speaking to focus on Eddie, then listened to its device.

"Hey, is there, I dunno, some way to communicate?" Eddie moved his hands back and forth, alternating between indicating the alien and himself. He took another step forward.

The alien stepped back, banging into the cart, rattling tools, and held out both hands. Then it whirled, snatched up a tool about a meter long and held it defensively in front of itself.

Eddie stopped and rocked back on his heels a bit, displaying his open palms and moved back a step himself.

Eddie could see that it had six fingers on each hand, with the index finger slightly pointed and longer than the rest. Its fingers worked in a multi-jointed manner that exceeded human digits by at least two. It issued the whooshing noise again, this time more harsh, rattling its carapace in a perceptibly more agitated manner.

Eddie tried to think. He had been hoping that the alien would be more receptive when it could see that he wasn't one of the creeps. In the midst of turning back to his friends, more of the aliens burst into the chamber. They were various shades of greens and blues from very light to near black. The new arrivals wore crisscrossing wraps like the first, but they had a more streamlined and disciplined appearance. Most important to note: they carried weapons of some sort tightly to their shoulders. Eddie jumped when they came at him and he could hear the footsteps of his friends pounding up the tunnel.

"No, wait!" Eddie pushed his palm at his friends and the other at the aliens. Both groups drew up short, unsure what to do.

"Eddie, get behind us."

"No. Give me my weapon."

"What are you—"

"*Give it.*"

Karen handed the creepwhacker over to Eddie. He turned slowly, the aliens looked intently at his hands. Eddie held the weapon loosely in one hand and took care not to point it in any way. He laid the thing down on the ground in front of him and backed away.

"Guys, put your weapons down."

"No way—"

"Jeff!" Eddie turned to his friend, using his hands to emphasize his point. "Put 'em down. *Please.*"

"Goddammit, Eddie." Jeff complied, driving the pike into the ground. Karen simply placed her bow and quiver in the dirt. She looked the most stressed of the three of them, pale and sweating, unarmed and unarmored.

When they'd all straightened and faced the visitors, the first of the nets blasted over Eddie. Knocking him off his feet, the soft mesh ensnared his limbs, keeping him from moving in much more than a wiggle.

"Hey, wait!"

Two more pops had Jeff and Karen under wraps.

"Jeff!" Karen squeaked as Jeff raged inside his netting.

The aliens snatched up the humans' weapons, gave them a cursory inspection, and positioned themselves two abreast to each of their captures. One was clearly the leader, giving orders to the group. They all bent simultaneously, picked the trio up between pairs, and started down the long tunnel at an impressive clip.

Back at the entrance they'd dropped into, the three of them were placed on the ground. At the flip of a switch, the netting retracted, each of the operators reloaded their devices. The humans stood, huddled under the opening, defiant.

The leader said something to his crew and waved them back. It gestured to the one who carried Eddie's creepwhacker and the soldier handed it over. Then the leader handed the tool back to Eddie. The same was done until each of them had their weapons back. Then it waved everyone back and pulled a cylindrical device from a sling on its torso.

Eddie could feel Jeff tense, his friend's right shoulder brushed his own.

The leader waved them back from the entrance again, shook the cylinder twice, and it extended up to the mouth of the hole with a loud snap. It twisted a ring at the base which released several hand-

and footholds along its length. The alien made a sharp noise, pointed at them, then pointed up, insisting that they leave.

"Fine. Let's go."

"You don't have to tell me twice." Karen started climbing the collapsible ladder.

Jeff followed, looking down at Eddie who was staring at the pointing alien.

Eddie's face betrayed his feelings, but he was doubtful the alien could read such human behavioral cues. "Fine," he mumbled and started climbing.

At the top, Karen and Jeff sat on the slope at the top of the mound. Eddie clambered out next to them. The ladder rasped off the edge of the hole and collapsed. They all yelped when the mound began to collapse in as well, making the entrance smaller and smaller until it had disappeared entirely, leaving only the mound of hardened dirt, much smaller than it had been. Low enough to drive over.

Scrambling to the bottom of the mound, they looked disconcertedly at the mesmerized creeps surrounding them and hustled to the truck. The three of them sat for several minutes, just listening to their own breathing. Karen and Jeff sat in the front seat, staring at the middle field between thoughts and reality.

Karen laughed first.

Jeff glanced at Eddie who cracked a broad smile. Soon they were all laughing, sides hurting, gasping for air, stomping their feet, slapping the dashboard, and pounding the seats. It was a full five minutes before they were able to stifle the giggles. Karen wiped tears from her eyes and looked at the boys.

Jeff turned in his seat and said, "I love you too, Eddie."

Eddie smiled and said, "I know," with a wink.

Karen watched the entire exchange with her eyebrows creased. "That was—" She reached out, cupped the back of Jeff's head, and pulled him in for a kiss.

If Eddie had a camera ready, he would've snapped a photo of Jeff's face when Karen disengaged from his lips. Eddie couldn't quite be sure, but he thought at least one of the emotions that ran across Jeff's face was relief.

"Okay, kids—if you're all done—where to now?"

Both Karen and Jeff looked at Eddie, but only the young woman rolled her eyes. After glancing at each other, they responded as a chorus. "South."

MINE

BY KYLE RADER

CHAPTER

ONE

"Come *on*, Timmy!"

"I can't go when you talk to me!"

"For cripes' sake! The Sleepers will have already taken the fort by the time you get done."

Hunter Thurston stood, one foot on a rock, back turned towards the struggling-to-pee Timmy Gagnon, his best friend since they could crawl. He peered into the forest where they spent every waking moment they could. If it wasn't playing *G.I. Joe* or *He-Man*, they were fighting hordes of the evil damned with sticks and rocks. In winter, it was sliding down hills from sun-up to sun-set, piling up snowbanks at the bottom of hills and hurling themselves into the white fluffy piles, unafraid. If it wasn't that, they explored the depths of the woods, looking for (and never finding) buried treasure, enough to lift them and their families out of the quiet desperation that life in the peaceful Upper Valley area of New Hampshire forced upon them. Not that Timmy or Hunter knew what that truly was, at least not yet, but as they approached the end of their first decade on the planet, it was seeping into their peripheries. The occasional empty stomach at bedtime, their folks telling them to crouch low when entering the town pool so the clerk wouldn't see them, these little things were beginning to add up. Soon, the hidden, unspoken shame would emerge, manifesting as the snickers and bullying by the other children at school when, upon seeing their hand-me-down clothes and backpacks that most assuredly did *not* have the most popular thing of the day on them, would peg them and place them in their social caste, never to be lifted.

But that was a lifetime away. Problems for other versions of themselves not yet come to be. All Hunter cared about was that Timmy would finish his piss so they could get a move on already.

A pinecone hit him in the shoulder. Turning, he saw Timmy, smiling, holding another in his hand. "Sorry. Had to. The Dreadnoks were about to run you over. I swear!"

"Ripper and Buzzer are going to be the least of your problems if we don't take the fort first," Hunter said. He stooped to pick a few pinecones from the ground and, after a moment's thought, chucked one at Timmy. "The Sleeper brothers always bring pebbles and rocks to throw and I don't feel like ducking those all morning to get in."

"Remember when they hit Joey right in the nose?" Timmy pantomimed an explosion emanating forth from his own, spitting and imagining literal buckets of blood pouring out with no end in sight.

"I sure remember the talking-to we got from his mom, and then ours later," Hunter said. "Not sure that it's something I'd care to repeat, so, can we go?"

They went (after Hunter reminded Timmy to zip up his corduroys) deeper into the forest, the sounds of their footsteps snapping fallen twigs and branches added to the ambient mixture of critters, birds, and the breeze that swayed the trees, causing them to creak and their leaves and acorns to fall. Neither boy noticed this cacophony of sound, not really. They'd spent so much time roaming around that they'd mostly tuned it out. Their attention was on their games, which evil, imaginary foe needed to be vanquished before their supper, opinions on the latest issue of *The Amazing Spider-Man* or *Action Comics*, or the apocryphal tale they'd heard on the schoolyard about the one kid whose brother's cousin was able to beat *Super Mario Bros. 2* without dying once. Trivial things all, but to a couple of nine-year-old boys, they were the entire universe. Things like a future living paycheck-to-paycheck and alimony and the state of the world? Those could wait, could take a flying leap at the moon. Timmy and Hunter had a fort to secure.

The "fort" was a local institution. No one knew who first built it. It'd been passed down from generation to generation of boys with a bit of wanderlust in their hearts. Located on the side of a small hill underneath a copse of white birch trees, the fort had been built up somewhat since its inception. Some industrious youths dug into the side of the hill until they hit root and rock, creating a kind of den. Others built upon this and constructed a makeshift deck, complete with railings, made out of scrapwood and branches. A roof and locking door were added after that, leaving a functioning clubhouse for any who wished to use it.

It, like the town in which it resided, had fallen on hard times since Timmy and Hunter's generation discovered it. The roof had partially caved in, and, if you had more than four people on the deck, it'd wobble, threatening a seven-foot tumble down the hill to the ground below, where decades of hurled rocks and sticks awaited. Timmy suggested bracing it with several larger logs, but it, like most proposed upgrades, went unfulfilled. Neither boy had the patience to put the work in; that wasn't why they frequented it. At the fort, you could just *be*, even if for a little while, even if you had to chuck rocks at the Sleeper Brothers. Nothing outside mattered. Not school, homework, or family squabbles.

The fort was safe.

Until it wasn't.

THEY ARRIVED TO FIND THE FORT ABANDONED. *GOOD,* TIMMY THOUGHT. They could dig in and keep the Sleeper Brothers out for eternity, or at least until they got hungry and went home for lunch.

There were two entrances up to the deck and den: a rickety old stepladder someone stole from their dad and wedged into the side of hill, hammering it into place, or (if one was adventurous enough) a set of handholds worn into the hill from decades of eager kids climbing to their sanctuary from the adult world. Timmy, possessed of a devil-may-care attitude, ascended the handholds while Hunter made his way up the ladder, moving inches at a time as not to anger the decaying wood and send him tumbling to the ground.

The den was a dust-and-dirt clouded mess that smelled of damp earth and wood. Timmy coughed as he cut through the motes hanging in the air, moving deeper inside where there were a few makeshift chairs and a wooden bench hammered into the roots of the trees overhead. He'd plopped down on one when he discovered Hunter, lurking at the mouth of the cave.

"Oh, right," Timmy reached beside him, into a faded maroon duffel bag, producing a flashlight. "Sorry about that."

Hunter walked into the dimly-lit den, taking a seat next to Timmy. "S'okay."

Timmy could tell from the look on his friend's face that it was rather *far* from okay. Hunter was the only boy in their class still afraid of the dark, a well-known fact that caused him much humiliation and bullying as a result. Timmy had even joined in on the teasing on a few occasions, not that he cared if Hunter needed a light on to go to sleep or not. It was more so that *he* wouldn't be lumped in simply by association, and thus, be bullied too. Timmy would apologize to Hunter each time this happened, but the coldness in his friend's eyes only seemed to get larger.

Eager to change the subject and, subsequently, cheer Hunter up for the inevitable war against the Sleepers, Timmy fished around in the duffel, the community storage shed for the fort, seeking the item that he heard Mikey Sleeper whispering to his brother Justin about that Friday at recess. The rules of the duffel were simple: whatever you put in, it remained for anyone to use; the flashlight, for example, and the mini first-aid kit and a *GI Joe* compass being prime examples. Snacks were always welcome, too. But, Timmy wasn't seeking a Butterfinger or a can of soda.

"Ah-ha!" Timmy said, smiling brighter than the flashlight.

"What?" said Hunter.

Timmy pulled the magazine out of the bag and laid it in his lap. At first, he dared no more than to touch its edges, fearing that it'd evaporate the second his greedy fingers flipped it open. "Mikey Sleeper said that his cousin, Rob Avery, and some of the older kids had used the fort this past weekend and they left *this* here. Boy, is he gonna be mad when he finds out we got to look at it before him!"

The *Hustler* showcased a nude woman pantomiming Christ's crucifixion. The blasphemy, meant to enrage adults such as Timmy's parents, folk who believed in the great "Moral Decay" of America, didn't mean a hill of beans to the boys. They flipped, eagerly, through the pages, moving past articles and crude cartoons to the object of their lust: the nude female form. Neither boy said much during this time, other than a low exhale or mumbled *wow*. They would've forgotten to breathe if not for necessity. They sat, legs touching at the knee on the wooden chairs, taking it all in. Though it wasn't cold, they couldn't help their arms and legs from shaking. There was a fear, ingrained in them by the adults in their lives, that told them what they were doing was wrong, *taboo*. Yet, it didn't *feel* wrong, taboo, not to Timmy, certainly not to Hunter, whose eyes threatened to leap from his face and take hold of the magazine for their own.

After a time, Hunter spoke, breaking the silence. "Did you know that you can put it there? In the butt?"

"What?" Timmy said, blinking a few times.

"It's true. My sister Michelle? She told me so."

"Michelle said that?"

"Yep-yep."

"How would she know?"

Hunter shrugged, taking the magazine from Timmy and flipping back a few pages. "She said the girls at her summer camp told her about it; said it's awesome."

"Huh."

"Yeah, would've thunk it? Michelle got mad when I asked her if she'd done it with Brent. Hit me upside the head and screamed at me to get out of the kitchen. I bet she has, though."

"Who knows."

"Would you?" Hunter said.

"What?"

"You know...with someone? Like that?"

"I dunno. I've never even had a girlfriend, Hunter, you know that."

"Yeah, I know. But, if you *did*."

"Maybe? Heck, I dunno!"

Hunter looked Timmy in the eye, holding the gaze a second too long. He hung his head, and pretended to be interested in the magazine, mumbling a half-apology towards him. "Yeah, yeah, yeah. Sure. No problem, Timmy. I get it."

"Listen. Hear that?"

Hunter craned his neck towards the entrance of the fort. "Hear what?"

Timmy took the magazine back and placed it into the duffel. "They're here," he said, snapping the flashlight off. "The Sleeper Brothers."

"Timmy...the f-flashlight?" Hunter said, cowering in the dim.

Ignoring Hunter's whines of panic, Timmy snuck from the fort to onto the balcony, pressing himself behind a piece of sheet metal hanging on by duct tape, shoelaces, and a prayer. Hunter, tumbling over himself, crouched behind him. There were some medium-sized sticks, pinecones, and rocks piled up in the corner of the balcony, ammunition to be used when someone's sovereign claim to the fort was challenged. The rules of this rural warfare were specific and simple enough: If a marauder was struck, they were "dead" and had to retreat behind a fallen pine tree and remain for a count of thirty, after which they could resume the fight. This continued until the defenders killed fifty people or the marauders were able to capture the "flag" of the fort; this "flag", nothing more than a re-purposed miniature New Hampshire state flag hanging on a string below the balcony, served as the keys to the kingdom. If taken, it won the right to the fort for the rest of the day. These rules, passed down from generation to generation, were sacrosanct. Any who failed to abide by them was shunned and banned from the fort for all time.

Timmy had an inkling that the Sleeper Brothers cared not for such things. They played rough in everything they joined in on. The last time they'd tussled, they'd brought a bucket of bolts and nuts, hurling them up by the cupful. Timmy didn't think they cared much for the fort at all, but for the struggle, the joy in *taking* something from another. Timmy couldn't abide a bully, thus he was prepared to fight until the bitter end to stop them.

His brown eyes squinted. He rubbed an itch out from his head, ruffling his short-shorn blond hair. He listened for the next crunch of fallen leaves, the next crack of a stick, gripping a large pinecone. Hunter sat back in the den, afraid. He always had trouble with this part. Fighting off imaginary foes? No problem. Real life violence, even that as playful as fighting for the fort? Hunter got queasy. He told Timmy that it was because he didn't want to "get into trouble," his family being one of the strictest in town, known for doling out harsh penalties whenever one of their brood screwed up. Most of the time, Timmy needed to goad Hunter into action, sometimes even by throwing something at his face. Seeing the fear on his friend's face, the way he hugged his knees to his chest, Timmy knew that this battle would be no different.

"Where are they?" Hunter said.

"What?"

"I mean, what are they waiting for?"

"Probably waiting to see you poke your bowlcut over the side and bean you with a sparkplug," Timmy said.

"Har-har, jerkface."

Timmy smiled, but it left his face near as fast as it came on. He was wondering the same thing. Did they really think to catch them unawares? The Sleeper Brothers were many things, but strategists weren't amongst them.

"Thanks for letting us look at the nudie mag first!" Timmy called out. Hunter giggled. "You wouldn't believe what's in here!"

"Y-yeah! There's one lady with one guy on either end!" Hunter, emboldened, let a low whistle out. "Kinda looks like your *mom!*"

The boys laughed, expecting to hear the high-pitched squeal that was Justin Sleeper's voice calling them every name in the book. Instead, nothing.

Timmy rose to his feet and peered out into the forest. He'd no way of knowing it then, but what he was about to see would change the course of his entire existence. Perhaps if he'd stayed hidden, asked Hunter to look instead, things would've been different, better.

Perhaps.

A WOMAN STOOD IN THE FOREST BELOW THEM.

She looked nothing like any woman Timmy had ever seen before. This woman possessed a malevolence that had the hairs on his arms standing on end and had every instinct in him, conscious and not, screaming for him to RUN, HIDE. Yet, Timmy did neither of those things; couldn't. He felt himself stuck in place, holding the wobbly railing on the fort and staring down.

The woman's hair reached her waist, obscuring most of her features save for whatever the slight breeze allowed to be shown. Of these, a patch of chin and nose appeared different the longer Timmy viewed them, looking full and vibrant only to change over to a jaundiced pallor of disease, washing away the former for the new, like ripples in a pond. Except for her eyes. Oh, Christ save him, those *eyes.* Even through the tangled mass of hair, they shone through, filled with something Timmy had yet to know in his short nine years on the planet: a malice so intense it was lustful.

The urge to jump down, despite the injuries he'd be certain to incur, and to embrace this stranger, grew from this frigidness, sprouting up like a sapling made from blackness. His grip on the unsound railing tightened. He'd pissed his pants at some point; he didn't know when.. The final few droplets were only just reaching his socks. The urges he felt flipping through the porno mag with Hunter, their knees touching, returned and were even more powerful. He knew, not felt, but *knew*, that he could fly, ascend through the treetops and circle back down. If he proved this, the woman would open her arms and be his for all time. He *knew it.*

The railing—little more than a fallen branch—creaked in protest under Timmy's weight. He rose to his full height, arms circling through the air to keep his balance. Loud pops sounded all around him. He didn't care. About anything. *Let it all fall down. I'm going to fly.*

"*Timmy!*"

He'd forgotten all about his best friend.

Hunter had taken hold of his belt, holding it and the floor of the fort, struggling to keep both upright. But Hunter was a scrawny boy—fifty pounds soaking wet. There was nothing he could have done to stop what had been put in motion, though he tried.

Timmy looked to the sky, seeing glimpses of blue and sunlight peeking through the canopy, thinking it beautiful, before the fort collapsed. The sound of Hunter's screams cut through the cracking of wood and the grinding of metal against stone. The serene sky flipped over for Timmy, replaced by the fallen leaves and branches on the ground, rushing to kiss his face with the tenderness of a cinder block. The air fled his lungs and the lights shut off, leaving him in darkness.

TIMMY SNAPPED AWAKE, UNSURE IF HE'D BEEN OUT FOR MINUTES OR hours. He felt terrible. His mouth hung loose and was filled with blood that refilled when he spit onto the soil. He'd lost two of his uppers—permanent teeth at that—a canine and an incisor. His left thumb was bent in the wrong direction. His right arm wouldn't lift and caused such pain when he tried that it stole what ragged breaths he could manage to take. He'd later discover that he'd not only broke his clavicle, but had separated his shoulder to such a degree that it'd never quite be the same, even after lengthy physical therapy. His legs worked fine, and while he didn't feel like it, he was able to crawl out from underneath the wreckage of the fort. His house was too far away. The closest place where he could get help of any kind was an auto repair shop a mile away.

A mile. He could make that. If he could only get to his feet, he could make it.

He crawled onto his knees and his stomach betrayed his gumption, causing him to vomit. It came out of his nose and was black and brown. He watched his tears plummet into a puddle of it, wishing that it would all *stop*.

"Oh…God…*please help*…," Timmy said, even though he wasn't entirely certain he believed in a God or any of that.

His stomach quieted enough that he could think, despite the pain. Crying, something he'd not done regularly since one of his uncles cuffed him upside the head at a holiday gathering after he'd dropped his cake, calling him a "pussy-little-bitch boy," would not stop, and Timmy saw no reason to harden himself, looming specter of Uncle George or no. The tears seemed to overflow his puke, forming a puddle deep and wide before him. Too deep and too wide. Impossible. Timmy shook his head, a mistake he regretted the second he'd done it, for it only increased the headache that lay behind his eyes. The pain brought clarity. The puddle of water was not from his tears.

The water lay in two indents—*footprints*.

"*Pretty.*"

The voice that spoke wasn't human. Timmy didn't have the vocabulary to know such words as nihilism and wanton. His body wanted to run for the auto repair shop and beyond, but the voice wouldn't allow for it. His limbs weren't his own, and twisted his aching, bleeding carcass around to face the owner of the voice.

She stood on the wreckage of the fort, hair brushed away from her eyes, revealing her face for the first time. It was not the face of the hag or ghoulish monster he'd dreaded, but one that he found rather intoxicating, almost beautiful. It was ever-changing, the ripples he'd seen from on-high fluctuated as she moved, swirling her features around until his stomach threatened him with a fresh round of nausea. A smell, wet and damp, emanated off the woman in pulses, reeking of decaying vegetation and flesh. Timmy noticed that she was soaking wet and wondered how that could be. The nearest body of water, the Connecticut River, was nowhere near, and yet water dripped off her like she was a rain cloud made flesh. Her clothes hung heavy upon her frame, slipping off her shoulders, giving him a glimpse of her pale skin, of the swells of her breasts. His cheeks flushed as he realized she noticed this.

"Pretty," she repeated, a wry smile formed on her face, revealing brown and green teeth so loose, that a few fell from her mouth and onto the ground. *"Pretty."*

Timmy opened his mouth to speak the many questions he had, but his words fled him the second he saw what she was doing to Hunter.

Hunter's torso was buried in the forest floor, held in place by the dripping wet hand of the woman. His legs kicked the air as she pushed down, sending him further into the earth, inch by inch. His screams were muffled and grew fainter until they couldn't be heard at all. The woman continued planting him until all that was left were his ankles; they'd stopped moving long before. With one smooth motion, the woman casually stepped upon the soles of his feet and stood there until they sunk within. All that remained of Hunter Thurston was a muddy puddle, swirling with a foamy, reddish mud.

"H-H-H—"

"Pretty." The woman moved towards Timmy. Her gait was serpentine, leaving behind a trail of bloody water. She stood head and shoulders over Timmy. He felt a surprising heat coming from her, one that coated him in sweat. His fingers twitched. His guts churned. The woman reached out and took his hand. Her touch felt like coarse paper. She placed his hand against her cheek and nuzzled it, cooing like a content kitten. *"Pretty."*

The woman's face contorted. She snatched Timmy off the ground by his shirt, tearing it off him, and holding him high above her head. Short, nubby claws formed at the ends of her fingers, each one dripping noxious, purple-tinged water. When the droplets struck his bare skin, Timmy felt a sense of…not calm, not peace, but the desire to *forget*. His family, the fort, *Hunter*, his entire life, to let it all be washed away in the plum-colored water. This apathy swelled in his chest until he was close to forgetting his own name.

That was when she cut into him.

Three grooves over his heart, straight down to his sternum, ending an inch above his belly button. There was pain, oh Christ, yes, there was pain. Timmy felt it all and cared not a whit.

The woman placed him gently upon his knees, regarding him as his head slumped and blood fell off him, soaking the forest floor. She raised his chin with two fingers, forcing him to hold her gaze, smiling cruelly at him, *into* him, once last time.

"*Pretty,*" she said. "*Mine.*"

BRIAN NEWTON WAS WORKING AN UNEVENTFUL SHIFT. THE TWO mechanics were hard at work on the backlog of vehicles they'd on schedule for the day, leaving him alone in the office, sitting on his ass, *waiting* for something to happen.

His chair squeaked as he rocked, watching the clock, willing it to move faster so it'd be lunchtime. He fantasized of the meatball sub he planned to order from the sandwich shop, along with the small cellophane baggie in his glovebox, containing the last of the ditch weed for which he'd paid his cousin far too much. Brian's existence was as such: doing the barest of minimums, getting paid a (scarcely) living wage, and going home to his studio apartment only to wake and repeat the whole thing over again. In the meanwhile, his waist grew larger, his ass fatter, and his once youthful, hopeful visage aged him far more than his twenty-five years should've accounted for.

Oh, how he wished for something to happen, something *interesting.*

Brian didn't look away from clock when the bells hanging on the door chimed. He suppressed a loud sigh of annoyance at the prospect of having to do *more* work than that which was required. "Help you today?" he said, wishing he was anywhere else.

There was no response, save for labored breaths and the sound of something wet hitting the floor.

Brian spun around to face the interloper to his solitary, slacker existence, eyes in mid-roll. "I *said* can I help yo—"

"I…I…th…there's been…an *accident*."

Timmy Gagnon stood there, blood streaked across his entire chest and soaking wet. His lips were blue and his teeth chattered. He'd one hand pressed against his heart atop the source of all the blood; Brian had never seen so much. In the minute Timmy had been standing in the office, a sizable puddle had already formed around the boy's feet. What stood out most, the thing that would chase Brian into an early grave, were the wounds themselves. While still open and weeping, they'd already started to close up, not *healing*, but *fusing*, turning the boy's skin the color of ash. Brian would recall the feel of the wounds most of all, the ghost of it would never entirely leave his fingertips. As he fumbled with some gauze from the expired first-aid kit they had in the shop, waiting for *real* help to arrive, he touched it. It was hard as granite, yet damp to the touch.

The next half-hour was a blur. Brian vaguely recalled calling for an ambulance and answering questions from the state police after they'd stabilized the kid and taken him to the hospital, but his mind made things muddled, giving it all a dream-like quality, almost as if it wasn't happening to *him*, but someone else. No amount of ditch weed could keep it at bay (and Brian would try heroic amounts), and no amount of booze, either. The wounded, bleeding boy took up residence inside his mind and refused to vacate.

Brian would quit the auto repair shop and pack what meager belongings he had into his rusted-out Pontiac Sunbird and drive halfway across the country, settling in another small-town in Indiana. The slacker, who wished for something, *anything* to happen, would live for only three more years, years filled with bad choices and worse food, until his heart gave out in his sleep one cold September morning while he slept.

Of those affected by the events of the day Timmy Gagnon emerged alone from the woods, his was a merciful end.

TROOPER LESLIE THOMPSON WASN'T IN A PARTICULARLY GOOD MOOD that day.

His Bruins ate shit the night before, knocking them further from playoff contention. He shook his head as he recalled the piss-poor defense that allowed the go-ahead goal to be scored. *Fucking losers,* he thought. If that wasn't bad enough, he'd been given notice that he'd been randomly selected to participate in a weekend seminar on the latest "de-escalation and sensitivity training," and participation was mandatory. Thompson had planned to head up to his campsite on Lake Francis in the North Country, sit by the lake with a tumbler of scotch and watch the world go by. He'd recently purchased a kit for a Mitsubishi A6M5 Zero airplane and was chomping at the bit to start assembling it. All of that, now on hold, because of some stupid kids running about unsupervised.

The kid, Gagnon, hadn't given anyone much, save for that there was one kid still unaccounted for. After five minutes at the scene—of which he made a big show of examining the wreckage of some sort of treehouse, grumbling and pretending to take notes—Thompson went directly to the hospital. He wanted to hear it straight from the horse's mouth, so to speak, even if the horse in question was nothing more than a scared shitless kid.

He pushed his way into the emergency room, letting his uniform and bulky frame inform the staff that he *was* going to get what he wanted, and if anyone gave him any grief, they'd be in for a world of hurt. It worked; it always worked. From the charge nurse, Thompson learned they'd admitted the Gagnon boy and were keeping him overnight for observation. Riding in the elevator up, Thompson stared at his blurred reflection in the sleek, polished metal of the doors, smirking as he plotted his plan of attack, and it *was* an attack, he knew this well before he was sworn in as a state trooper. Thompson believed down to the cockles of his heart that there were two breeds of people: *them* and *us*. He knew it was his destiny to take down as many of *them*, no matter where they resided or what they'd done, as he could, and that was what he intended to do, come Hell or high water. It didn't matter to him if they were "presumed" innocent; that was faggy, liberal rhetoric, lies that didn't reflect the reality on the ground. They were *always* guilty. Why else would he have entered their lives?

The elevator dinged. The doors slid open. Thompson's mood had shifted from grumpy to out and out mean. His temples throbbed, pulsing in time to his footsteps (more akin to stomping than walking), and his hands had formed into tight fists, seemingly of their own accord. There was justice to be done, *his* justice, and it would be seen through to the end.

"I'M STATE TROOPER THOMPSON AND I'VE GOT SOME QUESTIONS FOR you."

Timmy Gagnon's eyes went wide at the sight of Thompson pushing through the door to his room, so stocky he had to turn sideways in order to squeeze through. His mother, Lucy, a cigaretty, rail-thin woman whose blood ran thick with gas station wine and venom, rose and stopped the trooper from moving any further. "Hold on just one goddamned minute!" Lucy's voice was hoarse; she'd spent the better part of the day lining Timmy out for playing on that "goddamned death trap" and also not sticking around to look for Hunter, in addition to a plethora of other slights and grievances that had piled up in her mind, like leaving his dirty clothes on the floor. Things that did not matter, but could only come tumbling out of a scared and angry mother. "My boy has been through Hell today and he don't need no cop hassling him while he's lying in a goddamn hospital bed!"

Thompson gripped his gunbelt, smirking at Lucy, *through* her, to Timmy. *She can't save you from me,* his expression said. *Nobody can.* "Ma'am, I'm going to have to ask you to take a step back. This is a police matter and your son is a material witness. He *will* answer my questions. Whether it happens here or at the barracks in a small, windowless room, that depends upon what you do in the next five seconds."

Lucy held firm for those five seconds, five agonizing seconds in which the slow realization came upon both her and Timmy that she couldn't protect him from this bully of a man. Timmy's eyes filled with water as her shoulders slumped, defeated.

"Fine!" Lucy picked up her purse and stormed out of the room. "I'm going for a smoke. If you're still here by the time I get back, I'm calling the lawyers, the newspaper, hell, the goddamn Governor, and singing about how you're harassing my boy."

"Take your time, ma'am," Thompson said, showing his teeth to Timmy as his smirk grew into a cruel smile. "Take your time."

THOMPSON SMILED STILL AS HE SAT IN THE CHAIR LUCY VACATED. THE seat, still warm.

"Alone at last."

"I don't remember what happened, mister—"

"Trooper. Or Sir."

"—Trooper, *sir*. It's all fuzzy in my head."

"That's why I'm here, to help shake things loose. You went out to the fort with Hunter Thurston this morning, left his house around nine-thirty."

"Yes, Trooper, *sir*."

"Did you have any arguments with Hunter, today or otherwise?"

"We—were… friends. Been that way since as long as I can remember."

"*Were* friends."

"I…I meant to say *are* friends…like I said, things are—"

"*Fuzzy*. Yeah, I caught that part."

"Yeah."

"What are we going to find out in those woods, boy?"

"I…*sir*?"

"You know what I'm getting at, boy. Playing dumb isn't going to save you, not from me. It'd be better for you if you cooperated here and now and stopped this little game you're playing. *Much* better."

"I-I-I'm not playing a *game*. I-I-I can't remember."

Thompson leaned forward, close enough to Timmy that he filled his entire field of vision as if the room itself was swallowed whole from him. "I meet lots of people in this line of work. They all have a story to tell. Some tell them better than others, but in the end, they're simply that, boy; *stories*. This story? I'm finding it particularly easy not to believe."

"I'm n-n-not telling you a *story*, mister—"

"Trooper, boy."

"—Hunter's m-m-my f-f-frie—"

"Oh, he's your f-f-f-friend?!" Thompson clamped on the railing of Timmy's bed, shaking the whole thing. Timmy's eyes went wide from fear. His tears turned to full waterworks and he sobbed and sobbed. Thompson laughed a singular bark, shaking the bed again to snap Timmy's attention around. "Stop your bawling. I don't like being lied to, especially by some little punk who thinks he can cry and pretend his way out of trouble.

"Ever been to juvenile detention, boy? Sissy boys who cry for mommy? They make special projects out of them, and unless you can fight or you got cash to buy them off, it'll last the whole time you're there. Can you fight, boy? Got a trust fund? I didn't think so. Tell me what happened out there. What did you do to Hunter? *Answer me, boy.*"

Timmy, upset to the point where rational thought was smothered by emotion, couldn't respond in anything but blubbery, snot-filled sobs.

Trooper Thompson had had enough. Snorting, he pulled Timmy out of the bed. Timmy screamed as his stitches tore open and his I.V. lines popped free from his veins. Thompson threw him against the bathroom door, pinning him there with his gut and twisting his hands behind his back. This was the part Thompson liked the most: the bust. The feeling of helplessness when the perps heard the cuffs coming, the realization that they were well and truly cooked when the cold metal bit into their skin. It was as close to divinity as Thompson had ever experienced. He craved it much like the addicts of whom he'd busted more and more frequently. Who cared if they would get cut loose by a judge later on? He'd hound them until he found something that *would* stick, and thus get to feel the bliss of the arrest all over again. A successful prosecution and another bad guy off the street. That was all that mattered.

This kid? He'd break apart easily, Thompson knew this. Kid was a sissy-boy; probably still wet the bed and slept with a stuffed animal.

"Here's what's happening, boy," he said, his lips pressed against Timmy's ear. "We're going on a little ride, you and me, out to the fort, or what's left of it. I'm going to stand you there and make you watch as they dig out all the debris and together, we're going to watch as that boy's corpse emerges from it all. Maybe then you'll tell me what you did to him. Why? I don't particularly care. Save it for the shrinks and the judge. Any mercy you'd hoped to gleam from me is well and truly gone."

Thompson pulled Timmy off the bathroom door, slipping on something wet. *Great,* he sighed, seeing the yellow puddle (with spots of blood floating in it) his foot stood in. *Fucking pissed himself.* Anger rising to new heights, Thompson twisted the boy's wounded arm further behind him, causing him to howl in pain until his voice broke. "What did you learn just now, boy? You learned that Trooper Thompson doesn't get pissed on; *he* does the pissing."

"What in God's name is going on in here?" Timmy's doctor, flanked by the charge nurse and two security guards, stormed into the room. The doctor, a young, kind-faced Hindi man, strode right up to Thompson, causing him to let loose of Timmy, all but tossing him onto the bed on his separated shoulder. This, along with the violent handcuffing, would result in Timmy requiring two additional surgeries and months of physical therapy.

"This boy is a material witness to a missing persons case," Thompson was out of breath, sweaty. He glared rage into the doctor, bouncing on the balls of his feet like a boxer, seeming to dare the doctor to try to get physical, *welcoming* it. "He comes with me."

"He will do *no* such thing! Take those cuffs off him. This child is under *my* care, and I say he is not fit for travel of any kind."

"Doc," Thompson's voice dropped. His eyes went glassy. "You don't want to try me, not on this."

The doctor, unimpressed by Thompson's threats, stepped closer to him until their noses nearly touched; Thompson backed up half a step; it was enough. "Come back with an order from a judge should you wish to take this *child* from this place before *I* deem it medically safe. Until then, get out of here. Now."

Thompson all but swallowed his lower lip. He spit and took the handcuffs from Timmy, but did not release him. He snapped the free end to a handle of the frame, smirking as he dangled the key in front of the doctor's face. "You'll be seeing me again," he said. "Soon, too."

Thompson didn't notice that he stepped in the puddle of piss once more as he left. He wouldn't until he got into his cruiser and the smell filled up the car.

THE SEARCH OF THE FORT WRECKAGE DID NOT TURN UP THE BODY OF Hunter Thurston, nor did an extensive search of the surrounding area. If not for Timmy's own words that he was present, there would've been no evidence the boy was there at all.

The police declared him "missing, presumed dead" and let the case slip into the abyss of the Cold Case files, filed away alongside the supposed Connecticut River Valley serial killer and other mysterious disappearances and demises, only to see the light of day on the occasion when the files were moved from one storage facility to another, larger one in the mid-2000s.

The Thurston family refused to hold a funeral, holding out hope that someone out there would come forward and help bring their boy home. Hunter's mother, drunk, tried to break into the Gagnon house one night, months after the incident, demanding that Timmy tell what he knew. She was arrested (by Trooper Thompson, no less) but charges were not filed.

Eventually, life moved on for that sleepy corner of New Hampshire, and the disappearance of Hunter Thurston fell to no more than whispers and rumors, spoken in dusty corners of the general store or the smoking section of the parking lot outside the local high school. Even that ceased as the years went on, as life went on.

For Timmy Gagnon?

Nothing moved on.

CHAPTER TWO ❄

Lily Calhoun saw Timmy Gagnon sitting alone in the school library and knew that she had to talk to him.

It wasn't some wild whim or even meant to be a cruel joke, her being one of the upper crust of high school society and Timmy being…well, Timmy. There was a week left before they all graduated, a week left to embrace childhood before being let loose upon the world to make their fortunes, meager or large they might be, craft their lives, and stake their claim on the world they had been given. One week, to say the things always meant to be said, do the things always meant to be done. One week left, or so it seemed to Lily, to throw caution to the wind and do whatever the fuck she wanted.

On that particular Tuesday morning, during study hall, what she wanted more than anything was to hear Timmy's voice again.

She rose from her table, her social clique, and walked over. She found herself smoothing her blouse out and fiddling with her hair (*Should've worn a hat or put it up*, she thought), catching herself completely off-guard. She smiled, suppressing a laugh. That *she* would be fretting over what Timmy Gagnon thought? What had come over her?

Lily knew the answer to that question, knew it full and well, yet she dared not think it. Not yet. Thinking of it was close to speaking it aloud which would give it breath, *life*, and she wasn't sure she was ready for that.

Not yet.

"Hi, Timmy!"

"....Hi."

"Now, why is it that you've been back in school this entire year and this is the first time we're actually speaking? When everything is about to change and we're likely not to see much of each other, if at all? Seems rather cruel, don't you think?"

Timmy shifted in his seat, trying to hide within the confines of his beat-ass flannel shirt and even more beat-ass leather jacket. "I try not to."

They sat there for a few uncomfortable minutes, Timmy focusing on his book, not looking up from its pages, and Lily staring at him, into him. She pulled a stick of gum from her purse and popped it into her mouth, chewing with abandon. "I remember the time that big cop came and hauled you out of class in the...*second*? No, *third* grade. Slapped the cuffs on you right in front of my desk. Wow, was that guy mad at you! I don't even remember what they said you did—"

"Vandalism. And theft. Stole Ricky Patterson's bike then threw it through a plate glass window of the store his uncle runs."

"—right. I remember that day; think about it an awful lot. It gave me nightmares, you know? The way that cop—"

"Trooper," Timmy said. "Thompson. He's a prick and a fascist."

"—right, Trooper Thompson. The way he manhandled you, how scared you were, how *violent* he was? It stayed with me. All this time and I still wake up in the night thinking about it. Of course, I can't even imagine what it's like for you, Timmy."

"It's not the worst thing to happen to me," Timmy said. "Not by a country mile."

"You went away for a while because of that."

"One of several stints in the lovely up-state juvenile detention facility. I wouldn't recommend it."

"You did home-schooling after that, right?"

Timmy nodded. "Mom wouldn't let me leave the house unsupervised. She was afraid Trooper Thompson would find a reason to haul me back in. He's always looking for one, to this day. I'm surprised he's let me run around this long without inventing one."

"Huh."

"Huh what?"

"It's funny, that's all. That this one cop would keep coming after you. I mean, they never did find Hunter's body."

"Been real nice catching up, Lily, but you've got more important things to do than slumming it with the freaky town delinquent, so…"

"Sit down, Timmy Gagnon. Don't be mad with me." Lily halted Timmy's exodus from the table with the tips of her fingers, pressing gently on his forearm. It was solid muscle and felt like rebar underneath his skin. Lily found herself growing more excited when he sat back down from merely that, surprised that it worked even. She knew he was judging her actions, and might bolt from the table still, so she shifted around so that she, and only she, was filling his vision. Not the other kids in the library snickering and pointing at them. Not the librarian and study hall monitor, also watching with a morbid curiosity. Clearing her throat, she smiled. "What are you reading? Doesn't look like anything anyone is testing on, not that I'm aware of."

"It's not. It's private." Timmy closed the book and shoved it in his backpack. Lily caught a glimpse of the gold-lettering of the title etched on the spine, reading *Myths and Demonology*. "Reading…it's one of the only things that keeps things quiet. In my head."

"I get that. For me, it's skiing."

"Yeah, I heard that you won some competitions here and there."

"You been keeping tabs on me have you, Timmy? You stalking me, your ex-girlfriend?"

"*Ex-girlfriend?*"

Lily smiled, laughed. "Second grade. For about a week, maybe two. We held hands at recess, had lunch at the same table. You were my very first crush, Timmy Gagnon."

Timmy's cheeks flushed. He sucked on his teeth, the fake replacements tasting like plastic. He rubbed the back of his head, struggling to find the words. "I-I'm sorry. I don't remember that at all," he said, lying.

"It was a lifetime ago, right? You've had *other* things to deal with, more important than grade-school crushes."

"Yeah."

"Yeah."

Neither spoke for a time. The world went on around them. The onlookers, bored by the lack of action, turned back to their lives, their routines. Lily broke the silence, simply by talking, at first about anything, then to her skiing. Timmy watched her intently as she spoke of feeling the wind whipping across her face, the speed, the thrill of taking a turn, a jump, and felt something other than misery and self-loathing for the first in ages.

"It's freeing, really," Lily said, smiling. "Kind of addicting, you know? When I get out of here, I'm going to move out to Colorado, I think; Vail, maybe. Open up a restaurant, ski whenever I want. That'd be an all right kind of life to live, I think."

"You know your nose crinkles up when you smile, when you laugh."

"Shut up, it does not!" Lily laughed, playing at hiding her face from Timmy.

"It's cute."

"You think I'm cute?"

"Yeah."

"Yeah."

More silence followed. The words they wished to speak to each other hung between them, ghosts of regret and of want.

"So, hey, um, after the rehearsal walk tomorrow, there's going to be a big party; kinda a pre-post-graduation party out at Charlie Danforth's lake house."

"I heard."

"...you going to go?"

"I figured not, no."

"Why?"

"I'm not *technically* graduating with you. I'm four credits shy, thanks to Trooper Thompson insisting I stay the whole eight months my last stint in juvie. They're letting me walk with the class, but until I finish summer school, no diploma."

"Oh. That sucks."

"Also, I don't know if you noticed, I'm not exactly Johnny Football Hero around here. The last interaction I had with Charlie Danforth, he called me a 'faggot murderer' and spit on me. I doubt I'd be very welcome at his party."

"It's not *his* party, number one. Number two, it's for all of us, even you, Timmy. I think you ought to come. Maybe you can hold my hand again? Tell me about that book you're trying to hide from me a bit?"

"I...I don't know...Mom keeps me on a short leash. Trooper Thompson always seems to be about, you know?"

"You gonna let the mean ol' Trooper keep you in your mom's basement your whole life, Timmy?" The bell sounded for the start of third period. Lily snatched a piece of paper from her backpack and scribbled the address to the party on it, along with a time. "You decide you want to be more than what people think of you, meet me there. I hope you make the right choice, Timmy."

Timmy sat in the library until the librarian chastised him to get a move on. He'd get a detention slip for being late to third-period history, to be served the following Monday. He'd not serve it.

By then, no one would care about such things.

"*Can you believe this is happening?*"

Timmy couldn't. Not in a million years would he have believed it.

And yet, it was. He and Lily Calhoun, going at it, hot and heavy, in the back of her black Jetta, a bonfire raging against the backdrop of the lake and the party raging on in the background.

He almost didn't go; a last-minute crisis of confidence. His mother had nodded off on a combination of red wine and valium. His father was moonlighting yet again and, well, he hadn't shown much interest in his son since before the accident. *Before Hunter.*

It wasn't the fear of *them* catching him that caused his last second dilly-dallying. It was *him.* The one who laughed when they sentenced him to those long months in juvie, who took every opportunity to harass him—sometimes strip-searching him in public, who once took him behind the bank on Main Street and put his fist under his nose and told him that "his day was coming." Thompson. The last decade of Timmy's life was filled with the fear of seeing that fat-ass sauntering up to him, his hot-dog like fingers gripping his gun belt, chewing on a stick of gum. That the man wanted to harm him, Timmy knew full well. His shoulder still ached on cold and rainy days, in no small part thanks to the treatment he received from Thompson at the hospital.

Timmy thought of Lily's crinkled nose, how goddamned adorable it was, how it felt good to talk to her, to be fucking *normal* for once, and smirked at his reflection before ducking out his front door.

Fuck you, Trooper Thompson. Sir.

Part of him feared a prank. A *Carrie*-style act of cruelty that would result in the entirety of their class (and the hangers-on who crashed the party) to laugh and laugh until it was all there was in the entire world. He'd the cure for that in the form of a purloined bottle of wine and a couple of pills. He downed the bottle and snorted the pills in his car and headed into the party, to the spot where Lily told him to be, at the very time she told him to be, and lo and behold, there she was, looking fine as hell, dancing around the fire, her midriff showing as she spun around the flames.

Once she saw him, well, it was off to the races, as they say. There wasn't even time to say hello. Lily kissed him so hard their teeth smashed against each other. It hurt, but boy, did it hurt *good.*

She led him away from the bonfire, away from prying eyes and drunken revelers, to her car, parked next to a copse of pine trees, far enough away where they'd not be disturbed. Thoughts of a set-up crept up the back of Timmy's neck, but Lily quickly dissuaded him of these when she got in the back seat and threw her top and bra at him.

"Can you believe this is happening?" Lily said.

It was crazy. It was happening so fast. Timmy's head wobbled from wine and drugs, spun faster and faster. His heart beat so hard it hurt. How was this possible? How was this happening?

Lily fumbled with his belt, breaking free from his mouth. She smiled and invited his mouth to her breast. Timmy eagerly obliged. She hissed and moaned, rocking herself against him. "I want you," she whispered as her rocking turned ferocious. "I want you, Timmy. Now."

He didn't need to be told twice.

As he slipped his shirt over his head, as Lily's face—eyes half-closed, mouth slightly open and smiling—disappeared from his view, he felt her move in a strange, sudden way, almost like she'd a muscle spasm or cramp, causing her to shift away from him, nearly leaping off his lap. Strange, but no matter. He'd lay her on her back in the car and things would be all right. Perfect.

But the scream he started that day in the woods a decade earlier leapt out of his lungs.

It was *her*, looking back at him from the driver's seat, Lily's neck in her hands.

Oh God. THIS ISN'T HAPPENING!

Lily's head had been turned around backwards. Her legs spasmed and kicked against Timmy before her corpse slumped against him. The air in the car cooled in a flash until his teeth chattered. The woman's hands slid away, her claws carving through the leather of the driver's seat. The glow of the bonfire shone through the windows, muted from the heat of Timmy and Lily's passion, forming an odd-shaped crown behind the woman's head as she moved into the backseat.

"*Pretty,*" she said. A low snarl came from behind her black and green teeth as she tossed Lily into the empty seat next to Timmy with all the effort of throwing a piece of paper in the trash. She sat on him, her coldness robbing the last of Lily from him, and placed her arms around his neck. "*Mine.*"

His body betrayed him in every imaginable way, refusing to let him fight her off and get out of the fucking car, refusing to quell the lust he'd had for Lily, in fact, *increasing* it, transferring it to this...*thing* from his past he'd convinced himself was a bad dream. The woman laughed at Timmy, mocking his helplessness. She trailed her claws over the scars of his youth, ones she inflicted, reopening scar tissue long-thought healed over, as she took him in her hands.

"N-nooo..."

"*Pretty,*" she said, as she stroked faster. "*Mine.*"

"*Can you believe this is happening?*"

Words whispered to him in a playful, erotic context had been corrupted into something sinister, *wrong*. They haunted Timmy's ears as he drove the Jetta through the backroads of the county, too fast, swerving and skidding on the dirt roads criss-crossing the townships with populations too low and terrain—hilly and heavily wooded, even at the turn of the century—too cumbersome to maintain and pave as he drove with Lily's corpse lying on the floor.

After the woman had....

Once he'd come to his senses and realized what had truly befallen him, Timmy pushed the car door open and promptly vomited. His pants caught on the edge of the seat and fell down around his ass, further exposing him to the evening. As the vomit came, so did... *glimpses*...things the woman showed him as she violated him. They didn't make any sense to him. Stars and planets soaring, too close, overhead in a sky alien and strange to him. A vast expanse of forest, stretching to the horizon beyond, filled not with trees of wood and life, but of craggy stone and glistening teeth, pulsating with drool and tumors, filled with things, unseen and terrible, far worse than *her.*

And her...*oh ChristohGod*...the woman stood in a dreary, barren plain, filled with scarcely running water and shallow pools and marshes. A thick cloud of insects swarmed the air around her, feeding on the stench of decay. The water, brackish and swirling with an oily substance, rose to her waist as she raised her arms to him, beckoning to come and see. The water flow intensified, filling the marsh with the quickness of a flashflood. *"Pretty,"* she said. His cum dripped from her clawed hands. *"Mine."*

"FUCK!" Timmy almost didn't see the deer until he'd nearly run it down. He cranked the wheel and stepped on the gas, swerving around the poor, dumb beast, sending the Jetta into a fishtail. He stomped the brakes and turned into the skid best he could. The edge of the dirt road, a ditch several feet deep, drew closer by the second, the headlights casting shadows across it, making it appear like some gargantuan mouth, yawning. Timmy reached down and pulled the emergency brake while pushing the regular one to the floor, tears blurring his vision. Thankfully, *mercifully*, the car skidded to a halt at the ditch's edge. The stench of burning rubber filled the compartment. Timmy put the car in reverse and drove on, rolling all the windows down to rid himself of the stench. It remained still when he arrived at his destination.

It was a mine once, long since run dry and abandoned, leaving the town devoid of its riches and its waters polluted. Timmy only knew of it from the time one of his cousins drove him up there to get high. That time, they were in a truck with four-wheel drive, not a sporty, little car. The road, long-since reclaimed by nature, was a rocky, divoted waste, too much for the Jetta to handle. The car struggled for a quarter-mile before a pothole devoured the front wheels, snapping the axles, and making the car inoperable. Timmy collided with the steering wheel upon impact, breaking his nose. Spitting blood and cursing, he rummaged in Lily's trunk for a flashlight (the headlights, while still on, wouldn't carry the two-miles to the mine entrance), finding nothing but a pristine, empty space.

Lily was dead weight. The road moved to a steeper incline the longer he walked, making his terrible burden weigh all the heavier. Then, there was the mental weight. What was he doing? Should he not stop, turn right back around, and walk to the nearest pay phone and call for help? He'd not done anything wrong, not really. He could say that they left the party, drove to the mine, and got stuck. Maybe Lily got out to check and fell? Maybe that's how she broke her neck?

People might believe that. All I have to do is turn around right now and I can make this all okay.

Timmy's gut cut through the fog of wishful thinking. He *knew*, deep down, that no one would believe he didn't kill Lily. Once his name went out over the wire, Trooper Thompson would come down upon him like the wrath of God. The cop, that bully *pig*, he'd finally be able to put Timmy away for good and in doing so, save the goddamn world. In the darkening gloom around him, Thompson's visage appeared, brighter than the sun. That fucking smirk, his pudgy fingers hooked around his ill-fitting gunbelt, all present to mock Timmy. *I knew you were bad news, boy, and now, I will have you.*

"*Fuck you,*" Timmy whispered, spraying blood into the night air. "*Trooper Thompson, SIR.*"

The mine entrance was more or less shut up still. The wooden planks hammered into the entrance were stripped away, either by rot or thieves, but the chain link fence behind them remained, warped and twisted. Timmy kicked at the bottom corner, breaking through after ten kicks. He put Lily's body down as he peeled it back like a scab of rusted metal. It cut his fingers near to the bone, but he didn't feel it much. He was soaked in sweat and shivering. All he wanted to do was to sit down, just for a minute, but he knew if he did, he'd not be able to rise again on his own power. He squatted on the other side of the fence and pulled Lily through. She caught against the fence, becoming stuck. Timmy cursed and worked the fence, pushing the metal and ripping more of the chain-link free, but Lily remained in place.

Laughter echoed all around him. *Hers.* Timmy bolted upright, breath catching in his chest. He felt, not quite anger, but embarrassment, *shame.* He found himself crying from it, his tears further obscuring the near total darkness of the mine entrance. He couldn't stumble about in there for very long. He'd find himself tumbling headlong into a forgotten shaft to die alongside the vermin and Lily's corpse. He didn't know how far would be far enough, so he walked thirty paces and left Lily there, lying against the carved-out stone and dirt.

The car was a problem he couldn't solve; it couldn't be fixed or moved. He removed his shirt and wiped down the interior as best he could. He recalled half-remembered lessons about something called *D.N.A.*, and from the articles his father read on that so-called "Trial of the Century," but he didn't know much more than between the blood and his cum, he'd left more than enough to put him in the car. He rolled all the windows down to let the elements in, hoping they'd muddy the waters, giving him as much time as he could glom. He'd need every second, he knew. Thompson was waiting for him, even if he wasn't yet aware of what had happened. He waited nonetheless.

It took him an hour to walk down the mountain, another two to make it back to his house. His parents snored in the early hours, unaware of his presence. He packed a bag of clothes and lifted his mom's car keys, driving her Subaru to the bank where he emptied out the pitiful remains of his savings account, totaling around five hundred dollars. From there, he drove southeast, keeping to the speed limit, until the car ran out of gas, shortly outside of the Lakes Region. He parked the car behind a shopping plaza filled with derelict stores and disappeared into the surrounding woods.

He felt the woman's touch on him the entire time.

THEY'D NOT FIND LILY CALHOUN'S CAR FOR TWO WEEKS, HER BODY A month after.

Rumors hindered the investigation. Her friends mentioned some person, a boyfriend named Ramon or Roland, who lived in Lowell, Massachusetts, and that she might have run off to be with him. This turned out to be false; there was no Ramon or Roland in Lowell. Further interviews did mention Timmy, but these were met with skepticism, both from the police and the witnesses. Lily's best friend, Tammy Michaels, laughed at the suggestion that they'd be together.

"Lily might have seen him as something fun to play with, the whole bad boy thing, but it wouldn't have been anything more than that. She had a future ahead, you know? She was going places."

Timmy Gagnon? He was most assuredly going nowhere.

Trooper Thompson wasn't amongst the skeptics. Oh, he bought that Lily's interest was limited to a plaything, a quick tumble with the bad boy to piss off her folks. What he did not subscribe to was that Timmy would be content to leave it at that. He wrote report after report, asking for another look at Timmy's current whereabouts (rather suspicious that he'd light out at the same time, wouldn't you think?), another search of his house, further interviews, for that entire month, eventually landing a formal reprimand in his jacket and being delegated to desk duty on the graveyard shift.

And then a group of hunters discovered the black Jetta.

Thompson's heart was so full he nearly broke into song.

It would be a matter of time before the brass put him back on the case. He felt this in his bones and, despite wanting desperately to scream about how right he was, Thompson kept quiet, going to and from his desk, filing meaningless paperwork, smirking to himself as more details from the scene came in, details he'd pore over in his home, taking over from his model airplane hobby for a time. The lab couldn't confirm Timmy Gagnon was present in the car, but they couldn't rule him out either. That was enough for Thompson, *more than.*

He was brought in two days after they'd found the body. Thompson felt giddy. He kept quiet again as they told him he was on it, what the expectations of him were in his investigation. His conduct, they said, needed to be "beyond reproach." He nodded and made all the necessary placations. All the while, inside his head and heart, he was laughing at the brass, as he bashed their heads in with his flashlight. How dare they question *him*? The Gagnon kid; no, sorry, he was a *man* now. *No more juvie for you, bucko. Welcome to the show*—was trouble; he knew it a decade prior. Why didn't these fat heads listen? If they had, this girl (whose name he struggled to recall) would still be alive.

Thompson said none of these things. He went about his job, unleashed. Ready. The Gagnon family knew nothing, of course. He'd put both parents in the box for hours at a time and glean nothing from them. *How could they not know what their own kid is?* He printed up wanted posters, along with a reward for any information leading to his capture (the Calhoun family all too happy to contribute). He drove sixty miles in each direction, putting them up in every restaurant, post office, and liquor store he could find.

It was a matter of time. New Hampshire was so gosh-darned small, after all. Thompson figured he'd have the kid within a matter of weeks. Would the kid put up a fight, or when seeing Thompson coming for him, would the fear of God overtake him and the kid would collapse? Thompson relished either, lusted for it. At night, his dreams were of him killing Timmy in increasingly violent, intricate means. He'd masturbate to them upon awakening. He began painting the kid's initials onto the plastic bombs and armaments of his models, wishing they were live ordinance that he could drop on not only Timmy, but all the Gagnons, for surely the sickness, the *evil* that existed in Timmy lived in them all.

Yep, Thompson thought. *It's all over but the screaming, and I will hear you scream before the end, boy.*

CHAPTER
THREE

"*Hullo* there, young man."

Ernest "Lil' Ern" Bourgeous had lived in the Weirs since the day he was born. Hell, his mother used to tell the tale about how he was born "right out there" on Lake Winnipesaukee as his dad, "Big Ern," raced to get them to the shore and the hospital. Lil' Ern's life was filled with stories like that: apocryphal, each one larger than the next, and just as fun as the last. He'd one where he saw a Bigfoot shaking hands with aliens up North Country, another where a very famous celebrity ate no fewer than five hot dogs in one sitting at the beach before hopping in his big yacht to jet off to his big house the other side of the lake (Lil' Ern never would tell *who* he saw; that was all part of the fun). As the amount of years ahead of him grew shorter than those behind, the stories (and life itself) slowed, becoming a lot more serious, downright grim. The downturn of the Lakes Region was one reason, sure; the recession of the early nineties hurt the locals more than most cared to admit, Lil' Ern included. His modest go-kart track barely kept him afloat enough to ride out the winters. He'd been lucky to have gotten on as a dispatcher for a local ambulance company part-time (his time in Korea as a corpsman gave him a leg up on everyone else). That, and he'd work for peanuts without complaint. People he thought were doing all right for themselves he'd see lining up in front of the unemployment office or at the Market Basket the first of every month, carts filled with as much as their food stamps would carry them.

Then, there were the drugs. Lil' Ern couldn't tell you a reefer from an eightball, but he sure noticed the toll they were taking. People with sunken eyes, scabby arms, hands, and faces wandered around the Weirs. Crimes that "ought not to happen here" did indeed happen there. Burglaries, breaking and entering, even plain old vandalism, all had gone up in the decade since they'd elected ol' Slick Willie (of whom Lil' Ern did *not* vote for either time, thank you very much). Yet his experience with those in the throes of addiction had always been peripheral. Until that summer day when, upon arriving to open up the track for the day, he found one of his worksheds broken into and the boy sleeping inside.

"I said *hullo* there, young man," Lil' Ern said. "You ain't deaf, is you?"

The boy's eyes were wide. He looked past Lil' Ern to the door, gathering up the ratty sleeping bag and a hiker's backpack in his arms, ready to make a break for it. Despite his moniker, Lil' Ern was anything but *little*. He was as wide as the door to the shed and built of solid muscle. Even in his advanced age, he could still put up two hundred twenty pounds on the bench (without *too* much of a fuss).

"Boy, I ain't here to put you in a jam. Whatever your troubles are? Your business, not Lil' Ern's. I ain't going to hurt you none, so long's you don't try nothing on me. We have an understanding?"

"…I guess we do."

"Now, I told you my name. How's about you tell me yours?"

"…Zack."

"Zack." *A lie.* Lil' Ern shook his head. "Zack what?"

"…Just Zack…I ought to get going."

"You ought *not* have busted my window there. Them's ain't cheap, boy."

"Yeah, well...I'm sorry."

"Mm."

"You going to call the cops?" Zack/Timmy said, his body deflating, his eyes looking far away, ignoring the tears budding in them. Lil' Ern pulled off his Red Sox cap and scratched his freshly shorn head. *I could call the police,* he thought. *Mayhap I ought to...*

"There's some cardboard and duct tape in there somewhere," Lil' Ern said. "You patch up that window for me and we'll consider ourselves square enough."

"For real?"

"Did I stutter?" Lil' Ern turned to get about opening up for the day. Lots of kiddos and young people were expecting to race around his track and he aimed not to disappoint. He stopped his loopy gait at the top of the hill leading towards the main go-kart garage. "How'd you like to earn a little pocket money?" he called to Timmy.

"I-I'd like that very much, mister."

"Could use a hand around here, changing oil and tires, gassing up the karts, running the concessions and the like. It ain't much; twenty bucks a day, but it'll be in cash. Interested?"

"Yes, sir, I am."

"You fix up that window and come find me in the garage and we'll get you started," Lil' Ern said. "Oh. Only rule I got for you: can't have you sleeping on the property. Insurance company would pull my coverage."

"I get it."

"There's an old tent somewheres in there. You're welcome to it; consider it a hiring bonus." Lil' Ern turned with a chuckle.

"Why?"

"Pardon?"

"Why help me, mister? You don't know me from nobody."

Lil' Ern smirked, giving a little wink. "It's a helluva story, ain't it?"

AND SO BEGAN TIMMY GAGNON'S LIFE AT THE WEIRS.

It wasn't overly unpleasant. He'd work at the go-kart track from eight until six every day, doing odd jobs for Lil' Ern, and then he'd head off to his tent. He moved camp every few days, wary of the ever-looming threat of the police, of Trooper Thompson. The days were long and hot, but the nights would bring cool air from the lake. He'd enough money to eat every day, something he had to abandon early in his exodus from his hometown. *From the scene of the crime, don't you mean?* It wouldn't last. This life he'd stumbled into, the random kindness, was an anomaly. If Lil' Ern knew what haunted Timmy, what had been done, what *he* had done to survive it? The old man's kindness would end. His grey-green eyes would lose their twinkle of mischief and go cold, hard, as did everyone whom learned about Timmy.

He'd stay on for another week, maybe two, and then move on, hopefully richer and with Trooper Thompson none the wiser as to his whereabouts.

If not for the nights, Timmy might've deluded himself into thinking he was going to be all right. For the nights, his dreams, they belonged to *her*.

"PRETTY. MINE."

Night after night, she came for him. Sometimes he'd see her outside of his tent, lightly dragging her clawed fingers on the sides of his tent, laughing when he'd rush out, screaming and swinging the tire iron he'd taken from his mother's car. She'd not show herself to him, not directly. She'd wait until he fell into an uneasy slumber, in which she'd then conquer his dreams.

It was always the Forest, the one he came to think of as a giant, endless mouth permanently held open, wanting nothing more than to snap shut and swallow the universe. She'd take him by the hand

and drag him past the gnarled stone roots and rotting teeth, through deep and twisting paths, each growing tighter than the last as the Forest closed in around them. She laughed all the while, unconcerned for his safety or sanity. Timmy heard things moving all around them, caught glimpses of things of which if he'd gazed upon them, he knew he would never wake. They walked until his feet were bloody and shredded. When he finally collapsed, he found that the ground that rushed to greet him was not mottled with salivating teeth and unflinching stone, but muddy water.

Always the river. The pathetic, near barren waters that smelled sweet and sickly all at once.

The woman laughed at Timmy. She'd disappear into a puddle until all that remained was her face, ever changing. Sometimes it'd be Lily's face, eyes void of life and blood seeping from her nostrils. Other times, it'd be his mother, teachers, even Hunter, his dearest, long-gone friend and first to fall by the woman's hand.

The alien sky above would twinkle bright as the waters rose, seeking to envelop Timmy. He'd awake screaming as the oily stuff entered his mouth. The woman's voice, her *laughter*, would greet him as fresh as a slap to the face with a brick.

"Pretty. Mine."

"YOU BELIEVE IN CURSES?"

Lil' Ern put down his slice of pizza (sausage and pepperoni, heartburn be damned) and wiped the grease from his hands with a napkin. He chewed and swallowed before answering, a habit his mother, God rest her soul, drilled into him before Timmy's parents were even out of diapers. "I recall my grandmother used to believe that the Travelers and the Romani folk would do that to anyone they didn't like. Put a Hex on you and give you the ol' Evil Eye. Seemed like a bunch of nonsense to me, not to mention the casual bigotry from Grammy, of course."

Timmy nodded and finished his pizza, staring out the window, watching a late summer rain come down. Rainy days had been rare that summer, this being only the second they'd had. In both instances, Lil' Ern would invite Timmy into the main office and order pizza, a whole pie for each of them. Timmy was grateful, but Lil' Ern wouldn't hear anything in the way of thanks. "What else are we going to do on a rainy day *but* eat pizza?" he said as if it was the most obvious thing in the world. That day, Timmy was sullen, more so than usual. The nightmares were getting worse to the point where he'd started using drugs and booze to keep them at bay, to keep *the woman* at bay. He'd found a dealer who kept him whole in pills and rotgut in town, a risky move, he knew, but he was desperate for relief of any kind. Black hollows formed under his eyes. His skin was pockmarked with scabs and acne. He was jumpy, too. Lil' Ern dropped a pencil before lunch and Timmy all but lept out of his skin.

"I'm thinking I'm cursed," Timmy said.

"Why's that? Because you're down on your luck? That's life, boy, and it ain't nothing anyone can control. Oh sure, you get some say over it, but things greater than me and thee are out there waiting to toss a monkey wrench into our well-laid plans and dreams."

"It's more than that, Lil' Ern. I-it's kind of hard to explain."

"How's about you eat another slice and tell me anyway. You look like you could use it."

Timmy ate the pizza in three big bites, swallowing it with a sip of Pepsi, wishing it had rum in it. "Bad things happen to me, to people who get close to me. Not every minute of every day, but enough."

"Bad things."

"Real bad."

"And you think you're causing these bad things to happen."

"I don't think it, I know it."

"Uh-huh."

"There's...people, back where I'm from. They'd tell you that I'm worse than the Devil, that I ought to be taken out behind a building and shot."

"You don't say."

"What do you think causes thinking like that? Is it, I dunno, this weird collective unconsciousness? Or, is it more like a cold, and people catch it kinda like through suggestion? Listen to me, rambling on and on like a crazy person."

"Boy, you ain't crazy and you ain't cursed. What you are is *haunted.*"

"Haunted."

Lil' Ern nodded. "You've had a short life and it's mostly been all right, I'd say, relatively speaking, and yet, there's been enough awful that it's clung onto you like a barnacle, filled your head full of ghosts, and they're haunting your every waking moment, and, judging from the look of you, your non-waking ones too. Only way to get yourself un-haunted is to let them ghosts move on and lie where they belong: behind you. You get what I'm saying, boy?"

Timmy almost told Lil' Ern then. The deaths, the woman, the Forest of Stone and Teeth, the river bottoms. Somewhere, in the back of his mind, he heard the woman laughing at him and lost his nerve. "How?"

"How?" Lil' Ern blew an exhale out, blowing a small raspberry with his lips. "Hell, boy, if you can't figure out your own head, then you got to get some help. Therapy. Talk to someone once a week, every week, for a long while. Really put in the work and figure out how to come to terms with it all so you can—not forget, but forgive yourself. Given your situation, I'd say something that involved ain't in the cards for you, not right now."

Timmy's heart sunk into his shoes. "Probably not."

"You know something? Maybe what you need is what they refer to as a *placebo,* something that your brain *thinks* will help you out, but in reality, ain't much but sugar."

"What's the placebo for a curse?"

Lil' Ern grinned. "Come with me and I'll show you."

"YOU'VE GOT INTERNET HERE?" TIMMY LOOKED AT THE DESKTOP computer as Lil' Ern booted it up. It was cumbersome, blocky as hell, and took up most of the old metal desk it sat upon. He remembered from school that the first computers used to take up entire rooms, recalling black and white pictures in a textbook from the first Apollo missions. The one Lil' Ern had was a fraction of the size, but loud as a lawnmower when it started up, whirring and beeping.

"Of course I do. Even working on getting my own website up and running," Lil' Ern said as he connected to the World Wide Web. The sound of the dial-up modem was like that of a cat shrieking as it was turned into digitized bits. "My niece learned me most of it; still teaching me stuff. It's really interesting. I imagine it'll be even more so in a few years, but I'll be worm food by then. Young man like you? Ought to start learning how to code, once you get on your feet again."

"Your niece?"

Lil' Ern nodded. "Here. This is her website. 'The Blue Witch of the North,' or so she refers to herself in her *professional* capacity. Take a gander, boy, see what you think."

The website was crude. Several animations moved all at once, of pentagrams, trees swaying, fairies swirling around and around. They caused the site to move slow, making it hard to navigate. Timmy clicked on 'Services' and was taken to a plain black page with green text and a photo of whom he assumed was the aforementioned Blue Witch. She was small, pretty, with blue hair, fake elf ears, and a pierced nose. Scrolling past a lengthy section of how she claimed to "have heard the spirits since the day she was born," Timmy read about the things the Blue Witch claimed to be able to do (along with pricing points). They were the old standards: palm readings, Tarot, even seances (the most expensive).

"Your niece talks to ghosts?" Timmy said.

Lil' Ern laughed, shaking his entire frame. "She's an odd one, that girl. I don't believe in any of that stuff she's selling: love potions and divining the future and all that. But she's got a good heart and I love her to death."

Timmy kept scrolling through the website, finding nothing that made him believe the so-called Blue Witch had anything in her bag of tricks that would free him from the woman. He was feeling more and more discouraged, until he clicked on a link titled *Scenes from the Beyond*. What he saw caused his balls to retract inside of himself.

The first image was that of the Forest of Stone and Teeth.

It was but a pencil sketch, but there was no mistaking it. The gnarled trunks slick with ravenous teeth growing from them like tumorous flowers were present. There was only a brief line of text below the image, stating it was "the place in which the monsters are born and hold dominion."

Scrolling down, a picture of the boggy river bottom where the woman brought him was revealed; it too, an exact copy of his dreams. He heard his heartbeat—staccato fast—in his ears, for the picture revealed to him the name, of the river.

Lethe.

Outside, the storm crashed and raged against the building. "She's kicking up a fuss out there now, boy," Lil' Ern said, staring out the window to watch the sheets of water blow across the go-kart track. Timmy's mouth was dry, his words gone. It wasn't the storm. It was *her*, this he knew. He'd uncovered a truth that she'd not intended and she was now raging against this. The power shuddered and then blinked off. The computer screen, along with the Blue Witch's website, went dark. Timmy clicked on the mouse and hit the side of the monitor, all to no avail. "You bust that, you've bought it, boy," Lil' Ern said, shining a pocket flashlight in his eyes.

"Lil' Ern," Timmy said. "Where does your niece live exactly?"

"You find something to clear out your ghosts after all?"

"Yeah," Timmy said. A thunderboom rolled across the lake, whipping the waters up to a violent, choppy froth. "I just might have."

Trooper Geoffrey Wogen couldn't fucking stand Trooper Leslie Thompson. *Hated him* was a more apt description, if Geoffrey was being honest. That the man was an insufferable bully was well known amongst the Staties, as was the fact that seemingly nothing was to be done, or would ever *be* done about it by the brass. Trooper Thompson got results, even though his methods were questionable and his demeanor was that of a major league asshole, drunk on the power he'd gotten for himself. Geoffrey, like his colleagues, had taken on a policy of *enduring* Trooper Thompson whenever their paths crossed, doing whatever was needed to get him to move onto the next assignment and as quickly as possible.

That day in Laconia, it was Geoffrey's turn with the shitty end of the stick.

It took Thompson exactly one hour from getting Geoffrey's call to get there, one hour on the nose. He stormed into the building, refusing to check in with the front desk, save for a bellow demanding to see Trooper Wogen. No one questioned him. No one stopped him, demanding he follow standard operating procedure. They all stared, slack-jawed, pointing towards Geoffrey's desk. Thompson stood over Geoffrey as he ate his lunch (salad and mozzarella sticks, cornerstones of a healthy and nutritious lunch), huffing and snorting like a beast. Veins throbbed against his temples, beads of sweat rolled freely down his face, staining the collar of his uniform. "Where?" Thompson said. He smelled of airplane glue and stale coffee.

Geoffrey didn't have it in him to stand up to Thompson. So, chewing half a bite of tossed salad, he walked Thompson down to the interrogation rooms, to room 2B, where he had a real Emmy-Award winner named Rob Cross waiting.

"Standard low life," Geoffrey said as they walked. "A handful of DUIs, possession, possession *with* intent, good ol' B and E, even got him for public urination no less than four times. Nine times out of ten, he'd get processed, sent to county and see the judge for yet another ninety day stint, but *this* time, he said he'd something to trade, something 'worth my while.'"

Thompson's jaws ground his teeth fierce enough that Geoffrey heard the faint, repetitive clicking. He shoved Geoffrey aside once he buzzed the door open, rushing into the room to loom over a startled, hungover Rob Cross.

"You saw him?" Thompson pulled the wanted poster of Timmy out, holding it before Rob. "When and where. Now."

Rob, a doughy man with curly blond hair and a face mottled with moles, smirked, more out of surprise than mockery. He glanced to Geoffrey as if to plead for help, only to find himself shoved backwards out of his chair. Before he could cry foul, Thompson was upon him, hauling him to his feet and slamming him against the wall, his beefy forearm underneath Rob's chin, cutting off his oxygen.

"WHERE. WHEN. NOW."

"Trooper Thomps—" Geoffrey lost his voice when Thompson glanced at him, *through* him. In that instant, the rumors he'd heard about Leslie Thompson became verified, things spoken of over beers at the watering hole, at cookouts with other troopers, on long overnight shifts, things spoken of in hushed whispers, as not to give Thompson even a hint of hearing them. Geoffrey said a prayer when that gaze turned away from him.

"Tell me," Thompson said, pressing his full weight into Rob's throat. "Right now."

"O…Okay! I sell to him….sold to him yesterday….he's moving around, but camps over in the state campground last I knew… *please….*"

"Which one, asshole?"

"B-b-behind the…arcade…the big arcade…Funspot…"

"You know it?" Thompson asked Geoffrey.

"Sure. Pine Hollow."

"Fine. You're driving then."

Thompson let Rob Cross slide down the wall to sit in a puddle of his own piss. Geoffrey had questions, lots of them, but he sighed and followed Thompson to his cruiser. *Endure him, Geoffy, old boy,* he thought. *Endure him.*

TIMMY ALMOST GOT OUT OF THERE.

He'd gone from the go-kart track straight to the bus depot, spending what amounted to two days' pay for a one-way ticket to the North Country. The bus would take him as far as Lincoln; from there, he'd need to leg it or hitch his way through the Notch to Franconia, where the Blue Witch of the North lived. "She's got a great view of the Old Man," Lil' Ern told him as he jotted down her address. "Should take it in if you make it up there. Quite a sight to see." The Old Man being the famous Old Man of the Mountain, a rock formation that was on nearly every state document you could think of. Being the history buff, Timmy knew all about it, maybe more than most his age, and how it, like most everything else in the country, was re-purposed from the Indigenous peoples' cultures to be put on driver's licenses and the like.

He wasn't thinking so much of the Old Man on the walk back from the bus depot to the campground. He was thinking of her. *Lethe.* At long last, he'd a name for his tormentor. He wished he'd more time to search the library or use Lil' Ern's internet and find out more. Her presence was growing stronger by the day, by the minute if he was being candid with himself. Lil' Ern had become something of a friend to him, thus putting him at risk. *I've lost two people to this… thing,* he thought. *I'm not going to lose another.*

Possible salvation had him lost in daydreams. Timmy thought of the future, *his* future, for the first time beyond the next day, beyond whether or not he'd get to be warm, dry, hungry, or sick from withdrawals. Perhaps it wasn't too late for him? If this Blue Witch was the real deal, then once freed from Lethe's curse, why couldn't he start a normal life? Be happy? Timmy vaguely recalled having family—distant cousins of his mother's—out in New Mexico. Why not there? Far from the ghosts of Hunter and Lily, far from Trooper Thompson.

Timmy saw himself going to college, studying his beloved history, taking a semester abroad and studying in Europe, South America, heck, why not down to Antarctica? He saw his graduation, all smiles and warmth. He even saw a small college job for himself, working his way up from instructor to tenured professor, teaching his passion to year after year of students. A wife. Children. The house and the dog. All there, waiting for him. Christ, it was so real, Timmy felt he could reach out and touch it, and if he did, it'd become just that: *real.* He heard the laughter of his children playing, of his wife welcoming him home, and wept.

"GAGNON, GET YOUR FUCKING HANDS UP!"

The daydreams still tugged at the corner of Timmy's mind as he turned to find Trooper Thompson aiming a very large gun at his face. He still wore a sheepish grin as the laughter of his children washed over to that of Lethe. She appeared behind Thompson, floating behind him as he advanced upon Timmy, her head thrown back in uproarious laughter.

You...

Timmy's thoughts went to mush as Thompson brought the butt of his pistol across his face. The gravel walkway was as gentle as a drunken husband's fist. The sky above shuddered. Blackness closed in. Timmy watched Thompson, smirking, as he slowly pulled his handcuffs out. Thompson kicked Timmy in the stomach and chest several times, laughing. Timmy couldn't hear it. He heard nothing at that point, saw nothing but Lethe.

She waved as he slipped into unconsciousness, where she'd be waiting.

TIMMY WAS BROUGHT TO THE BARRACKS FOR PROCESSING AND HOLDING, until such time when he could be brought before a judge to determine where he ought to be tried for the murder of Lily Calhoun. Processing him took an hour; Geoffrey grumbled as Thompson didn't lift a finger to help. All he did was *loom* over the prisoner, smirking and basking in a self-congratulatory pride that was borderline masturbatory. By the time Timmy was placed in a holding cell, it was past six o'clock. The barracks were down to a skeleton crew by then: two support staff, one dispatcher, and one additional trooper, a woman named Sullivan, who was going to be on patrol. Counting poor, forgotten Rob Cross, still in the interrogation room, that made for seven people besides Timmy in the building.

Six would not see the sun rise.

"HULLO. I'M HERE TO SEE ABOUT POSTING BAIL FOR THE KID Y'ALL BEAT up at the campground." Lil' Ern was so angry he had to focus on keeping his hands from shaking. He spoke with a deliberate cadence, choosing each word carefully as to not slip into cussing, which he knew would get him either tossed on his ass or riding the pine in a cell alongside Zack. *Or Timmy. Or whatever the hell his name is.*

The officer at the desk looked at Lil' Ern once, then picked up a phone and whispered into it. Done, the wormy-looking man went back to the all-too important business of working on the day's crossword puzzle. *Civil servants in action.* Lil' Ern sighed. His back ached and he wanted to get to bed, and would've long since been tucked in for the night if not for his goddamn good nature. After Timmy collected his final day's pay and said goodbye, Lil' Ern got to thinking: *If he's heading up to see Callie, well, why not close down for the day and drive him up there yourself, you big ding-dong?* He arrived at the campground just in time to witness Trooper Thompson slamming Timmy's head against the roof of his cruiser. By the time he got out of his car, they'd screamed away, leaving behind a shocked crowd of a dozen campers and the stench of burned rubber.

"Who are you?" Lil' Ern looked over to see Thompson fast-walking towards him. *Looks like a constipated bull,* Lil' Ern thought.

"Don't matter none. If you want, call me a *concerned citizen* here to see about springing that boy you beat up." Lil' Ern slowly pulled his wallet from his pants, never taking his eyes off Thompson who, he noticed, had moved his meaty hand from his buckle to the butt of his gun. Lil' Ern shook his head and pulled out his money. "Y'all *do* take cash, yes?"

"Mister. That *boy* you're talking about is a suspect in two murders," Thompson said. "There won't be any bail before he goes before the judge, and even if there is, it'll be more than you can afford."

"Don't tell me what I can and cannot afford, young man. You ain't my bookkeeper."

"No, I'm not. I'm the guy who'll be more than happy to slap your ass in a cold cell right next to your dear *boy* if you don't get the hell out of my barracks."

"Do you often threaten people like that? Does it make you feel *big*? Fill up that emptiness you got in that rather *large* body of yours? Well, young man, you go right on with your threats and your puffed up chest, keep that hand of yours sliding towards that iron of yours—yeah, I seen it—let's see how well it plays when you pull it on an elderly, unarmed man, seeking to ensure a friend gets justice."

Thompson's face turned crimson. Beads of sweat arched across his forehead. His breathing became that of the bull Lil' Ern equated him to. "You had him working for you, yeah? Under the table... the state might have an interest in that little arrangement, not to mention that he was a fugitive. Harboring one of them is a big *no-no*, even for an elderly man, such as yourself. Yeah, I think I can make some time for you, old man."

Thompson came around the desk and clapped his hand on Lil' Ern's shoulder, pulling him back into the barracks. Lil' Ern didn't say a word as Thompson marched him back and all but threw him into a chair at his desk. He didn't say a word as Thompson, sitting down, grinning from ear to ear, started asking him questions: about the track, his business, relationship with Timmy. This went on for an hour. Lil' Ern was about to ask if he was being detained because, if not, he was going to up and leave and go speak to Fred Herbert, the local lawyer he'd used now and then.

The violence came before he got the chance.

It started with a drip splashing on the top of Timmy's head. Timmy, head hung between his legs, trapped between personal hells, ran his hand through his hair, feeling the dampness. He glanced up, thinking that it would be well in character for him to be stuck in a cell with a leaky pipe overhead. Instead of a brown stain of water damage eating through the tile, he saw nothing but smooth white lines.

Another drip fell outside of his cell, inches before the bars, followed by another, and another still, until a steady downpour was born, the water falling out of nothing before Timmy's eyes. The puddle stretched across the floor in moments. He curled into a ball on the cold bench, his fingers clawing at the air before his eyes. Glimpses broke through of the places he'd visited in his dreams and feared. Teeth. Stone. Decay. The River.

"*...please...no...*"

"*Pretty.*"

Lethe rose from the puddle, the water coming together to create her form and give her life. She caressed the bars of the cell, moving her hands up and down them. The wretched sound that came from her claws meeting the metal caused Timmy's ears to start bleeding. She giggled as he retreated from her in the cell. She reached for him through the bars, her fingers greedy.

"*Pretty.*"

"What in the *hell?!*" Geoffrey stood in the hallway, dropping the bag of fast food he'd brought for Timmy's dinner, spilling lukewarm fries and chicken nuggets all over the floor. His beady eyes went wide at the sight of Lethe. His mouth quivered.

"RUN!" Timmy said.

Lethe took three steps and was pressed against Geoffrey. She plucked his glasses from his face, twisting them around, examining them as a curiosity before throwing them over her shoulder. She touched his arms, then his chest, finally placing her hands upon his face. Timmy screamed and banged on the bars of his cell, yelling for help, to snap the trooper out of his stupor. Geoffrey stared at Lethe with a sheepish, sleepy grin, lost to her rippling skin and smile. She stroked his cheeks, cocking her head at him. She grabbed a fistful of his hair from the back of his head and held him close to her lips, his own hovering before hers, teasing him with pleasures he'd never experienced in this life. Geoffrey moaned, desperate to taste her. Lethe turned to Timmy, giggling.

"...NONONONONONO!!"

Turning back to the beguiled Geoffrey, Lethe revealed her true self. The alluring beauty she wore as a shade lifted, revealing a bloated, hideous drowned corpse, mottled with skeins of putrefaction and blackened, marbled flesh. The illusion broke the hold over Geoffrey and, upon seeing her, smelling the decay and dampness, he screamed—but only for a moment before Lethe's hand pressed over his mouth. She spun him around and slammed him—face-first—into the bars of the cell door. She pulled him away and repeated this, her laughter mixing with the sound of flesh and bone colliding with the thick metal, each strike emanating a hollow *gong*. The door bent from the impact, squeaking against the rest of the cell. She continued until his skull cracked open, spraying blood and pieces of bone all over Timmy. Lethe held Geoffrey by the neck, regarding his lifeless body as if seeing it for the first time, before tossing him into the hall, where he slumped against the wall and collapsed facedown, his blood pooled around him.

The secondary trooper, a man named Eastman, came running, shotgun in the ready position. He was a veteran, saw some action in Desert Storm. Seeing Lethe and what she'd done to his colleague made him hesitate, but only for a moment. It was enough. Lethe ripped the gun from him, taking his entire arm along with it. He fell to his knees, clutching at the fleeing blood, attempting to shove it back inside of himself. His complexion turned pale, and Eastman passed out shortly thereafter, dying in his sleep as his blood drained out of him.

Lethe disappeared into the barracks then, leaving Timmy alone with the bloody corpses. He put his fingers in his ears and shut his eyes, but this futile gesture didn't keep out the reality of what she was doing. She used her hold over him to make him *see, hear,* and *feel* each and every thing she did to the rest of the people in the building. He smelled Rob Cross's piss and shit as he soiled himself upon seeing her. He felt his neck snap underneath her hand—*his* hand, too. He listened as the dispatcher tried to explain the situation over the radio, begging for help that wouldn't come in time, heard the panic rise in his voice, making it crack. Lethe opened the dispatcher's throat and pulled his tongue through the jagged, wet hole. She kept the *send* button on his microphone on, so the rest of the Staties' network could hear his damp death rattle.

Then, she turned on Lil' Ern.

"...*nonononononononono....please...*," Timmy whispered.

Lil' Ern tossed the folding chair he'd been sitting on at her. It bounced off her head with no evidence that she even felt it, save for her laughter, now deafening. Lil' Ern threw a loopy left hook at her, connecting only because she allowed him to. It amused her; Timmy felt it. All of the carnage, how cruel and pointless it was, how it made

Timmy sick to his stomach, Lethe was *enjoying* it. She let Lil' Ern hit her thrice more. The old man was panting and all but doubled over after missing with a fourth. He looked at her, epiphany shining in his eyes, eyes that had seen worse horrors than Lethe in the hills of Korea a lifetime prior, and spit at her feet.

"Go on then and be damned, you—"

Automatic gunfire ripped through Lil' Ern and Lethe both, the latter seemingly bemused by the sensation and the former having the majority of his face simply *eradicated* in a puff of bloody mist. Lil' Ern was dead before he hit the ground.

"NOOOOOOOOO!" Timmy screamed, beating his hands against the bars of his cell.

Lethe turned, showing Timmy the murderer of the only person in the world he'd considered a friend. Her laughter twisted Timmy's stomach into knots. Thompson held the AR-15 on her, the shock upon his face turning to fear as she advanced on him even as he kept firing. When the screaming started, he'd left Lil' Ern to his own devices and made a beeline for the weapons depot, grabbing the rifle and several magazines of ammunition. When the rifle clicked empty, Thompson struggled to slap a fresh magazine in. Lethe knocked it and the weapon from his hands and slashed his chest open with her claws. He fell to the ground with a bellow of enraged pain. Blood turned the olive drab of his uniform dark in seconds. He pressed against the wounds best he could—red squirted through his fingers in time with his increasingly fast heartbeat—and reached for his pistol. Lethe plucked this from him too. She knelt on his chest, laughing as he roared in pain. She dipped her claws in his blood and then drew circles upon his brow, playfully swirling them into the creases of his skin.

"...*bitch*...k-k-k-kill you...f-f-fuckin..."

Lethe put a finger to Thompson's lips, hushing him. She rose from his chest, changing from her grotesque true form back to that of the ethereal woman. Thompson, despite his pain, despite his rage, found her rather beautiful. The final thoughts he had before slipping into unconsciousness was the desire to possess her for his own.

She returned to Timmy's cell after finishing off the cowering support staff in equally cruel ways. She took the broken door in her hands and removed it from the cage as if it was made of paper. She threw it into the wall with such force it became embedded. There was nowhere for Timmy to go. She cocked her head as he screamed at her, pressing himself into the furthest corner of the cell from her. She made no motion to approach him.

"*Pretty.*" Lethe said. "*Mine.*"

And then, she was gone.

Everyone was dead. Backup troopers were surely on the way. Timmy couldn't explain what had happened. He'd find himself lying in a pool of his own blood filled with holes from the heavy guns of the troopers. Escape was the only thing he could think of. He had to get north, to Lil' Ern's niece. *The Blue Witch.*

Not knowing where they'd put his belongings, Timmy resorted to looting the bodies. Taking the bus was clearly out now; even if he wasn't covered in blood and wearing prisoner's orange, every cop in the state would be on the lookout for him. He froze, panicked as the doubt of a successful jailbreak (*Jesus…how could this have happened…*) crept from his mind into his limbs, leaving him half-crouched over the body of the dispatcher. The glint of the fluorescent lights overhead on something metal—the man's keys—snapped Timmy out of it. The parking lot was filled with perfectly serviceable police cruisers, ones that were fast and, if he figured out how to turn the lights on, every car on the road would get out of his way. If he put the pedal to the floor and kept it there, he could be at the Blue Witch's door in under an hour and a half; an hour if the cruiser could haul serious ass. A little luck and they'd not notice it was missing for a while. *When's the last time you had ANY luck?*

Timmy rose to leave when a moan, low and pained, stopped him. Thompson wasn't as dead as he looked. He was pale and the bleeding had only slowed, his body not yet able to clot the flow. His eyes were shut. He kicked out with one leg and held his hands over his face, his fingers twisted into claws. Looking at the other monster in his life, Timmy felt nothing. He knew Lil' Ern lay in a heap mere feet away due to this man. Lil' Ern, the most decent person Timmy had ever met, dead because of this...*fucking cop* playing action hero.

Lethe giggled in the back of his mind as Timmy picked up Thompson's discarded pistol. He aimed it at the man's face, not sure how to even operate it other than point-and-pull. Could he do it? *Why not?*

The gun wobbled as his arm shook. *It's the weight,* a voice not quite his own told him. *You're not used to it. Hold it up with both hands. There you are! Nice and steady now. Aim down those little sights on the top. Good. Right between the eyes. Good. A moment's courage, Timmy, and he's gone. A small bit of pressure and...*

"NO." Timmy pulled the gun off Thompson, tossing it away. "I'm not going to do it, you hear me, *Lethe?*"

The scar upon his chest, given to him the day she pressed Hunter Thurston deep into the ground, caught fire. Timmy fell to his knees as the scar blazed with hot blue flame. There was no pain—the flames didn't even sear through his shirt. Instead, there was vision. Through the fire, Lethe showed him things about Trooper Leslie Thompson, *secrets*. As the flames died out and Lethe released him from the sights, Timmy knew Thompson better than he'd ever known another human before. And he hated it.

"I see you now," he said. "Trooper Thompson, *sir*."

He left before the desire to kill the man returned. Lethe's presence was absent as he drove north to his hopeful salvation.

Timmy had never been more afraid.

CHAPTER
FOUR

The Blue Witch of the North, aka Sally Levesque, began her day with the usual: confirming upcoming appointments, getting her herbs and crystals prepared for the day, checking emails. Banal tasks that the everyday small business owner had to do. Sally didn't mind them, but she wished she'd made enough money to hire on someone to do it for her so she could focus on the fun things; the readings, her Tarot, things that interested her. She was about to take her tea and then enter into some meditation out near her favorite tree when the police car raced up her driveway, skidding to a halt on the gravel. Her breath caught in her chest as she watched the flashing blue lights swirl around the hillside, her thoughts going towards the "special" mushrooms hidden underneath her bed and the eighth of marijuana in the dresser, not to mention the paraphernalia scattered about the back of her double-wide. She relaxed upon seeing the lights switch off, cursing herself for being a worrywart. Her modest grow was deep in the woods, unseen on the mountainside. Whatever this cop was here for, it wasn't her personal use illicit substances. Still, rather than give the officer an excuse to come inside and poke around, Sally threw on a sweater, put her dyed-blue hair in a messy ponytail, and stepped out on the porch to speak to the cop.

"Morning," she called, voice betraying none of her anxiety. Those who knew her said her smile could win over the hardest of hearts, a trait she used to her advantage in business and life. "Is there something I can help—"

Seeing the orange-clad boy covered in blood exit the car sent Sally running back inside. She slammed against the door, pressing her ninety-pound frame against it. The boy pounded on the door, screaming to see the Blue Witch. Sally fumbled with the chain lock, unable to make her hands perform the simple task of sliding it into place. *Oh God...Oh Christ, he's got a gun!*

The door burst inwards, knocking Sally to the floor. Her shoulder collided with her loveseat, causing a loud pop, followed by agony. Through a film of tears, she watched Timmy Gagnon stepping over the wrecked door, the shotgun gripped by the stock and held loosely at his hip, the barrel dancing near Sally's face.

"At last," Timmy said. A smile born of relief and sorrow found its way upon his face. "I need your help."

"Wh...what?"

"You *are* the Blue Witch? I need you to get to witching and get this *goddamn* curse lifted from me."

THE BLEEDING HAD, BY AND LARGE, CEASED BY THE TIME THOMPSON screamed onto the highway, heading north. His uniform stuck to his wounds, matting into his flesh, which had already the long, hard process of knitting his body back together. It hurt to move. Christ, even blinking was a goddamn chore. The paramedics tried to stop him when he awoke on the stretcher, but he wasn't a man to be deterred; even punched one of them in the face when he tried to push him down.

North. To that little bumfuck town outside Franconia. That's where he needed to be.

Thompson couldn't quite recall how he'd gotten hurt. The drive was lifting the fog, but not all the way. He remembered bringing in the Gagnon kid—*Kid? No. A...SHIT. Yeah, I like that. The Gagnon SHIT*— and starting to figure out which paperwork he could pawn off on Trooper Wogen (whom, last he saw, was a red, squishy mess on the floor) when that old fart came in and got in his face. After that, it wasn't so clear. Pictures of this and that: screaming, scattered gunfire, blood. Blinking sweat from his eyes (he couldn't stop, no matter how high he cranked the A/C), Thompson saw his house, the latest model ship he was halfway complete with (a *USS Indianapolis*), and then of himself, younger, thinner, at some kind of party, standing in a darkened room looking down at...*someone?*

Doesn't matter.

He knew where the Gagnon Shit (*heeheehee*) was heading. *How? Doesn't matter.* He'd find him and serve him justice. The old kind. Thompson smirked through the pain, wiping his brow with the back of his beefy forearm. The Shit would pay for those he hurt. How he got out of his cell and got to the gun locker, he didn't know. *Wogen probably handed over his keys,* he thought. *Trying to save his own scrawny ass. Didn't work out so good for you, did it, Wogen?*

Still, Thompson was surprised that the Shit killed that old fart. Even a mad dog needs friends now and then, don't they?

Wait...no. D-did it go down that way?

Thompson heard giggling—a woman's. He pushed the brakes to the floor, bringing the car to a skidding halt in the middle of the highway. Panting, he whipped his head 'round so fast, his neck muscles popped and seized. "W-who's there?" he said. The backseat, behind its protective cage, couldn't answer him.

The giggling came round once more, then vanished. Thompson blinked, rubbing his aching neck. He started the car again, pointing it towards the address where he needed to be. The directions were clear in his head, so much so he didn't need to have his map out on the passenger's seat, even though he couldn't explain *how* he knew them. The old fart said fuck-all before the Shit blew his head off, trying to hit Thompson.

I'm coming, Gagnon Shit. I'm coming.

"WHAT THE HELL ARE YOU DOING?"

"Smudging."

"Smudging?"

Sally's hand shook as she waved a white crystal the size of a ruler over Timmy. She kept glancing towards the door, to where the phone used to be before Timmy smashed it to pieces with the butt of the shotgun. *Keep it together, keep it together,* she repeated the mantra, one of many simple ones she utilized in her daily meditations (the other main was *Do No Harm, Leave Only Good,* but that rang hollow to her with a bloody, gun-toting man in her home). "This wand is cleansing your aura. When I sweep it off you it's like giving you a good brushing."

"Grooming for the soul?" Timmy said, a heavy sigh lurking behind his words.

"Something like that."

"And this really works?"

"It's one thing that could work, yes," Sally said. "You've not given me much to go on."

"I told you. It's complicated."

"Lying breeds bad energy. It's like junk food for a curse."

"Stop it. Stop this…waving around bullshit!" Timmy slapped the crystal from Sally's hand. She recoiled, walking backwards until her back hit a bureau. Timmy matched her, step for step, keeping the shotgun folded against his chest. "I am not here for the shit you hawk to tourists. I need *real* magic, do you understand? What's got hold of me has hurt…*killed*…I need it gone or banished or whatever."

"I-I don't understand!"

Timmy grabbed Sally by the wrist, twisting it behind her back. She screamed and flailed as he marched her through the trailer into a spare bedroom that Sally converted into an arts and crafts room.

An easel with a half-completed pencil sketch stood in the middle of the room, while the walls were adorned with dozens of paintings and drawings. Timmy sat Sally down at her computer desk and stomped around the room, eyes darting in his head, grunting like a starved animal until he found what he was seeking. He ripped the frame right out of the wall, sending motes of sheetrock into the air. He shoved the picture in Sally's face, pressing so hard, it caused her nose to bleed.

"THIS," Timmy said. "TELL ME ABOUT THE FOREST."

Sally blinked as the picture, her picture, came into focus. Trees made from rock, stone, and hideous, drooling teeth stretched out across a bleak horizon. Large planets and alien stars loomed overhead, staring down at the forest like malevolent eyes of angry, forgotten gods. "Th-this?"

"What is it? WHAT THE FUCK IS IT??"

"IT'S F-FROM A GAME!! A VIDEO GAME!"

"...what?"

"I-it's c-called *Curse of Gurthang*. It's one of the levels. I p-play it online."

"You're lying."

"No! I swear...i-it's where..."

"Where what?"

"...It's where the monsters are born."

Timmy dropped the picture and staggered backwards. He sank to the ground, deflated, laying the shotgun across his lap. Somewhere, deep within him, Lethe laughed at him. "...That's impossible...I've *been* there...I've seen the Forest...walked through it, with *her*...to that river, that one you've drawn that's hanging right over there."

"Th-that's not possible."

"And yet, it seems that it is. Lethe."

"Lethe?"

"That's her name. The one who's cursed me or *marked* me or whatever. She's been with me since I was nine years old. Killed my friend, my maybe-girlfriend, a whole lot of people down south." Timmy hesitated. If he told Sally that her uncle was amongst the dead, that he was partially responsible for it, then there'd be nothing to get her to help him, not even further threats of violence. *Could I do it?* He pulled his shirt down, showing Sally his claw marks. "Gave me this reminder. I don't know what she wants, why she chose me. All I know is she loves to see me suffer; craves it, I think. I can't go on like this…in misery, waiting for her to hurt more people. That's why I need you, Blue Witch of the North. Not to wave rocks over me, but to do some for reals magic, to fight this…monster and send her back to the Forest for good."

"Lethe isn't a person or a monster. It's a river."

Timmy nodded. "Makes sense…yeah. The water, the way her features kind of…wash over, like the current…a river…"

"But, it—"

"What?"

"Nothing." Sally held her breath, forcing the knowledge that it too was purely a myth, to stay inside her head. Whoever this guy was, he was sick. *Don't set him off by shooting off your mouth, Sally.* "The river Lethe is one of the major rivers of the underworld. It's said that all souls who find themselves there are supposed to drink from it before they can move on."

"What happens when you drink from it?"

"I-I don't know. Look, it's old, *ancient*, right? Lots of room for interpretation."

Timmy took the shotgun from his lap and aimed the barrel at Sally. "What's *your* interpretation then?"

"I…The river itself is about oblivion, where you go to wash away whatever or whomever you were in life. Doing this, you accept oblivion and sink in deep, knowing nothing else but the river for the rest of eternity."

"It's a punishment?"

"Maybe. If you asked me before today, I'd have said that it was more about letting go."

"Letting go?"

"All the trivial things about life. Once you get to the river, those things aren't supposed to matter anymore, so you drink or bathe in it, and move on to whatever is next for you."

"…It's in Hell?"

"Hell is a Christian construct and a true myth." The contempt in Sally's voice came out as a reflex, as if she were blinking or breathing. She dealt with being called a Devil-worshipper or Bride of Satan her entire life, and it never, *ever* ceased to infuriate her. So angered was she, that she didn't notice Timmy's grip on the shotgun tighten, his finger inch closer to the trigger. "The underworld is different. It's not about being punished. Whatever energy you put out into the land of the living is revisited upon you there. So, if you were mediocre, but not really bad or good, you'd drink from the river and fuck off to a giant meadow and wander about."

"And if you did bad?"

"Listen, this is one of *many, many* theories and m—*stories* about death and what comes afterwards. Things like this have been handed down way back to the oral tradition. We simply cannot know what is truth, not until we die, I suppose."

"Oh. It's real, all right. I've smelled the blood it's spilled."

"...*If* this...*entity* is real and has laid a claim on you, there are things that we can try to cast it out and send it back to the place it came from, the Forest of Stone and Teeth. We can create a Mirror Box and trap its essence within, or we can create a poppet or—or a talisman that will deflect Lethe from revealing herself to you on this plane. If that doesn't work, we—"

"I thought that was just a video game."

"I-I...This is all *very* scary to me, okay? Forgive me if it's a lot to take in."

"...I'm sorry," Timmy said. "For all of it."

"I..."

"I never should have come here," Timmy said. He wept, for he knew now what he had to do to make it all stop. "You didn't deserve this. None of you did, except for that shitheel cop anyway."

After it was done, Timmy walked outside and onto Sally's lawn. *You were right, Lil' Ern. That's a beautiful view of the Old Man.*

TIMMY WAS STILL LOOKING AT THE MOUNTAIN WHEN THOMPSON arrived.

"Gagnon Shit." Thompson was weary. A slight fever had set in on the drive up, a drive in which he kept the pedal to the floor and ignored every request for a status update that came over the wire. He was slick with sweat and blood. He didn't care. His grip on his pistol remained firm, his intent true.

"You ever see it like this? The Old Man of the Mountain?"

"What?" Thompson barked a laugh equal parts mockery and anxiety.

"I've lived in New Hampshire my entire life—short as it was—and this is the first time I'm seeing it. Oh sure, I've seen pictures galore. They can't quite capture the *majesty* though. It's something else. Nature has such beauty. Too bad we don't stop and appreciate it."

Thompson fired three times. The echoes were louder than the shots, rolling down the hillside, carrying all the way up to the Old Man and his ears of granite. Two of the bullets hit Timmy in the stomach, while the third struck him in the sternum. Blood streamed out of the wounds, soaking through his clothes and dripping down his legs and covering his shoes. He did not fall or look anything other than somewhat put out from them. Thompson blinked fever sweat from his eyes. "What the fuck?"

"The Abenaki call him Stone Face. Did you know that? The Mohawk say he is the spirit of a great chief who brought peace to their people through the love for a woman from one of the warring tribes. She left to visit someone and he died and his spirit became the Old Man, watching the horizon for his lost love for all time. History is neat like that."

Thompson shot twice more. The bullets ripped through Timmy and once more, he showed no signs of hurt. "Won't you fucking die, Gagnon Shit?!"

"I wanted to be a history teacher. Go to college. Learn as much as I could and try and teach that to kids. ... That would've been nice.

But, Lethe had other ideas for me." Timmy shrugged and turned back to look at the Old Man. "I'd not waste any more bullets, *Trooper Thompson, sir.* She won't let me die."

"*She?*"

"Lethe."

Thompson slid his pistol back into its holster. He shuffled his feet, trying to build up the nerve to rush Timmy, tackle him to the ground, and beat him to death. *Like a man,* he thought. *I don't need a gun to take you out, Gagnon Shit.* "I'm an officer of the law. You killed all those people, starting with that boy back in the eighties."

"Hunter. His name was Hunter Thurston, and he was my friend."

"Some friend. What'd you do with the body? Hid it *real* nice that we never found it. Imagine the bones are in some bear's den somewhere by now."

"Lethe took him. Pushed him straight into the ground, and into the Forest, I imagine."

"Sure she did."

"She did it because Hunter was in love with me. I didn't quite know what that was when I was nine. I knew *of* it, but I didn't understand the different forms it can take. I...I think that, maybe, I could have been happy...with Hunter."

Thompson spit bloody phlegm onto the ground. "I don't care, Gagnon Shit. Maybe you didn't kill that boy or maybe you did. I *know* you killed the Calhoun girl; found your prints and your spunk all over that car."

"Lethe..."

"Sure, sure, *Lethe* did it. Did she kill all those people at the barracks too?" Thompson pointed towards Sally's trailer, the windows acting as eyes, watching over the events unfolding on the front lawn. "She kill that one too?"

"No."

"No, *what?* Gagnon Shit."

"No, *Trooper Thompson, sir,*" Timmy said. "I killed Sally...I think.

"...I aimed the gun at her. I had my finger around the trigger. I don't think I *wanted* her dead, but she's dead nonetheless. Whether or not I squeezed the trigger or if it went off by pure accident...*Trooper Thompson, sir*, I can't honestly tell you."

"Lying sack of shit," Thompson said. "I'm going to put my fists through that lying face of yours until I bury your teeth in the ground."

"Goddamn you, aren't you *listening* to me? No, of course not! You had your mind made up about me the first time you saw me as a scared little boy. I was your white whale, wasn't I? Your John Dillinger? Pathetic."

Thompson rushed Timmy, screaming not words but guttural, vile sounds of hatred. Timmy turned his head slightly, looking towards the Old Man of the Mountain, taking in its beauty as Thompson tackled him. Thompson clambered on top of him until his knees were over his shoulders. He screamed as he brought his fists down on Timmy's face, again, and again, and again.

"DIE, GAGNON SHIT!" Thompson screamed in a voice not quite his own. Fear crept up and down his spine as Timmy failed to react from each punch. No tears, no cries of pain, only blood, and even that seemed to be an afterthought, even after Thompson broke Timmy's nose apart, splattering a crimson-stained blossom on his face.

"Wh—what the fuck *are* you..."

Timmy clasped his hand around Thompson's bloody knuckles. Thompson felt his entire body go rigid. His eyes rolled back in his head. He couldn't move, couldn't breathe. Everything turned white and gray, swirling into thick clouds until he stood in a darkened room, a room that he'd not set foot in since...

No.

"Yes, *Trooper Thompson, sir*."

Lying on a bed was a teenaged girl, sixteen if she was a day. On the bedside table, and spilling onto the floor, were empty cans of beer. Passed out on her stomach, she had her arms crossed over her face, content to sleep off the pursuits of youth, and surely would've done so and woken up with a bad hangover and possible prayer session with the porcelain god if not for another presence within the room. Leslie Thompson's face was the same at sixteen as it was when he'd met Timmy, save for slightly thinner around the jowls. The cruelty remained the same, gleaming and piercing. This time, it gazed on the unconscious girl as his portly fingers undid his belt.

The scene changed as his younger self climbed on top of the girl, to that of a slightly older version of Thompson harassing a classmate in the hallway of a school. Each boy wore a crewcut and a matching sweatsuit, the front emblazoned with the school's name (Underwood Military Academy) and logo (a griffin spewing fire). The boy Thompson bullied, a bespectacled, scrawny kid with a face covered in freckles, was ignoring the taunts, seeking only to protect a package wrapped in brown paper. They reached a flight of metal stairs and, as the boy tried to push past Thompson, he let his foot slip in front of the boy's legs. The boy fell, soaring through the air down towards where the unyielding metal greeted him. A hollow *clung* sound echoed up the stairwell from his head striking it. Thompson pulled the package, the precious item the boy wished to protect more than anything, from the boy's grip as he fell. He watched the boy's face as he fell, their eyes locking and holding each other close despite the distance between them. A stirring in his chest and his groin, equal parts horror at his actions and excitement for doing so, propelled Thompson's legs of their own accord away from the accident and up to his dorm room where he sat at his desk, staring at the package until the sun rose the next morning. It was then that he realized no one was coming to question or detain him. It was then that he opened the package. A model kit: that of an old Model T Ford, lay underneath the brown paper. Thompson opened the box and went to work, skipping the day's courses and mealtimes in order to finish it. Once done, he found himself weeping. It was the first time in his entire life he'd created something beautiful. Of the boy the model belonged to, Thompson heard he suffered a bleed in his brain and ended up in a home that catered to those who could no longer care for themselves.

The image faded and Thompson found himself in a swirl of fog.
"...W—How..."

"Do you think about that boy every time you complete one of your little models? Do you think of that girl whenever you fuck?"

Thompson turned, surprised to find Timmy standing upright behind him, staring into the heavy swirls of fog. Every wound Thompson had inflicted was healed, down to the bloodstains in his county-issued orange clothes. "I bet you do. Makes you feel the way you did when you got away with it."

"GET OUT OF MY HEAD!"

"We're not in your head. She showed me that, back at the barracks; Lethe. I think she was trying to get me to kill you then, and as much as I wanted to, I couldn't do it. I couldn't kill until the Blue Witch of the North an—and I'm not even sure if I meant to. You see, *Trooper Thompson, sir,* that's what Lethe wants from me, it's what she desired when she peeked through the cracks the river carved between our worlds. Lethe *is* oblivion, despair. She wanted me to embrace that, revel in it. Then, and only then, would she call me home."

"H-home?"

"Back to the river," Timmy said. "You never should have followed me. The consequences are yours and yours alone. Goodbye, *Trooper Thompson, sir.* Maybe you'll find a way home, but you'll never see me again."

Timmy walked into the mist. Thompson stared at his silhouette, growing fainter with each soundless step he took. He didn't understand it, *any* of it. His only friend, his *oldest* friend, anger remained with him, an old blanket comforting him. While it couldn't help him make any sense of what he'd just witnessed, experienced, it could help him with other things. *Gagnon Shit,* he thought, smirking as he pulled his pistol out, knowing in his heart of hearts that his aim would be true, that nothing would stop the bullets from ending Timmy Gagnon once and for all.

"I'd save those were I you," Timmy said. "You might need them where you're going."

The fog lifted, taking Timmy along with it. In its place was a vast forest, filled not with trees of wood, but of stone and teeth. The gun fell limp against Thompson's leg. His mouth hung agape. He stood in a clearing devoid of any life, only rock and granite-colored dirt. The trees tightened around him, their impossible branches moaned, sounding like obscenities being scrawled into a church window. Unseen things moved around behind them, staring at Thompson with baleful eyes. There was but one path forward, a narrow footfall with broken canines and bicuspids laying on the ground like fallen leaves, writhing in agony with their roots flailing for an anchor.

"I-is this...hell?"

No. This is where the monsters are born.

Weeping, Thompson walked into the Forest of Stone and Teeth. The grotesquery closed its curtains of saliva-stained rock behind him.

LETHE ROSE FROM THE MUD AND SHALLOW PUDDLES OF THE RIVERBED, greeting Timmy Gagnon with a smile and open arms. Gone was any pretense; she appeared to him as she was: a bloated, drowned thing beautiful to none.

Timmy stripped naked, feeling his burdens lift. The water only came up to his ankles. It was lukewarm and felt oily to the touch. Lethe embraced him, smelling of decay and insects. Timmy found himself not caring. It wasn't so bad.

"*Pretty,*" Lethe whispered into his ear. "*Mine.*"

They sank past the mud and into the hidden waters underneath. The water was clean, clear, and glowed with a blue light of which the source could not be determined. Timmy wasn't sure if he'd died or was still living. The water entered his nose and mouth, filling his lungs and stomach, but he did not hurt. Nothing did.

He was pulled further down by Lethe until they came to a grotto of stone and vegetation, warped and twisted. The leaves wrapped themselves around his legs, torso, and arms, holding him in place as the river churned around him. Lethe took his face in her hands and then, vanished.

Next to Timmy was a small boy. He stared ahead, eyes wandering this way and that, seeing everything and nothing all at once. He looked at Timmy and smiled, empty and devoid of emotion. Timmy knew this boy, once. What was his name?

What's my name? Does it matter?

...No. I rather think not.

The man who was once Timmy Gagnon, lover of history and books, floated in the river Lethe, underneath the Forest of Stone and Teeth, having forgotten everything and anything that came before. Oblivion was all that mattered.

CLICK CLACK

BY WILLIAM D. CARL

CHAPTER
❄ ONE

Click. Clack.

The sound reached Jonas through the cloudy miasma of a deep sleep, something tapping in the corner of a dream yet intruding upon the real world. Or perhaps it was the creaking resonance of reality interrupting his slumber. He lifted an eyelid, confirmed the expected darkness of the middle of the night and the familiar surroundings of his bedroom. He opened his other eye, taking in the space, wondering just what had awakened him, as he was usually a heavy sleeper. Across the room was his bookshelf, his desk with his laptop and speakers situated next to it, his folders and papers neatly tucked away from sight within drawers. His closet doors remained sensibly closed, and his heavy curtains prevented nearly all moonlight from invading the room. The other side of the queen-sized bed was empty. He ran a hand over the space, remembering times when it had been occupied. The sheets were cold to the touch and he winced.

Goddammit.

He thought he heard something again, an adjacent timbre, soft enough to have come from outside. He was alert now, vigilant and curious. Raising himself from his supine position, he switched on the bedside lamp. The small cone of light illuminated a third of the room while the rest remained veiled in darkness. No intruders; nothing had fallen from its place, like a book from the shelf or a pen from the desk.

But there had definitely been a sound, something just to the perceptible side of discernment. The idea of an unfamiliar noise interrupting his sleep while he was quite alone in the countryside pricked at him, like sharp fingernails pulling at stitches, and he felt his attentiveness sharpen. He got out of bed, crossed the room, and turned on the overhead light, eliminating any shadows where something could hide. Jonas knew he wouldn't be able to get back to sleep until he puzzled out what had made the racket; he'd watched far too many thrillers involving home invasions. He was wide awake, and his pulse beat in his ears, a trip-hammer of anxiety.

Moving through the house, he exited the bedroom and shifted into the short hallway. Across it, he turned on the lights to the bathroom, ascertaining there was nothing awry in the small white-tiled room. At the end of the hallway, the rooms split—kitchen and dining room to the left, living room to the right. Directly ahead of Jonas was the door to the basement. After he'd checked out the two larger rooms and discovered nothing, he opened the basement door and descended the steps. Washer, dryer, hot water heater, furnace—all was as it should be. Boxes were stored on raised plastic platforms, each meticulously labelled in black sharpie as to its contents. Christmas decorations, clothes meant to be donated, old DVDs and CDs. There were half as many boxes as there had been two weeks ago.

When Brad's possessions had nestled side by side with his own.

Shrugging, he headed back upstairs. Maybe he had dreamed the noise. He'd taken a couple melatonin gummies before bed, and he'd certainly had enough on his mind to trigger an auditory hallucination.

He couldn't stop thinking about Brad now. The way he had left. The unknown factors in the entire process of being dumped by a boyfriend of eight years. Even with their age difference, there were more similarities than differences. *Sometimes,* he told himself, *it's better not to know the details. Sometimes it's easier to remain in the dark.*

Having discovered nothing awry in the house, he passed through the kitchen and peered into the garage. Shelves of tools and boxes full of who-knew-what lined the walls, and a pool of oil had collected under where Brad's Honda had once parked. Once again, he could sense nothing out of the ordinary, nothing that could have made a sound so loud or unusual as to awaken him from his sleep.

Perhaps, it was outside. An animal in the garbage? A car turning around in his driveway?

Jonas pulled a pair of gray sweatpants over his boxer briefs and a RISD T-shirt over his chest. The shirt was beginning to get tight around his middle, and he reminded himself to start working out and eating right again. He'd been dumped, and two months was enough time to mourn while eating a pint of ice cream as his dinner every evening. He would need to lose this encroaching paunch if he was to be single again, if he was to attempt dating again, putting himself out there in a vulnerable position. It terrified him, especially at his age of fifty-four, ancient for a single gay man in New England, and he briefly considered saying "Fuck it" and growing old and fat, alone in his comfortable house in a comfortable sweatsuit eating all the ice cream he could stomach.

Stepping outside, Jonas switched on the exterior lights which flooded the front yard and driveway. He shook the phone in his hand, activating the flashlight. He scanned the area, moved to the side of the house where the garbage cans stood, covered and upright. Nothing had been bothered. Everything was in its place.

This is what happens when you move to the country, he thought. *Only one other house within miles, these two houses settled so far into the woods and away from the highway. It breeds paranoia.*

And yet...

Deep breath. Let it out and count to twenty like Dr. Shapiro suggested.

And yet, he felt the hairs standing up one by one on the back of his neck, a prickling sensation, goose pimples on his skin. A cool wind blew, and the towering pine trees that eclipsed his backyard on two sides swayed and swooshed in the breeze. They whispered to each other, secrets exchanged in the wind.

Suddenly, he was certain someone was observing him. He could feel the gaze of the hidden observer, someone watching with an intensity his skin detected easily. More goose bumps.

"Hello?" he said, his voice cracking in an embarrassing manner. "Anyone out here?"

He still felt as if someone was watching him, but he couldn't see anyone within view. He squinted, peered into the thick forest behind the house, but there was no one hiding in the shadows. His only neighbor's house, situated to the left, also seemed quiet. Mark Lyons and his wife Millie had lived in that house for thirty years, while Jonas had only owned his place for six. Their yard was immaculate, the grass mowed in perfectly positioned diagonal lines. The flower beds blossomed under Mrs. Lyons's dotage, although a few were beginning to wilt with the threat of the oncoming Autumnal weather. Mark was even building a stone wall around his territory using only stones and rocks he discovered on the weekly hikes he took to, in his own words, keep the old ticker pumping. It was still a work in progress, standing only about two feet high, but it was really starting to take form. He had managed to get the wall the entire way back to the woods, separating Jonas's yard from theirs. It had to be at least thirty feet in length, even though anyone could step right over it, moving from one yard to the other.

Jonah spied something pale on his side of the wall, a single stone, granite by the looks of it, about a foot by a foot and a half, glowing in the blue moonlight. It lay next to the wall on Jonas's side. He wondered if the stone had fallen, giving in to gravity and flopping onto the grass which, he shamefully noted, needed a good trimming. He wondered if that would have been loud enough to notice inside his house.

Jonas placed his phone in his sweatpants pocket and hefted the stone from the ground to the top of the wall. He saw the gap created when it had fallen, and he shoved it back into the slot where it fit nicely.

The stone was very cold to the touch, and there was a slick film enveloping it, probably some kind of lichen or moss. Mark Lyons wasn't worried about where he got the stones, but only that he was going to have a wall like so many other rural homes in Rhode Island. Jonas wiped his hands on his t-shirt.

This had to be the answer. The stone had slipped from its moorings and fallen to the earth with a thud. That's what had awakened him. That was the noise he had heard.

Only, he mused, *it hadn't sounded like a thud. More like something scraping, tapping. Like two stones tapping each other producing a clicking sound.*

He took a deep breath, relishing the cool September air. He could almost taste the crisp tones of Autumn coming on after a long, hot summer—apples, burning leaves. He was hit by a wave of nostalgia for his youth when the changing colors of the leaves had meant Halloween was coming, not the endless cycle of raking and mulching that preoccupied his Fall as an adult.

Brushing off his hands, Jonas turned and started back to the house. He'd taken a dozen steps before he heard the noise again, definitely coming from behind him. A scraping sound, a tapping. Click. Clack. Click.

And simultaneously, he felt someone's eyes upon him again. There was somebody behind him. He sensed it even as he stopped in his tracks. He caught the faint scent of something almost tangible, something darkly familiar.

He spun, hoping to catch the interloper by the short stone fence, possibly kicking the stones from their places.

"Aha!" he shouted.

But there was nobody there. The yard was empty. The pine trees whispered their riddles to each other.

Jonas headed back into his half-empty house to his half-empty bed and spent the rest of the hour in a bad space in his own head. He switched positions, tried with and without the blanket, chewed a couple more melatonin gummies, but he didn't fall back to sleep for several hours.

Outside, the stones vibrated and palsied, and the clamor they made was too muffled to hear inside the house, within his dreams.

CHAPTER

TWO ❄

Jonas had moved into the little ranch house six years ago, just when he and Brad had decided to attempt living together for a while. Marriage was still a distant notion, but they had moved beyond the "meet me at the bar" stage of their courtship, and he had wanted to see his boyfriend every morning and every night before bed. It had been good—really good. Until it wasn't.

In so many ways, the two men were opposites. Jonas was dark complected with short hair and comforting brown eyes. He stood six foot two inches and had a tight runner's body. At least, he'd boasted one at that time. Brad was short, a fireplug of sheer muscle with light blonde hair and Nordic features. They'd somehow hit it off after they met at an author's reading up in Plainville, Massachusetts. Despite their contradictory appearances, they discovered they read many of the same books (suspense and genre), adored the same movies (anything made before 1990, please), and firmly stood on the same side of the political spectrum. They laughed all the time with each other. They made dinner and went out and visited with friends. They were the couple every gay pairing aspired to be. An ideal.

Then, one day in late August, Brad pulled out boxes and a tape gun and packed his things, told Jonas he no longer wanted to be with him. He'd been preparing all day while Jonas was at work, and he surprised him with the announcement.

"But, why?" Jonas had pleaded. "Everything seems so perfect."

Brad had looked at the floor, shook his mane of golden hair, and shrugged. "This isn't what I want," he replied.

"I'll change," Jonas said. "I can become who you want, what you want. Just give me some guidance and I'll become whatever you need."

"It doesn't work that way."

"Did I do something wrong?"

"Well, you didn't do anything wrong, but none of this feels right to me. I don't know, Jonas. It's just time for me to move on. Maybe, it's time for you to move on as well. You don't know it yet, but this will be a positive thing."

"No, it won't," Jonas said, the tears finally arriving. "No! We were good together. I couldn't have been hallucinating."

"You were."

"It's the age difference, isn't it?" Jonas had twenty years of life experience more than Brad, and he recognized he had lived through so much Brad had missed—the AIDS crisis when his friends had all died, wasting away in hospital beds, the horrible Ronald Reagan administration, *Victor/Victoria*, for Christ's sake! It had never seemed to matter, but maybe his experience hadn't prepared him for the vicissitudes of youth.

Jonas had growled, thrown his hands into the air. "I give you everything! I bought this house so we could live together."

"Yes, you bought us a house. Way out in bumfuck nowheresville. I mean, Smithfield is a few miles away, but ... it's Smithfield! I feel isolated out here."

"We can move ..."

"It isn't only the location, Jonas. It's us. There's something lacking. There's a network of holes in the very base of this relationship, and it's all going to collapse on itself sooner or later. I am choosing sooner."

"Don't..."

He left. He loaded up a moving van with his possessions and he abandoned Jonas, alone with his crippling regrets, his second-thoughts, and his suddenly too-large house. Jonas had wept, had raged, had screamed until Mrs. Lyons had intervened from next door with a gigantic chocolate cake (which they had dutifully devoured together) and videos of 1980s slapstick comedies. By the time he was bloated with cake and watching *Airplane!* again, Jonas was feeling a little better. Mrs. Lyons, fifteen years older than he was, fifteen years wiser than he was, gave him a kiss on his forehead and left him alone.

And he had been all right, overall. The Lyons, his only neighbors for miles, checked on him at regular intervals, and he had his work as a copy editor which kept him busy. He even had thoughts of adopting a dog from the local shelter for company, but he had put aside such ideas until he was better grounded. He had been making definite progress.

Until this evening when something woke him and he had noticed the empty side of his bed and he had never felt so very, very alone. He thought he would take a look out back again, scope out the landscape, so he stepped out of bed and went to the back patio.

The overwhelming quiet of the backyard and the surrounding woods calmed him a bit, and he shut his eyes, inhaling the pine odor riding the breeze. He slowly let out the breath, inhaled again. Calm, balanced, tranquil.

The hairs on the back of his arms raised, and he had the unnerving sensation that he was once again being watched. He knew it was ridiculous; this wasn't a rational or explainable feeling. And yet, he knew there was someone watching him. He shivered; the breeze suddenly chilling him.

A twig snapped, and he opened his eyes to see Mark Lyons stepping over to the short stone wall separating them. Jonas exhaled with relief. It had merely been the old guy next door.

"Hello," Mark said with a half-hearted wave. "Can't you sleep? The missus and I were having problems with it tonight."

"I thought I heard something out here," Jonas explained, the ridiculousness of the situation overwhelming him. "Thought raccoons had gotten into the trash cans or something."

"Millie said the same thing. Got me out of bed to patrol the place and make sure. You know how she can be—a little too nervous for her own good. So, she hears something and I investigate and once again ... nothing."

"There was a stone that fell off the wall," Jonas said and pointed out the piece of the fence he'd replaced. "Fell right into my yard, but I don't think it would have startled anyone awake."

"Ah, the stones."

It seemed a strange thing to say, but Jonas let it slide. He said, "I believe I'll try to get back to sleep. Working on a new campaign, and the morning's going to come early."

"Ayuh, I'm with you there. Say, would you like to come to dinner tomorrow night? Oh wait, tonight? Say seven-o-clock? I'll have Millie make a spread. She could use the distraction."

"Sure. I'd appreciate a meal that didn't come from a microwave."

"Fine," Mark said with a grin. He touched the barrier with his toe, and it appeared to Jonas he was trying to show the wall remained solid. "We'll see you about seven."

"Want me to bring anything?"

"Just yourself," the neighbor said, turning and vanishing into his house. "See you then."

Jonas headed inside and closed the sliding door behind himself. He took another glance at the backyard, but he still saw nothing disturbing, so he switched off the lights and went back to bed. To his surprise, he immediately fell asleep and remained that way until the morning.

CHAPTER
THREE

J onas spent the next day working diligently at the new campaign he'd been granted, a print splash for a new line of pens aimed at the well-heeled schmucks who could afford a two-hundred dollar writing device. It was fun work, and it distracted him. He only thought about Brad when he had sipped his coffee in the morning, a daily ritual they had shared. Before he knew it, the day had passed and he was showering, getting ready for the dinner at his neighbors' house.

He liked the Lyons, even though they were quite a bit older and didn't have a lot in common with a middle-aged gay commercial artist who came from Boston. They were Rhode Islanders through and through, drinking coffee milk once a day, bemoaning the loss of the Pawsox, a local minor league baseball team. They were so essentially Rhode Island that Mark was creating this stone fence with his own hands and not hiring someone to do it for him. You could cut their accents with a knife; Mrs. Lyons sometimes reminded him of a longshoreman. But, like most of the residents of the Ocean State, they exuded a kindness and a distinctly Rhody sort of progressive compassion toward others. They had arrived at his doorstep on the first day he and Brad moved into the place, offering fresh baked cinnamon rolls and tea. He had adored them ever since.

At the designated hour, he was on their doorstep with a bottle of wine (he knew he'd been instructed not to bring anything, but wine didn't count), and Millie was welcoming him with a wide smile and a firm hug. She wore mom jeans and a paisley blouse that had probably been around since the 1960s. He couldn't help but grin and hug her back. She flinched a bit at the pressure.

"Oh, dear Jonas! It's so good to see you," she gushed, ushering him into the house. "How have you been? You look thin. Have you been eating enough?"

He assured her he'd been fine (a bald-faced lie) and he had been eating plenty of good food (ditto), and he followed her through the living room and into their kitchen. Their dining table was in the right corner of the spacious kitchen area with its wood block island and modern appliances. It all looked so burnished and shiny it put Jonas's own home to shame.

The smells reached him before he saw Mr. Lyons over the stove, staring into a boiling pot. "Hello," he said when he entered. "I brought a bottle of wine. I hope that's okay."

"Wine is always welcome," Millie said, taking away the bottle to open it and let it air. "We've got fresh clams and Point Judith calamari in a red sauce over linguini. Hope you're hungry!"

His stomach audibly growled at the pungent scent of garlic and tomato, and all three of them broke into a comfortable laughter. Soon, they were seated and shoveling the delicious dinner into their mouths. The wine he had chosen paired beautifully with the food, and he was glad he'd brought it.

"This is amazing," Jonas said. "Thank you so much. I think I needed this."

After he'd finished a second plate, Millie served coffee and a thin slice of blueberry pie she'd baked that morning. It was just as tasty as the main course had been, and Jonas complimented her on it.

"Pish posh," she said, refilling his coffee. After they'd finished, they remained around the table and Mark lit a cigarette. Jonas didn't know when he had last been so full and content.

"So," Millie said, her eyes darting to her husband. "Mark tells me you've heard things outside as well."

"Oh, for Pete's sake," Mark said. "You're going to ruin a good evening and bring up all this?"

"Yes, I am, and you can remain silent. I'm talking to my friend Jonas here. So, is it true? Have you heard strange noises outside in the night?"

Jonas nodded. "Yeah, well, last night at least."

"Did it sound like two rocks hitting each other, like someone tapping two stones together? Only, not hard and loud, but just ... tapping them? Like click click click?"

"That's what I heard exactly. It was barely loud enough to wake me up, but I went outside and didn't find anything. Other than your husband."

"She sent me out to look," he said. "I swear, every time she hears a bump or a scrape or anything, she sends me outside to prowl the neighborhood. And let me tell you, young man, at my age, when you're up, you are up for good. It's no use trying to get back to sleep."

His wife waved a hand in the air as though physically dispelling the notion. "He goes on and on about my sleeping habits, but I never have any trouble getting back to sleep. I roll over, close my eyes, and that's it."

"It's because you know you've got the bed to yourself for the rest of the night, you crazy old broad! You got the old man out of the picture and now you can sprawl out in bed any way you want to."

Jonas enjoyed their playfulness, the ribbing and good-humored bickering obviously a routine established by so many years together. They were an adorable couple, and they played off each other well—especially with an audience. Mr. Lyons leaned over and gave his wife a kiss, and she giggled, then scratched the area at the back of her neck where her graying curls landed.

"You know we're just bantering, don't you dear?" she asked. "We do that so often we hardly notice anymore. Oh, when you've been with someone as long as I've been with ... "

She stopped herself, putting a hand to her mouth, and Jonas saw the spots (were those new?) on the back of her fingers before he lowered his gaze to the plate on the table in front of him. Mr. Lyons glared at his wife for a second, concern in his expression. The room went silent, except for the ticking of the clock on the wall. A dozen ticks went by before Millie dared to speak again.

"I'm so sorry, Jonas," she said. "I didn't think. Blame it on a silly old woman and her loss of concentration. I don't know where my mind goes sometimes."

"It's okay," he said, his eyes still staring down at the table.

"No, it isn't." She reached across the table and took his hand, and he had to focus, finding her face in the midst of a flurry of unwelcome, trespassing thoughts about Brad. "I shouldn't be blabbing away at you like some crazy old coot about things you don't want to think about. This was supposed to be a nice night, and here I have to go and remind you of...you know who."

"It's all right," Jonas reiterated. "I can't hide my whole life. I have to confront it sooner or later. I guess I've just been ignoring his absence. Except late at night when I wake up suddenly. That's when I really become aware of things—the empty half of the bed, the empty half of the closet."

The empty half of my shattered heart, he thought.

She absent-mindedly scratched the back of her neck again. "Well, if you ever want to talk, you can come over anytime. We want to be supportive of you, Jonas."

"Yeah, we do," Mark added. "I'll even provide a good Scotch while we talk. That is, when you want to."

"No rush," she said. "When you're ready."

Mr. Lyons nodded, And Jonas thanked them both, stumbling on his words a bit as he grappled with the emotions of the evening. Now that the elephant in the room had been pointed out, the damn thing was stampeding around his head, trumpeting and bellowing for attention.

"In the meanwhile," Millie said. "What do you think is causing that noise?"

"I saw a stone had fallen off your fence into my yard," Jonas said, glad for the not-so-subtle switching of subjects. "I put it back, but something must have knocked it loose. Could a squirrel or raccoon do that? Maybe a cat?"

"There's no way a critter so small would be able to push those stones around," Mark answered. "Maybe a raccoon. They have those weird human-like hands."

Millie gathered the dishes and transported them to the sink. Jonas noticed her husband observing her, a concerned squint to his eyes, unwittingly scratching at an itch on his chest. All this scratching worried Jonas; they may have bedbugs, and he reminded himself to double check his clothing when he returned to his own place. It was making him want to scratch himself, even if his own itch was only in empathy.

"Well, I swear someone is shifting those stones at night," Millie said, traversing back and forth to the sink. "I've heard it the last three nights in a row. Click click click. Like rocks tapping each other or crab claws opening and closing. It's driving me mad!"

Mark leaned over the table and stage-whispered behind the back of his hand. "She's already there, Jonas. Mad as a hatter!"

"Oh, you!" she tossed a dish towel at him. "Just for that, you're washing *and* drying the dishes tonight!"

Jonas laughed, but after he had said his good-byes and taken his leave of them, he paused at the stone fence. The thing was only just above his knee, probably about halfway completed. He listened, holding his breath to try and detect the noise again. The only sounds he heard were the susurration of the pine trees and a distant hoot of a barn owl. A lone cricket sawed away nearby, and he just perceived the cars and trucks traversing the highway in the distance, past the woods. All the typical night sounds. Nothing weird. Nothing abnormal.

When he went into the house, he remembered the way Millie had been rubbing the back of her neck, and he removed his clothes and shook them out into the yard. Just in case. He didn't spot any vermin, but you could never be too sure. The last thing he needed was a bedbug infestation.

He spent an hour or so trying to watch TV, but even with an action-packed mini-series blasting on the screen, he could feel the stillness in his home like a physical presence. There was a hole there now, a human shaped void.

"Why?" he asked the empty room. "Just ... fucking why?"

Jonas had experienced loss before; this wasn't entirely new. Many of his friends had died during the early, terrible days of the AIDS crisis, and he'd had three long-term relationships which had each ended with half-hearted whimpers. This felt very different. This wasn't the diseased rot caused by a long, drawn-out death but more like the amputation of a limb. Sudden, unexpected, and throbbing with phantom pain.

He didn't want to continue thinking about it.

He couldn't help thinking about it.

He clicked off the television and collapsed onto the mattress. Despite his roiling emotions, he fell asleep relatively quickly, resting on his side, a parody of how he'd slept with Brad.

He scratched his left arm for a moment, chasing an elusive itch, and then he was snoring.

CHAPTER
FOUR

T he stones were moving again.

It was Jonas's first thought upon awakening and hearing the sound repeated ... click click clack ... like the previous night, originating from just outside. There was a scraping sound, stone grinding against stone, and he leapt from the bed, rushing outside in just his boxers. The cold air hit his skin and the sheen of sweat on his torso evaporated, causing goose pimples to break out across his arms and chest.

The stones were moving again.

He almost laughed; he was anthropomorphizing a fence, giving granite the will and ability to shuffle and stir on its own cognizance. It was beyond infantile.

Yet, here he was, nearly naked staring down a stone fence which barely reached his kneecaps.

And at the single stone on the ground at his feet, gleaming white in the moonlight. He heard it again, from the opposite end, and he hurried forward, scanning the rocks and the spaces in between them. The barrier was being made in the old-fashioned manner, using no mortar or grouting—just one stone placed carefully atop another, each aligned as perfectly as found stones could be, building it one at a time in the old Robert Frost method. Once it was assembled in as sturdy a manner as possible, moss or lichen or just gathering gunk would eventually glue it all together. But it seemed Mr. Lyons wasn't doing a particularly good job assembling the layers so they wouldn't tumble off each other. That's what it had to be, right? These stones were precariously balanced and now and again one slipped off the backs of the others.

Click. Clack. Click. Clack.

The stones were moving again.

As he watched, another stone slid and fell from its perch atop the others. It vibrated a bit, jiggling against the stones beneath it before it fell with a plop to the earth, nearly at Jonas's feet. He jumped back, eyes widened, brain trying desperately to process what he'd just witnessed.

"How…," he began, but the rest of the words didn't come, didn't matter at all. *How* encapsulated everything he was feeling at the moment.

The wind suddenly died. The trees stopped their incessant susurration, their long conversation concluded with a final sigh. The crickets stopped chirping, and the noise from the distant highway faded into silence. There wasn't a discernable sound to be heard anywhere around him. He couldn't remember ever being trapped within the walls of such a stillness, especially in Rhode Island where there always seemed to be a breeze stirring the atmosphere. His breath—in and out and in and out— was the only thing he heard.

It was as if the night had died.

Then, the tiny hairs on the back of his neck and the underside of his arms twitched and raised in an apprehensive awareness. With this unease came a certainty he was being observed. He could feel the pressure of someone's (or some *thing's*) gaze upon him, and he shivered, turning in circles in the yard.

When his regard met the thick woods, he stopped, squinting and peering into the obsidian darkness. The moon remained behind clouds, and he could perceive nothing except an abyss of shadow. Yet, he persisted absolutely convinced someone hid within that darkness, examining him. Every nerve ending in his body screamed the watcher was concealed within those trees and bushes.

"Hello?" he muttered, stepping toward the woods. "Are you there? What do you want from me?"

With every step he took closer to the trees, the air felt cooler against his perspiring skin. The breeze hadn't returned, and the silence still reigned eerily over the night. When he was within ten yards of the tree line, Jonas held his breath, listening. All he heard was his muffled heartbeat, fast in his chest like an encaged bird.

The woods didn't merely contain a darkness, but it appeared to have had all prevailing illumination sucked out of it. It wasn't merely a dark night, but a noticeable dearth of light. An absence. A black hole.

Then, he started as two bright, golden eyes became visible within the Stygian canopy. As hard as Jonas stared, he couldn't make out the shape of the person who owned those eyes; they remained obscured, but there was a sense of habitation, a feeling of something occupying space.

"Who are you?" Jonas asked, and he was ashamed at how his voice quivered.

He took another tenuous step forward, and the eyes blinked, went dark for a moment before opening again. He thought he could make out part of the person, a strong, muscular shoulder on the left side and part of a face. Details began to emerge, wrinkles around the eyes, the dusky, dark skin of an African-American, a bicep, tensed and veined with muscle. Behind that form, another shape coalesced into the vague outline of another man, tall and thin with yellowed eyes. Behind him, Jonas saw other shapes, fragments of male physicality—a hand, an elbow, a piece of a muscular leg. None of them came together to form a whole being, but there were several of them standing still in the shadows.

Behind him, a sound. *The* sound. Click click click…

He twisted in time to witness several of the stones in the fence drop to the ground, three on his side of the barrier and six or seven on the Lyons' side. There was nobody near them, no animals knocking them over. They just slid off and fell on their own accord.

Jonas spun back to the woods to find the eyes and the emerging figures had been swallowed up again by the darkness. As he waited, the moon emerged from behind puffy clouds, branches rustled in a gust of wind, and he saw several yards into the forest. The man was gone, like smoke in the throes of the prodigal breeze. Jonas stepped a few feet beyond the tree line, but he didn't see anything abnormal. They were gone, as if they had never been there.

Is any of this real? he wondered. *Am I losing my mind after losing Brad? Am I crazy with the grief? Could I be seeing things?*

When he touched the three stones fallen into his yard, he knew for a fact he hadn't been imagining it all. They modeled as proof, evidence of the strange happenings in the night. He kicked one with his bare foot. It felt strange, somewhat slimy.

He picked it up and returned it to its place on top of the stone wall, then he looked at his hands under the silver gleam of the moonlight. A thin layer of slime covered them. Rubbing them against his shorts, he sensed his hands were clean, but he headed inside to wash them under some soap and water in case … in case of what? In case the stuff was still stuck to him and could harm him in some manner? In case he touched his eye with a trace of that slime still on his fingers? In case that shit was haunted?

Suddenly, his hands itched.

He was halfway across the yard when he heard a voice in the night. "You heard it, too?"

Jonas jumped, his heart in his throat before he realized it was only Mark from next door, his hair a mess and wearing a ratty robe cinched around his paunch. Jonas was a bit embarrassed to be outside in only his boxer briefs, but he shrugged off the discomfort. This older gentleman wouldn't care how he was dressed in the middle of the night. He made his way over to the partially-completed stone wall and stood on his side, a victim of a sort of formality, an understanding that one stayed on one side of a fence at a certain late hour of night. Especially if one was clad only in his underwear.

"Yeah, heard it. And saw it," he answered. "It wake you up?"

Mark shook his head. "I sleep like the dead. But it shook Millie up, and she nudged me out here. Again." He motioned to the stones which had fallen into his yard. "You see who did this?"

Jonas shook his head. "I thought I saw someone in the woods, but it turned out to just be a phantom. Something I was imagining." He knew if he said and thought this long enough it would dispel the image of the dark man appearing and slowly taking form within the trees. He didn't want to think the word "ghost," and he wasn't about to say it.

"You sure you imagined it?"

"Yeah. Ninety-nine percent sure."

"Then how did the stones end up on the ground? Tell me true; it isn't you doing this, is it? You're not screwing around with my mind?"

"No," Jonas admitted. "But I saw them slip off and fall. Nobody was around, it just…happened."

"Like hell. I had those wedged in tight. Nothing would shake them loose except some kind of earthquake. Or human interference."

"I watched it happen, Mark. I was right here, and they just sort of…slipped off from their moorings and fell. The last one almost looked like it jumped."

"Jumped?"

"Well…" Jonas realized how absurd he sounded. "That's what it looked like. It sort of leaped. That one way over there." He pointed toward the farthest stone, about three feet from the fence. "I know it's nuts, but I swear … "

Mark picked up and replaced the stones, reintegrating them into their positions within the others. He grabbed hold of the wall and pushed, pulled. It remained solid. "See? This isn't going anywhere."

"I saw it with my own eyes."

"Stones don't move on their own accord."

"Well, these did."

With a sigh, Mark said, "I'm heading back to bed. Please don't tell Millie about the falling stones or the *jumping* stones. Or about phantoms in the woods you thought you saw. She's not sleeping real great right now. She's…not herself. Keeps hearing the stones moving."

"We've all heard it," Jonas said.

"Maybe. Maybe not. Still, don't bother her with the details. She'll never get any rest."

"Fine. But something is really weird about all this."

"You said a mouthful, buddy." He looked closer at Jonas before continuing, "And maybe you should get some sleep as well. You're looking pretty worn out."

Jonas nodded and waved as the older man stepped back into his own house and shut the back door. With a quick survey around the wooded area, he ascertained nobody lurked in the shadows, and he shivered as a breeze blew across his bare arms and legs.

Everything appeared to be as it should be—no apparitions, nobody watching him, no weird noises or self-destructing walls. All was quiet and still. Even the crickets and tree frogs started chirping again.

As he turned and headed into the house, falling into bed, he scratched the back of his left hand. The itch promptly went away as he collapsed into his bed, and he fell into a deep sleep, untroubled by nightmares.

CHAPTER
FIVE

Jonas was somehow very tired, and it affected his work. No matter how he tried to shape the previous night's experiences, he couldn't sculpt them into a final manifestation resembling anything other than a ghost story, a haunting. People disappearing, things moving on their own consensus—he wasn't one to believe in spirits or ghosts, but when confronted with so much evidence, it was hard to suspect anything other than the supernatural. Even though his conscience struggled with the very concept of ghosts—he had never been a man of a religious bent—he knew in his heart that's what he had seen. Those creatures in the woods, their figures half-transparent, half solid muscle, black as ebony. Who were they? Where did they come from? Most importantly, why were they in his backyard chucking stones about and generally acting mysterious? What had he done?

Passing a hand across his eyes, rubbing them a bit, he decided there'd be no work accomplished today. He was spinning his wheels, his mind returning again and again to the visitation he'd experienced. Those figures, the sound...click clack. Click clack.

Briefly, Jonas wondered what Brad would make of the entire situation. His ex was never very brave in the face of conflict, evidenced by his sudden abandonment of their relationship instead of fighting to keep it alive. He would probably have bolted at the first signs of the haunting, the sounds in the night.

Meanwhile, here was Jonas, desperately trying to rationalize what he'd seen. And failing miserably.

He was haunted. He had a ghost problem.

He decided to approach the only other person who had been affected by the sounds and the weirdness—his next-door neighbors. For a bit, it had appeared as if Millie had wanted to speak with him over dinner, to enquire about something, but her husband had stopped her. Now, in the light of the late afternoon, Jonas needed to know what she'd been about to ask.

Cutting through the backyard, he stepped over the low wall, noticing yet another stone had flown from its place within the construct. It gleamed in the sunlight, covered with a light film of some sort which glistened like slime. It lay on Mark's side, so Jonas left it, not wanting to touch the slippery surface. He was repelled by it, as if it emitted a rotten odor, as if it was rife with infection.

It's just a stone, he reminded himself. *Nothing but a piece of granite Mark probably found on the roadside.*

He turned, walked to Mark and Millie's back door, and rapped on it. There was a long pause, and he suddenly felt the tingling awareness of eyes on the back of his head. Someone was watching him again. His senses confirmed it. When he spun around to see if anyone was there, he was not surprised to find the yard empty and the woods dark and uninhabited. He didn't even hear any birds calling in the trees. Everything was still and quiet except for the easy breeze wafting through the needled limbs.

The door opened, and Jonas was shocked at Mark Lyons's appearance. Dark rings encircled his eyes, testimony to his lack of sleep, and his jowls hung loose. It had only been a day, but Jonas distinguished he was thinner than he had been only yesterday. His shoulders slumped, pushed down by the weight of a depression. His clothes hung loose on his frame, and his hair was unkempt, sprouting out around his male pattern baldness like weeds surrounding a rock garden. Dark bruises marred the skin on the backs of his hands and up his arms. One peeked out from the collar of the plaid shirt he was wearing. He'd buttoned it wrong, and it gapped in front. His breathing was ragged, as if he'd jogged to the door and triggered a minor asthma attack.

"Oh, it's you," he said in between deep breaths. "I'd ask you in, but…Millie isn't feeling well. Really, um, really under the weather."

"You don't look so great yourself," Jonas said.

Mark scratched at one of the dark patches, the bruises on his arms. His eyes darted to the woods then back to Jonas's face. "Feeling pretty rough, to be honest," he admitted.

"Can I do anything for you?"

"No, no, can't think of anything. How about you let us sleep? The quiet would do us a lot of good. That's all we need. Quiet and alone time."

Jonas was taken aback by the statement, and he frowned. He was never loud, never hosted parties or caroused. He suspected he was the most boring gay man for a hundred miles.

"I'll see you later," the older man gasped, turning back to his dark house and shutting the door in Jonas's face. His feet shuffled, barely lifting off the floor.

From inside, just before the door latched, Jonas heard Millie cry out, a sound of pain and agony. It chilled him, and he wondered just how sick she was. This was the cry of an animal caught in a trap, something about to gnaw off its foot to escape. It was a horrible sound.

Behind him, stone grated against stone followed by the firm plop of another part of the wall collapsing to the ground. Turning, he saw four stones on the lawn in the Lyons's yard. He'd entirely missed the other two which had dropped.

He shouted over his shoulder, "If you need anything, call me! I'll be here all day."

He sat in his kitchen and waited for the night to arrive.

CHAPTER

SIX

T he stone were restless that night.

As soon as dusk fell, Jonas heard them shifting, grating against each other, rattling like reanimated skeletons in coffins. Sometimes he heard the moist slap as they hit the dew-covered ground, but most of their tumbles were silent. The wind had also picked up, gusting and billowing in between short moments of calm.

Jonas put on a sweatshirt and a light jacket, and he stepped into the backyard, his heart hammering. He was terrified, but he didn't know why. Ghosts couldn't actually harm him, could they? So far, they'd just wobbled a few stones and sort-of-appeared at the tree line to the forest. It was spooky, certainly, but they had made no move to harm him.

He scratched at the patch of darkening skin on the back of his hand. It had become more noticeable, coloring like a bruise coming into full flower. He couldn't remember banging it against anything, but his mind kept returning to the weird, slimy coating on the stones he had handled, the ones he'd returned to their place in the wall. Could the slime be toxic? Could it also be the cause of the Lyons's sickness? So far, it merely looked like a bad attack of eczema, but Jonas had never suffered from eczema in his life. Why would it start now?

Jonas watched the stones vibrating, rattling against each other as if an earthquake were occurring. Gaps appeared between them, infiltrated by the moonlight. Some fell off, but most remained in place, clattering, quivering. The ones which had tumbled to the earth seemed to glow with a viscous luminescence. Jonas swore he saw one of them pulsing, breathing in and out. Alive.

"You're just a bunch of rocks!" he shouted. "You can't actually do anything."

The rattling grew more violent, and a wave flowed through the wall from the Lyons's house to the woods in the back. The stones actually rose and fell in sequence, a sickening parody of a crowd doing the wave during a sporting event. The noise grew louder as the wall pulsed.

CLICK! CLACK!

Numerous stones were tossed from their moorings. They were gaining distance and velocity. Soon, they'd be flying through the air like pebbles thrown by a child.

Mark Lyons emerged from his house, watching the crashing and settling stones in an awestruck stupor. His mouth remained open, and his cheeks drooped in the dark night, as if even they were exhausted. He waved his hands, shouting for the stones to stop it, to just stop it!

The absurdity of the situation overwhelmed Jonas, and he laughed at the old man. He knew it was a mistake the second the sound exploded from his lips, and he tried to bite it back, but it was too late. His neighbor, usually so kind and so amiable pointed at Jonas with a look as grim as a serial killer's.

"Don't you laugh," he said. "I got a wife in there dying and I'm sick and somehow these stones caused it. I don't know how, but it's not funny!"

"Sorry, sorry," Jonas said, hands held up in front of himself as if the old man was about to launch himself into an assault. "It's all so...weird. That's all. This entire situation. Why the hell is it even happening?"

He glanced over at the woods and saw the men were appearing again. As before, they were only partially visible, as if a mist snaked across them in various points, obscuring anyone from viewing them clearly. Jonas counted six of them, all male, most of them in their thirties or younger. They were muscular and every one was African-American, although their skin tone was so dark he didn't know which was melatonin and which was shadow. Their eyes were a jaundiced yellow, and their teeth were bared, lips curled back in silent snarls. Despite these facial expressions, they exuded a moribund sense of melancholy that seeped from them like perspiration. They reeked of sorrow.

Jonas pointed to them, barely breathing. He asked Mark Lyons, "Do you ... do you see them, too?"

"Yes."

"Are they...*familiar* to you?"

"No."

The figures faded in and out of the mist, some parts disappearing then coming back into focus, but none of them was ever entirely visible. They didn't move at all. Jonas watched them closely, waiting for one to blink or to inhale. They never did.

"What do we, um, do about them?" he asked Mark.

"How in the hell am I supposed to know? Get an exorcist? Find a ghost hunter? I don't know if there's anything we can do about them."

Mark grated inadvertently at the many spots on his arms. He didn't take his eyes off the men at the edge of the forest, though. Their stillness held him enthralled.

Suddenly, one of them took a step forward. The figure was entirely visible in the moonlight, unhidden by shadows or trees, and yet it still stared blankly with those hideous, yellow, glowing eyes. The ghost was naked, muscular, and scarred from head to foot with long, raised keloid scars.

The rest of the ghosts stepped forward, just a single step, emerging from the darkness of the woods into the pale blue light of the moon. As they became clearer, their scars became more discernible, and they were all covered in them. Many were practically thatched in ruptured tissue.

Jonas scrutinized them, squinting in the faint light. The skin between the raised scars was oozing liquids, dark and viscous. It wasn't blood, or it didn't appear to be, but the areas resembled seeping sores. These gleaming patches of skin reminded him of the late 1980s when many of the men he knew were dying from AIDS-related issues, their Kaposi sarcomas blooming like bruised flowers on their pale skin.

Jonas looked down at the back of his hand and his arm, really noting the darkening areas for the first time. Yes, they did resemble nascent sarcomas, but those didn't blossom overnight. They took some time.

He looked over at Mark, saw him scratching at his arms. The bruises on the older man were darker than his own, as well as more virulent. They marred his creped skin in multiple areas.

An idea began to form in Jonas's head, something crazy, something on just that side of horror.

These weren't bruises. They were symptoms.

Then, the lead ghost took another step toward Jonas, and the man retreated a few steps, alarmed by the sudden movement. The others followed their leader, one step closer, then a full stop. Eight or nine of them visible now. They were moving into Mark's lawn as well, and the neighbor stumbled backwards, catching himself on an Adirondack chair. His face was a mask of terror.

"What do they want?" he shouted.

Jonas cocked his head, waiting for more movement, to any kind of clue as to what the spirits desired. Every time, his eyes were drawn to the suppurating wounds, like wet valleys between the raised scars.

"Did you say Mrs. Lyons was sick?" he asked.

"Yeah," Mark answered, hesitancy in his voice. "She's got this skin rash, same as me."

"How bad is it?" Jonas asked, dreading the answer.

The ghosts took two steps, turning a bit and heading for the unfinished stone wall. Jonas recoiled, as did his neighbor at the sudden, jerky movements of the phantoms.

Those wounds on the lurking figures worried Jonas. More so than the fact that ghosts were gathering in his backyard. Those oozing gaps in the skin brought back multiple uninvited memories from a time when so many men were dying in hospitals where nurses were afraid to touch them, when people were paid to hold and rock babies, when a nation had ignored the decimation of a population deemed unworthy of sympathy. It wasn't just a feeling of hopelessness which absorbed him—then *and* now—but also a sense of unsolicited solitude. His friends had mostly died alone. He faced these ghosts, these spreading things, on his property, alone.

Well, there was Mark Lyons, but he'd been little to no help. He was a nice man, a kind man, but he was definitely hiding something. Every twitch of his eyelid and grimace telegraphed his closely-held secrets. There was a defeatism in his gestures which signaled concession. Depression made physical.

"Maybe you should take Millie to a doctor?" Jonas suggested, backing up as the ghosts surrounded the wall. They progressed in a fitful, irregular manner, as if Jonas was watching an old silent film, one subjected to years of rips and tears and missing frames. There wasn't anything natural about their sporadic motion, but there wasn't anything threatening, either.

But that didn't mean Jonas wanted to be any closer than he had to be. If these things *were* contagious, if they were spreading some sort of weird skin carcinoma, then he didn't want to get any nearer than he needed to be. There wasn't anything angry or violent in their movements, but their yellow glowing eyes exuded an innate sense of rage and betrayal that terrified him.

"I can't take her right now," Mr. Lyons said. He was halfway inside his sliding back door. "She refuses to go. And a doctor...a doctor wouldn't know..."

"But she is sick. With these markings, these...what, bruises?"

This stopped Mark. He raised his eyebrows, said, "You have them, too? Oh no..."

The interlopers stepped toward the wall again, moving in that weird manner. The wind picked up, shushing through the trees. The two little houses out in the country surrounded by the forest never felt so isolated. The darkness pressed in on Jonas.

"Can I see her?"

"I doubt she's even awake right now. It's hit her hard. She hasn't been out of bed all day. She just lays there."

"You really need to call a doctor. Or an ambulance."

"She doesn't want one. I think she wants to be alone, heal by herself, you know?"

"Can I see her?" he repeated.

Mr. Lyons flashed his eyes at Jonas, and they narrowed in the corners, crinkling with either suspicion or mistrust. "I don't know."

"We're friends. I only want to see my friend for a minute. It would make me feel a lot better."

"She is…really sick."

"Have you seen the back of my hand?" Jonas asked, rolling the sleeve of his sweatshirt up, exposing the weird dark blemishes running up his arm. "I have them, too. Not as bad as you do, but look."

"Come over," he said, waving Jonas to his side. The man's shoulders slumped. "I doubt she's awake, but we can see. Don't blame me if she's pissed."

Jonas followed him, keeping an eye on the restless spirits, which had reached the stone wall and were glaring at it with jaundiced eyes. He didn't think they were going to attack him as they appeared to be entranced by the stones and their unremitting click-clacking sounds. It was a terrifying sight, but Jonas's sense of danger had diminished. The all-encompassing feeling of dread, of malevolence, had been blown aside by the incessant wind. Now, the danger was coming from within himself on some microscopic level. He looked at the sore on the back of his hand and he would swear it was larger and darker than it had been at the beginning of the evening.

Jonas followed Mark through the darkened hallways of his house to the bedroom the old man shared with his wife. He didn't switch on the lights, and the scene was illuminated by the blue luster from the moon outside the window. Shadowy patterns caused by the fluttering lace curtains scurried around the room. Jonas was surprised Mark had left the window open, as the area was uncomfortably cool with the night air. Lacey impressions swept across Millie's features as the wind picked up again, a kinetoscope of ethereal puppet-plays.

She lay still beneath a sheet and coverlet. Her face, shadowed as it was, was mostly obscured, but Jonas saw the glint of something liquid around her eyes and sagging throat. Her breathing was loud in the room, and every inhalation caught on a jagged piece of interference, as though her throat had been lined with serrated blades. Mark groaned as he sat on the corner of the bed, reached out, and took her hand within his. He patted the back of it and whispered her name. When she didn't respond, he tightened his grip on her fingers, squeezing hard.

"Millie, Jonas is here. He's come to see you." He raised his voice to a rather uncomfortable level.

The old woman turned her head toward her husband, and some of her gray hair clumped and stuck to the pillow. As Jonas watched, the hair sloughed off her scalp. There was a patina of perspiration on it as well as a clear gel-like substance.

"Jonas?" she asked, her eyes not focusing.

"Hi Millie," he answered her, reaching out then retracting his hand when he thought about what horrors he might be contracting.

When she turned her head to see him, there was a horrifying moist squelch, and Jonas saw the appalling pustules on her face. Several had burst open and were seeping a nasty-smelling discharge which had dried into a crust around the wounds.

"Wish you...wouldn't see me...like this."

"You're still beautiful," Jonas lied. "Always."

Mark made a choking sound, gasping a bit, and Jonas knew he'd seen through the fabrication. It was terribly obvious this woman was deathly ill.

"You're charming, but...you're a liar," she rasped. "Charming...liar."

She fell asleep, her eyelids closing. Before this, however, Jonas had noticed the jaundiced yellow of her eyes, the same shade as the ghosts slowly surrounding the wall in the backyard. There was a connection between the two—between the specters and the dying woman—something to do with their health or the lack thereof.

Pulling Mark aside, Jonas whispered, "You need to get her to a hospital. Like yesterday."

"She won't go. Refuses to even think about it." Mark sighed.

"Why? Anyone can see how sick she is! Mark, she could die. Here in this house because you neglected to get her help."

"Don't you think I know that? Jesus, Jonas, but the woman is stubborn." He slumped in his chair, dropping her hand. "I can't bring myself ... to do it. I'm tired and scared and everything just seems so hopeless. All of it, just…fucking hopeless."

"What does she have?"

Mark fidgeted a bit, looked away from his neighbor. "What do you mean?"

"What disease is she sick with? Oh my God, aren't you scared? I mean, it looks like you have the same bug, Mark. You could be ill like her soon, and then what will happen?"

"It came on so sudden. I honest to God don't know what it is, but…it's horrible. Some sort of flesh-eating virus, looks to me. But I'm no doctor…"

"Then call one! Christ, I'll do it for you. Let Millie blame me."

"You would do that?" Mark asked, looking relieved.

"Mark, self-reliance is great and all, but sometimes you have to ask for help. Do you want Millie to die?"

He shuffled his feet. "No," he said.

"Do you want to die yourself?"

"No."

"Then stop acting like a petulant child. I'll call the doc in the morning, and he can be out here before the afternoon. What's his name?"

Scratching his chest, Mark moved over to a desk on the other side of the room and switched on a tiny lamp. He shuffled through a few papers before he found a business card and handed it to Jonas. He coughed a few times, and he caught a string of drool dripping from his mouth.

Jonas was instantly cautious and terrified. He had no mask covering his face. After living through COVID-19 and always wearing his face covering and social distancing, he now found himself in a single room with two very sick people—two very sick people with an unknown and thoroughly disgusting disease—and no masks in sight. It would be a miracle if he didn't catch this virus as well. Whatever it was.

As he backed out of the room, the situation rang his memory bell again, and he was swept back to the early 1990s when he would visit friends dying in the hospital. He'd tried to cheer them up, but they knew they didn't have very long, and he mostly had to sit still and try to deflect their anger. He was left with a distinct phobia of the visibly sick, the ones with open sores or gaping infections. He'd worked through it, striving to always remain positive, to hold their hands without flinching, to remain calm within the nightmare tsunami of the dead all around him. He had mostly succeeded. Mostly.

After backing away from the older couple, Jonas waved goodbye to them, and Mark waved back while Millie slumbered, her flesh glistening. Once he was outside, he turned to the ghosts. They were collected around the stone wall, watching intently as stones flung themselves off their perch and onto the grass. There were a lot of them scattered across the yard now.

As one, the spirits turned to Jonas, their yellow eyes blazing in the darkness. They kept still, and he noticed pieces of them devolved into mist, gaseous and clear enough to see through. The impending sense of danger and malevolence had returned, a sense of foreboding so thick it settled over the yards like a heavy fog. He felt their malice on his skin as he quickly withdrew to his house, little dew points of the hate-filled poison clinging to him, giving his face an unhealthy sheen. After he locked and secured the door behind him, he watched the backyard for a long time.

The ghosts moved slowly, purposefully, but they didn't approach the house or attack. Sometimes, they blipped forward, popping from one place to another, as if he was viewing a film with occasional frames missing. The longer he watched, the more assured he was they didn't mean him any harm or violence. They had some purpose in mind, but it remained locked in their collective memory, a prisoner of their ghostly machinations. Jonas breathed easier, felt his pulse slow, his blood pressure decrease. He suddenly felt very tired, and he considered the phantoms for a few more minutes before proceeding to bed.

He was asleep before his head hit the pillow, and he slumbered fitfully, dreaming of stones and ghosts and resolutions unknown.

CHAPTER
SEVEN

In the morning, the ghosts had disappeared, but Jonas still waited to go outside to investigate, prolonging the possibility of even more supernatural contact. He made a cup of coffee and drank it while eating a banana. He made his bed, ignoring the sweat stains on the sheets. He showered, shaved. Finally, he couldn't put it off any longer, so he unlocked the door and stepped into the backyard.

The stone wall was noticeably lower, since many stones had flung themselves into the grass or had been carried there, carefully arranged by spectral hands. In the middle of Jonas's yard, the stones had been used to spell out a phrase. Two words which made no sense to him.

HANT
ON

Jonas examined the words from every angle, deciding it did indeed say HANT ON, all capital letters, but he didn't have a clue as to what the phrase meant. He wasn't even certain it was English. He went inside, switched on his laptop, and brought up Google.

First, he learned it was the name of an international clothing producer, but he didn't think the spirits would work all night long to create a marketing gimmick. It was also the name of a horseshoe manufacturer, but that seemed even more ridiculous, with even fewer ties to the bizarre events occurring behind his home.

And then he discovered the word "Hant" meant ghost or bogey, sometimes short for haunt. This seemed closer, but "Ghost On" sounded too much like a Power Ranger maxim than a phrase used by malevolent spirits during a haunting. He didn't know how it all fit together, but the ghosts were definitely attempting to explain themselves. This was a message from the beyond; it had to be important. It had to be a clarification of a sort, yet he had no idea what it clarified.

But he knew someone who most likely did recognize what "HANT ON" meant. Mark Lyons had been hiding something, some awful truth that he knew. Why else wouldn't he contact a doctor for his poor wife? Why else would he act so shifty?

Realizing he'd volunteered to call for medical assistance for Millie, Jonas looked at a clock and saw it was six AM. No doctor would be in his or her office yet, so he shoved his cell phone and the business card Mark had proffered into his front pocket and stomped over to the Lyons's place. When he passed his neighbor's driveway, he noticed the tailgate of Mark's pick-up truck was down and a couple dozen of the stones were stacked haphazardly in the bed. He wondered if the ghosts had done this as well, another piece of their cryptic puzzle. He banged on the back door for several minutes, growing more and more worried, until he heard a faint voice from within.

"Come..."

The voice bore a vague resemblance to Mark's, but it was so weak and enfeebled that Jonas doubted himself. He opened the unlocked door and stepped inside.

"Mark?" he called out.

"In...here."

Jonas found his neighbor slumped into his easy chair facing a switched-off television. He had deteriorated dramatically since the previous night. What had looked like bruises all over his body had opened into seeping, gaping wounds. His hair, what was left of it, had fallen out, dusting the chair as if a pet had shed all over it. Sores covered his cracked lips and a disgusting orange and yellow pus streamed from his eyes, furrowing obscene tear trails down his melting cheeks. The room reeked of sickness and death.

Jonas was transported back to those hospital rooms from decades long ago, to his dying friends, to his well-meaning words which had ended up being entirely ineffectual. Death had followed him. After so many years, he recognized its stench, its toxic presence. Mark was dying. Flustered, Jonas remembered himself.

"Millie!" he exclaimed.

"Dead," Mark said in a voice which sounded as if it were filled with grave dust. "Died...last night."

Jonas rushed to the back room and gagged when he saw what remained on the bed. Amidst the covers was a human skeleton covered in gray and orange colored rotting flesh. So much of her skin and muscle had exuviated from her bones, and there was a sickening puddle of melted gore in the middle of the mattress.

This was beyond sickness. This was something overtly diabolical, something cruel and evil. Nobody melted into a pool of goo in the span of a single night. Nobody remained alive while their flesh liquefied and dripped from their bones.

As he headed back to the living room, he said, "I'm calling an ambulance for you. I'm not waiting for any doctor."

"Too late..." the older man said with a gasp, his voice thick with liquid. "Far...too late."

"Mark, do you know what's causing this?" Jonas glanced down at the darkening spots on the back of his hand and the ones on his arms. "Am I next? Is this happening to me now? What the hell is going on?"

"Let me tell you," Mark said, the awful words coming slow, as though forced up through a throat full of liquefying flesh. "It's my fault."

When Mark paused, closing his eyes, Jonas asked, "Do you know the words *Hant On*? Those words were spelled out in the stones this morning. Do you know what they mean?"

"Yes. It...explains everything. I understand now. Hanton... Hanton City."

Haltingly, the man explained, and Jonas couldn't control the chills shivering through his spine.

Not much was known about the village called Hanton City, Rhode Island's least famous ghost town. It was supposedly settled by loyalists to the British in the later 1700s, and people went there after the Revolutionary War to take refuge from the newly emboldened Americans, to be among like-minded folk. They'd built a small town and lived there apart from those who hated them and all they believed. Hatred is powerful, people can become vengeful and angry. It breeds violence. One day, everyone disappeared, leaving behind houses and furniture and animals. Nobody knew who evicted them from their property or if they had been murdered and dumped in the woods. Common assumptions ran along the hypothesis that angry locals chased out the loyalists, sent them back to England. They were just gone, and the town would soon incorporate into a leper colony.

The lepers moved in along with several priests who tried to aid them in their final dying days. But once again, prejudice reared its ugly head and the lepers were found dead, half-buried in a pit, a mass grave.

"This so-called legend was all based upon hearsay and rear-view history. I couldn't find any real written documentation about any of these rumors," Mark continued. "You know, it was also whispered that the place became a sanctuary for runaway slaves who had escaped their slave-masters in the South. They moved in after the lepers had died or were murdered. It didn't take long before all the poor inhabitants of Hanton City mysteriously vanished again, as the runaways were just gone one morning. Given the times, people didn't search for them. They assumed they had made their way farther north or runaway slave hunters had found them and returned them to the Hell of their so-called lives in the South. They were gone. Like the lepers were gone. Like the loyalists were gone.

"You ever hear people talk about a bad place? Somewhere—a piece of land or a specific house—where an inordinate number of deaths and sickness occur? Hanton City, after so many disappearances, became rumored to be a bad place, and everyone stayed away from it. Sensibly, it turns out. The small houses crumbled, weeds grew up, demolishing everything except the stones used to make the walls and floors. There was nothing left except the granite foundations and a couple of tiny cemeteries.

"Of course, there were all kinds of stories about the place, yet nobody actually knew where all the people went. Did they move on to a less desolate area, like the nearby growing town of Smithfield? Someplace not so wild? Did they die of some disease? Nobody believed they vanished because of a Roanoke-like mystery, but nobody was actually certain what had happened. Hanton City was just an overgrown area, full of vines and piles of perfectly cut granite. Granite which I knew was sitting there waiting for the taking, and I wanted it for a short wall enclosing the backyard."

Jonas closed his eyes and held his breath, sensing where the tale was heading.

"My trip to Hanton City hadn't taken very long; I had gone the last week in November, so the trees and shrubs were bare, allowing one to spot the paths. After a short drive and a shorter hike, I discovered an old homestead, now nothing but a stone frame, placed into the earth like a root cellar. There was an inch of brackish water in the bottom, but I slogged through it and retrieved the stones until I filled the back of my truck. I brought them back with me and over the past year, I assembled the wall. It must have taken them that long to track me down."

"Who? Who is out there at night?"

He took a deep, rattling breath. "I have a theory. If even some of the rumors are true, it fits. But, it's pretty bizarre."

"You don't think ghosts hovering around the backyard and passing on some sort of flesh-eating virus isn't bizarre enough?"

"You're right. Well, near as I can figure it, after the people who were still loyal to England were run off or killed, the town sat abandoned for a while. This was a town built out in the middle of the woods, far away from anyone. What better place to put people stricken by leprosy and other such diseases. There were a few documented leper colonies in New England, but mostly our forefathers stuck anyone with a disease like that on an island somewhere off the coast. Someplace where the patients couldn't infect the general populace. Now, there's this whole little town already built and empty. Good solid wooden walls and sturdy granite stone foundations and fences. Nobody was there except the rats and raccoons. They probably figured they could put it to some use."

Jonas nodded. "Makes sense so far."

"The lepers eventually all died out or were removed to the aforementioned islands. Maybe even with a forest separating the healthy folk from the sick, Hanton Village was still too close for comfort, and those ambitious locals took it upon themselves to rid the world of the infected. I suspect a lot of people died out there and were buried in pits. And they died slowly, because it's a creeping disease."

Jonas opened his mouth to protest, but the older man was correct. The symptoms were there for anyone to grasp. He shivered at the thought and mentally made a point to get to a doctor the second this haunting was over. Maybe even when this conversation was finished.

Mr. Lyons continued, pausing now and again with the effort of relating his tale. Mucous ran down his chin from his nose and lips, but he didn't wipe it away. He sniffled, persisted forward into his theory.

"After the lepers were gone the place was used by runaway slaves, a group of damaged people creating their own community, far distanced from their oppressors...or any whites at all. Rhode Island was a northern state, but slave-catchers roamed everywhere in those days, kidnapping Black people—even free men who'd never been slaves—and marching them back to the chains and horrors of the southern plantations. So, these ex-slaves fixed up the houses on those same sturdy, stone firmaments. They put together a small graveyard using the same ever-present granite to carve tombstones. They had a school and a church—you can still kind of see what's left of the steeple. They tried to live their lives peacefully and quietly. As you know, white America wasn't about to lay low and let a group of escaped slaves have anything remotely resembling true freedom. Still happening today if you ask me. But I bet those poor folks—people who'd thought they had distanced themselves from so much cruelty and rabid prejudice—I bet there were still threats and violence. There were probably men on horseback, their faces covered with hoods and sheets. They were harassed, but at least they still had some sort of dignity. The white men wouldn't have granted them the place called Hanton City if there wasn't some spark of charity in their hearts. Would they?

"And then those poor people started catching the disease that had been consigned to the corners of every building, in the water supply, in the very contaminated atmosphere of Hanton. They caught the disease and their skin started liquefying. They grew bruises and sores. Their hair fell out and their fingernails turned black and dropped off. I'd bet money they tried to get a doctor, but even in these so-called free states in the North, even here, nobody would go out there to help them. Whether people were afraid of the disease or they were merely averse to helping, they were left alone to die horrible deaths. Out in those woods. Waiting for any kind of help from their neighbors." He sneered the word as if it was distasteful in his mouth. "No help came, and I suspect they all died in those woods. And before they succumbed, their spirits died. Hope died. Religion, faith, innocence—all dead and gone. Melted away like the flesh sliding off their bones."

Mark asked for a glass of water, and Jonas fetched one from the kitchen. When he re-entered the living room, the stench of rot smacked him like a board to the side of his head. He wondered if that odor came from Mr. Lyons, decomposing as they talked, falling apart and suppurating pus and bile and something else dark and foreign.

"Thank you," he said, sipping at the proffered glass. "Anyway, they died out there, and their anger and fear and rage all seeped into the foundations of Hanton City. Contagion upon contagion. Rage upon sickness. All they had wanted was a place to live, to farm, to raise a family, and the white men had gifted them a place of death.

A bad place. They died knowing nobody was going to help them. They died consumed with anger and rage and despair, watching their children and animals perish before them, waiting for their final breath. All those emotions, all that turmoil, it imbedded itself into the soil and the walls...and the stones.

"I wanted a stone wall, one like all the others you see in Rhode Island, and I'd heard of the village. I didn't know any of the legends or history of the place, but I parked my pickup over on the side of the highway and hiked into the woods and into Hanton City. I took the stones, the ones steeped in this horrific history, and I did the one thing you should never do with the foundation of a bad place. I brought it home. In doing so, I've released the ghosts from that place, as well as the disease. I see you have the bruises now, there on your hands and your throat. That's how Millie and I started a couple of days ago, just before we hosted our dinner with you. Now, Millie is dead and gone. There's not even anything left of her that looks human. By the end of today, I will join her."

"I keep telling you to call a..."

"A doctor wouldn't do any good, my friend. Look at me!"

Jonas did as instructed, and he knew Mark didn't have long left in this world. Possibly only a few minutes. The skin was drooping from his face, dragging downwards and pulling off the skull in sections. Holes had appeared in the flesh, oozing liquefied tissue. The tips of his finger bones were exposed where his digits had dissolved and soaked into the armrests of the chair. His nose hung at a slant, precariously tilting to the left, as though it could drop off at any instant. The room stank of death and the familiar tang of rot—the smell of so many hospital rooms.

"You have it now," Mark said, breathing shallowly between words. "I can see it. From touching the stones. They pushed them off the wall somehow, and you...you picked them up. Touched them. Absorbed the sickness. As...as they planned."

"I'll get to the hospital..."

"No good. It'll do no good. There's no time. This disease, this... leprosy is incredibly virulent. I was fine two days ago, no symptoms at all. In just two days...it killed Millie, and I'm not going to last much longer. You know, don't you? You know what you must do? The only way to stop it?"

Jonas shook his head, scratched at a bruise on his arm. As soon as he touched his skin, he felt it was different. It was looser than usual. He shivered.

"You need to get the stones back to Hanton City. Before you can't anymore. Before you reach this stage. You need to restore the infection to that bad place, to remove it from here and then salt the earth where it started."

"I don't even know where Hanton City is."

Mark waved at a piece of paper on an end table near him. There were bloody fingerprints on the surface, and Jonas flinched but picked it up anyway.

"A map," Mark said. "It's almost half a mile from where you can park. Pretty far back. Take my truck, and there's a wheelbarrow in my shed. You must do this, Jonas. I started last night, but I'm too weak to continue. It's now up to you. Return the stones so the ghosts can rest again."

A swatch of skin from his upper lip to his chin slid downwards, separated from his face, and fell into his lap, exposing his lower jaw and teeth. He looked up at the ceiling and screamed, a rattling final cry of pain and resignation and despondency. His skin darkened as Jonas watched, split into cobweb-like cracks and fissures. Yellow pus streamed from the crevices. It was the most horrible thing the younger man had ever seen, and the final shriek of defeat and demise echoed in his ears. Before he knew what he was doing, he grabbed the stained paper, snatched the truck keys from the table, and ran outside.

The air in the dusk was sweeter than any he could imagine, the direct opposite of the pall inside the house which had assaulted all his senses. He gulped huge mouthfuls of the evening air, wincing. He realized tears were streaming down his cheeks, and he wiped them away with the back of his hand.

When he raised his eyes again, his vision was blurred, but he could see the dark figures stepping out of the woods.

Their flesh melting in globules like candle wax, dripping, bubbling.

Their flashes of white teeth behind curling blackened lips.

Their horrible yellow eyes.

A surge of hatred, despair, and sheer fury hit him like a tidal wave, rattling his bones, loosening his skin even more. He screamed into the night, a primal scream, a thundering echo from within his dying soul.

The ghost in the front of the pack, the one he assumed was the leader, smiled at him, raised a hand, pointed at Jonas's chest.

An owl hooted in the distance, and a coyote yipped. The wind stirred, picked up in intensity. The tall trees surrounding the two lonely houses waved in the breeze, whispered dark and primal secrets.

And Jonas ran to Mark's shed, pulled open the door, and removed the wheelbarrow.

It was time to get to work.

CHAPTER

EIGHT

The spirits observed Jonas in a clinical manner, unmoving, silent, brooding. There were nine or ten of them spread from near the crumbling wall where even more stones had fallen to the ground to the edge of the shadowy forest, invisible except for their glowing yellow eyes. A few women had joined their ranks, but they were also covered with wounds and scars. Their stillness was unnerving, and the gusts of wind shushing through the trees emulated a beast's heavy breathing — in and out, in and out.

Jonas retrieved the wheelbarrow from the shed and positioned it near the wall. He also grabbed a pair of work gloves and slid them onto his hands. He didn't want to touch the stones. He wondered now about how they seemed covered in a moss or a film of some sort. Could it be the infection coating the exterior of each piece of granite?

He was certain he'd contracted the disease, the accelerated leprosy which had killed his neighbors. As he bent over to work, lifting the stones and placing them in the bed of the wheelbarrow, he cataloged new aches and pains. He realized he was a man in his mid-fifties. He wasn't young anymore, but everything hurt more than normal—his arms, legs, back, fingers. It was a pain that invaded his joints on a cellular level. The soreness worked its way from inside him to the exterior. Some were short, stabbing pains—the agony of a tendonitis or aching muscle after an intense workout. Other twinges were more intense, throbbing like a migraine.

Jonas filled the wheelbarrow and maneuvered it to Mark's pickup truck, where he unloaded it, tossing the heavy stones haphazardly into the open bed. They clanged until the bed was covered in them. Then, Jonas heard the familiar click clack of the stones moving against each other; the sound which had triggered this entire obscene situation.

Click! Clack!

He made more trips back and forth, dissembling the wall and transporting the pieces to the truck. Before long the truck bed was full to the rim, and Jonas calculated there would have to be two more trips before the wall was completely excavated and removed to Hanton City.

As he slid into the driver's seat of the truck, he turned for a look at the ghosts. He hadn't witnessed any of them moving, but they were startlingly closer now. None of them lurked within the woods, hidden by shadows. All of them were in the yard.

The wind was picking up, and Jonas dreaded an oncoming storm. He hadn't had a moment to look up the weather report, but there were clouds partially obscuring the moonlight, and the wind increased a few notches. In his aching bones, he felt this was a good-sized nor'easter approaching.

Checking out the hand-drawn map, Jonas held it by its edges, not wanting to touch the grotesque stains which tarnished the paper. It wasn't difficult getting to the trail head of the hiking path that led to Hanton City, and he was there in fifteen minutes. He parked, pulled the wheelbarrow down off the pile of stones, and filled it.

Map in hand, he rushed into the woods, awkwardly pushing the cart ahead of him.

The path wasn't very clear, and there were two inches of fallen leaves to wade through. They were slippery and a layer of mud beneath the gold and orange maple leaves was muddy and difficult. Each step squelched as he took it, and he almost lost a shoe a few times.

All the while, Jonas felt his skin growing heavier, the aches and pains suffusing his body increasing in severity. The woods were dark, and he could barely navigate the wheelbarrow by the light of the moon, still mostly hidden behind clouds.

Using his phone as a flashlight, he checked and rechecked the map. The distance from the trail head to the ruins of Hanton City tracked at only about a half mile, but it felt like much further. Eventually, he reached the edge of two interconnecting low stone walls. Upon further investigation, he saw they were two sides of a foundation, that the other two walls were partially missing, and he knew he'd discovered the place where his neighbor had stolen the stones.

He took a step back, rubbed his forearms, as jolts of pain ran up his biceps and to his shoulders. This was the disease working its way through his body; he was certain of it. He may have been in his middle age, but he'd never had so many parts of him hurt at the same time.

It was accelerating. Time was running out, and soon he would be disfigured or dead. He dumped the wheelbarrow and rushed back along the trail to the truck. It took six trips, but when he'd finished loading the last cargo, he stopped for a moment, breathing hard with the exertion.

He took his first good look around at the ruins of Hanton City. It wasn't much, some low walls here and there, a stack resembling a chimney, a clearing that could have been a town square.

Yet, it had been a home to people. First, the loyalists, then the lepers, and finally the runaway slaves who'd been given the property by white men who had appeared concerned and caring. In truth, they probably wanted the Black men and women out of sight and out of mind, so they put them someplace in the woods. Someplace dark with a fiendish history. Someplace suffused with corrosion and disease. Jonas knew they'd merely shrugged when the last of the Black men died in the woods, succumbing to an infection they'd known had lingered there. He was certain they had known it.

The trees sighed, and Jonas felt the first raindrop hit his cheek as the storm made its way up the coast. He rushed back to the truck and tossed the wheelbarrow in the bed as he heard the first low rumble of thunder in the distance.

One trip down, he thought.

Back to the house. Wheelbarrow out. Fill it up. Take it to the truck. Toss the stones into the bed.

The work became rhythmic, routine, and he didn't pay attention to anything, going numb as the effort grew more strenuous. At some point, he realized it had been raining for a while, but he hadn't noticed it. His hair and clothes were drenched, and when he raised his head, he saw a filigree of lightning in the distance.

The ghosts were closer than ever to his home, even though he hadn't seen them move so much as an eyelid. After he'd reloaded the truck, he determined that there was at least one more trip to be made before the wall was completely disassembled and restored to the spot where the stones belonged.

He rubbed the back of his right forearm, and the skin ruptured open like an over-ripe plum, spilling a clear liquid down to his fingers. Jonas cried out in horror, removing his flannel shirt and ripping off one of the sleeves. He felt a chill as he wrapped the sleeve around the wound, tossing the rest of his ruined shirt on the ground. He grimaced as he smelled it, the recognizable scent of rotten flesh, of the dying.

His friends...

His reluctance...

His terror of sickness...

There was even less time than he'd thought.

He sped to the trail, whisked the stones as swiftly as he could to Hanton City, where he assembled them into the rough shape of the two final walls of the foundation. The rain was pouring down now, and the wheelbarrow got stuck several times as he traversed the leaf-strewn path back and forth from the truck. Eventually, he finished with this load, and he paused a moment, taking inventory of the various twinges all over his body while looking over Hanton City. Everything hurt, but he wasn't sure if it was muscular from exertion or something deeper. Was the leprosy invading his bones beneath the soft tissue?

As he turned, Jonas caught sight of a motion from the corner of his eye, a dark shadow amongst the other dark shadows. He spun on his heels to see two of the ghosts standing still about twenty feet away from him. A flash of lightning, and they disappeared, only to reemerge as the darkness resumed. The still figures were familiar to him—the two ghosts which had stood closest to the tree line and partially inside the woods.

It was working! They were coming home! He was bringing them home along with the stones.

He rushed back to the truck full of revitalized energy, and he had some trouble hefting the wheelbarrow into the bed. Once he was inside the cab of the truck and driving back to his home, Jonas noticed several more wounds had split open on his arms. Blood and pus covered his fists where the lesions seeped. He hadn't noticed it so much in the rain, but now, the discharge increased and with it came a new flare-up of pain.

"I'm doing it, Goddammit!" he shouted into the raging storm. "I'm doing what you want!"

He drove back to the house in the pouring rain, the windshield wipers barely able to keep up with the downpour. Skidding to a stop, he left the truck door open as he leapt out of the cab and grabbed the wheelbarrow, which slipped from his grasp and fell to the ground on its side. It took him a lot longer to load the last remaining stones into the back of the truck. The rain made them slippery, even with his work gloves on. Thunder and lightning startled him several times, and he kept glancing over at the remaining ghosts standing still in front of the woods. Seven of them now. Judging him.

Back and forth. Load and unload. Every muscle screaming out in pain. New wounds materializing all over his body as his skin cracked open.

He had to stack the final stones pretty high in the back of the truck, because Jonas wasn't certain how much time he had left. There probably wasn't enough time for a fourth run from the house to Hanton City; he would be dead by then if the infection continued to speed along its current route, so he heaped the rocks as high as he was able. Some slipped off, but he shoved them in the sides and the front seat. Anything to get this ordeal over and done with.

The drive back to the hiking trail stretched on and on. Even once he was parked, Jonas was so weary he could barely compel himself to move. He wanted to remain still, to listen to the rain on the roof of the truck, to close his eyes and finally rest. Away from ghosts and disease and lives full of half-empty beds.

But he couldn't do that. He knew if he shut his eyes for even a minute, he would never open them again, a victim of the entropic depression that had controlled Mark and Millie. He'd tumble into a deep sleep and melt away into a fleshy pile of goo. And he wouldn't give a shit that he was dying.

He was almost there. This was the last truckload of stones. He would soon be finished and then…what? Would the disease stop entirely and so he'd revert back to normal health? Would he be scarred by the ruptures in his skin and flesh? Would this even completely stop the ghosts? There was so much speculation, but it was all he had at the moment. Even when grasping at straws, even with the depression knocking at his skull, he tried to remain optimistic.

But it was difficult. The half mile to the ruins stretched out forever, and the muddy trails impeded his every step. His head was throbbing in agony, and his eyes were seeping a thick pinkish liquid.

With every load of stones from the wheelbarrow he placed alongside the molested shell of a house, he saw another spirit appear in the woods around Hanton City. They were joining their friends, returning home, reclaiming their place in this cruel world. Still, they didn't move, and the immobility grew eerier as each one materialized in the rain.

He abandoned the wheelbarrow in the middle of what had once been a road in the ghost town. His arms were far too weak to get it back down the pathway and to the truck. He said, "Screw it," and left it on its side amongst the weeds in a huge mud puddle.

He returned to the truck, revved the engine, and drove back to his house as the rain stopped and the sun began to creep up over the horizon. The world was filled with a brilliant yellow glow as if everything was healed and all that was damaging and corrupt had been washed away by the nor'easter. The water pooled in long patches alongside the roads.

Jonas parked, got out of the truck, and stepped through the back door of the Lyons's home. He had hoped to see the two of them, fully restored and rosy-cheeked, bustling out to greet and congratulate him. Instead, he found the chair Mark had been sitting in with a crusty skeleton sitting in the center of it, the chintz stained with various fetid bodily fluids. In the room where Millie had been sleeping, he discovered another set of bones surrounded by a puddle of yellow and red slime which stained the mattress and sank deep into it—all that was left of his neighbor. The overwhelming reek of death and putrefaction engulfed the place like a stench-ridden shroud, and he hurried to the backyard, his shirt sleeve/bandage pressed to his nose.

A single ghost remained stationed like a sentry in the yard; Jonas supposed all of the others had returned to their home with the stones. The final sentinel was the large man, tall and broad-chested, the first one Jonas had spotted all those days ago. He was half enshrouded by the trees, which waved in the wind, casting net-like designs across his ruined, sore-filled face.

"I did it," Jonas called to him, and his voice was low and raspy, a victim of the horrible weather and the progression of the disease. "I returned all the stones to your home. You can go now. It's safe to go back."

The figure stood still, and not even the constant wind disturbed a hair on its head or a flap of material from its ruined clothes. It persisted as a specter outside of time. Jonas tried to read its facial expression, but its visage remained a besieged battlefield of scars and wounds. A fine mist wavered before it, enshrouding its countenance.

"I did…all you…wanted," Jonas croaked. "This has…to stop. Now. It can't…go any further."

Something on the right side of his face twitched, and Jonas experienced a sudden change beneath his hairline, a perceptible deficiency. Glancing down into the grass, he saw a wax-like object surrounded by dripping ooze. He raised a hand to the edge of his right cheekbone.

"Oh, God…"

His right ear had fallen to the ground, and a steady stream of pus bubbled from the crater resulting from its absence.

The contamination wasn't stopping. It was actually accelerating, even as the wraiths vanished from his yard. In the end, it didn't matter. None of it mattered. Nothing he did ever fucking mattered.

Jonas felt a forfeiture in his spirit, a crushing despair and sense of futility pushing so hard he collapsed to his knees. There was a wet sound as he dropped. He weakened as his soul lost its will to live.

This is how it feels, he thought. *To be utterly powerless and in the thrall of someone…something you cannot control. This is what it is to live under the whims of another force, another race, another character. Ultimately, this is what takes you down and destroys you. This feeling, this sense of helplessness. No matter what I do, I will suffer and die. No matter how strong I am, I will suffer and die. No matter how white or male or privileged or wealthy or successful or American I feel, I will suffer and die.*

As so many have before me.

He had observed enough death in his past that he knew when the turning point came, when the victim realized it wasn't worth struggling to hold onto life anymore, when the patient succumbed to the warm, welcoming arms of oblivion. He'd been a witness in his time. He didn't need a mirror to know he had exceeded this point.

It explained so much, including the reluctance of his neighbors to seek out the help of a doctor. Their hope had been breached, and now Jonas experienced the same feeling. His will to survive tumbled like bricks in a shattered castle wall. Or stones in a fence toppling to the ground.

"I...don't understand," he said. "I...returned the stones. Your home is back...where it belonged."

There was no answer from the still figure, even as the light from its yellow eyes dimmed.

The sun rose above the horizon, a yellow and orange glow haloing the tops of the trees of the woods. Shadows stretched out toward Jonas, who stumbled a bit before retaining his standing position. His legs were wobbly beneath him. His skin was clammy and cold and it itched intensely.

The final crumbling wave of hopelessness and despair washed over him. He wanted to cry, but his tear ducts were already ruined.

I will suffer and die, he thought again.

With a final look at the ghost, he saw it fading with the encroaching dawn.

It would return. When night came.

But Jonas knew he would never see it again.

He stumbled to his home and entered the back door, which was still unlocked. Along the way, he lost his other ear and a long flap of skin from his face. His shoulders were dusted with his hair, which was falling out at an alarming rate. He didn't shut the door behind himself. What was the point?

He was nearly blind by the time he found his favorite chair, facing the windows. He slumped into it, mirroring the posture of Mark next door in his final moments. As his eyes gave out, he saw a single object in the front yard, a white and green stone dropped and abandoned in his rush to move them all back to Hanton City. When the dawn light struck the granite, it created a sun flare, and then Jonas was blind.

He hadn't finished his job after all. He had missed a stone, and now it was too late. He wondered if the results would have been different had he noticed the overlooked stone and restored it to the bad place, the place where people had been sent to die, far from the contented, unblemished consciences of the locals. He wondered if its restoration would have been soon enough, if he would have merely been scarred a bit or if it wouldn't have altered a thing.

At least, it's over, he thought in his last moments. *At least it won't go on to infect anyone else with its evil. There was nobody left to hurt.*

He opened his heart to the darkness beyond.

And darkness took him.

CHAPTER
NINE

Brad parked his car and stepped out into the driveway. The home he had tried to make with Jonas was dark, the bright sunlight gleaming off the windows and obscuring the interiors. Several birds chirped in the trees of the woods surrounding the place.

It had only taken a few weeks for Brad to realize he had made a terrible mistake when he'd left Jonas. He'd attempted to forget the older man by rushing into fumbling, awkward sex and a few short-lived relationships which only served to remind him of all that had worked so well with his former lover. He had fought it for two months, but he had finally admitted he had been happier in the rural boonies with his Jonas than in any city he'd visited.

He had made a terrible mistake, and he'd returned to rectify his error.

Heading to the door, he saw the neighbor's truck parked crookedly past the driveway and onto the lawn separating the houses.

The grass had deep ruts where the truck's tires had rolled, and there was something white and out of place in the front yard. He reached down and ran his fingers across the square-shaped flat stone.

It was cold to the touch, and a slimy film coated his fingertips. As he brushed his hands against the legs of his jeans, he thought he heard someone sigh loudly behind him. He spun around, but there was nobody nearby. Deciding it was only the wind, he headed to the front door.

His key didn't fit, and he knew he shouldn't be surprised Jonas had changed the locks. His fingertips tingled, and he wiped them on his pants again.

"Jonas?" he cried. "Are you home?"

He walked around the house to the backyard, where he was shocked to see the stone wall Mark Lyons had been building was gone, leaving only a long trench in the grass. It exposed the soil, and earthworms and centipedes wriggled in the damp earth. He shivered. He hated creepy-crawly things. It was a part of why he despised the country, why he didn't like this place. The things that lurked underneath the surface always slithered out one day.

The back door was open, which was incredibly weird.

"Jonas? Honey?"

There was no answer except for the sound of that sigh, a real exhalation of utter hopelessness. He spun around again. Nobody was there.

The skin on his fingers itched.

Squinting, he thought he saw a dark figure standing still in the woods. When he blinked, it was gone, and he shook his head. His imagination had always run rampant out here in the countryside.

Yet, the man he loved was inside this house, and he needed to be with him, needed to see him, needed to feel his touch, his lips. He had always loved the feeling of Jonas's skin against his.

"Jonas?"

He stepped into the dark rectangle of the opened back door.

His fingers itched, as did his forearm.

He wondered if he should wash his hands.

And he was inside the house, swallowed up by the darkened rooms.

His heart was full of hope for reconciliation, and he was practically humming to himself when he saw the thing in the chair in the living room.

The back door slammed shut as he started screaming.

Outside, the stone moved, flipping itself over and over on the paved driveway like a dying fish out of water.

Click clack.

Click clack.

Click clack.

Click Clack.

THE RED HIKE

BY KRISTIN DEARBORN

Elena didn't like hiking. Certainly didn't like hiking in October. She didn't like waking up at four o'clock in the morning to the sound of Charlie clapping his hands, "Time to get up, ladies! Adventure awaits! Let's go, we're burning daylight!" There was decidedly *no* daylight to be seen, most all of the light coming from the soft orange glow of an analog clock in Natalie's living room.

Elena groaned, maybe a little bit still high. It was okay, she just had to move her body and an impossibly large backpack to the van and then she could go back to sleep.

She had to remember she was here for Natalie. Here because Charlie was something of a piece of shit. Natalie'd been trying to make a name for herself as an outdoors influencer, which seemed odd for a girl who'd spent all of college high on their apartment sofa, staring at *Stardew Valley*. She'd given in to Charlie's (pathetic) advances and was a changed woman. Now she managed a Burger King, and every penny was earmarked towards *hash tag van life*. A "real job," she said, would be too confining, wouldn't let her up and leave when "the mountains were calling." This was all great, Elena loved this for Natalie…just without the Charlie part.

She hauled herself off the couch and stretched. They were off on an adventure, she was going to make it fun. A producer had noticed Natalie's posts with their oceans of hash tags, and said that if she did a video about some hike in Southern Vermont for Halloween he'd pay her for it. Then their friend Crystal told Elena that Charlie hit Natalie and somehow Elena said she'd come on the hike even though she didn't know shit about backpacking, like maybe she thought she could protect Natalie? Whatever, it was now 4:30 in the morning and Elena shivered and stepped into Natalie's beloved van. They hadn't fully converted it over to #vanlife; Natalie and Charlie had gotten so far as to pull out the back two rows of seats, and there they'd piled the camping gear for the trip. Elena lay down in the backseat and passed out as soon as they pulled away from the Burlington apartment building. Strange unremembered dreams swirled and skirted around her as she slept. She woke up disoriented, the van off, red flashing light illuminating the seat of the van. A moment of panic snaked up Elena's throat, but before she could choke out a word, Natalie said, "Coffee?"

The red was a stop light, blinking red because it was too goddamn early for it to use all its colors. They were in Bennington, parked on the outer edge of a Starbucks parking lot.

Elena rubbed the sleep from her eyes and used her phone to order from Starbucks. Natalie dressed her in a pair of hiking leggings, she had trail runners which Natalie and Charlie said would be fine. An activewear t-shirt with a fleece. In her pack she had a down jacket with a hood, a pair of fleece pants to sleep in, light gloves and heavy gloves, a light hat and a heavier hat…she wasn't sure what to expect out there. A lot of walking. Exhaustion. Whatever, she said yes. She needed to see what Charlie's deal was and get her friend out.

In the lobby of the restaurant, Natalie told her to put her phone on low battery mode or airplane mode to save power. "I have a charger, so we should be able to charge overnight, but the less you can use the better." It went unsaid that Charlie's phone, a blocky top of the line iPhone with the screen the size of a small tablet, got first priority. This was the main device which would be filming their star. Elena's phone was smaller, a few generations older, didn't have the three cameras. Other than Natalie being Natalie, she couldn't imagine what she would be taking pictures of out there. Her brain wasn't kicked into high gear yet. She needed coffee. Natalie said they had all the food covered, and she wondered if that included coffee. A barista called her name, and when she went to pick up her latte, he brightly said, "You going hiking?"

"Yeah!" She added more enthusiasm than she felt, 'cause he was cute. Shaggy bangs in his face under a toque, a ring through his lip. Name tag: Trevor.

"Where you headed?"

Proud she remembered the name, she said, "Glastenbury Mountain."

"Oh, no shit. Be careful out there."

"Why's that?"

"Have you heard the stories about what goes on out there?"

"I mean," Natalie sent Elena many links to prepare for the hike, and she'd meant to read them, she really had. When Natalie had been talking last night Elena mostly had been fixated on Charlie, wondering what Natalie saw in him. She scraped her memory bank. "A bunch of weird stuff? A ghost town?"

"My dad remembers my grandfather talking about being part of the search party for Freida Langer."

"Who?" Elena said.

"Hi there," Natalie butted in. "My name is Natalie Montclair, and I'm doing a video about the hike and the hauntings, would you mind if I record your story?" Natalie. Waifish, blonde, an outdoorsy little pixie.

Trevor smiled at her, "Yeah, that's cool." He glanced over his shoulder at the other barista.

"Can you back up, introduce yourself, and tell us what your father told you?"

"Uh, sure. I'm Trevor Daniels, and I was just saying I remember my dad telling stories about being part of the search party for Freida Langer."

"Tell us about it," Natalie encouraged, her phone held out towards Trevor. Elena glanced around the store to find Charlie and saw him glowering by the door.

"Okay, so Freida Langer went missing in 1950, right around Halloween. She was out with her husband and some other family members, she was like fifty, they were hunting, she was super outdoorsy. The story goes that she went out on a hike with some people, fell into a creek, said she wanted to run back to the camp site and change her clothes, she'd catch up with them. Her husband was at the tent, never saw her. No one ever saw her again."

"Until her body was found?" Natalie prompted.

"That's the wild part. My grandfather went out to help look. He was one of three hundred people out there. Dogs. Helicopters. Airplanes. They went out five times. They were good searchers. They never found her."

"Wait," Elena said, "Natalie just said—"

"This is the crazy part," said Trevor. "In the spring, they found her body. It was right where they'd been looking. Grandpa said he'd walked over that spot himself on two of the searches and he swears to God—and he was a believer so that's a big deal—swears to God that she wasn't there. They could never find a cause of death."

"She didn't just…freeze to death?" Elena said. She didn't know how forensics worked, or how they had worked in the 1950s.

"If she'd frozen to death, my grandpa would have found her. They searched there."

"Ladies, we need to get moving," Charlie said.

"I'm working!"

"Either way," Charlie said, "we have a long-ass walk in front of us. Travis will be here when we get back." *Trevor*, Elena thought. Charlie'd heard him say it as clear as the rest of them.

"One more question," Natalie said. "Have you ever seen or felt anything spooky in those woods?"

"Nah, man. Because I won't go out there. And I definitely wouldn't go out there in the red coat you're wearing."

Natalie glanced down at her red North Face jacket. "Thank you Trevor, are you on Insta? Can I find you when the project comes out?"

"Yeah, Trevor Daniels. Is this like a professional production or something?"

"Sure is. Now we have to go," Charlie said.

"Watch out for maneating rocks!" Trevor called after them, as Charlie ushered Natalie and Elena and their coffees out of the warm suburban atmosphere of Starbucks and out into the Vermont October morning, where it was still dark, and the cool of the morning bit at their faces.

"Maneating rocks?" Elena said.

"You *really* didn't read any of what I sent you, did you?" Natalie said.

The van was warm when they piled in and smelled a little bit of old outdoor gear musk. Trevor's story was creepy, sure, but it was his grandfather's story; 1950 was seventy-two years ago. If someone killed that Freida woman, they were either dead or not much of a threat. Maybe she should have spent more time with the articles Natalie sent, or maybe, since they were here and she was committed, she should just think about the beauty of nature. She drank her latte as fast as she could, thinking also that sixteen ounces of steamed milk sloshing in her belly might not be the best thing.

Charlie ground the van to a stop in a small parking lot, just past a cheerful Green Mountain National Forest sign. They'd be hiking on both the Long Trail and the Appalachian Trail. If the trail was worn down by all those thru hikers, it had to be kind of easy, right? Charlie threw open the back doors and the cold air swirled in.

"You have to start cold," Natalie said.

Elena asked her to repeat herself.

"Don't get all bundled up and hit the trail. Start with minimal layers on, so when you start warming up you don't just sweat through everything."

"I really don't want to be making camp in the dark this afternoon, and the days are short. Let's hustle, girls, come on."

"Is he always like this?" Elena muttered.

"Only when I'm not moving fast enough."

"How often do you move fast enough?"

Natalie laughed and rolled her eyes.

Elena polished off her latte and left the cup in the cup holder. Morbid thought: if they disappeared on the mountain like Freida, the time and date stamp on her cup might be an important clue for investigators.

"Hike your own pace, Elena. We'll be filming and talking, but we'll match your speed. You should always have eyes on one of us, got me?" Charlie said.

"Okay."

"And if someone does get separated, we'll always wait at the next intersection. First intersection is in 1.3 miles, a spur trail to the Melville Nauheim shelter. There will be a privy there and fresh water, if anyone needs it, or needs to take a shit. When you need to pee, pee in the woods."

They thrust a pair of ski poles into her hands—no, trekking poles—and she dumbly accepted them. She hated to part with her puffy down jacket and stuff it into her pack, but they told her to. Shouldering the weight was heavy, but it impressed her how with the belts cinched the weight melded with her own.

And they were off.

Natalie was talking to the camera in the civil twilight; Elena hovered behind Charlie, trying to warm her body by moving it. Her latte sat in her stomach like a brick. She pulled out her phone, switched it to low power mode and airplane mode. Six thirty. The sun would be up in another half hour. She expected to see light on the horizon to the east, but the trees seemed to take the glow of her headlamp and swallow it whole. The leaves illuminated in her headlamp, a tangle of color wet from the night before's dew. The red maples stood out like spots of blood on the path. Lucky, she supposed, it hadn't frozen.

She tuned Natalie out as they started walking. She kept her gaze and her headlamp on the ground at her feet, stepping around rocks and over roots in the trail, trying to avoid pockets of mud.

Natalie stopped talking, Charlie turned his light down, and silence draped over them like a big, damp blanket. He stepped aside and made her go in front of him, which was annoying because she knew she'd only be slowing him down as the trail became steep quickly. Natalie got farther ahead of her, and Charlie gave her a fair amount of distance from behind. Her breath came ragged as they gained elevation, and it became all she could hear, an affront to her friends' physical fitness and the quiet of the morning. Cold wasn't a problem anymore, and sweat ran down her back, pooled between her breasts, and wet the back of her neck. The silence of the forest, unseen outside the cone of light of her headlamp, reached around her, crushing her, and every gasp and every crunch of her shoes on the path felt like an insult to the woods around them. She realized she was deep in her head, but for the first time in a long time, it felt nice.

Dawn crept up on them, the forest going from black to shades of gray, the leaves only illuminating their fire when directly lit by a headlamp. Elena realized she no longer needed her light. A glance at Natalie and Charlie showed her they'd flicked theirs off, Natalie pulled hers from her head and stuffed it in a pocket.

As the light grew stronger, Elena marveled at the forest. She couldn't imagine getting lost here because she couldn't imagine stepping off the trail, couldn't fathom how someone could navigate the sheer abundance of the trees. They seemed to reach towards the trail, taking as much space as they could, leaving only a little for the humans on the mountain. Natalie stopped up ahead and panic flared in Elena. What was wrong? Why stopping?

The movement warmed her legs and the walking had become a rhythm. Stopping felt wrong, made the pack grow heavy on her back as she leaned on the trekking poles.

"This is the turn off to the shelter. If you gotta shit, that's the place." He pointed at a small trail off to one side.

Elena *did* feel like a visit to the privy was in her best interest, and wondered about what they'd said about not peeing in the privy. She would do all her business at once, she had no idea how to even separate the two, and she really didn't want to pee outside. Not with Charlie around. Oh Jesus, would there be toilet paper?

"Do you want to go first?" Elena said.

"We need to be quiet in case there are people still at the shelter. It's early, they may be making a leisurely morning of it." How did Charlie always sound so goddamn condescending? Elena hadn't realized how close they were to the shelter, and was particularly thankful when they arrived and found the odd structure empty. It housed four bunks, but two of them were extra wide and seemed to also serve as seats for a table. Elena saw a mouse scurrying into darkness.

"Is that like where we'll be sleeping?"

Natalie did want to go first, and pulled a zip lock bag of toilet paper out of her pack. Elena must have looked worried, cause she said, "Don't worry, I got ya," before disappearing down a trail towards a privy.

"Pretty much."

"Don't, like, bears come in? Or other animals?"

Charlie reached down and dialed the condescension up a notch. "Only if you're stupid enough to bring food in with you. You should always hang a bear bag out of reach away from where you're sleeping. The animals don't want us, they want our food cause they think it's an easy meal."

"Okay, but we're, like, going to be sleeping where bugs can get us…" Her sentence petered out.

"It's October. You'll be fine."

She tried to change the subject.

"So we're a mile in?"

Charlie grunted an affirmation.

"So only ten more to go?"

"I'm going to go take a piss."

Elena shrugged the pack off, her back sweaty already, and perched on the edge of the shelter. She could still see Charlie's red jacket, standing out in the colors of fall. The day was overcast, a disappointment because she thought it was going to be nice. The gray of the sky leaked down to the earth, the fog cutting the visibility.

When they stopped talking, the silence threatened to crush them.

Weren't there supposed to be birds and bugs and other things out here, singing and squeaking and doing nature things? Not this oppressive silence that sat on top of them like a dumbbell. It made Elena want to shout as loud as she could.

Natalie talked to her about shouting. Showed her instead that on the chest strap of her pack and again on her headlight, tiny whistles were built into the design.

"Why?" When she asked Natalie why, Natalie didn't make her feel like a moron. "If you need to yell for help, this will save your voice. I've never even used them." In her apartment she'd blown into the headlamp buckle, and sure enough, a loud clear whistle sounded.

Charlie came back, didn't say anything, fiddled with his phone. Elena didn't dare mess with hers, wanting to preserve every scrap of battery. It wasn't the newest iPhone so the charge kinda stunk, but it wasn't as bad as her last iPhone had gotten. Natalie came trudging back, and passed the baggie of TP over to Elena.

"Is it gross?" she hated herself for asking. Felt childish.

Natalie wasn't fazed. No condescension from her. "It all depends. It's a compost toilet in the woods at the end of hiking season, so kinda? But I feel like it's better than a porta-potty at a festival. I look forward to hearing your assessment."

Elena walked, feeling light without the pack or poles, down a slight hill and out of sight from the shelter. She thought she heard Charlie and Natalie talking, but the mist and the forest quickly garbled all sounds. A sign for water pointed off uphill and Elena realized she'd left the pack with the whistles back at the shelter. If she got lost, she'd have to scream.

The brown privy appeared in front of her, raised up, a crescent moon carved in the door. The wood looked rough but clean, and when she opened the door it didn't stink. It *was* much nicer than a porta-potty at a festival. A bucket of wood chips sat to one side with instructions to dump a handful in after you did your business. She peed in the privy, even though she wasn't supposed to. A sign on the door told her it was bad for the composting.

She chucked the wood chips down the hole, wiping her hand on her pants and hurried out. The shelter seemed farther away than she remembered—had she taken the wrong turn towards the water? All the trees looked the same. Why had Natalie let her go anywhere alone out here? She wasn't sure she could get back to the car if she had to.

An ember of panic smoldered in her chest, threatening to ignite. Then she crested a steep rise that she remembered, and there was the shelter, there was her borrowed pack. Natalie lounged next to it like she was at a five-star resort.

"Ready?"

She'd kinda hoped to be able to rest for a while, but apparently that would come in another ten miles. Why on earth had she agreed to this?

Because, she told herself. *Crystal said Charlie hit Natalie, and you needed to see for yourself what was going on.*

"Ready."

She shouldered the pack. Already it didn't feel quite so oppressively heavy, and once it was in place she absorbed its weight. Add the trekking poles and she was ready to go. She'd be sore tomorrow and the day after for sure, but maybe not too bad.

There were a lot more miles between now and then.

They walked. It felt like forever. Charlie's irritation was palpable every time Elena asked that they stop, every time she shrugged her pack off. In contrast, Charlie never sat, kept his pack on, and paced around them like an irritated shark. Sometimes Natalie sat with Elena, sometimes she pulled out her camera and monologued about the forest primeval. Elena grappled with her breath and her heartrate and tried not to listen to Natalie talking about missing persons, strange hairy creatures in the woods, UFO sightings, and possible theories.

Mid-morning, the mist burned off, and bright sun flooded the crayon box of leaves all around them. As the sun shone, it became hard to balance the tales Natalie told with the glorious Vermont fall around them. Elena watched the couple. Her mission, she reminded herself, wasn't to solve a haunted mountain, but to evaluate her friend's relationship and get her help if she needed it. Charlie was a pretty shitty boyfriend, but he took photograph after photograph of her, filmed where she needed him to be. The amount of content he gathered would make for a pretty neat YouTube video.

How would Charlie feel when Natalie had millions of fans rather than thousands?

They walked. Her quads were stone, and she sweated through all the clothes. The cool fall air was a balm washing over her.

"The shelter is right up ahead," Natalie said. She'd led the hike from the front most of the day, with Charlie looping around behind Elena and heading up to film Natalie, alternating. She hated when he was behind her, felt like he judged her every foot placement and every rasping breath.

"What shelter?" Elena managed.

"Goddard. This is it!"

"We're done?" The little building squatted before them, a sturdy roof covering the sleeping area and a porch. Benches were built into a front railing. The inside was dark in the long shadows of the afternoon, but Elena imagined it as dry and out of the wind. She'd never imagined so looking forward to lying down on a hard wooden floor.

"Oh, it wasn't so bad," Natalie said, trying to be encouraging.

The shadows grew longer, but there was still plenty of daylight. Elena overheard Charlie muttering that they should have been able to do the hike in five hours. Looking at her watch, it had taken over eight. She was proud of herself. They'd done it.

She headed across the clearing to the little shelter, rounded the corner, and…

A body lay inside.

Huddled in a pathetic ball in the back corner.

A scream simmered in her throat but she couldn't make it come out.

He was a mess of long matted hair and bright hiking clothes, a giant thru hiker backpack nestled with him and a vibrant but dirty blue sleeping bag.

The corpse opened his sunken eyes.

Elena never got her scream out, instead backed away, bumping Charlie and stumbling back.

"There's someone in there."

"Yes, Elena, that's how these shelters work. First come, first serve, and sometimes we have to share."

"It's okay, Elena," Natalie said, kinder. "What's wrong?"

"He...I...He looked dead. Then he opened his eyes." She lowered her voice, not wanting him to hear her. There was something else about him, though. Something familiar. Like she'd seen him before. Maybe up in Burlington?

Elena fought the temptation to burst into tears. She was so tired, Charlie's condescension grated on her, and the start the man gave her...It all felt like too much.

"Hey man, how are you?" Charlie strode over to the shelter, and acknowledged the other hiker.

"He's just curled in the back like a wounded animal," Elena said.

"I hope he's okay," Natalie said, more by rote than any real compassion.

He's not.

Elena heard a soft murmur of a voice from inside the shelter, saw Charlie step back and frown. Natalie went to his side, both of them dropped their packs as far from the guy as they could get. Elena followed, not wanting to be alone.

"Are you hiking southbound?" Charlie said. The man in the corner didn't look capable of hiking anywhere. It wasn't that Elena had imagined they'd have the shelter to themselves (though this late in the season, she kind of had), but she thought that anyone sharing the shelter would be hale and hearty and ready to hike.

"Nah man, I'm just here for a little while."

Charlie's brow furrowed. "You all good?"

The man thought on it a moment. "I don't think so. I haven't felt so good. This isn't really a good place."

Icy prickles danced down Elena's spine, made worse by the fact that she was drenched in sweat and they'd stopped walking. She wanted to put on the camp clothes Natalie insisted she bring along. The idea of something dry and clean was like heaven. She'd imagined changing in the shelter out of the wind, but not if there was a stranger in there.

"I'm Badger," the guy said.

Charlie went tense. If she hadn't been watching him closely, Elena never would have noticed. "Charlie."

"OMG," Natalie squealed. "When Charlie hiked the first hundred miles of the AT, they called him Badger. Trail names are given, and they said Charlie was mean as a Badger and he *hated* it. I guess weird is fitting on a haunted mountain. Let's get changed into some dry clothes," she murmured. "I don't really love his energy." They went around the side of the shelter, into the howling wind, and changed as quickly as they could. When they came back, Charlie crouched in front of the fire pit, frustrated.

"The wind comes from every angle. Can't get the fire to start."

Natalie held up one finger. "Hold that thought." She grabbed her phone, used it first as a mirror to preen, then pressed record. Elena felt like a bedraggled rat, unclear how Natalie could look so fresh.

"The Abenaki were the first people to make their home in this part of Vermont. They called this summit the place where four winds meet, and tended to avoid it because of erratic weather patterns, the winds switching direction. How's the fire coming, Charlie?"

He grimaced at the camera. "As a matter of fact, Natalie, I'm having a bit of trouble getting it started for the very reason you mentioned. The wind keeps creeping in from different sides and blowing things out."

Natalie swept the phone over the camp, catching Badger in the video as she panned past.

"We're here just about at the top of Glastenbury Mountain. We have time to make dinner, take in the sunset from the top of the fire tower, then do a little exploring tomorrow before we come down. I'll check in in a bit. Bye!"

Elena looked at her phone. Zero bars. Of course. She wanted to sit, wanted the comfort of a man-made structure, but didn't want to be so close to Badger. She had to, she finally decided, and went to sit on the bench on the shelter.

"You came," he said.

Elena, wanting to be a good friend, pressed record on her phone, and tried to subtly point it at him.

"What did you say?"

"It's been lonely here. I've been here a while."

Charlie came over, puffed up and given up on the fire and come over to protect his women.

Badger squinted at him, like there was a joke in his head he didn't want to share. "There's a cairn nearby. Really cool. You should check it out."

Elena held her phone steady. She really didn't want to stay here with this crazy guy all night. Her legs ached and all she wanted was to sit for a while…without worrying about being murdered.

"Yeah," Natalie said. "We're definitely going to check out the cairns."

"Cool, cool," Badger said.

"It's pre-colonial," Natalie said, looking into her camera. "The stones aren't from here, the rock isn't anything that's found in Vermont. And they're big. Big and old. Native American maybe, Abenaki, but they want nothing to do with this place. Archaeologists are pretty sure they're not burial mounds. We're going to go check them out."

"I can show you where they are." Badger struggled to get up, but flopped back down into his little nest. "Just off the summit—"

"How about you rest up, and we'll come and get you if we're having trouble finding it," Natalie said.

Elena thought she saw blood on his hands when he tried to stand.

Natalie turned off the recorder on her phone and Elena did the same, but kept it close. Natalie went to Charlie, put a hand on his back and leaned into him. Neither Elena nor, presumably, Badger, could hear them.

Charlie's body language made Elena uncomfortable, coiled tight like anything could and would set him off. She imagined him hurting Badger, and then, with a clenching in her gut she imagined him hurting Natalie. Again.

Elena stood up, her legs squealing in protest. The idea of going down already made her want to wail. She wanted the fire going, and then to curl up in her borrowed sleeping bag. Her calves felt like rocks and her knees protested.

"We're going to find the cairn and then head to the fire tower," Natalie said.

"Should someone stay here with our gear?" Elena tossed her head to where Badger curled in the shadows.

"He's fine, and if he's not I certainly wouldn't leave you with him!" Natalie said.

"He's just high. Or sick. Probably both. Shouldn't be out here," Charlie said.

"You really think it's okay to leave our food and sleeping bags with him?"

"You want to carry them again?" Charlie said.

"People out here are fine. Hikers would never jeopardize us by fucking with our gear," Natalie said.

"But he—" Elena started.

"Then just stay with the gear and quit whining," Charlie snapped.

Elena bit back her words. Whatever. Charlie knew best.

"Charlie, stop it. Elena's coming with us, and we're only taking the filming gear. Are we ready?"

To hike again? To move? No, never. Elena resisted the urge to ask how far it was.

"Cairns first, while we have light. Sunset in the tower is going to be epic."

"Less epic with no fire to come back to." Charlie kicked at the fire ring with his boot.

Natalie changed the subject. "When we get back I'm putting my crocs on, can't wait to get out of these stupid boots. But no one wants to see me in crocs in my video."

"Really?"

"I don't want to see me in crocs in my video!"

How could she still be acting like things weren't seriously fucked up? Even if Badger weren't here spreading his bad vibes, Charlie was a fucking asshole.

"This way to the cairns."

"Do you want me filming?"

"Not yet, the website I was looking at says they're a little tricky to find."

She didn't dare stay behind with Badger, so she followed at a distance. Would she even be able to get herself home tomorrow? Ugh, and what even was home? Her parents would make a big fuss over her being sore, over her being "into" backpacking now. Her dad telling her stories about trying to hike with his frat brothers in college, the time a moose chased them off Mount Waumbek in New Hampshire.

Elena followed Natalie and Charlie off the trail on a flat, wooded plateau. She didn't know much about hiking or outdoors stuff, but leaving the trail was how you got lost. She peeked at her phone, where one bar flirted with her, appearing and disappearing. Elena shoved the thoughts out of her head like she shoved pine boughs away. The ground here was mossy and spongy, and the wind did seem like it came from all directions at once. Never again, Natalie. Never again.

"Here!" Natalie's voice sounded too far away, and for a moment when Elena looked around she couldn't see either of her friends (if she could call Charlie a friend). Panic fluttered in her throat, but then she saw Charlie's red jacket and hurried in his direction.

Elena came up short behind Charlie. The cairn wasn't what she'd expected. Stones, neatly piled, surrounded a dead pine tree in a ring. They came up taller than Charlie's waist, and thick green moss covered them. The placement was so intentional, like an ancient New England stone wall. Charlie turned on his phone to film, and Elena did the same, from a different angle. She caught Natalie in profile, her hair tugged back into a messy bun. She looked perfect, playing the right part in her red North Face jacket. She started to talk to the camera, Elena watched for a moment, then looked away, back over her shoulder.

"What the fuck?" Charlie. In the moment it took for Elena to turn back to him and Natalie, at first she thought he sounded mad.

She realized he sounded afraid. She realized Natalie was gone. She blinked. Still gone. She struggled to suck in a breath.

"What happened?"

Charlie glared at her. Hate gleamed in his eyes. He spat at her like she were some kind of idiot. "She disappeared."

"What are you talking about? Natalie!"

Charlie thrust his phone in her face, the screen had gone dark. Elena's phone was still recording. She stopped and rewound, watching what she'd captured. Natalie reaching out to touch the cairn, placing a hand on it. The image shuddered, like an old VHS tape with magnetic interference. Natalie gone. She went back, watched again. Handed her phone to Charlie and took his. He'd put the passcode in, and she watched his recording. Clearer, more polished with his fancy phone, but the same result, Natalie talking, looking at home in front of the camera and in the woods, a nauseating shudder, then nothing.

"She winked out of existence."

"I don't get it," Charlie said, apparently too distracted to be mean. "This is going to sound stupid. This all sounds stupid. We read something about rocks that eat people."

"The rock didn't eat her," Elena said, but what did she know? She went to the cairn and before she could stop herself, she placed a hand on the stone Natalie reached for. Charlie shouted at her.

Nothing happened. The moss was cool, pleasant to the touch, though a little more coarse than she'd expected. She pulled her hand away like she'd been burned. Looked at Charlie. Put it back. He took a step away.

"Why...?" He took another step away, his heel getting tangled in a thick, tentacle-like root jutting out of the moss. He fell, landing on his butt. Elena put another hand on the cairn, groped at it, felt around.

Why indeed? Why didn't it take her like it had taken Natalie?

"Tell me about the rocks," she said. Charlie stood cautiously; all his bravado gone. The rocks sat silent, their mossy backs reminding Elena of an ancient turtle.

He shook his head. "It's just a story. Just like all the other bullshit out here. All just stories."

"I don't think so."

She thought of the barista in Bennington. Her gaze landed on Charlie's red coat. Her coat was one of Natalie's, big for Natalie to layer under, but just the right fit for Elena. Bright blue. Something about the color red, they'd said, right?

"Come here, Charlie."

"Why?"

"I have an idea."

"To get her back?"

"I think so." Or to follow her. She couldn't accept that the rocks *ate* people, that was ridiculous. Rocks don't eat. Yet the rock as a waypoint between here and somewhere else, that actually made sense to her. Natalie had to have gone *somewhere*, right?

When Charlie came close, she grabbed his sleeve, and put her palm on the mossy surface of the nearest rock.

Nothing happened.

"What the fuck did you do? My phone is dead." Charlie peered at the screen of his phone. Elena'd killed her own phone, it wouldn't light up or turn on at all. *At least they were conserving battery*, she thought ludicrously.

"Put your hands where I can see them," someone said.

Badger, Elena thought, but she and Charlie turned to see a man in wool trousers and a plaid shirt with an old-looking rifle pointed at them. In his other arm was Natalie, one of his large hands clamped down on her mouth, keeping her quiet. Her eyes were huge and luminous in the gloaming.

"Three in one night. My lucky day."

Elena expected Charlie to charge him, to attack, to funnel all that rage he carried around with him at something actually productive. If they tag teamed the guy, they'd be able to get Natalie away from him.

"Come on, you all. Back to the resort." He relaxed his grip on Natalie and pushed her towards a thin herd path.

Resort?

"You can't shoot all of us," Natalie said.

"No, but I figure shooting one will do the trick and the rest of you will fall in line."

Elena was sure he was right. They headed off in single file, Charlie first, then Elena, followed by Natalie, the gun trained on the back of her head, held in two hands now. Twice, Charlie let wispy pine boughs slap Elena across the face (or maybe they were fir, she could never tell the difference) before she watched for them and caught them, holding them back before they clobbered Natalie in the same way. They left Elena's face wet and a little bit smelling like balsam fir. It contrasted with a smell of woodsmoke in the air, one that decidedly hadn't been present before they touched the stone. Elena watched Charlie, still carrying himself with all his anger, shoulders hunched and head down. He marched ahead, and when he stopped, she caught herself before she plowed into him. They'd reached a clearing on top of a hill, a valley spread out before them.

It couldn't be right, not in the world where they'd entered the woods, because Natalie showed her the map, showed her the great expanses of green all around them. No towns. Not the bustling little community before them. A stream wove its way through the center of the valley, followed down the mountain by railroad tracks, shiny and new looking. A couple on horseback rode through town, the woman sitting side saddle. A wooden bridge crossed the stream in the middle of town. Dominating the entire scene, perched into the hillside sat an imposing four story building with a tall clock tower, glowing orange in the fading light. Across from it looked like a hotel, back behind were people's houses and brick kilns pumping out smoke. All the trees here were cleared away.

"This is 1898," Natalie whispered, close enough to Elena for her to hear. "There's going to be a flood. Any day now. It's going to wipe out the railroad tracks and the town will die."

The gun jabbing into her back shut Natalie up.

1898 meant time travel. "No," said Elena, "that's not possible."

"It's not on the map anywhere. Not for more than a hundred years," Natalie said.

"Shut up," her captor said.

"Where are we? What year is this?"

He laughed at her like she'd told the funniest joke in the comedy club. "Yer in Glastenbury. And you just said when. Just like you said the flood is coming. Seems like you have all the answers, little miss."

Elena couldn't tell if he was placating her, teasing her, what his angle was. She opened her mouth, but had nothing to add. Charlie stared down at the town, his face slack.

Down below, a trolley car puffed out steam, and a string of well-dressed men, women, and children boarded it. Snatches of their laughter drifted up the hillside.

The man marched Elena, Natalie, and Charlie down the thin path until it met up with a rutted road running along the stream, on the other side from the railroad tracks.

The man led them across a bridge. A string of folks passed by, the women in long skirts with colorful blouses and jackets with puffy sleeves, boater hats perched atop their heads. The men wore open jackets with turned down wingtips at the collars, bowler hats atop their heads. They ignored Elena and her friends, and Elena stared at them. No one spoke out for them, no one stopped their kidnapper and asked him to rethink what he did to them. The people rushed for the trolley, hurrying but still talking and laughing. The trolley would wait for them.

Their captor shoved them onward, and they went into the hotel through some kind of staff entrance, opening to a basement. Most of the bigger buildings were built into the hillside, above them was a grand porch where the men and women in fancy clothes presumably had recently sat, taking in the fall leaves, sipping cocktails.

That's where I belong. The entitled thought took Elena by surprise, but she didn't walk it back. They all had to stoop to get through the basement door, and the hallway inside was dusty wood. It smelled like fresh cut wood, despite the dust. The walls around them were bright, not yet weathered.

"Change. Clothes are on your bunks. And if you try anything, we know where to find you." He shoved Natalie and Elena into a room and closed the door behind them.

Natalie ran for the door. "Charlie!" Only silence met her.

The transition would have been a great time for Charlie to throw his weight around...nothing.

Three bunkbeds, three bunks tall, lined the walls of the room. For the moment, they had it to themselves.

"Natalie, what is all this?'"

"I think we know where all the missing hikers have been going."

"Here?"

"Seems like. I was reading about Glastenbury before we left. I know we're in 1898 because I'm a nerd: they logged all this area extensively before that, and then when there were no more viable trees, someone had the bright idea to run a railroad up here and make it a resort. The resort was open for exactly one summer, in 1898. In late October, I don't remember the date, there was a huge storm and a mudslide and it wiped the railroad out. Everyone here was stranded, could only walk down. They could never afford to rebuild the railroad, and the town just...died. Everyone moved out." Natalie thought for a moment. "When the storm comes we can use it as a distraction, go back to the stones, and hope they send us home."

Elena gaped at her. Watched her friend strip out of her North Face and Patagonia gear into linen underthings and a woolen skirt and blouse that looked like a maid would wear it. Natalie scrunched up the clothes.

"Wait," Elena said. "Keep your jacket. There's something about the red that makes the stones work. It didn't pull me when I touched it without Charlie." Elena changed out of her borrowed clothes. The shoes were too big and her feet swam in them. She was cold already. And so, so tired. Maybe they'd get to sleep before someone put them to work.

Natalie balled up her red jacket, stuck her multi tool in the pocket, and tucked it in a corner under one of the bunks.

"Did you read any stories about people just...arriving in the woods around here? Like they'd come from another time?"

"No." Natalie thought about it for a moment, grimacing as she laced her own shoes. "But maybe we wouldn't? Someone like that would be afraid, and might hide. And there was Freida Langer, who we were talking about in Starbucks. She disappeared, but then showed up totally randomly in a spot where people searched before. So maybe? Maybe we can get back through."

"Freida Langer was dead, though, right?"

"Yeah. But maybe she didn't do as much research as I did before, you know? We kinda know where we are, when we are, and we think we know how to get back, yeah?"

"Yeah. I'm tired. My body. From the hike. I don't know what I'll do if I have to keep going today."

Natalie fished a protein bar out of the ball of clothes she'd wadded up on the bed, and handed it across to Elena.

"Charlie must be losing his shit."

Charlie deserves to lose his shit, Elena thought. "He'll be all right. I notice he's not running his mouth at our captor."

"Seriously? Now?"

Elena looked around the empty room. She was tired. The line between her brain and her mouth was taut and short. "Crystal said he hit you."

Natalie took a deep breath. She looked like she wanted to say something, she paused, then said, "It's okay."

"Is it true?"

"I know how it sounds. It's not like that."

"Tell me about it, then."

"Here?"

Elena tried the wooden door and found it locked. "Not much else we can do until your friend comes back for us."

Natalie thought for a few moments. "He's insecure. So, so, so insecure. I just wish he'd work on himself, help himself. Therapy, or a job, or anything. I busted my ass to get the money for the van together, and he treats me like I owe it to him."

"Why not go?" Elena tried so hard to keep the judgement out of her voice.

Tears welled up in Natalie's eyes. "It doesn't matter now. Not if we don't get out of here."

"We are going to get home. It will matter. Talk me through it. I can help."

"It's going to come out wrong, I know it. So bear with me and don't call me a selfish bitch until I'm done, okay?"

"I'd never call you that."

"If he had a job we'd be tied here. He's a really good photographer. He takes good video, and he edits well. Right now, I can work fast food, and then we can pick up gigs when we need to. This video was supposed to get us out of Vermont. I thought that if we had some success and he had producer credit, he'd stop being such a dick. Sometimes he's really sweet. When he gets out of his head, when he gets out of his own way, I really love him."

"I get it," Elena lied. "When this is done, you can hire a photographer."

"But I want it to be him, you know? But him not being an asshole. The good side of him. The one he only shows me when we're out in the woods."

"I didn't see that side today."

"You make him nervous."

"Why?"

Natalie buried her face in her hands. "Can we not do this? I get it. I hear myself. It doesn't make sense. I'm dumb. I'd call me dumb if this were a movie."

"You wouldn't call a friend dumb if they were telling you this."

Natalie breathed out her nose. "Guess not. But I'd tell me to get out."

In the silence, Elena slipped into her own head. Men who hit. Angry men. Something simmered there. Something ready to boil over. Elena hated being around it. And she thought the angry men knew that, too, and used it to keep women out of their spheres.

Sometime later, seven other women came in, all talking over one another, then stopped when they saw Elena and Natalie on the bottom bunk together. They leaned on one another, as much for physical warmth as for comfort.

"That's my bunk," a tall woman said, not unkindly.

"We didn't know where to go," Elena mumbled, as they got up. Her legs, set from sitting for a bit, howled.

"Where are we?"

"Did you come in from the woods?" The women talked differently, *talked funny* Elena wanted to call it, but that wasn't right, or kind.

Elena and Natalie nodded. "You?"

"Jessamyn did." The lead woman pointed.

"What year? What year did you come from?"

"1986. But that doesn't matter."

Elena said, "Why doesn't it matter?"

"Time doesn't matter."

"If you're from 1986 you know there's going to be a flood and—"

"That's where you're wrong. There won't be a flood. The storm comes and...everything resets. A huge clap of lightning and it's spring and we're welcoming the first trolley of tourists and everything has to be perfect."

"You'll see, it's soon," someone else said.

Elena realized she was shaking her head, but what good was it to be in denial? None of this made sense.

"Two days til the storm," another woman said.

"Who's doing this?" Natalie said.

"I know you've a lot of questions, but the sooner you just settle in, the easier it'll be on ye both."

"I don't want it to be easy. I want to go home!"

The women shook their heads sympathetically. "I know, dearie. We have some fun. Tonight's a night off, all the guests went back down today and they won't be back until the spring. We'll have dinner soon, then plenty of time to get you two learned about what your jobs are. You start as housekeeping here in the boarding house, if you're lucky you can make it up to the casino."

"Has anyone made it home?" Natalie said.

"We don't know. No one who's run has ever come back. I'm mostly sure that's 'cause she's caught and killed them." The women took turns answering, like a Greek chorus.

Elena latched on to that single pronoun. "She. Who is she?"

"Rest. You've had a shock today. It was a good day to come, we can ease you in. Middle bunks here and here are free."

Elena and Natalie retreated to one miserable middle bunk, sticking together, and watching the women chatting amongst themselves, laughing, even. One took their 2022 clothes and carried them away somewhere. All except the hidden red jacket. "You have everything you need out of here?" she asked before she went. "Can keep some small things, but they'll notice if you hold too much back."

They took their phones out of instinct, even thought they were inert hunks of glass and metal. Elena wouldn't give up the phone, regardless of how useless it was.

The evening passed. They ate in different shifts than the men. Natalie tried to find Charlie, but the other women gently kept her in the room. She tried to fight them, but they were firm. *Too much trouble,* they said, if she went out of the room.

Natalie argued she was fine with that, willing to take on whatever it entailed, but one of the women spoke up. "Not just trouble for you, trouble for all of us. The sooner you sit tight and calm down, the better off you'll be."

Elena and Natalie shared a bunk and Elena remembered being a foolish little girl and telling her friends she loved them, "dearly not queerly," a feminine prototype of "no homo." It seemed so silly and petty now. Natalie sobbed herself to sleep, and Elena wished she could, but no tears came.

Morning came early to the windowless room, and Elena and her screaming, aching legs were sent to tag along with a woman called Rachel, bringing meals to the guests on the upper floors. Midday they transitioned to turning the rooms over. The lush feather beds and bright airy spaces made her back ache even more. In 2022 if someone opened a place like this, the tourists would go wild for it, chamber pots and lack of running water or not. She imagined staging a photo from the bed, catching the clock tower of the casino in the frame. "Killing time in Glastenbury, Vermont. I'll try my luck later in the casino, but for now, cat naps in sunbeams."

Rachel started the morning professionally enough, showing her where to find the cleaning products, showing her a few tricks to make the work go faster.

Then she said, "Elena. You're going to get out of here."

The words pierced Elena's consciousness like a spear. Hope, that fickle bitch, jabbed at her.

"Natalie? Charlie?"

"You and Charlie go back. He attacks you and gets shot. Natalie is a huge mystery...She goes back and posts a picture of herself on one of your social media sites wearing this." Rachel gestured to her woolen maid's blouse. "But no one ever finds her."

What?

"And you?"

"I don't know. I'm from 2150, so I could read about your news story. I've never met anyone from further in the future than I am who was willing to tell me anything. We try not to talk about the future to people, they insist on not talking about our homes at all, say it just gives false hope. I just...I had to tell you."

Elena wanted to cry...She couldn't imagine being the catalyst for the escape, it had to be Natalie or Charlie. But Charlie attacked her and was shot? Shot by whom? None of it made sense.

"I'm sorry, that was a lot. Let's get back to cleaning up the room. If she hears us talking like this...it won't be good. So just...I guess keep hope and watch for opportunities."

"Who is *she*?"

"Lenore. I don't want her hearing, or one of her goons. I've already said too much."

Rachel turned her back on Elena, and Elena wanted to pounce on her, demanding she tell her everything. But she bit her tongue.

Elena and Rachel were on their third room when there came a clatter of horse hooves from outside. "That's Lenore," Rachel said.

Elena snuck a peek out the window and saw a severe woman, dressed in what Elena imagined was high fashion for the day, dismount the horse she'd ridden side saddle. She wore a fascinator over a low bun, and a scowl on her lips.

"Who is she?"

"In charge."

"But—"

"They say her hearing is extra good. Don't let her catch you asking about her."

"Why is everything such a stupid secret around here?" Elena knew her voice rose louder than it should.

"Because we're slaves. Slaves in some kind of pocket dimension, where Lenore is in charge. And as long as people go to the top of that stupid mountain in October insisting on wearing red, she'll have a never-ending stream of workers. There's no running away; in this universe there's only this resort and trees. I don't know where the trolley gets its tourists, but that way is closed to us. Pam tried to take it and never came back."

"You don't think she's living in New York City or something, with a new identity and a new life?"

"No, I do not. I tried to run once and her hounds brought me back, starving and exhausted. These woods aren't particularly life supporting."

"Did you go back to the cairn?"

"I couldn't find it."

Elena bit her lip, then turned to dust the vanity. Stared at herself in the mirror. The last remnants of the mascara she'd put on the day before they left (she hadn't showered before the hike, and hadn't done a good job washing her face) clung to her lashes. In the maid's uniform, not the kind you'd see as a slutty Halloween costume, but rather a dull, off-white woolen tunic-type dress, she looked painfully plain. She regarded herself as the door to the room banged open.

"You're one of the new girls?"

Lenore stood shorter than Elena imagined after seeing her dismount the horse. Her shoes had a sensible low heel, which meant without them, Lenore was positively diminutive.

"Yes, ma'am." Elena wasn't sure where it came from, but seeing Rachel standing ramrod straight, for now at least, Lenore would receive deference.

Lenore nodded approvingly. "Have the other girls made you feel at home?"

"Yes, ma'am."

"And told you the rules?"

Elena cast a fleeting glance at Rachel. "Yes? To never discuss where we come from?"

"Yes would suffice. You come from here. You are Glastenbury now. Our little town can't run without workers like you."

Elena nodded.

"Do you have any questions for me?" Lenore said, in a tone that suggested the correct answer was "no."

Instead of answering with another "yes, ma'am," Elena said, "How did we get here? What is this place? How long do we stay and work?"

"I'm not sure I heard you."

Rachel kept her face impassive.

"What kind of a place is this? Time travel? How do I get home?"

"This is your home. I'll be gentle, and it'll only be five lashes. Any other questions?"

"Lashes?"

"Six. Any questions?"

She shook her head, but that wasn't right either. Lenore cocked her head. Elena managed to croak, "No, ma'am."

Now Lenore smiled, big and wide like the Cheshire Cat. "Perfect. I do so appreciate all the hard work you're doing for us."

She swished out of the room, and closed the door behind her. Rachel and Elena stood motionless for a few beats.

Then Rachel said, "Are you simple? You're going to get whipped. Do you have any idea what that's like?"

"I'm from 2022. Of course I have no idea what a whipping is like."

They transitioned to the next hotel room and Elena lost herself in the work. It was easier that way, only thinking about dipping her rag into the bucket of now cold gray water and scrubbing at the pine floors.

In the afternoon a bell in the clocktower rang, and Rachel shot a look at Elena.

"We're going to gather outside. You'll get your punishment. You and whoever else didn't watch their mouths today."

"*Today?* Like this happens every day?"

Rachel nodded. "There's always something to talk about. Not every day someone gets whipped, though." Elena must have been making a horrible face, because Rachel said, "You'll be okay. She knows it's your first day here. It'll basically just be making an example of you."

Elena wasn't sure if this made it better or worse. Would it now hurt more than she expected cause she assumed they'd be "taking it easy" on her?

ELENA LEARNED THAT AFTER THE FIRST BITE OF THE WHIP, HER EARS rang with a high-pitched whine and her vision started to go gray. It felt like a house of cards being built on her back, stacking pain on pain on pain in different angles and different dimensions. She wasn't sure when it ended, and even though the number was only six she lost count and at some point she sank onto the dirt and no one bothered her for a while. She didn't pass out.

Spit dripped out of her mouth and her fingers gripped the dirt. Three days ago she'd been concerned about whether or not to get her nails done. Now her whole back throbbed and spiraled with a pain like she'd never conceived of. She couldn't tell if she was crying or screaming, her throat felt raw, but she was breathing through her mouth, sucking in great gasps of air.

After the whipping, Lenore said a few more words. Elena couldn't hear them; her ears only registered a high-pitched keening. Tinnitus or her own wailing, she didn't know or particularly care. When Lenore finished, the sun sank below the tree line and the temperatures dropped. It was Rachel who came for her.

"Natalie," Elena said. Something awful must have happened to her if Rachel were the one coming to her aid. Right? "Where is she?"

"I didn't see her. She wasn't at the circle. Neither her or Charlie."

Charlie, jealous again of someone other than him getting attention? Even here with all this, was he dominating Natalie.

"Did she notice?"

"Not sure. If she did she didn't let on. Are you hungry?"

Though she'd worked a full day, the thought of food made Elena's stomach roil. "Lie down. Rest. Is there something for my back?"

"I'll help you to the infirmary. Can you stand?"

"Did they ever whip you?" Elena hoped Rachel's answer would distract her as she took the other woman's strong hand and struggled to her knees. Every new movement was a new twinkle of agony in her back. She imagined the pain as Fourth of July fireworks, the ones that start with a big burst, and trickle lots of little bursts, falling to the ground until they wink out. But a new firework would rise to take their place.

"Everyone has," Rachel said.

Everyone.

"If she's in a mood for it, she circles like a shark. Tries to get someone to say the wrong thing and when they do, she gets them."

"She kills them?"

"She does. Usually around when new folks come through the woods for her."

"People try to escape?"

"Either back to where they came from or out into the forest. Anyone who's come back just says they were lost in the woods, wandering in circles. Never finding roads or houses or seeing any sign of people or animals. These woods are a ghost."

"No one has found the cairns again?"

"No one who's come back."

NATALIE, HER RED NORTH FACE JACKET BALLED AGAINST HER STOMACH, held out her compass, and looked up at the stars. The moon, just like at home, was an absent friend this time of the month. Wind whipped at her, icy and mean. As she walked, it seemed to come from all sides at once. She couldn't turn her back to it, it kept pushing her face, first from the left, then the right.

She'd tried to get Charlie to come.

"You saw what happened to Elena, didn't you? Do you want to be next?"

She didn't. That's why she took the opportunity to run. She thought he'd come. He'd help. Thought he'd be there for her and do something, anything, other than cower and judge.

She needed to confirm there was a way to get home, thought about all the missing persons from the area. People like the college girl who went missing and the little boy who were never found, but Freida Langer was found—had made it back to her own time—and another guy, a hunting guide's body was found. Natalie hypothesized that people who could navigate the woods were able to find the cairn.

Langer was dead with no apparent cause of death, her body too badly decomposed to get an accurate read. The guide had been shot once, in the back, apparently not in the location where the body was found. Natalie had hoped they'd both made it through. It hadn't taken long to hike to the resort from the cairn, so she thought she could get to the cairn, confirm that it worked, and go back for Charlie and Elena while poor Elena had their attention. The leather shoes bit at her feet and she pined for her hiking boots. She hurried over the deer path they'd used the day before.

She put her compass away; it swirled and lurched, trying to find its bearings and failing miserably. Must be like the cell phone, ordinary laws of physics didn't quite work here.

The herd path and her memory would have to do.

She paused, crouched, a momentary respite from the wind, which lashed the brush all around her. Her ears stung with the cold. The woolen outfit stood out bright in the starlight and she didn't want to be seen. Glastenbury glowed below her, nearly every window of the hotel lit by lamplight. The resort preparing itself for a new season of guests, one that never should have come. The scene before her shimmered, going hazy around the edges.

For a beat, Natalie wondered if she'd been poisoned, but instead understood it had something to do with the liminality of this place.

She needed to find the cairn, needed to get out of here. If she couldn't get home…She'd cross that bridge when she came to it. There had to be a way. A way home, to her own *when*.

She pulled the puffy jacket on, the October night so cold she could see her breath in front of her face when she exhaled. As long as she kept moving, she'd be fine. Another pause to study the stars. They were in the same place as they were back home, at least. If they'd been different, twisted, she didn't know what she would have done.

Charlie taught her the stars, and for that she was grateful. Before his careful tutelage, they'd all seemed about the same to her. She'd never been able to see the constellations everyone always talked about. The big dipper, sure. Cassiopeia was a W, and the seven sisters had the stars packed so closely together they made their own light. When he pointed out Orion, she felt like a fool for never seeing it before, his belt so clear in the night sky. Then Cepheus appeared, over Cassiopeia. They all fell into place after that.

She used them to keep track of where she was. When she reached the line of the trees, the forest swallowed her whole. While the trees did help at cutting the wind, they swayed all around her, leafless branches whispering above her. Every so often a trunk groaned, and she remembered Charlie telling her to stay out of the woods in high winds. Something crashed off in the forest…A tree falling? If someone came up behind her, she'd never hear them over the sounds of the wind. Even if they didn't, the susurrus of the branches above her might drive her mad.

She kept a Gerber multi tool, one that Charlie gave her, and used it to slice notches into the trees as she walked. Their escape needed to be as simple as possible. She couldn't be worrying about where to go, which way was right when they were running for their freedom.

It took time to score the trees.

When hiking with Charlie, Natalie tried to stay in the moment and trust the trails. In most of the places she'd been, trails were clearly marked and well defined. But as she neared almost every intersection she first became impatient, itching to check the All Trails app on her phone, then when it felt like they'd travelled the prescribed distance, she started to doubt. Most of the time she could, and did, slide her phone out of her pocket and check the GPS, and she'd never yet been off track.

Charlie scolded her for using her phone on hikes, telling her she should be present, be in the moment, unless she was actively working. She wasn't sure she cared anymore what Charlie thought.

While everyone was distracted with poor Elena's fate, she remembered his face, pale and haunted, as he shook his head "no," indicating he wasn't coming with her on this escape attempt. She wondered how she'd found him handsome. When she met him freshman year of high school, he'd still had all his baby fat. Through college he'd made it his mission to rid himself of it and more. Today he'd looked gaunt. Like Glastenbury had already taken him and was wasting him to nothing.

How dare he not come with her, not be here to help her, to act as lookout? How dare he treat her the way he'd been treating her? Her anger propelled her through the trees, gashing into them with more fervor.

She could leave him here.

The thought reflected off her at first, not even an option. But...

She couldn't.

She'd miss...what? The attitude? Him butting in when the producer from the production company was talking to *her*, offering her a gig? She chewed her lip so hard she could taste blood.

She remembered the way Elena looked at her, trying to be supportive but pity loomed large on her face. Had she thought... Did she think she was fooling her friends? Friends she saw less and less often? Natalie shook off her shame and kept going.

With the marks on the trees and the trail, most of the other workers (*slaves*, she reminded herself, this was literally the definition of slavery) could find their ways out on their own. She'd have done her part, her responsibility was mainly with poor Elena, Elena dragged here almost against her will, who wasn't even all that excited for the trip if everything had gone to plan. She was only here because she was worried about Natalie and about Charlie doing something to hurt her.

She knew it was wrong, but also knew that her mom loved her dad even though she threw beer bottles at him and punched him and kicked him. But they always made up. They had three kids and had been together almost thirty years. It just happened sometimes, she thought. But did she love Charlie enough to put up with being a victim to his mercurial emotions?

Not when he wasn't by her for something like this. He'd been a shit ever since she signed the contract for this gig. She supposed he'd been a shit beforehand, but he really amped it up, especially in front of Elena. She thought about the impromptu Starbucks interview—the show would have eaten that up, they shouldn't have stopped talking just so Charlie could keep the hike schedule he had in his head.

The anger pushed her. She didn't want to be out here. If they'd whipped Elena for…Natalie didn't even know what, hadn't gotten close enough to even talk to her, to ask her why, what would they do if they caught Natalie slipping back into the town? The anger carried her. Natalie pushed forward, scrutinizing what she could see of the path. There, a hobnail boot print, and next to it the print from a modern hiking boot. She pushed forward, and cut into a tree with extra vigor.

With no watch and no GPS and not even a view of the sky to tell how much time had passed, Natalie decided she would notch four more trees then turn back.

Three more.

She let time stretch out, then notched the second to last tree. When she looked up from the bright pine gash, she thought she saw something up ahead. A pile of stones. She rushed forward, her shoes tangling in a root and she wobbled, almost falling, but there ahead was the cairn. The wind, she noticed, had stopped. Its absence meant Natalie was suddenly warm in her jacket after the sustained chill.

The cairn looked exactly like it had in 2022 when she first saw it, covered in a thick pelt of soft moss. Almost innocuous, not even particularly sinister. She expected when she saw it again for it to be thrumming with an ancient evil. But no. Just a mossy, pile of rocks. She checked to confirm that she was wearing the red jacket, as though she needed to. But she had to be sure before she placed her hands on the rocks.

It was still night, still dark. The glimpses of stars up through the bows of the trees still looked the same. She fumbled in the jacket pocket for her phone...a dark brick.

Then she remembered to turn it on. She'd tried in Glastenbury proper, but it stayed dark. Now a big, bright apple glowed on her screen.

She was home. She could be back to the van in a few hours of hiking. The key was tucked in the exhaust pipe. She could go home, she could get in the van and just drive...The world was her oyster.

Her phone woke up and caught a bar of signal. A few sorta but not really concerned texts from friends; *you back yet?*—that kinda thing. She pointed the camera at herself, with the cairn clearly in the background, didn't smile, and snapped a selfie. She glanced at it, and though it was dark and pixelated, both she and the cairn were clear enough. Not sure what she hoped to prove or communicate, she uploaded the photo to Instagram.

CHARLIE TRIED TO PUSH THE MENTAL PICTURE OF ELENA OUT OF HIS mind. When the first lash struck her, he'd peeled away, back to the men's dorm room. Natalie would be pissed, he was sure, but he just couldn't. No one else was in the dorm, everyone eating—dinner after a public flogging? What the hell had Natalie done? What had he let her do? All of this was a stupid idea, starting with bringing Elena along at all. The girl was beyond useless. He hated the way she'd huffed and puffed along the hike, and he hated the way she kept stealing glances at him.

He'd wanted to do a cool hike. Mount Marcy, the highest point in New York. Work towards all the four-thousand-foot peaks in New England (Glastenbury Mountain didn't even rank on the hundred highest list) or better yet leave New England all together, get the hell out of here, away from all the so called friends who pried and harassed them. Wouldn't real friends keep their noses away from his and Natalie's business?

The man who slept on the bunk above him—Gareth, though Charlie had tried not to learn his name—poked his head in the door. "New guy," he said.

Charlie raised his head but didn't respond.

"Lenore wants to see you."

"Why?"

Gareth snorted.

"Not for me to ask why. Lenore says get the new guy, I get the new guy. Come on."

"And if I don't?" Charlie hated himself for the little tremble he couldn't keep out of his voice. Gareth, a hard man from years of hard labor and primitive food, sighed.

"You saw what happened to your friend today."

She's not my friend, he wanted to say. Instead, Charlie slid awkwardly off the center bunk.

Colburn, who had the bunk below, slammed Charlie into a wall when he'd put a foot on the other man's bunk to steady himself as he ascended this morning.

Charlie let Gareth lead him out of the boarding house, up a well-trodden dirt path towards the Casino on the hill. This, he realized, was part of the town for the tourists. It presented as cute and cozy, everything neat and tidy. Every window in the Casino was lit, and the clock tower stared down at the almost-town like an ever-watching eye. It made his skin crawl. They bypassed the sweeping veranda of the Casino, with its wicker chairs and cigarette stands, spittoons and potted plants. This late in the season the plants would have to come inside soon or they'd die in the Vermont winter.

Built into a hill, the back entrance of the Casino, the servants' entrance, opened into a hallway clearly not made for public use. It was similar to the first-floor boarding house hall, roughhewn, still smelling like fresh pine, not yet weathered. They walked to the far end of the hall and took a narrow steep staircase all the way up to the fourth floor. They emerged in a cramped kitchen—it couldn't be for the Casino and its restaurant, not up here and this small.

Private apartment, then. Must be Lenore's. Gareth took him as far as a plain door.

"Good luck." Gareth rapped twice on the door, then retreated back where they'd come. Charlie stood alone in the kitchen. He wondered if a flying leap out the window would kill him. He decided on the downhill side it would, maybe not so much on the up hill side. Fucking Natalie.

The door before him opened, and he took a step into opulence. A walking contradiction, the butler looked like a craggy old Vermont dairy farmer that someone shoehorned into a suit. "Sit. Lenore will be in to see you presently." He spoke like a man given lines to memorize in a play.

Then the butler left.

There were three chairs in the parlor (he didn't specifically know if this was a parlor, but it looked how he imagined a parlor would look), and he chose the least grand of the three, feeling like the dirt on his clothes would soil the velveteen fabric. He perched on the end. An array of portraits and paintings cluttered a wall over patterned silk wallpaper. Most prominent was a painting of a bearded, barrel-chested man posing in Civil War attire, matched only by a painting of the Casino at dusk. Both the man and the clock on the Casino seemed to bore into Charlie, to watch him. He broke the staring contest with the man first, turning his gaze down to his simple leather shoes. They'd been worn before, maybe by someone who'd been whipped like Elena.

The click of the parlor door was so soft, Charlie didn't immediately turn. Equally soft was the whisper of Lenore's slippers on the thick rug. She was fully in the room when he finally lifted his head.

"Hello, Charles."

Charles. His grandmother called him Charles, insisting his father was the original Charlie. He'd hated it. On Lenore's lips, it sounded like honey tasted. More mature than the nickname he'd chosen and stuck to his whole life.

After a beat, he stood. He was pretty sure that was what he was supposed to do, yeah?

"Oh Charles, you can sit, we aren't nearly so formal as that here. What do you think of my town? And what about those of you who've moved here?"

As though he'd carefully decided this would be his new home.

He hesitated.

Lenore sat in the chair closest to him, arranging her ample skirts, lowering herself with a grace that women in 2022 never bothered to learn. He admired her long neck, and her straight posture. She could balance a book on her head. Natalie and Elena spent all day staring at their stupid phones. To think, if they cared, they could look like this.

"I know you didn't choose to come here, Charles, and for that I'm so, so sorry. But I think you'll find you like it here. Most people can't see the advantages, most aren't wise enough to see the benefits of a place like Glastenbury."

"Benefits?" he echoed, then regretted it.

"What have they told you about this place?"

No one told him jack shit. Admittedly, much of that was likely his own fault, he'd rejected the friendly overtures from the other men on his first night here.

"Nothing?" A smile played at her full lips. "Oh, you're just what I'm looking for."

Of course he was, he thought automatically. How could he not be. What if he'd come here for a reason?

"Let me tell you about my father," Lenore said.

Charlie—*Charles* imagined Natalie saying that, and imagined all the boring bullshit she'd spew about her dad who was a CPA and once ran two thirds of the Boston Marathon before spraining his ankle. Lenore, though. He leaned in, ready to listen.

"My father was also named Charles. Charles Glastenbury the fourth. He came north to Vermont after fighting in Maryland in the Civil War. He was a decorated colonel but wanted to choose a path of peace after everything he'd seen, all the fighting and cruelty." Charles thought of Lenore whipping Elena, the sparkle in her eye and the way her lips curved up into a smile. "He found a whole town for sale here in Vermont. They'd plundered the land, cut down all the useful trees, and were in dire straits. My father bought the town, brought the railroad here, brought workers. He built this beautiful casino, the general store, the hotel...

"He wanted people to be able to enjoy the beauty of Vermont.

"One storm ruined it all. A mudslide in an October storm took out the railroad. It had been so much work, so expensive to lay the tracks, he could never afford to rebuild it. The one season was successful, but not so much that he could bring back the railway.

"He took his life in the clocktower when he realized the town was isolated here and his dream was dead. That next summer, no tourists would come. I tried to keep up appearances, to keep his death a secret, but the workers trickled out one by one. Our family kept one slave, a woman called Beth.

"I caught her trying to run away. A torrential downpour, she still couldn't hide from my hounds. I was ready to have them tear her to pieces, when she said she was descended from the witches of Salem and could grant my greatest wish. How did she know my greatest wish? Even though my cloak had soaked through and my horse was tired, I decided to entertain her.

"She told me of a place on the mountain. With the right words, words from her grandmothers, I could go back. Back to the beginning of the summer. I called her a liar, but she led me to a stone cairn on the mountain. All she asked was to be let go...She said she'd stand nearby, and if it worked she would disappear as I went back in time, if it didn't I could let the hounds have her. Charles, I imagined my dogs would be chewing her bones for dinner.

"My cloak was red—that would help, she told me. She said I needed to place my hands on the stone as she said her words. It sounded like nonsense, but if she tried to run or cheat me, the dogs would be on her. If she embarrassed me, she'd never walk off this mountain. I took off my gloves and laid my bare hands on the wet, mossy rocks, expecting to hear the snap of a twig as she ran off. Instead she started a rhythmic chant.

"The next I knew, it was a bright summer evening, no longer dark at five in the afternoon. My horse was gone, the dogs gone, Beth gone."

"And that's how we got here?" Charles said.

Lenore's eyes narrowed after being interrupted. "Are you familiar with the story of the Monkey's Paw?"

"No." *Was that like the horror movie about the service monkey that went crazy and killed everyone?*

"It's about a mother and a father who make a foolish wish, that their son, killed in the war, would come home to them. The granter of wishes is a literal soul, and in the story the son returns. They never specified that he not have been killed. Likewise, I wished to relive that great summer of 1898, to start it over. And so I have, each October when the mudslide and the flood comes, at midnight the clock resets to June 21st, and the trolley brings the tourists, and I show them the time of their lives. I didn't wish for my father to be here with me, he's still lost."

"You can't go back to the stone and wish?"

"Going back to the stone doesn't work for me anymore without Beth's words. And as you and your friends saw, for anyone else, it draws them here."

"How can you escape?"

She laughed. "Escape? Why would I want to leave? It was frustrating at first, but I have everything I need here, all my whims are met, and I'm amassing a small fortune."

"A fortune you can never spend."

"Somehow, the money renews with me. Each summer I can send for new and different things, all new dresses, the finest Worth has to offer. It's paradise here."

"You don't want to go home? Back to your time? Back to your people?"

"I had one person and he died here with me. My time is full of backwards imbeciles with no foresight. I'm a god here. I'll never go." She paused. "And if you are as smart as I think you are, you'll stay too, and find that helping me is much more fun than being my enemy."

ELENA MUST HAVE PASSED OUT; WHEN SHE CAME TO, A FEW OF THE other women were in the dorm. She lay face down on her bunk, her raw back exposed to the cool air. The pain morphed into more of a throb, dull…until she moved.

"Natalie?"

"Not here," Rachel said.

Elena struggled up on her elbows and her back screamed.

"Where? Where is she?"

"Haven't seen her since before…" Rachel vaguely gestured at Elena's back. "I thought she was there, but then I couldn't keep tabs on her. I was more worried about you."

"Thanks," Elena murmured. She wanted Natalie. She wanted to go home. She'd even take Charlie. She asked after him.

"I don't know, I'm sorry."

"Did she leave me here? Did they leave me behind?" It made sense, they both were more adept at traveling the wilderness than she was, she'd only slow them down if they'd brought her. But it still stung. Her back stung, her psyche stung…It was how slavery worked, she remembered. Take all the hope away. One would expect it to come from the enslavers. From Lenore. The additional betrayal from her friends stabbed even deeper.

She didn't want to be the kind of person who gave up, didn't want to acquiesce…but none of the other women in this room were lying prone, flayed open. Or at least, they weren't today.

"How many of you have been whipped?" She asked Rachel.

Rachel answered with a dry chuckle. "All of us, at some time or another."

"All of you? Like, literally?"

"Lenore invents a reason for everyone to taste her whip. Keeps us all in line. The real question is how many of us have been whipped more than once."

"And?"

"Not many. Most learn how to navigate her moods, give her what she wants to hear."

"What about the last woman who slept in this bed?"

"I think you know the answer to that."

"I don't. She could have been killed by the whip, run away and vanished…" (*Maybe even back to her own time*, she hoped.) "…or maybe she killed herself."

"Or she got promoted and lives in one of the cottages by the stream."

"Is that what happened?"

"No. She threw herself off the clock tower."

This statement might have made Elena cry if she had any tears left inside her.

"This is really it, then?"

Rachel shrugged. "For now. Keep your hope." Elena wanted to know who'd been here the longest, how many cycles they'd seen. But what good would the answer get her? "You should get some rest."

"Work tomorrow?" Her back wouldn't nearly be healed enough to get up and move around.

"We'll bandage you up. She also gets mad if you bleed through your uniform. The punishment for that is more whipping."

"That's insane!"

"Keep your voice down. This whole thing is insane. Get some rest."

Rachel left her then, climbing into her own bunk. Elena liked it better when Natalie was here with her. Natalie and Charlie, striking out into…what? She wanted to think nasty thoughts at them (especially Charlie), but she wanted Natalie to make it. To get somewhere. To be free.

Wanted her to be free so much so that when she woke up to Natalie gently touching her arm, disappointment washed over her.

"I thought you got home?" She couldn't believe she'd fallen asleep, but even more so couldn't believe Natalie was here. "Where were you?"

Natalie pressed a finger to her lips. "I did get home."

Elena's eyes went wide. "Why are you here? Why are you back?"

"I came back for you. Your back…I'm so sorry I left, I used you as my distraction. Everyone was watching, and I didn't think I'd have a better shot. You were right, I just need the red jacket—something red—to get home.

"It's already started raining, the rain that's going to flood this place out. Tomorrow afternoon the mudslide is going to wipe out the train tracks. We go then, when the chaos happens. Everyone will be running around like chickens with their heads cut off, that's when we can go. It's going to wipe the trail out, but I left marks on the trees. We should be able to find our way."

"You actually got there? To our time? How do you know?"

"I made an Instagram post. My phone worked. People are a little concerned about us, but not what I'd call worried yet. No one is going to be out looking for us."

"I guess that's good. I'd hate to have someone wind up here."

"I think most people are smart enough to not wear red."

"Come on, that's not fair. How many things are actually haunted?" After this experience, she wasn't sure; what if there were more haunted things out there? What other myths and stories were true? If one pocket dimension existed, how many others were there?

Natalie, it seemed, travelled the same path of thoughts. "Who knows." She was quiet a moment, and in the dark Elena could picture her chewing on her lower lip. "I don't want to tell anyone else."

"We have to help them." Not save Rachel? Or any of the other women who'd tended to her after the flogging?

"I don't know who we can trust. If we tell the wrong person—" Natalie made a sound. A little hitching sob. "I don't know if I even want to tell Charlie."

The words were like an ice bath. Elena made her repeat herself. "I've been thinking about him the whole time we've been here and… he's not a good person."

"That doesn't mean he deserves to be abandoned here."

"If I can find a way out, he should be able to, too, right? And I marked all the trees. We can leave a note for them, there's a path."

"The trees won't be marked if the mudslide is what causes the timeline to reset, right? The trees will go back to how they were?"

"It doesn't matter. If I could figure it out, then anyone can. Right?"

Elena didn't answer.

"Right? Come on…if we tell the wrong person, we're stuck here forever."

"I guess."

"Let's get some sleep."

Elena was pretty sure neither of them actually slept. In the morning, a heavy downpour blanketed Glastenbury. All the workers roused before dawn, and shuffled sleepily to the mess hall. Elena's back felt tight, and as promised, Rachel bound it with extra layers of linen, slathering some kind of salve on first. Elena hoped it was something from 2150 that would reduce the scarring. She imagined herself home, having to explain why she wouldn't wear a bathing suit or tank top in public ever again. Better than being here. Anything was better than being here.

"After lunch," Natalie whispered, just before they parted ways. The workers fanned out to their jobs, Rachel and Elena to prepare guest rooms on the third floor. Today they worked in a room painted sunny yellow. It provided a nice contrast to the dark clouds outside. Elena wondered what it would be like to stay here, to simply ring the little bell by the bed if she needed anything. Unlike the previous mornings, today dawned warm. Not in a nice way. A fetid warmth that promised bad weather up ahead. Elena guessed the storm was the slap from the tail end of a hurricane that had already battered Florida and the Caribbean. If those things existed in this world. Maybe the first time around that's what the storm was, but otherwise it only existed here.

Rachel kept stealing glances at Elena, until finally she said, "What's she up to? Where was she?"

Elena remembered the bite of the whip, thought of Natalie's haunted face, thought of Lenore. Could she trust Rachel? Maybe, but she couldn't risk it. Even though the first part of what Rachel said had come true: how did she know Rachel wouldn't run to Lenore first thing?

"She's ashamed," Elena said. "She wasn't a very supportive friend. When Lenore started...hurting me...she ran. Hid in the basement of the Casino. Didn't come out until the middle of the night."

Rachel slanted a glance at her, and Elena feared her lie burned red on her cheeks.

"She apologized a thousand times last night, but it doesn't matter. None of it matters, does it? I don't think this is a place where people have the capacity to be good friends."

"Not if you don't let people in," Rachel said.

A prickling crept down the back of Elena's neck, igniting the tips of her wounds.

"She's kind of a bitch," Elena mumbled. "The whole thing was stupid. The whole hike. Coming out here was stupid."

"Your disappearance is part of why I was out there," Rachel said. "Natalie's post on Instagram—you know Instagram, right?"

Elena nodded, forgetting that Instagram would be as archaic as Dead Sea scrolls to Rachel. Natalie would like to hear that in the timeline where she vanished forever, she still managed to be famous, turning into a legend that endured.

"Natalie is the selfie queen. We were here 'cause she was making a vlog—like a video diary thing—about the haunted woods here."

"I know. I read all about it. They were able to get some of the footage off your phone when you got back, the cloud, you were the only one who wasn't fully encrypted. It looked like B roll, assuming Charlie shot the real stuff."

Elena just nodded.

"The timeline didn't make sense. Natalie's final Instagram post came 48 hours after the last time your phone was backed up. Like she got back one last time. Last night."

"She said she went and hid." Elena didn't need to fake the tears that swelled in her eyes. She shrugged away from Rachel, which hurt her back, and busied herself making the bed. Why hadn't she thought that some of the other workers here would be like Natalie, people who wound up here because they were curious about the mysterious disappearances and phenomenon? It gnawed at her. Should she tell

Rachel everything? *Ugh*, she wasn't cut out for the cruelty here. Her hands shook as she went about her work, between that and her back she moved slowly, meaning Rachel picked up her slack.

A few minutes before they broke for a quick lunch of plain sandwiches, a horrendous crack of thunder rent the sky. Rachel let out a little yelp and looked embarrassed after. They hadn't spoken since earlier. Elena felt Rachel watching her all morning, less a comforting presence and more a keeper. How would she get away? It was now after lunch, and the storm kicked up outside, just the conditions Natalie said they'd be escaping into.

"I have to go to the bathroom," Elena said.

Rachel shrugged at her. "I wouldn't want to go out there."

"It must have been something I ate." Elena laid a hand theatrically on her stomach. As she said it she realized they'd all eaten the same thing. "Or my period." She bolted out of the room, through the ritzy nice hallway to the staff hallway. On her way down, she passed Charlie. She froze, stared at him. Contempt oozed off him, like he wasn't even trying to hide it anymore. It made tears spring to her eyes. Did he think less of her because he'd seen her whipped? What the fuck? He could have helped her. She didn't say anything, rushed away, careful not to trip over her too-big shoes on the narrow stairs. She looked back and found he hadn't moved. Would he say something? Something kind? She looked towards him expectantly, but he turned his broad back on her, and went about his business.

Was Natalie really going to leave him here? It still didn't feel right to Elena, seemed too cruel, even for someone like Charlie. She hurried; she *did* go to the outhouse first, praying to a God she didn't believe in, one she'd never given much thought to before touching the cursed rock, that this would be the last time she pissed in this damned hole in the ground. She wanted toilet paper, real toilet paper. She wanted fast food, real junky garbage, all calories and no substance.

She was so close, all she needed to do was meet Natalie under the clock tower.

The air felt warmer than it should for almost November, ripe with humidity and an electric, pre-storm smell. The sky above swirled iron gray and white, a pregnant storm ready to let loose. As she crossed the wooden footbridge over the stream, fat drops fell on her.

Already the brook below her had swollen and the rocks that were visible when they'd gotten here were underneath brown water. The wood of the bridge was slippery, and she used the log railing to steady herself. These shoes…She wondered what they'd done with her trail runners. A man passed her, but his head was down, keeping an eye on his footing and keeping the rain out of his face. From the west, thunder rumbled. Almost unconsciously, Elena counted before she caught a flash in the sky. Close and coming closer. Good. Let it come. Let it wash this place off the map.

She didn't care that it would regenerate immediately, she wanted it gone off the map.

She looked downstream at the railroad tracks, the trolley tracks which she knew would be the weak point. In her world when the tracks washed out, there was no money to rebuild and the town died, the few residents moving away one after the other until no one was left and Glastenbury was nothing more than an empty square on the map. The rain began in earnest now, soaking her wool shawl almost immediately. It smelled like she imagined a sheep would smell. In the Casino, the lights burned bright, and if she hadn't known better, she would have thought it looked like a cheerful place to shelter from the rain.

A hunched form stood in front of the building, facing up at the clock tower, protecting something. Natalie. She curled over the red North Face jacket, desperate to mask the bright color.

"Hurry. We don't have much time."

Elena nodded, and they moved upstream, past the Casino, off the nice, well-trodden path, where it grew narrow. Natalie half jogged and Elena fell behind. Her feet screamed in the shoes, the lacerations on her back threatened to split open, and her legs still hadn't quite recovered from the initial trek up here.

Elena kept up as best she could, but she could still see the town when she begged Natalie to slow down.

Natalie did, but she watched the rocky trail behind Elena, scrutinizing it. Elena looked uphill, not wanting to look back. She saw the bright white of one of the cuts Natalie made in a pine with her knife.

"I saw Charlie," Elena panted. "I passed him on the stairs when I was coming down."

Natalie paled. "What did he say?"

"Nothing. Just glared at me. Like it was my fault we're here. Like it was my fault I was…" She couldn't say whipped or flogged, and let her voice trail away.

"Try and get your breath. It's all straight up and we have to be quick."

The rain helped, in that it muted the sounds of their voices, but it also made it hard to hear what else was in the forest. They hadn't gained the altitude yet for it to completely close in around them, the woods where they were now were still young, traumatized from the dramatic deforestation that would be the town's downfall.

"We should get moving," Natalie said, shielding her eyes against the rain and peering down the trail.

The sound of a twig snapping was almost but not quite masked by a boom of thunder. The storm was closer now.

"Come on," Natalie said. "Someone's coming."

Elena's skin crawled and her throat threatened to close. She tasted iron panic. She couldn't go back there. She couldn't have them hurt her again. They'd kill her for trying to escape.

"Go ahead of me," Natalie said.

"I can't, I can't follow the trail."

"Watch for the notch marks."

She didn't have any red on. If they got separated, she'd be fucked, just lost in the woods. Even if she found the rock pile, she couldn't make it home without the color red. Behind her, a scream. Sounds of a struggle. Natalie said to go on ahead, but what if she needed help? What if the jacket needed help?

Elena turned under a crash of thunder and headed back down the trail. Facing this way, she couldn't see Natalie's marks on the trees, but she could follow the sound of footsteps and light grunts of a struggle. She rounded a corner and found Natalie and Rachel scrapping.

"Rachel?" Elena cried.

She warded off Natalie's blows.

"Stop! I just want to come with you."

"What did you tell her?" Natalie snapped.

"She didn't tell me anything. It didn't take a genius to figure out the two of you had something planned. Where's your boyfriend?" Rachel said.

"We broke up," Natalie said.

"You're leaving him here?"

Natalie, still panting from the altercation, dropped her gaze to the ground. "He's been talking to Lenore and...It's just better this way."

"We should hurry then. If he's been talking to her, and if he knows you're planning to escape—"

"I'm not an idiot, I didn't tell him I was planning this."

"He knows you, though, and probably he can guess?" Rachel said.

Natalie tipped her head up to the sky, letting the rain pummel her face.

"Let's go!" Rachel said again. "You saw what she did to Elena when she asked some questions. We can't let her catch us."

"Okay," Natalie said, reluctant. She resumed her place in the lead, and resumed her fast pace.

"How did you find us?" Elena panted at Rachel.

"Don't talk, save your energy. And you're not exactly subtle. I just followed you. I passed Charlie, too, must have been right after you did. He didn't look happy."

"Never looks happy," Elena wheezed.

"I hope she knows what she's doing."

"She does. Smartest person I know," Elena said.

They trudged on in silence. When the woods swallowed them it grew darker, a permanent dusk even though it was only midafternoon. The branches overhead kept the rain off. The leaves underfoot were slippery and each of them had fallen at least once. They climbed in elevation. Winds whipped at them, first from one side, then the other. There was no way to lean out of it, and their clothes weren't warm. As the storm approached and they walked higher, it felt more like November. Elena's shoes rubbed her feet raw on the heel and the bottom of her big toe. Her feet were cold and the little toes were numb. She could worry about all of it when they were through the cairn. She'd soak her feet in Epsom salt—soak her whole body in Epsom salt and not go out for a week. She remembered she'd be going home to her parents' house and not back to her cozy apartment, and didn't even care. Her mother would let her use the soaking tub in the primary bathroom and wouldn't bother her.

Elena walked into Natalie, who'd stopped without a word. Rachel came up behind Elena, and woofed a little gasp.

"What?" Elena whispered.

"The trees." Natalie sounded defeated.

Elena looked. Really looked. Every single tree bore a score mark identical to the one from Natalie's knife. The trail was lost.

Rachel pulled up abreast of Natalie. "Come on. You got yourself there once with no marks. You can do it again."

"But someone knows we're out here!" Natalie scrutinized Rachel, her drenched black hair, the wool and linen garb they all wore clinging to her body. "Who did you tell?"

"Stop it. You're wasting your energy. Find us the trail. Ignore the marks."

"I had stars last time. My compass is shit, it's not working out here at all. The rain's dropped leaves over the trail. I can't do it."

"The cairn was near the summit, right? Can we, like, go up until we can't go up anymore? And then…" her voice trailed off because her suggestion was dumb.

"We have to," Natalie said.

"And we have to hurry. I hear someone coming," Rachel said. "I'd rather be lost out here than go back. I'm not going back. I won't."

Natalie took one, long, last, lingering look. "Okay. Up. I think when I came through I went this way," she pointed, "so if we head that way and kind of trend up, we'll get to the top eventually."

"Okay." Elena would have followed her friend anywhere, even before this. She was the best chance any of them had to make it out of here. They resumed walking over the rocky ground, but not as quickly as before. Natalie wasn't as sure of herself, a far cry from how she'd seemed on the trail on the way up to the mountain.

"Come on, Nat, you got this!"

Natalie, who Elena knew hated to be called Nat, glared over her shoulder, then smiled. She nodded, and pressed onward. Lost was better than captured. Lenore would make sure they didn't have another chance to escape.

The thunder came faster now, the lightning above strobing at times. Maybe its glow would give Natalie the light she needed to find the true trail. Still they climbed. Sometimes they heard things in the woods with them, branches snapping, the shuffle of feet in the leaves, but whenever Elena looked around she saw nothing, and kept pushing her poor body onward. What she wouldn't give for one of Natalie's protein bars. Her stomach yowled in agreement.

No leaves clung to the trees, but a rich tangle of underbrush made it hard to move through the terrain. Sometimes Natalie found them ways through, sometimes they fought against it. Elena pretended not to notice the way she shook her head, as though she was sure they were on the wrong path. Still, each tree bore a white notch bitten out of it.

Rachel took up the rear, seeing Elena was struggling and wanting to keep the party together. Elena heard a sharp cry from behind her and wheeled around.

A man—maybe Elena had seen him before, maybe not, with the homogenous clothing it was hard to keep anyone straight—had an arm wrapped around Rachel's neck and pulled her back, dragging her off her feet.

In that moment Elena forgot her feet, forgot the pools of lactic acid screaming in her muscles. She ran. Dipped to pick up a rock the size of two fists, and in a fluid movement, swung it at the man's head.

His eyes popped wide and he let Rachel slide from his grasp. She dropped, holding her throat and sucking in big breaths. Elena hit him again; this time her rock came away bloody. She hit him again.

He crumpled to the ground and now he was even easier to hit. She ruined his face and it was hard to see. Her eyes stung and everything was blurry but she had to get off this goddamned mountain. She couldn't be here anymore.

Friendly hands looped around each of her arms and pulled her back. Her first reaction was to swing at them too, but it was Rachel and Natalie, and when Elena realized, she went limp. The adrenaline fled from her and all parts of her screamed, her shoulder howled in protest, she was sure she'd torn open the lashes on her back.

"I can't see," she mumbled.

Someone wiped at her face with something soft and sheep smelling. Blood. She'd gotten his blood in her eyes. Her friends turned her away from the mess she'd created.

"Him or us, Elena," Natalie said.

"Thank you." Rachel touched her throat.

"Who was he?" Natalie said.

"One of the men. I don't know how long he'd been here. He'd gotten in with Lenore. She doesn't talk to us, whips us, but the men she'll speak with and…I don't think it's magic, but they'd do anything for her."

"They're all idiots," Elena croaked.

Natalie might have been crying or it might have just been the rain on her face. "Come on. Up we go. We must be getting close now."

"Really? Or are you just saying that?"

"Does it matter?"

Elena guessed not.

They walked.

Elena started shivering, her teeth chattering and body shaking. Walking provided some warmth, but it wasn't enough. She didn't remember it being this far when they came down from the cairn, marched at gunpoint. She hadn't been thinking straight then. Was she now? Wasn't that one of the first signs of hypothermia, going a little loopy? It didn't matter, she needed to put one foot in front of the other. The leather chomped into her flesh with each step, her back screamed until all the misery blended into a background hum and the world was only walking.

Natalie let out a little cry, pointing. Her marks on the trees were back, alone. Whoever cut up the other trees had grown lazy, assumed they wouldn't make it through, and had given up on marking the forest. Natalie went faster, leaving Elena and Rachel further behind. Elena struggled onward, Natalie carried the red coat, they couldn't get through without it.

The underbrush trembled as a particularly virulent flash of lightning lit up the whole area, and something bowled out of the woods and took Natalie down.

Not something. Charlie.

Beyond her, Elena saw the cairn. It hunkered benignly, green moss blending against the brown forest so that it barely stood out. "There!" she pointed for Rachel.

Charlie tackled Natalie and hit her, Elena saw her head snap back.

"You think you can leave me?" he said. "I'm moving up in the world. We're done."

The red coat dropped to the ground and Natalie struggled to get her hands in front of her, to ward him off. Something flashed in Charlie's hand.

Natalie stopped struggling.

Elena knew Charlie was a pure seventh generation Vermonter, had grown up with a father who withheld love and affection but taught him the land. How to fish, and how to hunt. When Charlie lashed out with the knife, he knew where to slice in Natalie's torso.

Even if Elena could get Natalie through to 2022, would they be able to get medical help in time? They were eleven miles from the nearest road, and cell service was spotty. Rachel guided her around the fighting couple and to the cairn. She pulled a knife of her own.

Elena's heart sank; she'd trusted Rachel, Rachel from the future who'd helped her and put the salve on her back. The knife in Rachel's hand flashed and she slashed out...at the meat of the palm of her hand. Bright blood, bright red blood welled up. Rachel looked at Elena, dropped her knife, and placed her hand on the stone.

She winked out of existence, as though she'd never been there.

Elena squeaked, reached for her, but of course there was nothing there, no evidence there'd ever been anything there, not even a smear of blood on the wet, mossy stone. Rachel was home, back to her time, which meant Elena and Charlie were alone.

The wind howled through the trees, and the last stubborn oak leaves dropped with the rain around them. Rain pattered the ground, so loud, everything was so loud. Charlie, soaked and now bloodied, raised his head at her. He held up the red jacket. "You want this?"

Elena reached down for Rachel's knife, and did just as Rachel had done. She stared at Natalie. Her friend's eyes were open and when the rain hit them, she didn't blink.

Charlie dropped the jacket and charged and Elena put her bloody palm on the rock and...

IT WASN'T STORMING ANYMORE, THOUGH THE SKY OVERHEAD WAS A light gray. Elena stumbled back, soaking wet, and landed on her butt on the damp leaves. She scrambled away, bracing herself for Charlie to follow her. She didn't expect an arm to snake around her neck from behind, for the stink of an unwashed person to waft over her. She lashed back with Rachel's knife, and the person grunted.

Elena spun around to find Badger holding his arm, glaring at her. Badger. Charlie.

"You're not supposed to come back through. None of you are!"

Now that Elena knew, she couldn't believe she hadn't seen it right away, the cruel eyes and the arrogant set of his chin, even emaciated and shaggy. How stupid had she been, even when Natalie told the story of Charlie's trail name.

Elena backed away from him, knowing the cairn sat behind her now. She didn't want Charlie coming through without her seeing him.

"Just let me go."

"No no no, Lenore wouldn't like that one bit. No one can get away and no one can know."

Thoughts scudded through her mind. She needed the packs from the shelter, needed to get dry. She needed to see if she could call for help. She needed to get as far from here as possible, and needed to stay clear of Badger and Charlie.

She didn't let herself think about going back to look for Natalie.

Badger came at her again. What she'd done to save Rachel was an animal reaction, but the adrenaline wasn't pushing her anymore, now it was barely a gentle shove. Yes, she'd smashed that man's face in with a rock, but killing the scraggly hiker in front of her didn't seem right either. If she killed Badger here and now, would Charlie wink out of existence in the pocket dimension, or was that realm protected somehow?

She ran, it seeming in the moment like a better course of action than fighting. She thought she remembered how to get back to the lean to, the path here was more trodden than it had been in the past. Badger—she couldn't think of him as Charlie—tackled her and Rachel's knife slid from her fingers, coming to rest on a pile of leaves just out of reach. She snapped her head back and though it rattled her brain, she felt his nose crunch against her skull. He went limp. This Charlie was weaker, wasn't right in the head. She squirmed out from under him, able to push his body off. She kicked him, but with the stupid leather shoes it hurt her just as much as it hurt him. He curled around himself like a pill bug.

Killing him was murder, and here murder was a real-life thing with real consequences. That was, of course, true when she'd been on the other side of the cairn, but her slowed thinking pushed her to rationalize the consequences. So she ran again.

There was the fire tower, its top shrouded in fog. There was the trail, the Appalachian Trail and Long Trail, marked with familiar white blazes. That way was the shelter. She could hear something behind her, Charliebadger dragging himself along after her. Her problem wouldn't stop when she got to the shelter, she couldn't change her clothes or call for help if she were being attacked. Couldn't get out of this wet wool, the useless linen that seemed to be starting to freeze.

She remembered a whistle, what Natalie told her about three short blasts. It hung from the strap of Natalie's pack, easy to get to. She blew. Waited. Repeated the distress signal.

Charlie reappeared, blood pouring down his nose and covering his chin and chest. Blood also blossomed in his arm where she'd cut him. Three more sharp calls from the whistle.

No one was out here. No one would help her. Help wasn't going to come. No one—

A loud sound rent the afternoon, echoing across the mountains. A rifle blast. Charlie stopped in his tracks, dropped to his knees, and spilled over to his side. Elena huddled against the packs and saw a man and boy, dressed in camouflage and blaze orange. The boy carried the gun, his eyes wide. They ran to Charlie, who lay still on the ground, then saw Elena, and rushed to her.

If it were a horror movie, Charlie would have risen up and slain them as well, but he stayed where he was.

"What happened?" the man asked.

Elena made a decision. "I don't remember."

It was widely thought that Charlie had killed his girlfriend and hidden her body somewhere in the Glastenbury wilderness. They brought out tracking dogs, but a heavy rain interfered with the search. They confidently tracked to the old pre-Columbus cairn and lost the track. He'd never wanted Elena along on the hike, so why he didn't kill her first, they couldn't figure. Police found a journal where he ranted about Natalie's popularity on Instagram and TikTok, raging both that he wanted to keep her for himself and that he was the one who should have been loved, that he was unappreciated for being behind the scenes. Elena was incidental. No one would believe her, and she couldn't be held responsible if anyone went through the cairn again, so she stuck to her story. She remembered the hike, remembered getting to the shelter. She didn't mention the other hiker. The next thing she knew the man and the boy, bear hunters, had shot Charlie and were trying to see if she was all right. Why was she dressed like that? She didn't know. Couldn't she remember anything? No.

Her story wound up online, added in to the mythology of the window area over Southern Vermont. Over time, and with willpower, Elena began to forget for real. She did her best to push the people and the place from her mind. Maybe the police were right, and she'd just been caught up in an abusive relationship and a fit of rage.

She saw it though, when she woke up from dreams in her Arizona desert apartment. The clocktower in Glastenbury, its face glowing orange against a late autumn sky.

ACKNOWLEDGMENTS

One morning in September of 2022, I finished reading a manuscript by my friend and fellow author, Kyle Rader, which I enjoyed so much that I started thinking about proposing we work on something together. By afternoon, he and I concluded that an anthology of New England-based horror novellas was the thing, and by suppertime that night, we had our lineup of incredible writers in place, one for each state in New England. I pitched the project to Cemetery Dance, who agreed to take it on, and set a deadline for everyone that somehow, magically, was met by all. It couldn't have gone more smoothly, apart from my brain shutting down almost completely when I tried to come up with a title for the anthology, which Kyle helpfully provided during a brief brainstorming session. I may be the editor, but this book owes a lot to Kyle Rader, and I am forever grateful for his thoughts, advice, and enthusiasm.

Gratitude is also due to Kevin Lucia at Cemetery Dance for *his* enthusiasm, not just for this anthology, but really for the genre overall. I don't know if I have ever met anyone with as much passion for horror as Kevin, and it's wonderfully infectious. Between his own stellar writing and his work for CD, he has truly become a force in horror publishing and I'm proud to have played a small part in it.

I am equally proud to have my work published alongside the extraordinary stable of writers assembled in this volume. Every single one of them was first choice and I remain as ecstatic now as I was when they all eagerly agreed to contribute. I have long been an admirer and fan of Rader, Carl, Silvia, Nunnally, and Dearborn, and I can rest well knowing no one could possibly read the stories herein without becoming every bit as much a fan as I am. Gigantic thanks to them all for bringing their very best to this project. They are magnificent writers all, and they all made my first outing as an anthologist a dream.

Ed Kurtz
Connecticut, Autumn 2023

ABOUT THE AUTHORS

WILLIAM D. CARL IS THE AUTHOR OF *BESTIAL*, *PRIMEVAL*, *OUT of the Woods*, *Three Days Gone*, and *The School That Screamed* as well as the novella *Safe Places*. He has published short fiction in over fifty anthologies and magazines, including *In Laymon's Terms*, *Out of the Gutter*, *The Many Faces of Van Helsing*, *Damned Nation*, *Retro Horror*, *Skin & Ink*, and *Wicked Weird*. He lives with his partner of 32 years and one rather large hound dog in Pawtucket, Rhode Island. By day, he is a book buyer for An Unlikely Story, and by night he watches far too many crazy movies to enumerate. He likes pie.

GHOSTIES AND GHOULIES AND LONG-LEGGEDY BEASTIES AND things that go bump in the night: that's **Kristin Dearborn** in a nutshell. A life-long New Englander and horror writer, Dearborn earned her MFA at Seton Hill University. She's been on the horror scene since 2010 with her short stories and novellas, and has contributed to a number of anthologies. Dearborn is the author of *The Amazing Alligator Girl*, *Sacrifice Island*, *Woman in White*, *Whispers*, *Stolen Away*, and *Trinity*. If

Dearborn is taking a break from all things blood-curdling, she's likely scaling mountains, zipping around Vermont on a motorcycle, hanging out with her dog, or gallivanting around the globe looking for her next novel's horrifying inspiration.

ED KURTZ IS THE AUTHOR OF *THE RIB FROM WHICH I REMAKE the World, Bleed,* the *Boon* trilogy, and other novels. His short fiction has been honored in *Best American Mystery Stories* and *Best Gay Stories* and he has written for film magazines like *Paracinema* and *Fantasm Presents.* Ed lives in Connecticut with his partner, author doungjai gam. *In the Cold, Cold Ground* is his first anthology as editor.

ERRICK NUNNALLY WAS BORN AND RAISED IN BOSTON, Massachusetts, and served one tour in the Marine Corps before deciding art school was a safer pursuit. He enjoys art, comics, and genre novels. A graphic designer, he has trained in Krav Maga and Muay Thai kickboxing. His work has appeared in several anthologies of speculative fiction and can be found in *Apex Magazine, Fiyah Magazine, Galaxy's Edge, Lamplight, Nightlight Podcast,* as well as the novels *Lightning Wears a Red Cape, Blood for the Sun,* and *All the Dead Men.* Visit erricknunnally.us to learn more about his work.

KYLE RADER IS THE AUTHOR OF THE NOVELS *MY BFF SATAN, Kegger,* and *Four Bullets.* He lives in New Hampshire with his wife, son, and dog, Scrambles. He can be found at kylerader. net or @youroldpalkile on Twitter.

MORGAN SYLVIA IS A METALHEAD, AN AQUARIUS, A COFFEE addict, and a work in progress. A former obituarist, she is now a full-time freelance writer. Her fiction and poetry have appeared in several places, including *Pseudopod*, *Wicked Witches*, *Northern Frights*, *Under Her Skin*, *Haunted House Short Stories*, *Endless Apocalypse*, *Twice Upon an Apocalypse*, and *The Final Summons*. She is also the author of two novels: a horror novel, *Abode*; a fantasy novel, *Dawn: Book 1 of the Aris Trilogy*; and two poetry collections, *Whispers From The Apocalypse* and *As the Seas Turn Red*, which was nominated for an Elgin Award. She was also one of the co-writers for Realm's werewolf audio drama *Undertow: Blood Forest*. Sylvia currently lives in Maine with her boyfriend, two tuxedo cats, a chubby goldfish, the cutest rescue dog ever, and a pet banshee. You can follow her at www.morgansylvia.com.

CEMETERY DANCE PUBLICATIONS PAPERBACKS AND EBOOKS!

THROUGH A GLASS, DARKLY
by W. H. Hussey

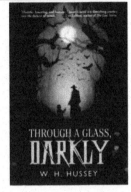

Steeped in classic horror, this chilling contemporary tale deals with secrets long buried, festering guilt, and haunting loneliness...

"Horrific, haunting, and humane, Hussey's novel is a disturbing journey into the darkest of minds."
—Tim Lebbon, author of *The Last Storm*

THAT NIGHT IN THE WOODS,
by Kristopher Triana

Scott Dwyer invites three people from their past to honor a dead friend's memory. They share a dark secret that has troubled them for decades. Now it's time to face their traumatic pasts. Together, they must unravel the mystery of what happened in the patch of forest behind Scott's house, a place once known as Suicide Woods.

"Kristopher Triana is without question one of the very best of the new breed of horror writers."
—Bryan Smith, author of *68 Kill*

Made in USA - North Chelmsford, MA
21528_9781587679407
10.21.2023 0548